RADIO

J · RUSHING

RADIO

A Novel

Print ISBN: 978-1-7346508-0-8

eBook ISBN: 978-1-7346508-1-5

Published by J. Rushing

First Edition: May 2020

This is a work of fiction. All characters are fictitious.

Any resemblance to actual persons, living or dead, is entirely coincidental.

Cover design and layout by Kelcey Rushing

jrushingwrites.com

For my wife,
for so many reasons.

Only in thought is man a God;

in action and desire we are the slaves of circumstance.

- Bertrand Russell

RADIO

J · RUSHING

FRIDAY

6TH JANUARY

1928

1

DINNER AND A BITTER DRINK

The evening of my death was supposed to be civil. I assumed the only loss I would risk involved words and ideas. It was an outrage to end the night with the loss of my body.

The tables at *L'Embuscade* were draped in fine white linen, the chairs filled with stuffed egos. Ours hosted the two most inflated: the Twins, Artemis and Apollo, in their matching ivory and gold splendour. His three-piece, double-breasted ivory affair glistened with gold buttons, a gold silk tie, and gold cuff links. Artemis shimmered in a short, tight dress of ivory sequins arranged in overlapping scale-like semicircles, each rimmed with gold. An homage to her antiquated armour no doubt. Her golden hair was just as short and tight. The Twins were always together, always matching, and always preening over one another. Deviants.

"And who have you brought to our table tonight, you cad?" Artemis's question dripped with poison as the words in turn dripped from her scarlet lips.

"This is Alina, but don't bother with conversation. She speaks neither French nor English." I patted Alina's pale hand. The Slavic barmaid gazed at the Twins with warmth and nodded in an attempt to engage. Hopeless, of course.

"Interesting choice of company, M," said Apollo, his dark blond goatee blending with his tie as he looked down his nose at her through round, gold-rimmed glasses.

"My company and our business need not mingle, nor is our business hers."

"Wise, I suppose. But why bring her at all?"

"A fine meal deserves good company, Apollo. *That*, I had to bring with me."

"You wound me, Marduk."

"If only."

I sat across from them in my decidedly unflashy umber tweed suit with my date, whose pale pink dress also underwhelmed. The room oozed with chic modern flourishes. Straight lines and moulded glass light fixtures, mirrors and brass, liquor and jazz. I hated much of the jazz at that time. Too damned upbeat. Like whiskey, you could find the good stuff after digging past the plebeian tastes of most.

The menu was merely a prop as I prepared myself for the primary-school lesson I was about to give, again, on population control and subterfuge. We had been over every detail of their imbecilic plan but the rationale of my objections to the Mentium's undertaking somehow failed to find purchase in the minds of my fellow members of the Upper Echelon. It was almost as disappointing as the bastardization of my machine, my radio, and my vision for it.

Tonight was my last attempt at reason. I would do everything in my power to make them understand the world demanded we remain in the shadows. Like the vampires we created, exposing ourselves to the light would be our end. That point was an inarguable truth, but it was not the truth they wanted to hear.

"*Garçon!*" Apollo's offending word rang through the room and a red-faced waiter strode toward us. Apollo received looks of reproach from a few of the more thoughtful patrons but he was as oblivious to the judgement of the masses as always.

Apollo styled himself a sun god; being served fuelled him in the way sunlight fuels a tree. Especially when those serving are constantly reminded of their place.

The slender waiter arrived in full penguin regalia. Draped towel and thin, waxed moustache, of course.

"*Monsieur*, you have chosen?"

Apollo cast a glare upon him, a challenge to the penguin to prove himself worthy of the great Apollo and his cherished sister.

I quickly scanned Alina's mind while the Twins played with the waiter then I ordered for us both and the man scurried away. I opted for Dalmore as an aperitif. The whisky was needed to tolerate those two.

The Twins were the self-elected leaders of the Upper Echelon, which in turn led the entirety of the Mentium. They derived their power from each other. Not their *mental* powers, those were gifted to them and to all our kind by some unknown workings of the universe. No, this power sprung from their trust in one another. The rest of those like me — Broadcasters as we now termed our subgroup of humanity — live rather guarded, solitary lives outside of our official Mentium business.

We naturally seek relationships — we're human after all — but we find giving our bodies much easier than giving our trust. The Twins' trust ran deep, affording them a consistent, steadfast ally. Allies equal power and power can tip the scales in one's or rather, a pair's favour.

What they didn't possess were intellects to match their influence. Crafty, yes, capable, of course, but they lacked foresight and an understanding of the consequences of their actions. Just look at the ridiculous religion they created. A child's dream of excess and privilege.

"Come now, M, how can you be so disturbed by these plans?" Artemis, her chin on her hand, clearly bored with the issue. "This is a return to form, by your own creation no less. We've spent centuries using manipulations just like this."

"True, but it's been centuries since we've been that heavy-handed. This isn't about blowing the dust off old tricks. We operate in an entirely different time. A different world."

"No, just a different you," said Apollo.

"Change is about more than the physical," I continued. "More than just our bodies evolve. The minds of the Monos have changed. Our minds and thus our ways *must* adapt too. Showing them monsters and demons then swooping to the rescue isn't going to work. This isn't the Middle Ages."

"They are the cattle they've always been," he said. "Why do you fight us?"

"I simply find the idea of our extinction unsavoury."

"Oh, do stop being so damned dramatic." Apollo pinched the bridge of his nose. "Evolution? Extinction? What is that to immortals?"

"A delusion. You've killed Mentium yourself. You know full well we're not immortals."

"Pedant," said Artemis.

The drinks arrived, blocking my retort. We ordered food, Apollo with the same venom as before. My Dalmore was gone before Alina had even touched her Aviation. The Twins sipped their Lillet Blancs and eyed me like school children waiting for a lecture.

I obliged. "This plan cannot go forward in its current incarnation. It's insane to think otherwise. My radio was never meant to be used for something this overt. This blunt."

"Overt? This is what we do, Old Sport," Apollo said. "We take what we want and we do so by force. Physical or mental, it's always been force." He placed the sculpted ivory mouthpiece of a cigarette holder in his mouth and lit it with a slow drag. The opposing end was of course gold. Always ivory and gold. Always predictable.

"Old Sport? Have you been reading? How very academic of you." I swirled my empty glass as if a spontaneous refill were possible.

Artemis cut in. "Scott's book should be required reading for all of us. Gatsby knew what he wanted and through manipulation, *our* brand of manipulation, he got it."

"You're proving my point," I said. "Our manipulations have been subtle for a millennium, as were Gatsby's. He manipulated the social order and created a suitable environment for his plan. He influenced the right people to do what was advantageous for himself and his goal. What you're suggesting would be more akin to Gatsby walking up to Tom, shooting him in the face, then carting Daisy off over his shoulder."

"As he should have," said Apollo, his attitude sullen. "Gatsby didn't achieve his goal, did he? Had he been a bit more proactive, a bit more, assertive…"

Apollo resembled Fitzgerald but by face alone. They shared a jutting chin, big eyes, and a narrow nose. Apollo's brawny physique and lack of creativity were obvious deviations.

"What you're suggesting," I said, leaning in and placing a finger to my temple, a cue to switch to a purely mental conversation, "Is not assertiveness, it's foolhardy. Times have changed. Look around you. We live in an age of science." We only allowed each other's mental voices in. We knew better than to fully open our minds to each other; far too many cards to conceal.

"Spoken like a scientist," said Artemis, without speaking. She rolled her eyes and sipped her drink in a motion as smooth as ballet.

"And as a scientist I am telling you that inciting mass hysteria under the pretense of godhood is not going to work on the minds of modern Monos. People's first thoughts will fall toward rationality. Toward realism. They'll never believe the words of anyone claiming to be gods."

"We are their gods," said Artemis.
"Were," I broadcasted into the minds of the Twins. To the outside world, our table was silent and Alina's palpable boredom projected that to the surrounding crowd. "We'll all look like fools at best or, more likely, be hunted down as monsters."

"What rationality do you see in them?" asked Artemis, waving her empty glass in the air. "Look what they do to each other. They're still recovering from the last war. Monos believe what we want them to believe. They always have and always will. They crave the fantastic. The gods of old, back to restore order. They'd be lined up like it was some Chaplin picture. They're hungry for it. They're ripe for this deception. For our return. Look at their art, their music, their literature. They've never stopped loving us."

"You're wrong. They love fragments of what we were. There's no memory of what it was truly like."

Apollo took a long drag from his cigarette and let the smoke flow from his nostrils. "Save your breath. You've already been overruled.

The Upper Echelon voted in your absence. It was unanimous, save for you, of course."

"Yemoja and Cernunnos voted with you? Tian?"

"He said unanimous, didn't he?" said Artemis.

"It isn't unanimous unless all vote. No me, no decision."

"We don't see it that way."

I rubbed my face. "Millennia of prior precedence states otherwise. And why did you agree to this dinner if you had no intention of listening?"

"Think of it as a final gesture of goodwill. Besides, public humiliation is always more satisfying, Old Sport." Apollo's laugh escaped his trademark caustic smile.

"Enough of this farce," I switched back to verbal speech. "If you'll excuse me, I need to relieve myself."

"I'm sure you do. Don't worry, we'll babysit your date for you," said Artemis, her gaze that of a constrictor as she eyed Alina.

"Be nice."

"Never."

I strode off toward the WC and descended the spiral staircase. The men's lavatory was empty and I took up temporary residence in one of the stalls, readying myself for business but not in the manner one might assume.

Far from believing my success was inevitable, I planned to increase my odds. Odds matter little if the game's already been played but Alina could still be useful. Information is currency.

I closed my eyes and focused in on my date. My consciousness, a skater on a pond, skimmed from mind to mind until I located hers. Then, I entered.

Alina's mind was ablaze with irritation. I couldn't blame her. She was far from my date. She was a hired hand or, to be accurate, a hired set of senses. My initial plan was to use Alina as my camera and make my own 'talkie' of the Twins' discourse while I was away. This would give me time to dismantle their objections. I'd hoped to be one step closer to stopping them from ruining our livelihood.

Shutting out the distraction of her internal whingeing and whining,

I pushed deeper into her mind until I could feel what she felt, see what she saw. And it made my breath catch.

There, in my chair, sat Izzy. His black hair was thick with pomade and a crisp grey suit hugged his lean body. The subtle Shippo design of his red silk tie glistened. Izanagi sat with the poise of a Shogun, a quality I'd admired once.

His presence at dinner was not part of our plan. Why the hell was he there?

"He's been planning it for weeks," he said as my food was laid in front of him by the still shaken waiter. The wood-handled knife for the Twins' shared *côte de bœuf* clattered next to Apollo's hand as the waiter set it down. "He assumed I'd assist him, and to be fair, my acting has been impeccable. And I have helped him in my own way. To the benefit of you and your vision of course."

"Leave us!" Apollo said and the thin penguin waddled off to lick his wounds. Apollo sat fuming, and not just his cigarette. Both hands gripped the edge of the table making his fingers go white.

"Sabotage? Izanagi, he wouldn't dare," said Artemis, her face flushing as she spoke.

"Oh, he would, and did," Izzy said as he stabbed at the steaming *gratin dauphinoise* meant for me. He lifted a hefty bite to his smug little mouth and chewed with relish. "This is M we're talking about. He's drawn up schematics, visited key sites, it's all ready to go. The great Marduk won't stop until he sees our plan fail."

Our plan? My protégé and accomplice was now in the act of becoming my replacement. I almost admired the play, but my rage wouldn't allow it.

Apollo sat motionless. He stared into the table as if looking for answers. Simpleton. I had premeditated treason. I had prepared for treason. The protocol was clear. What was there to think about?

I willed Alina to focus on the Twins. I'd spent years working alongside Izzy. The last thing I wanted to see in that moment was his conniving face.

The pair sat close, whispering. At first, their focus was on each other — typical — but as their conversation progressed their gaze turned toward Alina. I couldn't make out what was said save for their last sentence.

"He's watching. He's using the girl," said Artemis, her eyes burning and locked with Alina's.

There was no time to react. Apollo's powerful hand slammed down next to his plate and the glint of the steak knife's blade had little time to register before the damage was inflicted.

As the blade slid into Alina's chest, I lingered inside her long enough to see the heads of all the diners in the room begin a slow pivot in the direction of the Twins. The faces wore the blank stare of statues not the mask of shock a normal person would don. Their minds were no longer their own.

I pulled out of her brain and regained my composure. "This won't end well."

The wood veneer of the toilet stall was a prison and I flung open the door, seeking escape. A man in his mid-twenties stood at the sink. The water was running but his hands were at his sides, dripping.

Damn it. I took a tentative step forward. The tap of my shoe against the tile rang out in the now-silent restaurant. His head rolled toward the sound. His face, stone. Just like the patrons above.

I said nothing as I tried to sidestep around him, though my eyes were trained on his. My motion became a trigger and at the top of his lungs he called out in a booming monotone, "Here! He's here."

The boot knife I always carried was drawn in one practiced motion. I pushed him back with a second. The water pooling in the sink transitioned from clear, to pink, to red as the dying man's body lay across the white porcelain.

The sound of tinkling metal and breaking glass rang from the floor above. I stepped through the open door of the WC to the stairwell. At least twenty people in evening attire crowded around the top armed with silverware and the jagged necks of wine bottles. All with the same lifeless faces. All under the control of the Twins. All awaiting commands. At the head of the mob stood the penguin, a corkscrew between his fingers. At the sight of me, the crowd surged. There was already one dead man that evening and I was prepared to make it a dozen if need be.

"This will be your mess to clean," I yelled into the dining room, shaking my limbs like a fighter before a bout. As the mob reached the bottom of the spiral, I lunged. With quick, precise movements, I set about opening the throats of the first five to descend. The corkscrew caught my cheek as the penguin fell among the bodies that, like branches in a river, formed a temporary dam. The others pushed on, thrusting their makeshift weapons toward me. The blood of the fallen coated their finery.

"You dare betray the Mentium?" Apollo's grandiose voice carried through the room. "You know the consequences. Is your pride worth all this? Make this easy on all of us."

"I'd rather not," I said, dodging a bottle of cognac.

I tried to force my way into the mind of a tall man at the top of the stairs, and caught a fleeting glimpse of the area above. My chances of escape were nil. Everyone had left their tables and flocked toward me. Everyone but my three fellow Broadcasters and my dead camera. They sat, directing their newly-formed army. Whether their goal was to kill or capture me I didn't know. Decorum in our little guild called for my capture but the Twins were a bloodthirsty pair and I couldn't trust their restraint.

"I am not turning my back on the Mentium," I blurted while ending another two lives to stem the flow of groping, mindless assassins. "I'm turning my back on this idiocy. I'm turning my back on you!"

"*We* are the Mentium." Artemis spoke the words as if it were a universal truth. I had no more words for them.

I stepped back from the pile of bodies to catch my breath. My situation was hopeless. The Twins had control of every mind in the room.

"Damn it, damn it!" I slashed at a new throat, then another. Then, a moment of clarity. Their control was total within the room but not necessarily outside.

I groped for the thoughts of anyone nearby. Anyone who might have a view of the restaurant. There, walking opposite *L'Embuscade* was a woman huddled beneath an umbrella, and I settled into her head. Through the front facade, I could see the angry crowd within, and what would prove to be my deliverance.

The frigid winter night meant that no outside tables were in place, leaving visible a dark, rectangular patch on the sidewalk. A metal door. A supply room in the basement had an exterior entry point. I was standing in that basement.

Pulling back and focusing again on my own senses, the glint of a brass doorknob flashed below the stairwell. That had to be it.

Once underneath, an accurate kick near the knob sent the door swinging and stale air spilling out. Inside, a single bulb burned, illuminating bags of onions and potatoes piled around the room. Kegs of beer were stacked near the metal supply doors leading outside. A keg became a stool, my arms, battering rams, and with great effort the supply doors opened. I lifted myself out into the night.

Icy rain was a shock compared to the heat inside, and the cold spread as I ran down the slush-piled boulevard. The wind tore at my face, filled my lungs, and they burned as if black with frostbite. Still I ran. Comfort was not in the cards for me that night.

2

SACRIFICE

The blood would not be enough. The cuts, evidence of nothing. Still, I was desperate.

My fingers flexed against the straight razor while I weighed options. The hulking Eunuch had come too close to catching me, too close to alerting others so I squeezed at his neck with the crook of my arm and thrust our struggling bodies into the deserted, decaying dressing room of that forsaken burlesque theatre. It would have to do. I had no intention of reaping the rewards for my treason nor continuing to run through that bitter Parisian night.

Oil lamps, perched above each mirrored table, drenched the room in a whisky hue. A cabaret raged beyond the red velvet curtain as we thrashed about backstage. Its cover, a stroke of luck on that unluckiest of nights.

The razor glinted next to my face as I pulled my arm tighter. He slammed my spine against the rear of the stage, my head grazing the curtain. The heels of his Oxfords dug at the floor, forcing my vertebrae against the wooden edge. Lightning bolts of pain coursed through me as he twisted and pressed but I held firm.

I'd have slit his throat had his body not given out first.

Panting, I let his bulk roll off me and I smoothed my hair. I kicked at the brute, then grabbed him by his suit lapels and dragged him toward a row of steamer trunks. Five more Eunuchs and three

Mentium Underlings were mere blocks away.

The largest trunk was empty enough and I stowed his body inside, covering it with makeup-smudged clothing before locking the lid. Now it was my turn.

"This will not end here." The words fell like marbles as I pulled at more costume boxes, readying myself for the next tragedy. "I will not end here."

Putrid mustard slacks and a sequined aubergine jacket replaced my high street suit. Disguise, no matter how repugnant, buys time.

I settled before a makeup table and took in my reflection. "Artemis, Apollo, you degenerates. I won't forget this."

Clumps of hair fell to the filthy floor. With each stroke of the razor, I looked less and less myself. "This had better bear fruit."

Once I'd hacked my hair and moustache to a crude stubble, I scoured the unkept room for what could become another makeshift casket.

The black of a small storage door beckoned from beneath the stage as the crowd cheered the clamorous show above. I glanced back at the door, knowing they were close. My limbs, still burning from the sprinting and the killing, carried my hunched body into the sanctuary of the darkness beneath the stage.

High shoes at the end of long legs shook the boards above as I lay sprawled against a canvas-draped crate in the near dark. Bright lights streaked through gaps and illuminated the dusty air before me in sheets of cycling colour.

I began the ritual as I always had, though the implement was one of convenience rather than ceremony. With the straight razor, I sliced deep into my right thigh. Then my left. Slow breaths through the nose, tongue pressed tight to the palate — no screams.

My helplessness disgusted me. Trust in Izzy — dangerous, fleeting trust — brought me here, brought me low, but I would rise.

The wrists came next. Small cuts along the arteries, not across. Efficiency is key. The draining of blood is not like the draining of a bottle. One feels neither empty nor lighter. One feels cold inside, warm at the wounds, and a sense of fear that squeezes the mind like I'd squeezed the Eunuch's throat. It's irrational for someone who had lived so many lives, yet each time I felt it. It's human.

More blood, black in the darkness, coated my skin. Each finger, a stalactite dripping into a pool of my own creation. My life flowed from opened wrists as I fought to keep my body calm through the agony and rage.

The acrid smells of electric stage lights and backstage oil lamps blended and fouled the air, as did the sound of French words over American jazz. All of it sour in my lungs and ears.

"That's it… that's it." The pain of the flayed flesh waned. I'd learned early and with haste to detach from it.

The right angles of light that shaped the small access door in front of me were the only things that were right on a night gone so wrong. The stage, a tomb, one with an audience just beyond, focused on the burlesque in front of them while my grotesque body lay below.

That night was about escape. Escape from my kind, my fate, and from my body. There was still much for me to do.

The dancers continued to pound from above. A tremor of anger joined the ever-present convulsions. Before me, covering my body, that hideous *costume de cirque* soaked up the last of my vitality. The humiliation was worth the time it purchased.

Another tremor shook me. This time a half sob, half laugh. Who would this fool? The police? Certainly, but the Mentium? No. The Twins would find this jester's corpse amusing and pitiful. What would Lilith think?

"Their amusement be damned," I said, as the music continued to pulse above me. I'd cherished this particular body and worked hard to keep in top form. There is a link between body and mind. Neglect of one sacrifices the other. That night however, necessity called for the sacrifice of one to save the other.

This death was a damned theft and they would pay for my loss. The ledgers would be balanced, but not before I stopped their lemming march toward our destruction.

As I prepared for the final cleaving of flesh, the cold engulfed my legs and a fog wrapped my mind. One must battle the fog at all cost.

Clarity is critical before transference.

More shaking. I abhor the shaking. It's so bestial. So raw. The body twitches, seizes, and jerks. Every single time I fought the shaking and every single time I shook.

The blade in my hand tapped against the floorboards as I pushed my back higher against the crate. The clamour above me stopped, or I perceived it stopping. Had they come or was it the blood loss?

The Mentium would hunt me without end and I had little time remaining before they destroyed everything we'd built. I needed more time. Time! Everything was about time. Time and action.

Blood glimmered around my bare feet. Just beyond, through that right-angled opening, a large mirror reflected only the total black of the small door at the back of the stage. My body was obscured, but oh, sweet sadistic fate…

A rivulet of blood trickled out of the dark polygon and into the amber glow of the dressing room. A macabre little path leading toward a macabre little scene.

My body was all but found but I'd make them fucking work for its identity. Lowering my lids, I took in the feel of this body one last time.

With both weak, shaking hands, I placed the razor against the bridge of my handsome Roman nose, wincing as the blade cut with its first touch. I cringed at the utter uselessness of the reflex.

"Do it." The dark blade, millimetres from my eyes. "Do it then get to work."

I tensed, pulled down hard, then drew a final line across my neck, silencing the escaping scream before my arm fell limp.

Leaving the body is not difficult. Letting go is easy if one knows how. If one is practiced, experienced. I'd let go so many times before.

This was different. I was casting off into the dark. There had been no time to choose a new body, no time to prepare. My consciousness was both archer and arrow.

The archer was blind.

The arrow flew anyway.

3

MÜD

"The stage… my body…?" said a voice that was not mine, but left my lips and resonated in my head… yet, not my head.

Small hands scraped at mud-caked eyes. Unsure hands that lacked control. I opened my new eyes and a kaleidoscope of spinning colour and blurred lines surrounded me. A swirling, flashing tapestry smothered me where I lay and the incessant pulse of that awful Jolsen tune attacked from all sides.

Toot, toot, Tootsie, Goo' Bye!
Toot, toot, Tootsie, don't cry,

Two slow, difficult breaths and all came into focus. The world felt familiar. The night felt real yet somehow hyper-real. Walls of buildings rose around me and it was their limestone faces that were suffocating in colour.

Red dominated the drizzle-streaked air. Not red, rouge. Bright rouge from modern neon lights. Le Moulin Rouge, Le Mirliton, Place Blanche… no. I was at the foot of Montmartre and the archer's aim could not have been worse.

Kiss me Tootsie and then,
do it over again,

I had cast myself miles away, and toward home no less. Our temple stood mere blocks from me, full of my brothers and sisters of the Mentium. My enemies.

Cold, pale earth coated a black wool suit. It wasn't my suit but it wrapped my shoulders, rather, those shoulders. Small shoulders that used to belong to someone else.

The mud had seeped through to the skin, my new skin, and despite a great deal of protest, I willed that half-numb body into motion. The weight of the muck hung from every limb as I brought the body to its feet. Everything was wrong and yet an inexplicable feeling of peace forced itself on my consciousness. It was no time for calm.

I found myself encircled, no, boxed within the exposed foundations of a soon-to-be building with lights bleeding in from above, just as I'd been seconds before, in another place, in another body. That body was gone and all that had to be done would be completed within a new, frail figure.

When somebody says goodbye to me,
I'm sad as I can be,

Steady, freezing rain turned the snow-crusted construction site to mire. I should have felt cold. I should have; but did not. I should have ached but did not. Taking possession of another body was, by its nature, unpredictable, but doing so at random… removing a random life… I couldn't begin to fathom the ramifications. Nor did I care to. Every tentative attachment to the brain brought with it more calm, more peace, more confusion.

Time. I could have purchased more time if only the Twins had listened, but they never listen. A month? A week? Days? Just enough to break their pride. The Twins did not see reason; they only saw power. And Izzy, that turncoat, saw power through them. Fools. All of them.

He seemed to take a lot of pleasure,
saying bye-bye to his treasure.

Izzy. That bastard. He was as blind as — *how could I have been so blind?* That snake. The scheming and secrecy would have been commendable had it not been directed at me. The great Izanagi, pupil, confidante, usurper.

I searched the short, scrap-wood fence for an exit. The warm buzzes from my dulled senses were disconcerting. The severe lack of coordination in this new body, more so. Mobility was vital. Wolves devour the weakest fawn and the Twins with their Eunuchs and Underlings were howling.

As if by instinct, I gathered a soiled hat, a derby, from the muck and placed it back on my head. I took a few shaky steps toward the bustling street beyond the walls of the construction site. Something was most assuredly not right.

There's always an adjustment period when assuming a new body, but every attempt to deepen my connection to the physical brain was met with an aggravating blend of numbness and flashes of acute sensory information. With feet that felt laden with far more than mud, I stepped past the fence and out onto the sidewalk where Place Blanche exploded into view.

Automobiles zipped along a boulevard that had belonged to horses not long before. Crowds of people flowed around every corner like water in the gutter. Colognes, perfumes, tobacco, liquor and the smoke of the street corner chestnut roasters filled my head. The brightness of the lights sent me reeling and I reached out to steady myself against the side of Le Mirliton, a club I knew well. My filthy hand slid across a poster advertising Josephine Baker's next performance.

"Apologies Miss Baker," I meant to think, yet heard myself say. "You deserve better. I deserve better. This… body. Who the hell have I gotten myself into?"

What did it matter? It was my new skin. My small, weak, useless prison for the foreseeable future, drowning in lights and debauchery on a snow-crusted, rain-soaked street.

"My love!" I pressed my back against the wall. Lilith's scent, my dear, glorious, Lilith, exploded within my over-sensitised nose. In my shock, I lost control and my new body slid to the ground. With Lilith at my side we could make short work of the Twins and Izzy and put the Mentium back on course. I managed to look up as the smell passed and a woman with auburn curls glared at me. Auburn, not raven. Not Lilith.

Watch for the mail, I'll never fail,
If you don't get a letter then you'll know I'm in jail,

"Damn this night and damn this song and, and, just… fuck!"

Heads turned and gasps sounded but no one dared come near this soiled miscreant. I set about composing myself and as my consciousness took over, so too did the eerie calm.

Boulevard de Clichy lay at my feet, its edges lined with distracted minds, distorted minds, minds twisted by white powder from the new world and dragons from the old. Dragons one chased at the behest of a flower. A poppy.

"Pitiful," said a man, staring as I groped the wall to regain my feet. Yet he hadn't moved his mouth.

My powers were weak and control was nonexistent. All standard for a fresh transference. Only the most basic functions were accessible as I began the glacial process of regaining my strength.

Other minds flooded my head, their thoughts and feelings a mental gyre. Among the throngs of merrymakers, I was tuning in without control — at random, everyone at once. The visions were vivid but blurred. Thoughts of liquor, food, sex, loving, loss, regret, and pleasure. New Year's festivities rang fresh as 1928 was born just days before. I was sharing those thoughts and feelings and memories. No. I was *experiencing* them. It was chaos but still I suffered that insufferable calm.

The minutia of my surroundings pleaded for my attention as I ambled along with languid movements. I wanted to run but the body wanted to sway and stroll and gaze. Frigid raindrops reflected the surrounding light and crashed to the ground in their thousands like the burning biplanes of the great war. The muted snare cracks from within the clubs echoed distant explosions. I was transfixed by the beauty amid the horror.

Heightened senses, deep interest in the average, the calm — *unbelievable.*

A chemical dragon had coiled itself around the brain of my

new host, hoarding its powers and rendering it useless. My own consciousness, now a knight trapped within and shaken by the revelation, tried in vain to slay the beast.

I focused my consciousness inward, trying to wrench control of the body from the drug. The harder I gripped the more the calm consumed me. Of course it did. I pulled back from the brain though I couldn't escape the opium's gravity.

Chemicals can only be slain by the passage of time. I knew this. I'd seen into opium-soaked brains before. I'd manipulated them and used them. It was quite another thing to find myself living inside one. My future had somehow become even more bleak.

I swayed and wove a twisting path through the crowd as I gazed at the hypnotic rotation of the red mill and began to ponder Lautrec. The brown paper, the palette, the rough yet lively lines… the excruciating blast of an automobile horn ripped me back to reality. All eyes were on me as I scurried out of the street and into the tree-lined median of Place Blanche.

Again, I pulled back from the brain, managing to keep control of only physical and motor functions. *Get control, M.*

I forced my new eyes to search the faces of those around me. Did I know them? Did they know me? Did they know this body? The Mentium would be looking for me. My body was new, but my consciousness was the same and it was raw and open to anyone who could sense me.

As I turned to flee, light became translucent streamers that fluttered and waved. It was as if a parade was taking place for no one but me. A long sigh left my chest. The thoughts were peaceful, but that peace was frightening and I strained to keep myself separate from the tainted grey matter.

"Not again," I thought and heard the body say. My mud-slicked back fell against the trunk of a sycamore and my shoulder hit the ground. Serenity, a blanket over everything as I sat up and lay my head against the wet bark. I was a wanted man but the opium was trying its damnedest to force relaxation. I let my eyes fall closed.

New sights dissolved the calm into panic. Wool-clad incubi peered at me. Their heads at once human and inhuman. Some bore animal teeth, others the shimmer of fish scales. All sneering and scoffing at me, a clay-coated golem amongst respectable creatures, there to partake in unrespectable things.

As if by mental muscle memory, I reached out to manipulate their minds. To make them go away. Nothing. I was castrated of my power. Kicking hard at the ground, I pressed my back into the tree but slipped, coming down hard on my hands.

"Leave me alone!" I wailed like a child. It was despicable.

More eyes from more monsters pored over me, and I swung wildly to ward them off. The sycamores above me began to bend, their bare branches like gnarled hands reaching for my throat.

I cowered on the snow-caked ground in the middle of Place Blanche between Le Mirliton and the competing clubs of *Le Ciel* and *L'Enfer*, Heaven and Hell. "No, impossible! Stay away!"

L'Enfer was adorned with carvings that would sow unease in the most sober of minds. Crudely sculpted bodies groped and crawled around the entrance like the archivolts of a cathedral. The door itself a gaping mouth with burning red eyes, ready to devour the souls of all who entered. I understood that these pitiful creatures were stationary. That the mouth was benign and the eyes glowed via electric light. I'd entered that mouth many times. I knew its true nature but my new eyes showed me a twisted fantasy.

It was a scene befitting Dante and dread devoured my euphoria. The bodies writhed, whipping limbs out at passersby. The door was a flicking tongue and the eyes peered deep inside of me.

The vision before me elicited both tears and laughter. Confusion. Confusion was omnipresent.

The first cane strike to my foot woke my new body. It had been sleeping. Opium dreams are the stuff of legend. I now knew why. The second strike landed with more force and I scrambled to get to my feet.

The thoughts of everyone within three blocks sang in unified chaos, and I cringed as if in pain. The thoughts of the cane-wielding Mono held nothing but reproach and judgment. I had never in my life more willingly accepted disdain. He didn't know me. He wasn't looking for me. He wanted me gone as did I.

I couldn't allow the process of fusing with the brain to continue. I needed to, but could not. My consciousness had to act as captain, guiding his battered ship through its self-inflicted chemical storm. My dependence on that drug-addled brain made every action like trying to waltz on sand.

I again attempted to keep myself detached from all but the body's motor functions, which meant that interacting with people was impossible, at least without being devoured by the dragon once more. An inevitable outcome. Ignoring the cane wielder, I fled down a quieter, darker Rue Blanche.

4

CLEANLINESS AND GODLESSNESS

In my filthy state, I was a beacon for attention. Sanctuary was paramount but my own apartment was no longer an option. The Mentium were undoubtedly waiting, watching, and ready to abduct and question any who approached.

In the pockets of that muddy suit I found the bulge of a wallet, and the points of keys made themselves known. I stepped into an unlit doorway along Rue Blanche and wiped my hands on the brick facade to remove enough mud as not to ruin the only evidence of who I now was.

Inside the ageing billfold I discovered I was occupying the body of one Delbert Chambers. Delbert, an American, had his papers on him — his *carte d'identité* — with an address, which meant that I now had a place to hide. Like this new body, the Mentium wouldn't know this address. It was across town, not far from where my old body lay limp. It should have been a simple journey but opium, the cold, and a need to avoid people in that bustling city all combined to turn an evening stroll into my own small slice of hell.

The disapproving eyes of aristocrats and prostitutes alike washed over me as did the icy rain. Again, I tried to turn those eyes from me and again I was helpless. An hour prior I would have made them choke on their tongues or shit their pants. Anything to take the focus off of me. Monos are good for little save providing us with our needs. In that moment, I needed privacy and could make none for myself. They were all as useless as I felt.

I continued on down Rue Blanche, a slug, leaving a trail of silt in my wake, only adding to the spectacle.

It took days, sometimes weeks for any of my kind to fully settle into a new body, even under ideal circumstances, and nothing about that night was ideal. It was difficult to put one unsteady foot in front of the other as I rode that body down the dim street, let alone try to formulate any plan of action.

Try as I might to stay detached from Delbert's brain, my consciousness kept attempting to merge. Each time the effects of the chemicals altered my thoughts; each time I was forced to pull my *self* to freedom. With each taste of peace the dragon offered, there was a pull to sip more. I couldn't allow myself to partake, at least not willingly.

"Just keep walking." Were my lips moving?

I ached for warmth and a wash. My new body's ability to feel the cold was beginning a slow return as the *Église de la Trinité* and its central fountain came into view.

The square in front of the church was vacant save for a drunk on a bench. The fountain in its icy stillness could bring my new body back to a somewhat presentable state. I looked too disgusting to be inconspicuous; stealth is vital for a man on the run. Despite temperatures that hung just above freezing, I made my way toward the water.

At the edge of the fountain, its three marble angels towering over me, I scanned the surrounding streets for more prying eyes and judging minds. Sensing none, I emptied all my pockets into the derby along with Delbert's watch and set it aside. Looking up, the statues' smiles took on a mocking angle. I sneered back at them then recoiled. Embarrassment swept over me. The dragon was winning. I hate to lose.

I slammed my fist on the edge of the fountain, leaving a pale stamp. I tore at my clothing and grit my teeth against the cold I knew was coming, then tried to slam my fist once more but I'd settled in again and the calm wrapped itself around me.

Logic dictated that I leave my clothes on. I'd be soaked either way and the opium wanted to know what an ice bath would *feel* like. I was so unfocused it was a mockery.

"Enough!" I grunted and ripped back out of the brain. All my anguish flooded back. I hated. I hated all.

The beggar rolled on his bench underneath a dirty wool blanket. He was dressed. He had clothes. I needed his clothes.

"Excuse me," I said as I guided the body toward the large man. His eyes shot open and stared at me with a mixture of fear and anger.

"What do you want, *monsieur*?" he said, sitting up and holding his blanket under his chin.

Reaching for my powers I said, "I need your clothes. You'll give them to me."

He burst out laughing. The slight stung more than my impotent abilities and I struck him above the ear. He stood, and my new body only met his shoulders. My face met the back of his hand and I tumbled backward.

I was livid despite the calm's fresh advance. I was tired, embarrassed, frustrated, and stuck in that inebriated body. Opium be damned, my rage flared like alcohol on a fire and, rising to my feet, I screamed "I need your clothes!"

As my voice echoed through the deserted streets, its sound was followed by the creaking of window hinges. I turned a slow circle as myriad clothing began to flutter downward. Handfuls sailed from every direction. I'd managed the first control of minds since entering Delbert's body and it couldn't have come at a better time.

While the drunkard discarded his coat, I manoeuvred Delbert's body around the square sorting what looked reasonable both for a small man in his twenties and for the chill of the evening. Once I'd collected wool trousers, a rough jumper, socks, and an overcoat, I returned to the fountain.

Stripping off Delbert's muddy clothes, I braced for the chill to come but as my hand reached through the surface of the water I was reminded of the opium blanket my body still wore. Naked and with haste, I washed face, hair and arms as the garment-strewn square was already enough of a spectacle. The mud sent a pale, menacing cloud through the dark water. I was glad it had moved on to menace something else.

The clean clothing was like velvet against my drug-enhanced nerves. As I finished pulling them on and stuffing Delbert's belongings back into pockets it struck me that I had called for clothing but not shoes or a belt. The trousers barely had hips to sit upon let alone an arse. I returned Delbert's soaked brogues to his feet and stumbled, pants clasped tight in hand, until I found his dripping suspenders.

The apartment dwellers stood at their open windows and stared out with vacant eyes. The drunk shared their pose.

"Close them and go away." I said, trying to send the command into their minds. Still, they stood.

"Go away!"

Still nothing. Powers in the minutes after a transference are like a new fire trying to catch flame. Sparks, flickers, lots of smoke, anticipation, and irritation.

"Damn you all."

I turned and swished Delbert's felt derby in the murky water and gave it numerous good shakes, then placed it back on my head. Wool is warm, even when wet.

My only goals were to find Delbert's apartment, dry off, purge the opium, and think. I'd been cast out, sold out, and forced out of my own body.

All who had a hand in my downfall would pay.

My dinner guests most of all.

5

THE WEIGHT OF WORDS

"I can feel you Marduk," said a voice that crept inside my head. "You damned fool. How could you have done this to us? To yourself?"

The voice was not mine, though I had no doubt of the owner's identity. Our minds linked through the aether as I crossed in front of *Printemps* department store. Her intrusion startled me, and I leaned against the nearest building in order to focus. I was mere blocks from the fountain and already she had found me. Or at least my mind.

Word travels fast amongst the Mentium but I was taken aback by the speed at which my demise had spread. Phantom perfume had raised the spectre of my love when I first woke in this body. Now, the presence was real and inside my head.

I squeezed my eyes shut to cap their lenses. To provide her with a view of my location or a reflection of my new face was not yet prudent. I needed her help, but I had to be sure she'd give it before I revealed myself to her. For now, I'd give her only my words and hope the thirty-odd minutes I'd possessed the body would provide little memory information for her to take.

"Lilith," I thought to myself and thus to her, "you found me. Excellent, listen, we need to move quickly. This whole night's gone wrong."

"What's wrong is your betrayal."

"My betrayal?" The words crushed me under their weight. "Darling, you can't be serious."

"Do not judge me, Marduk. You're the one who turned your back on your people. On me."

Was she in on the plot? No, I wouldn't believe that. Still, I was a helpless rabbit and the Mentium were hounds. There would be Eunuchs and Underlings crawling all over the city searching for me and now my Lilith, chief strategist of the Mentium, had joined the hunt.

"How can you side with them?" I asked, squeezing my eyes tighter and placing my hands over my ears to cut out even more sensory information. I focused in on her mental visage. Her obsidian hair, toned, lean frame, always wrapped in green and always ready to act. "After what they've done to me?"

"Stop playing the victim. You did this to yourself. I side with the Mentium in all things just as you should," she said, with tones of disappointment and duty. "How could you have been so stupid, love?"

"Pots and kettles, Lilith."

"You've made an absolute mess of this. The Twins are going insane and Izzy is already out guarding your radio. Don't make the situation worse. Turn yourself in and let me handle it. It may not come to… entombment," she said. Her pause, a proof only of our bond.

"Entombment," I said, "Now who's being stupid? Lilith, I doubt I'd live long enough to be entombed. The Twins want me dead. You know that's true. Look, I need you to help me or leave me be. I have no time for this."

"I choose neither," she said.

"Dammit, Lilith, you aren't fool enough for this. You know damned well the Twins are driving us to ruin. You can't be a part of that."

"How can I not?" Her words stung. "Everything we are is built on the Mentium. Our survival is the Mentium. I serve the Mentium, not your schemes."

I could feel myself scoff and I'm sure she could too. Despite her words, Lilith's booming mental voice was a comfort, drowning out the cacophony of thought surrounding me. A shoulder collided with mine, so I pushed Delbert's back harder against the stone wall. My eyes remained closed but I could feel the swirling air as pedestrians passed. I strained to pull as far from Delbert's brain as I could, but I suspected Lilith would sense the air as well. She'd know I was in a crowded location.

"If the Twins go through with this the Mentium is finished. I need you, my love, please."

"We cure our ills from within. Just as we always have. There was a vote and there is protocol to follow. The Mentium survives through protocol."

"Damn the vote. I wasn't there. That's out of protocol, isn't it?"

"I have my duty."

"Think! This is lunacy. This is— this is apocalyptic for us." Thinking was painful. "The damage… you want to protect the Mentium and its fucking protocol then, please, help me. Your duty lies in protecting what we've built, not overseeing its ruin. Dammit, make the sane choice."

"I am," she said, and I wanted to scream though I had control enough not to send a wail echoing through the streets. " I'm making the only sane choice. I want the Mentium to survive as much as you. Unlike you, I'm unwilling to stoop to treason. Fucking hell, M. Treason? How could you put me in this position? You knew what was at stake."

There was nothing to say. Of course I knew what was at stake. I knew what I chanced to lose — including her — but following the Twins down their dark path would mean losing all. Either option was a risk. Yet I would choose my own risks rather than have them forced onto me.

Focus was a struggle. The last of the rain again demanded attention, though this time through touch. I could feel those particles on my hands and face stroking me, licking, tingling, tickling me as my world burned. Distracting me while I once again grew cold and damp.

All blame fell to the drug. I had no idea how many hours prior Delbert had used the opium. All I could do was float downstream and wait. My newfound impotence was revolting.

"Enough with this silent treatment, M," she said. "Dammit, listen carefully. The entire temple is in chaos right now. The Twins ran to me after your escape. First for info on you, then for advice. They're listening to me. I've been given free rein over the search. Let me bring you in. I know I can secure a lighter sentence for you. I can get you blindness or maybe you'll just lose your hands. I can get you into a new body in a decade or two. Decades, M, what are a few decades? I know I can convince them to take entombment off the table. Time will set things right."

I caught myself pounding the wall with the edge of my hands. "They… want… me… dead, Lilith! You can't do anything for me once I'm in their hands. I need you out here."

It was she who now took pause. Her anger toward me, toward the situation, flowing through our connection.

"We found your previous host," she growled. "Bloody purple jacket and all. Know that I will find you and I will make sure you see *proper* justice for what you've done."

"If I was in danger of capture, you'd have me already," I said, using all my focus to feign my usual arrogance. "Until you identify this body I'll be in the wind and you won't be able to take me to your new overlords."

"I serve no one but the Mentium."

"Keep telling yourself that."

"Run, my little snake-dragon. Run and hide. You know I love a chase."

Snake-dragon. If she only knew how much of the dragon I was feeling that night. What used to be a symbol of my power was now what hindered it. At least what fledgling powers I possessed.

"Pardon, monsieur!" A hurried Frenchmen bumped into me, arm in arm with a woman bundled in sable. Jolted back to the physical world, I checked the faces of those moving past. For once I was glad not to see hers.

If my lover had forsaken me, was all lost? No, Tian, my mentor, would help me. I couldn't fathom why he'd voted the way he did, but I knew he would always come to my aid. I needed to see Tian, but first I needed shelter.

Jumping back in the saddle in a manner less metaphorical than I would have liked, I marched on through a thickening crowd and tried to blend in as best I could. Prey use camouflage to their advantage and the predators were close.

Within minutes, I was adjacent to the grand facade of *Le Palais Garnier* and desperately trying to avoid the brightness of its glow. My eyes shied from the intensity of the light, the drug still wreaking havoc on my senses. My pace slowed, my anger and fear dimmed, and my mind became transfixed by the elegance and beauty before me. It was difficult to look away, to focus on anything else through the drug.

Its golden statues, newly illuminated by electric light, pointed skyward as if to welcome the last of the frosty rain. A clear, cold patch of sky sailed over the colossal building, venting what warmth remained at street level as the night continued its quest to see me freeze. The massive oxidised dome perched in the centre of the palatial opera house reflected an iridescent green. Ravel's *Bolero* had recently debuted and that night's performance was just letting out.

The throngs flowed past me and their thoughts continued to pour into my mind as they had since inhabiting my new body. I'd mustered the strength to block some minds but only sporadically.

In order to sense my consciousness, Lilith — the Mentium's equivalent to a field marshal — had to have been close, likely even in that scattering crowd. Lilith Desjardins did so enjoy Ravel. It's a pity I had to commit treason and die on the night of a performance.

Shaking away my chemical awe, I continued my awkward trudge along the sidewalk as the Haussmannien streets absorbed the flood of well-to-do descending the staircases of *Le Palais Garnier*. French in their finery, elegant English, and an assortment of continental *crème de la crème* scurried through the slick stone streets. My mismatched, dishevelled state was an ill fit for the surrounding opulence. In spite of the opium I sank deeper into the brain to regain more control of my motor functions, and thus a modicum of composure.

My drug-addled gait was less conspicuous than the loose control I'd been employing. I continued to plod past the sea of muted peacocks in a desperate attempt to add distance between Lilith and myself. She may have been done talking but she was still hunting.

"Keep going," I thought and the body whispered to me. "Ignore all of it. Keep going."

There were more eyes here. More people, yes, but it was their eyes that concerned me. The Mentium were looking for me and they'd search with more than their own senses. I'd employed one camera that night. They had millions at their disposal. My saving grace was that they didn't know into whom I had slipped. I had to keep it that way, though my inability to mask my mind was no help.

I straightened my body, slowed my pace, and tried to look as ordinary as possible. It was all I could do. I was also shivering again. It was the second time that night I had found myself shaking. I hated the shaking.

6

THE KITTEN

Le Louvre stood sentinel to my left as I crossed a silver, ice glazed *Place de la Concorde*. Its stones, wet and slick from the rain, glistened in the lamplight as they froze with the plummeting temperature.

The transplanted Egyptian obelisk at its centre called back to a simpler time when the reach of the Mentium was confined to the locale in which we found ourselves. That time came to an end and what was to come, what I had to prevent, involved nations.

The Mentium's power had expanded a thousandfold with the birth of my radio and I would not tolerate its abuse. There's a difference between steering the ship and commandeering it outright. We'd retired as captains of society and promoted ourselves to admirals far too long ago.

I stopped midway across a deserted *Pont de la Concorde.* In the distance shone the garish Citroën advertisement that stained the steeple of Eiffel's tower — the broadcast antenna for my radio. It was a testament to the tastelessness of Monos. At the tower's peak, the spectral spotlight swept the sky, extending far into the night. It was a reminder that the power of my device would bring chaos to cities as far away as Bergen, Moscow, even Cairo. I couldn't imagine Ma'at standing for that.

"My triumph and my undoing." I muttered as my eyes followed the arc of the light.

Gripping the frigid concrete railing, I peered downward into the abyssal black of the Seine. The undulating water flashed at its peaks with the amber of streetlights that lined the river's banks. The sight was stunning and again I grew infatuated, though thankfully for a reasonable amount of time. The opium continued its too-slow fade and I had been moving with ever-growing fluidity. My senses had become less active and my preoccupation with the frivolous was beginning to wane though the drug still burned. Its twisting of reality now came with merciful subtlety.

The clarity that grew as the dragon began to uncoil from the brain prompted a more thorough investigation of the man I had become. In time, the memories stored in his brain would become accessible, but for now, physical clues were my only aide.

I withdrew the items and placed them on the wide rail in front of me for closer study. Aside from the wallet, identification card, watch, and keys, I'd found some pocket change, three jazz cigarettes, two well-used tortoiseshell plectrums, and a half dozen business cards. 'Del Chambers' they read. 'Guitarist, Arranger, & Composer.' I was relieved to see that he used the moniker, Del. Delbert was as dreadful as his twiggish body. I was also heartened to see that the addict had a profession though he had neglected to translate his business cards into French, so his competence was still in question.

My breath rose in a thick fog as I pocketed the items and placed the watch on my new, pale wrist. The air began to sparkle and I spun a lazy circle, taking in the effect. This wasn't the drug. It was snow. The temperature had dropped below freezing. This too, I studied with a serene smile twisting my face.

Move, I thought. This time only thinking.

I had to increase my pace. Lilith and the Mentium would not stop. Exiting the bridge to the southeast, my steps toward Del's home fell as if they were habit. As if I had always known the route.

I approached *Gare D'Orléans* and its massive clock loomed over me, showing 12.17am. I had been Del for over an hour, wet and chilled for just as long, and knew I couldn't survive the cold much longer.

My new body shuddered.

I am sick of shaking tonight.

My muscles locked, then my legs crumpled underneath me. I cycled through the possible causes as I continued to quake.

"Not now," I pleaded to no one. "What is this?"

The drug, the transference, none of that made sense. I wasn't sure whether I should pull away from the brain or dig in deeper.

Three great convulsive waves tore through me and my control over the new body blinked in and out like a toddler at a light switch. Panic exploded within me, but I managed to get to my knees. A final flash of something, not pain or pressure but just as intense, lit my skull like a lightbulb. My hands gripped my head through my hat.

It was as if my consciousness was a magnet, pulled from a ferrous base and then released, slamming back. An invisible hand, toying with me. No, not toying, struggling. It was as if something had awoken within me.

The explosions in my head burst again and again. I crumpled onto my side in the street, still shaking and still gripping my narrow skull.

Bearing down, I did everything I could to secure my tether to the brain. It was a frightening, foreign experience. I'd never felt anything like it. A man of my years rarely felt anything new. But something new was happening. Then the words came.

Leave me alone… The voice, though weak, echoed in my head.

Who…? I thought. Someone was with me. Someone was inside my head. Not broadcasting into my head. Actually inside.

"No. Impossible," I said aloud. "You could not be…"

Bern… Where's…

"Stop it! No… No! You're supposed to be gone. You have to be gone!"

Please. I'm scared.

"I'll bury you," I said, again out loud. "You cannot be in here with me. I'll… Argh!"

The shaking slowed and, now foetal, I opened my eyes to the frozen street. He was still there. Somehow Del was still inside.

I'd shoved him down into the subconscious and hoped he'd stay buried, but I'd need to deduce some permanent solution soon. I'd just picked a fight with some of the most powerful humans on the planet. I'd have to fight the pull of that damned opium in the coming days.

Now, I had someone to fight inside me as well.

"I just need to get out of this snow and think!" I kicked at a brown ridge of slush near the curb.

"Betrayal, suicide…" I kicked more snow, "Drug addicts, voices in my head! My life is some hellacious story from some damned pulp rag." More snow. "No plan, no friends, no idea what to fucking," snow, "do," snow, "next!" Snow, then my hands went to my knees and I tried to catch my breath. Apparently there wasn't enough opium left in my system to cap my frustration, though it still rocked me back to calm now that the show was over.

As I panted mumbled oaths, there were no words from within. My head-mate was silent but Del's instincts again spoke. That instinct prompted a turn away from the river and pointed toward his home.

I rubbed the bridge of my nose and squeezed my eyes shut. Whether out of self-preservation or some desire to make nice, the addle pate was helping me.

"Fine," I said, raising the collar of my overcoat against the snow and walking onward.

After five frigid minutes, instinct drove me onto a darkened Boulevard Raspail. The weather had exacerbated the desolation of the street. Desolation was perfect. Desolation was beautiful to me that night. Desolation was safety.

Only two blocks in, the muted slap of a new set of footsteps began plodding behind me. I had earlier asked myself how the night could grow worse. I regretted that question.

This has got to be a jape. I slowed to a confident walk, or the best my inebriated, shivering legs could muster. I threw my shoulders back and tipped my elbows out to seem larger. Futile of course but I had to try.

I used the bay window of a storefront as a mirror to see the stalking creature. Shadow obscured their face, but their posture and their mind were easy enough to read. The man was a thief, but I had no time for such trifles.

I trod on for three more blocks. The thickening snow swirled as the coal-smoked breeze flowed around building after building on its journey into the open air above the river at my back. The shops that lined the street had long been closed and only a select few lights remained within apartments above. The minds of their occupants bellowed their distracted, inane thoughts but those thoughts provided proof that the two of us were alone on the street. It was better that way. Privacy.

I approached an alley that I, not Del, remembered from past shopping excursions in that neighbourhood. It would suffice.

I slowed further still, allowing the distance between myself and my assailant to decrease. A sharp right turn and I plunged into the dim passage. He followed. My consciousness was prepared but I held little trust for the body. My movements had to be simple and they had to count.

A brick wall, covered in a rough stucco, blocked the end of the alley. Refuse overflowed its containers, as expected, and it was then that I set about removing at least one nuisance from my night.

"*Ton portefeuille,*" called a juvenile voice from behind, demanding my wallet. Below me lay a broken apple box and an assortment of spent tin cans, their detached lids scattered across the ground. I turned and backed myself against the billowing garbage. Both hands groped the air in a show of surrender and as Del's thin arms climbed past my face I began to second-guess my decision to confront the rogue. I'd been in control of nothing that night and if I could not control this situation how could I hope to end the Twins' plan?

"*Ton portefeuille, maintenant,*" the young man demanded in a tone that feigned dominance. The little light that penetrated the dark of the alley was too dim to see the blemishes that certainly covered his face. He could not have been more than nineteen. I remained silent.

As expected, he stepped closer. From his breast pocket emerged a medium-sized pen knife and he brandished it as if it were Excalibur itself.

"*Maintenant!*" he said again, adding a puppyish growl. He was rattled by my refusal to play along. The calm provided by the lingering drug aided my cool demeanour. Any positive was welcome at that point.

Still I said nothing. Frustration tensed his body which only served to annoy me. I owned frustration that night.

His posture, his stance, his breathing, all signalled an impending strike. I held my ground and remained mute though it was difficult to hold my arms aloft. What little muscle clung to Del's chilled bones were already sputtering out. It was pathetic.

"*Putain!*" he spat and charged. He held his knife firm but far from his body, blade pointing up. Amateur.

As he lunged, it was time to execute my grand plan. I flopped backward onto the piles of garbage. It was the only damned manoeuvre that drug-ravaged body could manage though my timing proved true.

The boy's sophomoric attempt to push his knife into my ribs dissolved when I dropped, and he sailed past me and onto sacks of kitchen scraps. I lay supine on the cold wet ground groping the pile of tin cans and secured the first sharp edge I could find.

He lay on his belly trying to push himself up while I rolled to my knees then threw myself on his back, pinning him to the stinking filth.

"*Monsieur!*" he said, contorting his body in desperation under my limited weight. Weight I shifted over and over to keep his hips to the ground.

"*Monsieur, s'il vous plaît, s'il vous plaît! J'ai une famille, une bébé! S'il vous plaît!*"

"Enough. *Tais-toi,*" I said then continued in French. "Fate is the consequence of choice my friend, and you've chosen."

Just like I had chosen.

My words fell quietly into his ear as one of my hands struggled to keep a grip on his blond hair. Pulling his head back, the other hand pressed the jagged can lid to his throat and drew it from left to right.

When his fight faded, I dropped his face into the bags of garbage and reached for the knife in his hand. He was twitching when I pushed the blade between his ribs, just to the left of his spine. I hate the twitching. A few twists of the steel destroyed his lung and heart, ending both the boy and the delay he had caused me. With my hand on the back of his head, I pushed my unsteady body back to standing then stooped to retrieve the blade.

"Will this night never end?" I asked him as my own ribs heaved and my lungs sucked air. Falling and a small bit of grappling proved too much for Del's deplorable fitness.

I wiped the blade on the dead Mono's trousers, folded it, and placed it in my own pocket. He wouldn't mind the stain.

A pen knife was not much more than a toy, but it was better than nothing when fierce kittens like my young friend were about.

I left his body with the rest of the refuse and continued the long trudge toward my new home. In less than two hours I'd secured my new body's first kill. Though killing has always come easy for me, having spent lifetimes creating omens I'd label that an ill one. Del's body was not suited for killing.

The night was cold and growing colder. My own shaking was ever-present. I needed to take Del home. I had a lot to think about along the way.

7

MY RADIO

"Excellent soirée, M," said Ma'at, taking a fresh glass of champagne from the table next to our guest of honour, Gustav Eiffel. She wore a white silk dress and red sequined headband holding up a blue feather over her bobbed, obsidian hair. "This is quite the moment for you."

The old man sat motionless in his favourite chair. Motionless save for his eyes. It was 1921 and he'd just turned eighty-nine. Eiffel only invited the most notable of science's elite to join him in his simple yet elegant apartment at the top of the tower. I invited myself and a few of my closest associates for a combination solstice and inauguration party.

"It is," I said, waving my own drink at the other guests. "As times grow more complex, so too must our tools." A dozen of us were squeezed into the tiny apartment, not counting the two herculean Eunuchs acting as waitstaff. Whether they scrubbed the floor or guarded our lives, we preferred them big.

Those with invitations that night were we ten of the Upper Echelon, Izzy, the sole Underling, and of course, dear, terrified Gustav.

"And what a tool," said Tian as his hand gripped my shoulder. His current berobed body was Chinese, of medium height, medium build, and was aged sixty-seven. Most of us acquired new bodies after reaching forty-five but Tian liked to live full lives and rarely changed bodies before eighty. He said it aided in better understanding and thus the manipulation of those who held most of the wealth in a population.

"You've really outdone yourself," he said. "Saving this iron monstrosity from the scrap heap was a stroke of genius."

"Genius? From you no less. I'll take that." I raised my glass to his good taste.

"Of course you will," said Ma'at, linking arms with Tian. "Please, don't encourage him."

"It certainly doesn't take much," he said, patting her hand.

All in the Mentium were fond of Tian save for the Twins, who weren't fond of anyone but each other. As the oldest of our lot, Tian was everyone's grandfather figure no matter the age of the body he inhabited.

"If truth be told, though it needn't be, it was really Marconi doing my work for me," I said. "His trans-Atlantic broadcast set a lot of minds racing, myself included. All I had to do was make sure that the conversations had by those that mattered stayed on course."

"Well, with this radio of yours, we'll finally repair what the Monos have so badly broken," said Tian.

"Repairs are sorely needed," said Ma'at. "That war was embarrassing and costly and we can't afford to let our guard down again."

"Here, here," I said.

The Great War was the first major failure for the Mentium in centuries. We'd been taking our hands-off approach to societal control to an unhealthy extreme. The Monos in turn took their petty squabbling to their own extreme.

In the aftermath we resolved to put things to rights with more targeted control. It was necessary to expand our power and yet maintain anonymity and invisibility within society at large. My research into radio and the adaptation of its technology provided the solution we needed.

On December 24th, 1921, our inaugural broadcast coincided with the inaugural broadcast of Radio Tour Eiffel, the first state radio station in the world. Controlled by us, of course. "With this," I said, placing my hand on an iron crossbeam and by extension, my radio, "our reach is now the continent, not just our surroundings. We have a cannon with the touch of a feather."

"A feather?" said a drunk Apollo as he and his sister sauntered over to us.

"Why would you load a canon with feathers? Think big, my good man."

"Whispers have always been more powerful than weapons, Apollo, and now we have a whisper weapon. It's just glorious," said Tian, visibly proud of himself and of me.

"We prefer it when a weapon deals a blow," said Artemis, the smoke from her cigarette puffing with her words.

"This is a tool, not your sword," said Ma'at, "its impact only matters so long as it aides the building process, or in our case, rebuilding."

Ma'at squeezed my arm and with a roll of the eyes, moved to secure a chair before the Twins could rebut. She knew better than to follow them into an argument. Being correct rarely matters when the odds are two to one.

As she walked away, I too took my leave. Tian could fend for himself. I procured another glass of champagne from a Eunuch's tray as the brawny man lumbered by in his tuxedo.

"Tonight is a momentous occasion," Tian said as I stepped toward Lilith and Yemoja at the back of the room. "You twins just relax and celebrate. M's radio will leave the Mentium, no, no, the world, no, *everything,* forever changed."

If only he knew what was to come.

Beyond the massive iron girder that bisected the room sat Yemoja in aquamarine satin and Lilith in emerald taffeta with a chessboard and an air of tension between them. The scene reminded me of the clash between ocean and land.

"Must you always do battle, love?" I asked as I rested a hip against Lilith's shoulder.

"Battles never stop, darling, and this one has been marvellous," she said, reaching down to rub my leg but never taking her eyes off the board or her mind off of her strategy.

"Marvellous for you," said Yemoja. Her dark eyes did leave the board long enough to greet me then sneer at her opponent.

"Going that well?" I asked.

"Ha, that depends on the heart of your question." Yemoja moved her bishop. "This is one of the best games I've played but I can tell she's toying with me."

"Toying with you?" Lilith said, leaning forward to move her rook. "No, dear, I've beaten you. Checkmate."

"Of course you did," Yemoja said, then snapped her fingers toward a Eunuch who extended a full coupe in a hand the size of a bear's paw.

Thank you, sweetie, she thought to him then turned back toward Lilith. "You know, chess originated in Africa."

"Then I should expect more of a challenge from you."

"With that, I leave you," I said, kissing Lilith on the forehead then taking Yemoja's hand.

"How do you put up with her?" she asked.

"The secret is to not engage," I said. "We haven't played chess since the 1750s"

"Weakling," said Lilith.

"And you still love me." I bowed to them both and turned to leave.

"I have a lover in Lagos who would jump at a chance to play with you," said Yemoja as I stepped away.

"When do we set sail?" asked Lilith and the sound of their clinking glasses rang out behind me.

At the windows of Eiffel's cosy abode stood Izzy's sleek figure chatting with Cernunnos' brawn. Between them and myself sat bearded, boisterous Radegast in full black tie, wine bottle in hand. At his side burned Kali in a beaded orange dress and black sable coat. I say burned because everything thing about the woman was heat and fire and energy. Radegast was bearing the full brunt of her laughter as did the ivory beads around her neck.

"And then the raja said to me, 'Teach me! Teach me your secrets!' Then he," she said, shaking her head and waving a hand in front of her face.

"Stop it, I can't, I can't" said Radegast between guffaws. He put the wine bottle to his mouth then handed it over to Kali who drank deeply. I raised my glass to them then left them to their stories.

"M," said Izzy and motioned me over with his head. "Cernunnos was just asking me about our next steps."

The tall redhead extended a powerful hand to me as I joined them.

"Damn fine machine you've built here, M. Izanagi says you'll be in full swing in a day or two. When do I get my turn in a chamber?"

"Patience, old friend," I said, and he was my friend, at least as friendships go in the Mentium. "Everyone will take shifts in the chambers. Izzy, can you shuffle some names around on the schedule? I think Cernunnos might enjoy next Tuesday's broadcast to Edinburgh."

"I think I can manage that," he said. "Anything else?"

"Not tonight, Izzy. You need to worry about your current mission."

"And that is?"

"You're an Underling at an Upper Echelon event. Get drunk, eat as much as you can, and regret nothing."

"Will do," he said.

"Oh, also, could you get us fresh champagne from the Eunuch?"

Izzy shook his head and took our empty glasses.

"What are we doing in Edinburgh?" asked Cernunnos, handing his over.

"Technically, nothing," I said. "Our operatives in Edinburgh won't be involved. The entire operation will be based here in Paris. King George will be at Holyrood and we have a few suggestions for him. Care to climb into the good king's head?"

"From Paris to Edinburgh? Incredible," said Cernunnos as he stared out the window over the city of light.

◆ ◆ ◆

By 1923 our work swelled to a pace of nearly two dozen transmissions a week. We could influence a vote in Prague, order a killing in Madrid, and convince a Russian minister to hire one of our Underling operatives all on the same day, and all from within our own temple in Paris. Every message was subtle and efficient. For some that wasn't good enough.

"Have you finished?" I asked Izzy.

My lab lay in the cavernous double-height basement of the Mentium's temple. Daylight glowed from frosted windows at street level. Ours was a temple in function alone, ostentation was something to be avoided when operating an unseen society. Despite this, 36 Rue Gabrielle was a palatial red brick and plaster corner tower with upper views over the entire city. Sometimes we couldn't help ourselves.

"Of course I've finished," he said, hunched over a pile of schematics. Other low-level Mentium technicians bustled around him. "Triple checked."

His meticulous, pomade-laden hair glinted in the afternoon sun as he looked up from his work. "New couplings were installed last week. We'll need to check here," he said, pointing at one of myriad caverns in the catacombs below Paris. "Or here." Of course this chamber was on the opposite side of the map, "in order to inspect them in person. The terminals may have been corroded from the start or the couplings themselves may be faulty."

"Well spotted, Izzy." I paced around the wires and equipment of the lab. "How much longer?" We were in the middle of a transmission to quell an uprising in Hamburg against the Weimar Republic.

"Done," said Artemis as she sprang from her chamber within the sunlit brass and glass signal collector and went to Apollo who had been sitting, bored, while his sister worked. The two never entered the radio together but were always present for each other's sessions. Paranoiacs.

"Can't this thing do more?" she asked placing a pale arm around her brother's shoulders. "I'm feeling creative. Let's give those sots on the Majestic a voyage to write home about. A kraken would do nicely."

"You've got to be joking." I said, not bothering to look at her. It's obvious now that she wasn't.

"Vision, M. You lack vision," said Apollo, taking his sister's hand and moving toward the door.

"I assume we're no longer needed," said Yemoja as she pulled the copper helmet from her head and stepped from the signal collector.

The collector stood four metres tall including the four glass insulator pylons that came to a peak in the middle. There was space for five Broadcasters within the body of the amplifier. A Broadcaster would stand on heavy rubber matting in one of the five coves and lean against the red tufted-leather backboard. Comfort is expected when expense is trivial.

"Yes," I said, waving her over. "You're done."

She stepped close and both Kali and Kukulkan emerged from the amplifier and followed. Kukulkan, in his powder blue shirtsleeves, took his Homburg from a hook and placed it on his head. The red feather in its bow was bright and big.

Each Broadcaster had been chosen for their given skills. Yemoja boasted the longest range; Kali produced the most vivid visions, and Kukulkan came in a close second, though he was not a part of the Upper Echelon. All Mentium below the ten members of the Upper Echelon were considered Underlings. Operating at such a high capacity meant recruiting select people from their ranks to transmit along with us.

"What's wrong now?" asked Kali, leaning against the table near Izzy with both arms, "I'm surprised you keep fouling up. We barely got those krauts sorted."

"There appears to be some disconnect in the catacombs," I said. "Don't worry, Izzy will scurry along and take care of it. Did everything go as planned?"

Kali shrugged. "Other than this tin can crapping out on us, yeah, everything's ducky."

"Yemoja," said Kukulkan, "that manoeuvre you pulled was exquisite. Can I get a lesson?"

"The conduit?" I asked. It was a technique of Yemoja's own creation and it was the perfect example of subtle dominance in action.

"Of course," she said in her practiced faux nonchalance. "I just had to find my microphone and loudspeaker, or in this case, *Lautsprecher.*"

"Please, spare us," said Kali. "You're good and you know it. Cut the bashful shit."

"Izanagi," said Yemoja, ignoring the slight, "when is the follow-up transmission scheduled? My own schedule is quite full."

"Tomorrow, Yemoja, tomorrow. I'll make sure the radio is functioning at one hundred per cent by morning. If that will work for you, of course."

Yemoja was the second most ancient of us behind Tian. Seen as a mother figure, her steady nature and blunt manner commanded respect. Izzy paid her an exorbitant amount of reverence.

"Noon would be splendid," I said, giving Izzy a small, mocking shake of the head.

"I can't do noon," said Kukulkan. He sat atop an adjacent table, his snakeskin shoes up on a chair.

"No one asked you, Underling," said Kali. "Or me for that matter but as long as you get this damned radio working properly, I won't cast a kitten."

Kali, unlike Tian, never stayed in a body past the age of thirty-five. She fancied herself a perpetual post-teen and tried to stay practiced — with varying degrees of success — in the lingo of the era.

"Noon will be fine," said Yemoja to Izanagi, repaying his respect with some of her own. To me she gave a smirk and to the others, a nod, before disappearing from the room.

"She's always on the move," said Kukulkan, his s's lingering and blending with his Guatemalan accent. Regardless of host, his lisp always surfaced.

"She is indeed," I said. "If you'll excuse us, Izzy and I have a meeting scheduled."

"Not so fast." Kali thrust a red-nailed finger against my chest. "Get this fixed and get it done quickly. I'm tired of these issues. I'm not climbing back into that thing until it's hitting on all sixes."

"No machine is perfect," said Izzy.

"Certainly nothing built by you two," she said, heading for the door.

"I'll cancel my lunch plans," said Kukulkan on his way out.

The technicians continued their work, tidying the lab and resetting the chamber for the next day's transmissions. This left Izzy and me alone at the table.

"The Twins need to stop asking to put on a show. My radio is not some kind of cinema projector," I said, resting against the table's edge.

"It could be. Easily. You know that," said Izzy. "Don't you ever dream of seeing what our creation can really do? We haven't even scratched the surface of its potential."

"It'd be fascinating, but the thought is asinine. Just because a motor car has a top speed doesn't mean it's advisable to reach it. Not only would pulling some damn fool stunt draw attention and interest from the Monos but the Reformed could catch wind of it."

"What could they do? They're on another continent. They haven't been active in Europe for decades."

"That doesn't matter. If Coyote sent just one of his bastard followers over on a sailing, they could blow the damned thing up. You know they're not above sabotage. Use your head."

"Yes, my liege, I beg forgiveness." Izzy, bowed over and over. "A thousand pardons."

"If only you actually revered me so. Then maybe I wouldn't have to put up with your drivel all damn day."

"Oh, you love my drivel."

SATURDAY

7ᵀᴴ JANUARY

1928

8

COHABITATION

Steam rose from warm electric streetlights, yet another modern addition to this ancient city. Exhausted and nearly frozen, I stopped, quaking amidst the thickening snow in front of a prosaic brick apartment block in *Le Quartier Croulebarbe*. Mold and signs of wear hung like decoration. A concrete placard above the door dated the building to 1893. It was far too new to look that old.

Pain flared in my joints as I removed Del's damp identification from my soaked trousers. In the amber glow I double-checked the street name and building number. Triple checked. The place was ghastly but I could finally get warm.

I reached for the door handle and placed a hand on the soiled brick wall to steady myself. It opened with a click and I hauled my frigid, tired body inside. A brass frame containing names and apartment numbers hung on the cracked plaster wall to the left. Delbert Chambers/Bernard Hammond #32.

Bernard. A second tenant. Damn it. More killing. More hassle. Don't be home.

The worn carpet of an un-level spiral staircase led me to the front door of Del's apartment. There, on the landing in front of the door, I took a breath and readied myself to deal with this Bernard if need be. I doubted that I could, unless he was just as frail as his roommate.

I took a moment to try and sense any minds that might be inside but felt none. Still, I didn't trust myself or my powers. With the kitten's penknife in one hand, keys in the other, I slid the brass into the lock. It took a shoulder to get the door open.

Three quick, awkward steps into the darkened apartment, two seconds to listen and observe… Just me. The door closed with a scraping thud and I groped for the light switch.

Small electric sconce lights illuminated a meagre two bedroom apartment. Old, ill-treated furniture filled the main room. There were empty wine bottles arranged near the door. Two music stands stood in the corner near the kitchen.

At the back of the apartment I found two bedrooms. The room to the right was well kept and simple. Someone had made the bed with care. A chest of drawers held toiletries displayed in neat rows. A line of old, carefully shined shoes sat at the foot of the bed. I hoped this would be mine. I felt I deserved some good fortune that night.

I turned and opened the other door. Abject chaos. If there was a place for everything, then nothing was in its place. There was, however, a diamond in the rough. A large, immaculate guitar with a sunburst finish sat in a stand against the far wall. I knew it was a Gibson L5. I knew that the violin-esque f-holes cut into its arched top were a recent addition to the world of guitar manufacturing and that it was designed by a man named Lloyd Loar. Above all, I knew that I loved that guitar as if it were the grail itself. I knew this because Del knew this. Each was a part of Del's physical memory. Memories that were becoming mine. This disaster was Del's room. My room.

I took a seat on the bed and gripped the edge of the mattress. "Of all nights," I said to no one. "Of all the bodies in all of Paris… This cannot be happening. I don't deserve this utter bullshit."

My anger bubbled like a pot on the stove. Any opium induced euphoria had passed. I stomped into the kitchen where I set about brewing some coffee. Warmth and calm were my top priorities.

Back in Del's bedroom, I stripped off my sodden clothes, hung them in his closet, and pulled out a mustard yellow jumper and a pair of brown corduroy pants, the seat worn paper-thin. Mismatched wool socks — the only two I could find — finished off the ensemble and went a long way toward bringing my body temperature up. The catastrophe of a room did nothing to aid calm.

After pouring myself some of the dreadful percolator coffee, I stood in the middle of the sitting room and stared. I had no idea where to begin. Nothing was as it should be. Del's body could not have been more ill-suited for my purpose. Nor his clothes, that room, his life, none of it. Nothing had gone in my favour. I required a body that could move, fight, or at least defend itself.

Instead I was Del Chambers, and everything Del Chambers was, comprised my new existence. I had to find a new host. I could not stay in such a body, but time was an inescapable trap. It would be two weeks at an absolute minimum before I could rid myself of Del. The Twins' near-sighted farce of a plan would come to fruition before then. Del Chambers, for better but assuredly worse, would be the one who prevented the coming disaster. Or he would die trying.

Coffee in hand, I returned to his room and perched on the twisted blankets that draped his bed. A tarnished brass alarm clock with a single bell sat on his nightstand and informed me it was nearing two o'clock. I pushed an ashtray through a pile of empty pistachio shells to make room for my mug then put my feet up and took a few calming breaths. My insides turned but intestinal trouble was the least of my worries.

For the next hour, I focused on my new body. It took five attempts to turn inward before I could manifest a true presence inside the mind. Once there, I followed nerve pathways into each of its parts, checking to see just how well this vessel could perform under pressure. The results were less than inspiring.

Lilith crept into my thoughts, figuratively, as I continued evaluating Del's body. She knew me better than any other. We had been rivals since before the birth of our organisation and lovers almost as long. Her understanding of me as a being would have proved quite the advantage for my little succubus, if only I had any intention of being myself. Therein lay the singular benefit of my circumstances. Del was the antithesis of who I had always been. In public, I would need to live his life as he would, while working to achieve my goals and stay out of sight of the Mentium. Del's inconsequential life would serve as excellent concealment. Finally, a positive.

The effects of the drug had burned to coals but I still felt some of both its figurative and literal heat. A minute spark of hunger, though not for food, flared in the brain. After my inspection of the body, I became fully integrated into my new brain. There was no pulling back now. All of the body's cravings were now my cravings until I managed to move on.

Unsteady limbs and a shifting mood were a vast improvement from the hours prior. I returned my focus to the corporeal world and leaned my shoulders against the headboard, attempting to take a moment just to breathe.

I… who are you?

"Stay down!" I spat.

Del's consciousness was disoriented yet it was again interfering. Stronger measures were necessary. I took a deep breath and again turned inward.

A dark cityscape stretched out before me. It more resembled a disaster zone than a metropolis, and I assumed the form of my previous host — brown tweed suit and all. This was not my standard mental avatar, but I didn't want to scare the man any more than he already was.

Del's mind was as disorganised as the rest of his life. It was a patchwork of experience, as if a junk collector was allowed free rein over an entire world. One building however, stood clean and strong and beautiful. A concert hall with bright lights and a grand marquee. "Del Chambers" was emblazoned across the glowing sign. Below that sign paced the man himself. He'd surfaced out of the subconscious and appeared dazed and lost.

As I approached, he jerked his body away from me, cowering in front of the theatre door.

"Del. How are you still here?" I asked. The question was rhetorical.

"What's happening? What is this?" he asked, fighting back tears. "Level with me man, I got the screaming meemies over here. Am I dead? Please, just tell me something."

I stepped forward, which sent him into a frenzy. He clawed at the theatre door, gripped the brass handle with both hands and pulled with all his might. I made sure the door remained closed to him, I focused my thoughts near Del as he desperately yanked and pulled. I steadied myself and with a pitiful amount of effort, began building a mental construct. On any given day this would have been a thoughtless task, but so soon after a transference it stood at the edge of my capabilities.

First, a golden frame materialised, then as I bore down, the space began to fill. First with a blue haze, then something more opaque, until a free-standing, blue wooden door had formed.

"Del?" I said.

He gave no response but instead continued to fight with the theatre door.

"Del, please. DEL!"

He looked up at me, eyes wide. I was pointing at the blue door.

"Try that one."

Instinct took over and he threw his body at it. He had turned the handle and swung the door open but managed to catch himself before stepping through. His fingers were pale as they flexed against the frame. A swirling sea of clouds, memory, lightning, and horrors, awaited him on the other side.

It was his subconscious.

He stared at the scene, transfixed and terror-struck and I used his distraction to end the situation, at least for the night. I placed a firm hand on his back and pushed. He fell and the door slammed closed. I'd locked him into his subconscious and hoped it would quiet his interrupting.

The world of Del's mind was now mine to command and I wanted none of it. With thought, not hands, I ripped the marquee off the theatre. As it hung, suspended in mid-air, a sound called from outside the body. My concentration wavered and the marquee fell.

Though I was inside the mind, I remained tethered to the senses. The sound of the front door opening pulled me back to the physical world.

"Del? Del are you home?" asked a voice from the entryway.

This was not the time for introductions.

"Del?"

A tall, sturdy, African American man stepped into the room. His clothes were as worn as Del's but were pressed and free from stains. This, I presumed, was Bernard.

"Del, Jesus, where the hell have you been? I've been out looking for your ass all night! You know I worry when you run off like that." He paused, studying Del's body as it sat on the bed. "Are you… dammit, man. I knew it. You let me run around in the cold while you're out kicking the gong around?"

A decision had to be made. I could pretend to be Del despite having no time to study his mannerisms, his speech patterns, any of it, or I could reach for the pen knife and hope to slip it between his ribs before he knocked it from my feeble grip. Neither were viable options so it fell to a third.

I stood on exhausted legs and stepped through the disorder of the room. His jaw was broad and shaved close. A single day's stubble rose from the skin. I focused on the area where his mandible bent up toward his ear and kept my eyes locked on that point. There could be only one attempt.

"Bernard," I said, giving the man a grin while continuing my stare and readying my body, "good to see you. I was just—"

"Bernard? You know my mom is the only one who—"

My small fist landed true and the big man fell.

9

HEAVY LIFTING

Bernard was heavy. I cursed Del's weakness as I pulled the man out into the sitting room by his wrists. I had no time for yet another bump in the backwater dirt road my life had turned into. What was I going to do with the man?

Near the window stood a chair. A short, rounded affair covered in a tattered, faded pink damask. I placed it in the middle of the room over a worn knockoff Turkish rug.

Next, I searched the apartment for some sort of cord. There was no point looking for anything in Del's room. Bernard's turned up nothing. I was tempted to use his ties. Silk is strong after all.

In a kitchen drawer I found a half spent spool of jute packing twine. It would suffice.

Slow, unconscious breaths singled that he was indeed alive. One less body on the tally that evening, at least for the time being.

My back screamed as I hefted his weight and took a few steps. After three ridiculous cycles of this, I finally lifted him into place. My old body would have completed the whole affair in one motion.

All the jostling caused him to start coming around. This would not do. Moving behind the chair, I wrapped a slender arm under Bernard's chin, his trachea and carotid arteries buried in the crook of my elbow. In any other circumstance, Del's small stature would have been disastrous but Bernard was still hovering just above conscious.

I had a narrow window in which to act.

As I squeezed and restricted his blood flow, his body again went limp. A few seconds and around three kilograms of precisely placed force can render anyone unconscious. Any human body, even my new, puny vessel could deal out a measly three kilograms of force.

I set to work binding Bernard. I tied his chest to the back of the chair, his ankles to the legs, his wrists behind his back, and all of it together.

The work exhausted me but had me fully awake. The minuscule pull of the remaining opium in my system couldn't provide enough influence to steer my mind back toward sleep.

I sat on the dilapidated couch across from Bernard. It, too, in that fleshy pink damask. What should I do with him? I could kill him and remove a possible complication. I could lock him away in some deserted part of the city until I had achieved my goal. Why hadn't I killed him? Was Del still exerting some force in the brain? No, logic told me Bernard could be of some use. He could earn his life by aiding me. We would see if he would be up for the task.

His tidy habits already established him as the better of the two men in this apartment. When he woke, I would interrogate him. If he proved adequate, I'd utilise him as my assistant. As I had no strength to speak of, and I seemed to be utterly alone in my undertaking, I'd need someone to provide whatever aid I required. There were inherent risks to that plan but it would increase my odds of success if I had someone at my side.

The idea of being alone swelled in my head. The Twins' behaviour held no surprise, nor did the lack of fight in many of the other members of the Upper Echelon. Self-interest reigned supreme. It was a trait we all shared. Not particularly noble, but what is honour to immortals?

It was Izzy and Lilith who provided serious blows to my sense of trust. And Tian. I couldn't fathom how the oldest and wisest of us could side with the Twins. It made no sense. He'd seen every flaw in their scheme. We'd discussed at least that much.

To shield him from retribution, I'd left him out of my treason. Just as I had done for Lilith. I'd chosen Izzy instead and I'd chosen poorly.

Still, I had assumed that at the very least, Tian would have recused himself from the whole debacle. Why had he engaged? Why had he chosen this nonsense?

I resolved to find out. As I was Izzy's mentor, so Tian was mine. He may have sided against me, but I knew I would always be safe in his home. While I might not have had anyone on my side, I wasn't alone.

I rushed back into Del's room and searched his closet for a heavy coat that better fit his frame than my borrowed mantle. Donning a moth-eaten dark grey overcoat, I returned the damp derby to my head. Making one more trip into the sitting room, I attempted to enter Bernard's mind; he was far from waking. Satisfied, I relieved Bernard of his wallet and left him to slumber.

10

SEEKING HEAVEN

"Here we are, *Monsieur,*" said the taxi driver as he pulled the motorcar to the side. As requested, the driver stopped five blocks from the building that housed Tian's apartment.

"*Merci.*" I handed him money from Bernard's wallet. Breath clouds and snow circled my head as I stepped into a quiet street on *Île Saint-Louis.* With my hands in the pockets of my overcoat, I began my walk. Deserted streets greeted me, and I was glad of that. Tian had a love of the water and of quiet and there was no location more suited to those demands than the smaller of Paris' two natural islands, situated just east of the towering Notre Dame.

The snow was falling much harder, a thick blanket covered the ground, but this time I found it beautiful not deadly. What a difference dry clothes and coffee can make.

Homes and apartments, four or five storeys high and squeezed together, lined the street as I left the first footprints of the night in the fresh snow. The buildings were dead. No lights, no sounds, and after a cursory scan of the area, no waking minds.

Unsure if my ability to block my consciousness from others was functioning at all let alone well, I was encouraged at my growing ease in sensing and sorting out minds of Monos. I didn't need the nightmares of others interrupting mine. The strengthening of my powers happened at a standard pace now the opium had faded but nothing else about my situation was standard. Any growth was a positive.

All seemed as it should for 4:30am on a snowy Saturday morning. Until I saw my first Eunuch. First one, then two more, lurking at the front door to Tian's building. They hadn't seen me.

I shuffled and knelt behind a hedgerow, my weak calves burning within seconds, and reached out with my mind, groping with my consciousness for others. I felt over a hundred sleeping minds as well as the three simple Eunuch minds. It was odd to see the group near Tian. He'd voted in favour of the Twins after all and they couldn't think I was a threat to him.

The Eunuchs posed a problem. I couldn't best them physically and Eunuch Minds are structured in such a way that they can only be used by one Broadcaster at a time. Whoever gave them their current directive, namely watching for me, would have to release them before I could step in.

The last thing I wanted was to be stuck out in the snow for the second time and I wouldn't turn around either. Tian would give me the answers I needed. He would help me understand what had happened at the Twins' sham meeting. He would know how the others felt and why they voted the way they did. Most importantly, he would know what to do about the opium. He could help me cope. He'd studied the drug and its possible applications.

There was no time to dwell over dragons as I kept my eyes and mind fixed on the Eunuchs. The squeal of a bad hinge and hard boot heels cut the night and the cherry of a cigarette emerged from the dark doorway. His details were too dim to make out but the shape of his hat was enough. Kukulkan took a place among the Eunuchs. I had been fond of Kukulkan. No longer.

The Underling stared ahead as my mind dissolved into fear. Aside from the Eunuchs, we two were the only waking minds. I hadn't sensed him. He, like all Mentium, like Tian, kept their minds closed to others unless the need to open arose. Lilith had found my consciousness and barged into my head because I could not keep her out. On that dark street, Kukulkan was oblivious to my presence. The realisation that I was blocking my mind was sweet relief. I was still hidden but I was no closer to Tian.

Think. I had to think. How could I get to him without being seen? The Eunuchs couldn't read my mind but they'd be suspicious of anyone who came near, and Kukulkan would be scanning for any new person to come into range.

A distraction was in order. I reached out again, and this time picked up on a random, wakeful mind. A man, thirty-two, fit and intelligent, his name was Claude, second floor apartment to my right.

It was as good a time as any to attempt entering Claude's mind to plant a few directives. This could barely be called broadcasting but it was all I felt up to.

I closed my eyes and, with far too much effort, sent my commands from my mind to his. Claude went to his closet and dressed, then walked outside and over toward Tian's door. The three Eunuchs turned their focus to the man and Kukulkan stamped out his cigarette. The man, per my instructions, continued his forward march until I was convinced their suspicions were sufficiently piqued.

"Kukulkan, let's talk," I said through the man's mouth. I held up his hands, gesturing for calm.

"Nothing doing, traitor. You know we have to take you in." He said, stepping closer.

"I was afraid you would say that." My words fell from Claude's mouth, then I sent the man on the run of his life.

All four men launched after him. Their quarry was found. I, in turn, launched myself toward the door to Tian's building. I could hear their collective footfalls echoing into the distance as I grabbed for the handle of the door. It was locked and I should have known it would be. I reached out specifically for Tian. He would have naturally had his mind closed to outsiders, but I hoped he'd hear my signal. It was a silly hope, but I was desperate. I called out to him again and again. Nothing.

Switching tack, I searched the building for any wakeful mind. All were asleep.

I slammed my fist against the door frame. The Eunuchs would return soon but I wasn't giving up. I had to reach Tian. I needed answers.

My focus shifted toward finding a new concealment point but as I turned to move off, something gave me pause.

Above me, directly across from Tian's apartment, a light flicked on. A single, open window was illuminated. I doubted that hitting the doorframe would wake someone and I couldn't fathom why anyone would leave their window open to the cold on a frozen January night.

The silhouetted figure of a woman stood in that window. The interior light passed through her curly hair and I could see that she was holding something. Further details were impossible to discern. I checked her mind but it read as if asleep. A sleepwalker? I stood staring up, and she down, for an uncomfortable amount of time. At last she began to hum the main melody of *Ambush on Ten Sides*.

The tune wrapped me in memory and the accuracy of its title was not lost on me. My initial shock at hearing the song turned to admiration. The likelihood that anyone on *Île Saint-Louis* knew that song, other than Tian himself, was nil. That crafty old man had left me a clue.

We often hummed a butchered version of that difficult traditional Chinese song as a duet during the many philosophical retreats we took together. That is, once the volume of wine surpassed the volume of our ideas and the stroking of beards began.

I loved picking his brain for wisdom and he was one of the only Mentium I knew who doled it out so freely. He harboured less of the inherent, self-sustaining mistrust than any other Broadcaster I had known.

Time is one of the only factors that separate we Broadcasters. The Mentium constantly grows its small but strong numbers as more of us are born but everyone starts at a year zero. Tian's year zero was over five hundred years before mine.

I hummed the bars back to the woman in the window and she disappeared from her perch. The light went out and I crept to the doorway of her building and waited. Light footsteps rang out from inside then the large oak door opened.

The woman was in her forties, her dark, curly locks tied behind her head, and she wore a long, white nightgown. Well, not so white.

Before any other details, her smell struck me first. She reeked of old urine and her nightgown was tainted with a large, light yellow stain.

"How long have you been waiting for me?" I asked.

She looked at me with bloodshot, unblinking eyes.

Again she hummed the first bars and again I echoed them.

"Sunday. *Gare du Nord.* 13:37. *Étoile du Nord* to Amsterdam. Your ticket," she said and brought the item she had been holding up between us. I grabbed hold but it took her a few seconds to release the locked, strained muscles of her fingers. She must have been waiting hours, maybe a day.

"Does he mean for me to run?" I asked.

"Answers," she said. "Guidance from your elder."

I smiled at that. He often called himself my elder, just to rub it in.

The woman began to sway.

"Please," I said. "Is there anything more?"

She fell to the ground, exhaustion taking hold now that her mission was complete. I pulled her inside the doorway and left her there. It was cold but she wouldn't freeze. The sun would soon rise, and she'd be found.

The ticket went into my breast pocket and I walked at top speed until I was out of sight of Tian's door, then I sprinted across the bridge and into the Latin Quarter where I raised my hand for another cab.

"Thank you, old friend."

11

EXISTENTIAL PONDERINGS

"Coyote, that ingrate. How did he slip through our grasp?" I asked, pouring myself another porcelain cup of *baijiu*. It looked like white tea but walloped like whisky. I needed the distraction.

"Our grasp is weak. Our touch is light. We were not prepared for such rebellion," said Tian. He sat in yellow robes in his mountain retreat outside Beijing. Ma'at, Lilith, Izzy, and I had chosen to join him. We all needed a vacation, and to escape Paris for a time. The five of us talked below paper lanterns in his open-air sitting room. The green of the trees outside offset the reds and golds within. A low table lay between us holding a clay jug full of the tasty beverage.

"Then should we not strengthen ourselves?" asked Izzy. He, too, wore robes, but those of his native Japan, and the breeze that stirred the leaves outside also slapped at the fabric as he stood behind his chair. We all had opted for silk robes. The sight of westerners was no surprise to the locals because we were not seen. Inside Tian's small palace, we were served only by Eunuchs. Outside, we projected ourselves as loyal Manchurians and thus, for all intents and purposes, were.

"No," said Tian, sipping his own *baijiu*.

"No? Surely now is the time to steel ourselves," said Lilith. She sat on the floor between my bent legs with an arm over each thigh, a cup dangling from one hand. "Tian, we've never faced a threat like this. We have to destroy them."

It was 1732 and we'd just come through a massive schism in our ranks. It proved to be the first successful uprising in our history, and it was all the doing of Coyote, the trickster. There was never a more apt moniker than his.

A few centuries prior, when Europe was expanding into the Western Hemisphere, the New-World gods were inducted into the Mentium.

The fresh recruits included deities from Patagonia to the Arctic Circle. The Meso-American gods were an easy sell, as were most South American gods. Their religions were more similar to those of the old world in their structure. Their brutality and the scope of sacrifice, especially living, was a thing to behold. Amassing wealth and power was as much their aim as it was ours.

The North American gods, however, struggled to assimilate to our way of life. You, see, the gods of North America and many from Australia and the Pacific tended to seek balance more than gain. Yes, these Broadcasters lived off their worshipers but the amount taken was minute, pitiful in comparison to their Aztec, Mayan, and Incan cousins.

Coyote openly challenged the Upper Echelon within decades of his induction into the fold. It was endless. It wasn't more than a century before the disease of his ideas had spread within the Mentium. Many of the lesser gods from Africa and Asia, even some of the old Euro-Pagan gods sided with the Trickster and his Ameri-Pacific stalwarts. Their aim, they claimed, was to seek a more equitable system. They wanted to let the Monos determine their own fate, regardless of our profit or their ability to do so. I think what they wanted was to free themselves from the rule of the Upper Echelon. Either way, this could not stand.

"No," repeated Tian in his calm, focused demeanour. He was the founder of the Mentium. He'd travelled the world in search of the most powerful among us, not to bring us to heel, but to help us see reason. He envisioned our order, and his word was tantamount to law. He was the father of the Mentium and a father to us all in many respects. More so to me. He'd given me so much over the centuries, but his wisdom, his respect and his trust meant more to me than anything I'd acquired in my long life.

"Musicians," he continued, "use precision and grace to create the exquisite. They dare not fight or build with those same hands or they risk their ruin."

"What does that have to do with our situation?" asked Ma'at.

I, however, understood. "Advantage versus disadvantage. Risk versus reward. Specialisation," I said.

"Marduk is correct. Very good, my son," Tian said as a Eunuch, his mind freshly castrated, poured more of the distilled sorghum beverage into his cup. "Our system has become one of nuance, but that nuance comes at a price. No decision is free of consequence. To fall back into old ways, ways of force, would only serve to disrupt our delicate web. One cannot go to war in secret. To believe otherwise is folly."

"I do not believe Lilith is speaking of war," said Ma'at. "If we are decisive, can we not snuff them out before it comes to war? Can we not destroy them while their rebellion is young?" She set her empty cup on the low table between us.

"Young? Dear child," said Tian, "their rebellion was young decades ago. When Coyote convinced the likes of Mulungu and Vishnu of his beliefs, his rebellion had matured. When they chose to separate, they did so because of ideals, not their leadership. The only way to end them is to wait them out. Fortunately for most of us, we have the time."

"I mourn for Vishnu," said Ma'at. "His punishment was deserved but I mourn."

"As do we all. No one wishes entombment on anyone but he knew the cost of treason," said Lilith. "What a waste. What a fool."

"He fought for his beliefs," I said, rubbing her shoulder.

"That doesn't mean his beliefs weren't foolish."

"Fair, but we know belief is built on a seed of truth. No matter how far from reality one's belief grows, there must be a kernel of truth that one can cling to."

"What logic do these… oh what do they call themselves?" asked Ma'at.

"The Reformed," said Izzy with a wry grin.

"Right," she said, aping his smile. "What kernel of truth do these

Reformed use to build their beliefs? It all seems too ludicrous."

"That might does not make right," I said. "That tradition is not sacrosanct. That just because a system functions, does not mean there is not a better system."

"Are you suggesting they're right?" asked Lilith, craning her head around to look at me. "Are you saying their treason was justified?"

"Not at all. Just that they aren't entirely wrong. Their kernels of truth are generalisations. It's easy to rally around broad ideals but harder to justify them. I would never suggest they have utility for the Mentium."

"Yes," said Tian "but they one day could."

"Surely you're joking," said Izzy, his hands gripping the back of his carved chair.

"Not at all. Where these Reformed lost their way was in their willingness to abandon the Mentium. If they disliked our ways, it was their duty to show us a better path, not to blaze their own. I would hope that any of you would step up and protest actions that risk the Mentium. The Mentium as an entity is far greater than any system or strategy we employ. It must be preserved at all costs for it is what preserves us. Change is inevitable. We have changed our ways in the past and will do so in the future but through the change, the Mentium must live on."

"We are all agreed to that," said Lilith.

"The Reformed have chosen to become less than we are. Their ideals, by their own design, make them weak," he continued. "They are a wound. We must keep the Mentium as healthy as possible until the Reformed are but a memory, a scar."

Later that evening the two of us were alone, walking along a wooded path lit only by the moon and fireflies.

"This wound is deep," said Tian. "It is sad how quickly our brothers and sisters lose faith."

"They're fearful. That's all."

"Are you, my son?"

We walked on. The sound of our sandals against the hard earth beat out the seconds between his question and my answer.

"No, not of Coyote but I do fear for us. Lilith is right. We need to strengthen ourselves but the nuance you speak of must be maintained. Can it be done?"

"Oh, yes, and you will do it."

"Me?"

"Marduk, my boy, you know very well that brain of yours won't stop until you've discovered an answer. And you will, in time. I have faith in you. It is logic, not passion that has seen us through. Logic will prevail in this too. We will prevail. The world needs the Mentium as much as we do."

I hoped he was right. I needed him. I needed his guidance and reassurance. I knew I was on a righteous path, I just needed to hear him say so.

The world did need the Mentium. I believed that. Monos could never rule themselves. In that, the Twins were right. But to have the Twins be those rulers? That had to be stopped and I had to honour Tian's mandate to bring logic back to our secret empire.

12

QUESTIONS

"You need to stop struggling, Bernard, or I'm just going to kill you and be rid of you," I said, standing in front of the angry man. "It is Bernard, isn't it?"

"Stop talking like that. And you know damn well what my name is… Delbert! There. How do you like that?" He said as he strained against the packing twine. "Del, what the hell is going on?" With each pull and jerk, Bernard tightened his own restraints.

"Answers come later. Now, since we've been thrust into this predicament, it would be prudent to get acquainted. It will aid my final decision."

"Decision? Acquainted? Del, knock it off. I don't care how hopped up you are. This isn't funny."

He wasn't understanding. What could one expect from a Mono? Almost no Mono-Receivers ever had the fortune, or curse, to know my kind existed. I took a seat on the couch opposite Bernard.

"Yes, Bernard, let's start with Del."

"Why do you keep calling me Bernard? And why are you talking in the third person?"

"Because we've just established that that's your name. Pay attention."

"Del, listen to me. You've got to think your way through that shit," he said, staring into my eyes. Concern and annoyance painted his face. He was fighting the twine less but cringing more. "You've called me Bernie since the day we met. Since we were little. You remember?"

"I'm sure Del remembers and I'm sure he does call you Bernie."

"Del, you've never been like this. You on something new?"

"Yes, Bernard, in a manner of speaking. Del has never experienced anything like this and, truth be told, neither have I. It's quite new for the both of us." This was already becoming tedious. "Look, I have never called you Bernie, ever, because I'm not Del."

There was a long silence as Bernard studied me, his sturdy body, a better fit for me by far, was tense against his restraints. His anger simmered just below the surface. Then… the eruption.

"Oh, come off it!" he said, tugging and twisting at the twine around his wrists and ankles with such force that his chair danced below him. "You know what? Go to hell. I don't need this. Let me loose and sober up. I mean it. Let me loose. I need some air."

I permitted myself a long sigh. It was going to require more than words to convince him and I felt less and less inclined to do the convincing.

"Let me out, Del. Now!"

Despite my annoyance, I couldn't blame the man. Living with an opium abuser meant living with a liar. It meant living with someone you cared for but with all the foundations of trust washed away. Unstable. Volatile. Dangerous.

A demonstration was in order but with my abilities still so weakened, it would need to be brief and to the point. Still, Bernard had to be shown that my behaviour wasn't drug related and that I was indeed, not Del. After he had that knowledge, his reaction would seal his fate. I needed help but not from one who would be a liability.

I let my body slump, cradled by the couch, and closed my eyes, turning inward and securing what amounts to mental footing. It was time to broadcast, fully this time.

"Hey, Del. Where'd you go?" he said, panic creeping into his voice. "Don't fall asleep on me, man. You gotta let me go."

I didn't feel any influence from Del's consciousness. He was still repressed, which meant I was free to work.

When talking to Lilith, she was in my head so she did most of the heavy lifting. There on that dismal sofa, I'd get my own exercise. I took a breath and, to paint a physical picture of a most decidedly non-physical act, filled my mental lungs and prepared to shout.

My eyes opened and focused on Bernard's. His were a deep brown and as I stared, I entered his mind. This is by no means mandatory, but I've come to learn that a little dramatisation goes a long way in the demonstration of one's skills.

Bernard, can you hear me? I said without speaking. The lips of my new body remained unmoved. My voice, my previous voice, calling out to him.

"Who said that? Who's there?" his eyes darted from door to windows and back, then settled on me as his thoughts spun through the possibilities. He was analytical, along with being strong and determined. That meant the score was three to zero in favour of becoming my assistant.

Bernard, there's no one here except for you, me, and our mutual friend Del. I sat frozen, staring, focusing on the task at hand.

Terror filled Bernard's eyes.

"Jesus, dear god, Jesus, what's happening?" He jerked and pulled at the twine and made the chair dance across the floor. He looked like Jack Johnson against the ropes taking body shots. He had Johnson's frame, though with more hair and less muscle. Bernard's manacled minuet ended with a crescendo of strain then subsided.

Wait, did Del slip me something? Did that little shit drug me? He glared at me, at Del's body, his jaw set.

"No Bernard," I said, this time out loud. "No one slipped you anything."

"Whoa, whoa, whoa." His saucer eyes and lip quiver made me suppress laughter. So typical. "How… how did you know what I was thinking?

I'm inside your head Bernard. I responded, once more without speaking. *You're sitting in your living room, Del is tucked away inside his subconscious and I've now taken up residence inside his body. I am speaking directly to your mind, reading your mind, and trying to decide if you're worth more to me alive or dead. Those are the simple facts of our situation.*

"Simple?! Jesus, am I dead? I think I'm dead."

"Bernard," again switching back to a physical voice both from exhaustion and annoyance, "you are not dead, yet. Del is not dead.

None of us are dead. We are all alive, real and existing in the same reality. You've just been introduced to a new aspect of that reality. Most are a bit taken aback."

"This is magic." He began to rock. "Definitely magic. Okay, okay, okay… So, are you some sort of demon? Is this voodoo?"

"No. To a Mono like yourself, it may seem like magic but that's because you don't understand. We will of course rectify that if I let you live. What you are experiencing is science in the same way that all things are science."

Bernard's head swung back and forth in slow negation of my statement. He stared at the ground as if it wasn't there. His chest heaved under his pressed suit and strained at the buttons of his shirt. I didn't need to read his mind to know what he was thinking but for curiosity's sake, I did. He was sorting the facts and didn't like their arrangement.

"Bernard! Come back to me Bernard," I said snapping my fingers in front of him.

"Don't kill me. Please, just, just, okay, I… fine I believe in you, you're real, okay, just don't kill me. And don't kill Del. Please."

I crossed Del's pipe cleaner legs and draped my arms across the back of the couch.

"First, I'm not Father Christmas, your belief is not necessary. I exist whether you believe or not. Now, I have a few questions for you."

"Anything, just, just don't kill me."

"Your favourite author?"

"What?"

"An author or I'll put this," I said, pulling the kitten's penknife out of my pocket and opening the blade, "between your ribs."

"Oh, god, uh, Doyle! I like Doyle!"

A fair answer.

"Can you run at least a mile without stopping?"

"I think so. I mean, sure. If it keeps me alive."

"Good. Twelve times twelve?"

"Um, 1…144."

"If Del's body should come under threat of harm, what would you do?"

"Whatever it takes. Del's my best friend. Please don't, just don't hurt him."

I looked at the knife in my hand and placed my index finger on the spine of the blade. A slow smile spread across my face and with a quick jerk I pressed the blade to my throat.

"No, Jesus, no! You bastard! Don't hurt him. Stop it!" Bernard thrashed at his binding and lunged at me, bringing himself and the chair crashing down on one side.

"He's done nothing to you. Please. Just stop. I'll do whatever you want. Anything just please don't hurt him." Bernard's fear and rage were melting into helpless terror.

I uncrossed my new legs with a kick and stood, lowering the pen knife to my side.

"Thank you," he said with a quavering sigh.

I gave a nod then walked around behind him.

"No, come on. No, please. I swear, I'll do what you say. I said I'll do anything!"

"Relax Bernard," I said, standing over the heap of body and chair. "You're going to be okay. You've just secured your own life. I think you'll be helpful or more to the point, valuable."

"Valuable?"

"You clearly love Del. You clearly want to preserve his safety. It stands to reason that as long as I'm inside Del, you'll work to preserve my safety as well."

"Sure, whatever you say. Just please, don't hurt us."

The blade of the pen knife slid between his wrists and he flinched. I pulled and he flinched again as the twine fell to the floor. I repeated the steps with the ankles then folded the knife and dropped it in front of his face.

"What are you doing?"

I said nothing and retook my place on the couch. Bernard righted the chair and picked up the knife.

"Take it. Do what you will. I can't overpower you in this ridiculous body."

He studied my face then the knife then sat back down in the chair. "But Del..."

"Precisely, Bernard," I said with a clap then returned my arms to the back of the couch. My chest and neck were wide open and as safe as a lamb with its shepherd. "That was just one last little test. Now, we have much to discuss, you and I."

"Bernie," he said, looking up at me with lingering fear but more important, resignation. "Would you please call me Bernie?"

"No."

He bristled at my response. I could understand. It was but a small courtesy that I purposefully denied him.

"Look, do what you want but everyone calls me Bernie. Always have. I don't go by Bernard. My mom..."

"Yes, your mother is the only one who calls you Bernard. I know."

"If you know, then what's the problem?"

"Tell me, what does Del call you?"

"Bernie."

"That's precisely why I won't. I'm not Del. It would behoove you to remember that as our partnership moves forward," I said, picking at a frayed hole in the upholstery.

"Partnership?"

"Yes. You're going to help me with a situation in which I've recently found myself."

"What are you talking about? You take Del from me, you were going to kill me, and now you're asking me to be your partner? I thought you just wanted my protection."

I leaned forward, resting my elbows on my knees, my face closer to his. I had to seem genuine.

"First of all, I'm not asking, Bernard. As I said before, I'm not going to kill you and Del is still very much with us. We two cannot share a single brain and so I've placed him inside the subconscious. He's safe, but to restore him to his normal state I need your help. And yes, that includes more than protection."

Again he shook his head but this time his expression was pure anger.

"Blackmail. This is all blackmail."

"No, well yes, but not really blackmail. Reality. I could have killed you but didn't. The knife is still sitting in your lap but you won't raise it to me. The truth is, if you don't help me, I'll be forced to do the work myself, in Del's less than healthy body and that, I'm sure, will not end well. If you don't help me, your world is going to see war. A war far worse than the Great War. My bridges have been burned, so to speak, and I need an ally I can trust."

"Worse? What the hell is going on?"

"Tell me Bernard, are you hungry?"

"Hungry? Jesus Christ! You've got to be kidding me. I don't need food, I need answers."

"How about both?"

Everything about Bernard froze in a pose that screamed frustration. His mental gears ground, trying to assure himself that it would all be okay. I know because I stole a quick peek.

"Do I have a choice?"

"A yes then?" I said, standing and moving into Del's room. I grabbed a dry hat, brown this time, still a derby, and his heavy wool jacket and returned to find Bernard still glued to the chair, the knife still across his thigh. His mouth was still frozen in that twisted half shock half confused state that makes for the darkest of comedy.

"Bernard. Food. Answers. I require one. You want the other. Let's go."

He rose and placed the knife on a side table. "Fine, sure, what the hell. If you can get Del to eat something that would be great."

The sentence took me aback. I took a moment and evaluated how I felt. I should have been hungry. With all the walking I'd done, the work this body had done to keep itself warm, I should have been able to eat a goat. I needed to eat yet I felt no hunger save for opium. I already felt a small longing for the drug.

"This body must eat," I said.

"You aren't wrong there."

"Well, then it's time for a *petit déjeuner*. Is *Le Select* okay?"

"Yeah," he said, taking tentative steps toward the wrought iron coat rack near the door. "Yeah, sure… but I've got a lot of questions and you better talk."

"Yes of course, but do you also have money? I don't seem to have any with me. I will of course return the favour."

He paused as he donned his jacket. "You sure that wasn't Del talking?"

"Positive."

He patted the pockets of his pants then his jacket.

"Oh, sorry, of course you have money. Here." I handed back his wallet. "I needed cab fare."

"You stole my wallet?"

"And now it's back. Don't worry, I'll return your money in due time."

13

BREAKFAST

A typical blend of minds dotted the brasserie. *Le Select* was one of many ports of call for wayward artists, literati, intelligentsia, and those who wanted to soak them in. Being one of the only eateries open twenty-four hours a day turned the green light of its sign into a beacon for wakeful minds with much to think about and much to discuss.

As Bernard and I entered, the interior lights cast their glow on no more than ten customers. 5:30 on a Saturday morning was a lean hour for business but a superb time for privacy. The fact that it had once again begun to snow only helped our situation.

I led Bernard to one of the rear tables, an overeager waiter followed wearing the standard white shirt, black waistcoat, and tired expression.

"*Bonjour messieurs,*" he said as we took our seats.

"*Un moment s'il vous plaît,*" said Bernard with a commendable French accent for an American. The waiter nodded and scampered off as if he'd expected the request. Bernard was calm and feigned nonchalance, though unease wrapped him like cologne.

"Nicely done, Bernard. Americans usually make a mockery of themselves when they speak French."

"Well, I live here now and I've been taken in pretty well. It's only right that I do my part and learn the language."

"I'm assuming Del isn't quite so fluent."

I knew the answer but wanted to learn more about Bernard's

perspective on his friend. Part of the routine when settling into a new body is to scan your host's physical memory for any useful, unknown skills. I hadn't found much French in Del's head. I hadn't found much of anything useful to tell it true. At least not on the surface.

"Why do you want to know about Del?" he asked in a suspicious, fear-spiked tone. "Does it even matter?"

"An odd question," I replied. "I'm in the man's body, I'd say it's pretty damned important to know who he is. Now, I'm going to need you to try to think clearly, Bernard. Can you do that?"

"Yes."

"Good, now about Del."

Bernard took a deep breath. The air smelled of wine, brandy, and duck fat.

"Del, well, Del can get by. He knows how to ask for what he wants but isn't much for conversation. At least in French. In English… that's another story."

"How is your relationship? It would seem your friendship is a bit strained."

Bernard looked down at his hands while his thumbs rubbed the cuticles of each finger.

"We've been best friends for twenty years. Back in Chicago we did everything together. Music was always our dream. Just to play, you know? We don't care about fame. Just want to pay the bills doing what we love. We both live to perform, there's nothing like being on stage, but neither one of us play an instrument that gets the limelight."

"You play…"

"Why don't you just read my mind, smart guy?"

His voice was quiet and uneasy, but the barb still rose from his words. Brave, given the circumstances. I couldn't help but smirk.

"A valiant jab," I said. "But you do remember I was going to kill you not one hour ago."

"You won't kill me. You need me. I'm not going to pretend that I'm not afraid of you but I sure as hell am not going to make a show of it."

I liked the sound of that. It showed strategic thinking, boldness, and above all else, meant that I would be spared the nuisance of coddling him.

"Well then, to answer your question, after entering a new host, it takes time to reach full strength. Some abilities come quickly, others take days or weeks. To be honest, my demonstration was a bit draining," I lied. It had gone better than I'd anticipated, but I wanted to hear the words Bernard chose to speak rather than taking the information for myself.

"Host?"

"In time. First, my original question?"

"Fair enough. I play the bari sax. Baritone sax for those not in the biz. It falls in with the bass more than singing with the altos but I like it that way. Both Del and I love the pulse of the rhythm. You know, getting locked into the groove. It's why he's so devoted to guitar. Was devoted..."

"The opium?"

"Yeah, and some cocaine too. Now, don't get me wrong, I'm no prude or saint or anything, I've dabbled, but I don't like losing control. Del, well, he likes it. I mean, really likes it. He says he's more creative. That shit's sucking him dry though, man. He was like my brother now he's like my child. We came here to make it big. Now I'm just trying to make sure we can both eat and keep the lights on."

The weight of the words was hard to ignore. "Why haven't you kicked him out and moved on? You're clearly the better man."

"You're a real bastard aren't you?" His eyes locked on mine then sank to the table. "What kind of question is that?"

I let the silence fall. I was a bastard to most, and an outright villain to others, but I'd let Bernard make up his own mind.

Our attentions shifted to the menu though my new body showed no sign of hunger. My weakened state required that I eat anyway. Fuel in, energy out, simple chemistry though the task of eating would prove anything but simple.

As if by some impossible teleportation, the waiter appeared over my shoulder. *"Vous avez choisi messieurs?"*

"Oui, un café crème, deux oeufs, cinq merguez, et des frites," I said. The waiter nodded, his expression a mixture of remembrance and disapproval.

"Pour moi, un café et deux croissants s'il vous plaît," responded Bernard with a kind expression. As the waiter left the kindness faded.

"Your turn. Start talking," he said, centring his gaze on me. The look seemed natural to him. How many times had Del seen that face? I still wasn't sure how much to divulge so I spoke in broad terms and left the minutia for another time.

"Where shall I begin?" I asked.

"Try the beginning."

"Wait," I said, realising what had just occurred. "What catastrophe did I just order?"

Bernard cracked a smile, the first genuine smile I'd seen from him. "You just ordered a Del Special. You sure he's not pulling any strings?"

"How can such a small man consume so much?"

It appeared that Del's proclivities were able to manifest despite his repression and despite the body's indifference to sustenance. Another potential pitfall.

"It's been a while since he's eaten like that," said Bernard. "The drugs have had his guts all balled up for the past few months. He'll go days without eating then binge when he's feeling right."

I made a mental note to start reconditioning Del's body with healthy habits. "Okay, the beginning," I said. "Which would you like? I've had many."

"Start with your beginning. Where are you from?"

"That my friend, is a difficult question. For a number of reasons actually."

"I have lots of time. I have nowhere to be until the gig tonight. And I'm not your friend."

"Well, I won't bore you with details—"

"Stop talking and talk," he said. He was irritated, frustrated, and had no trust in me. Excellent. I needed an ally who could think for himself and his shift from stunned shock to assertive questioning was encouraging.

"Bernard, please, we don't have time to dwell on all my past lives. Even if we had years in which to discuss them. In reality, I haven't been *from* anywhere in a very long time. Technically I was born in the central region of what the British have dubbed Iraq. Iraq, I could rant for days over that debacle."

"Debacle? What's wrong with Iraq?"

"If you ever meet someone from Bretagne or Catalonia, ask them if they're French or Spanish. Their answer will provide yours."

"Okay, so you are, *were*, what, Persian? Wait, you know what, you're right. There's time for this later. Next question. Why are you in Del's head? How are you able to do that?"

"That's two questions," I said, trying to relieve tension. Bernard preferred that the tension stay as it was.

"Let's start with the latter," I said. "I'm able to exist within Del's brain because my consciousness is different than the vast majority of the population. I'm what we now call a Broadcaster."

"Who's we?"

"Patience, Bernard. Now, there are three levels of human cognition, technically four, that exist rather than the singular idea preferred by both philosophers and scientists. You, as far as I can tell, are what is known as a Mono-Receiver, meaning that you can only perceive your own mind. Over ninety-nine percent of humans are like you. Next, we estimate that about two hundred thousand people worldwide belong to a group known as Multi-Receivers. These are your mind readers, your mediums, and your fortune tellers. The powers of a Multi-Receiver can range from random flickers to extreme accuracy. Finally, you have my kind, the Broadcasters. The names for these categories are quite new. Our order likes to stay cutting edge. The advent of radio provided an excellent, more accurate analogy for the functions of consciousness."

"Radio? Not sure I understand."

"Human consciousness is like a radio signal and your brain, the brain of a Mono-Receiver, can only tune into one. The second level, the Multi-Receivers, those that aren't charlatans at least, can receive their own 'signal' as well as 'tuning in' to those of others. These are the

'Madame Esmereldas' and the 'The Great Mindinis' of the world."

"Okay, I think I follow, like radio stations."

"Precisely."

"But what about you? You're a… Broadcaster?"

"Yes. I, and those like me, are not only able to tune in to the consciousnesses of others but we can transmit our own signals to them. We can make others experience things, do things, and believe the things that we want them to. We can also, as is the current situation, move our consciousness to other bodies."

The waiter arrived with our breakfasts and set them down with a practiced nonchalance unique to brasseries. As soon as my plate made contact with the table, I set to work devouring the culinary abomination in a manner that defied decency. By the third bite, my drug tainted bowels began to protest but eating was not up for debate and I'd be damned if I was going to let the discomfort stop me from doing what was necessary.

I focused my mental energy on soothing and distracting the body while I let Del's instinct and bad habits control his hands and mouth. Broken yolks mixed with the red grease of the *merguez* sausages into a heart stopping sauce.

"How?" I surveyed the carnage before me.

Bernard responded with only a shocked expression.

Two slow, deep breaths and I again let Del's muscle memory attack the dish with deliberate fork strokes. Swine would have taken greater care with their food. As I sopped up the last of my yoke concoction, Bernard took the second bite of his first croissant.

"Okay, I don't care what you say, I just watched Del eat."

I looked at my empty plate and greasy hands with a feeling of disgust. At least my new, malnourished body had eaten. "Yes, well, his habits do seem to be surfacing. Usually that doesn't happen."

"Why not?"

"This is the first transference I've experienced where the previous consciousness remains attached. Their memories are usually all that remain. Before this, I've always been alone inside."

His eyes were full of accusation as he asked his next question. "What happens to the previous owner?"

I understood what he was doing but there was no point in deception. "The untethered consciousness is cast out into the aether."

"So you kill them? Is that it?"

"Not at first. Theoretically, their consciousness could return to the body after I vacate."

"Theoretically? Why don't they?"

"Because the body is terminated after use for both ease of exit and anonymity. Anonymity is paramount to the Mentium."

"You kill them."

"Yes. The body has to be severely weakened for the transference to occur. Leaving the body near the moments of death ensures a smooth transition."

"So, you're a murderer?"

"Among other things. At least to your kind," I said as a pang of discomfort spread through my abdomen. My stomach was not happy. "Murder is a term used by the consumed. The consumer deems it part of survival. In order to stay alive, we Broadcasters must find new hosts. It's as simple as that. Does the eagle murder the fish or the cow the grass?"

"That's different. Murder is about taking a person's life."

"No, that describes killing. Murder is an idea created by those who feel wronged. Murder is about two things. First, it's about robbing a living thing of time within their body. Potential time, remaining time, time one assumes they rightfully possess. They do not. No one owns time and one cannot steal what is not owned. If one was to die today, those who would mourn them would weep and say they had their whole life yet to lead. Years, decades, all speculation."

Bernard chewed another piece of croissant, his eyes never leaving mine.

"Now, the second aspect of murder has nothing to do with the deceased. It lies with the selfish drives of the bereaved. They have been robbed of time with their loved one and thus feel wronged as well. They have been made to feel uncomfortable. You can see this selfishness at every funeral. The body is left to decay for days until their loved ones can work the funeral into their plebeian lives. If a funeral were really in honour of the dead, the body would be rose-covered and subterranean within hours."

"What does this have to do with anything?"

"We Broadcasters do not pander to the selfish whims of Monos. We kill when it prolongs our survival. We kill to protect ourselves. We kill when it's convenient and to our advantage. We do so without remorse just as Del's body ate those pork sausages without remorse."

Still he sat in silence, tearing into the second croissant, still staring. I finished my lukewarm coffee while I stared back. I wasn't about to be judged by a Mono.

"You said four," he said once he'd finished chewing.

"Four what?"

"Four types of humans. Mono-recievers, Multi-Receivers, Broadcasters, and..."

"Spectres," I said, finishing his sentence and hoping it would end there.

"And? What are they?"

"Ghosts."

He dropped his gaze and rubbed his neck.

"Look, cut the crap. I'm not a fool so please stop treating me like one."

"You may as well think of them as ghosts. They are the only things that haunt the dreams of Broadcasters but thankfully, we kill them all."

"All of them? Why would you do that?"

"Because they cannot be contained or trusted or controlled. Spectres are the rarest form of humanity. A liberal estimate would be a few dozen births per century. Low numbers make for easier eradication and we eradicate them because their power far exceeds ours. Multis and Broadcasters can block their minds from others. It's what will make my movement throughout the city possible in the coming days. Spectres can get into anyone's head at any time for any reason. The damage they can cause… we haven't left any alive long enough to know the true extent of their power."

"Long enough?"

It was my turn to be frustrated. "Children, Bernard. When Spectres are children, they have a terrible time masking themselves. Better to nip them while they're buds than to suffer the thorns later. Fish in a barrel and whatnot."

"You murder children. I'm sitting here with a child killer, protecting him..."

"Yes, yes to all those things. Get used them and move on. Dwelling will only cloud your mind, and do not for one moment think that your opinion of me or my kind matters in the least. If it becomes a problem I'll remove you as well."

Deep breaths and cold glares were the only thing between us until a group of 'ossified four-flushers' in their mid-twenties entered the brasserie, all shouts and guffaws. The pretentious men, a bit too much Manchester leaking into their attempt at a London accent, took up residence at a booth across the room from our table. The staff cringed at their drunkenness and the volume of their voices, but the boys were too inebriated to care. It was approaching dawn and their party was at an end.

As they ordered food to soak up bad decisions, Bernard spoke again. "So why did a murderer choose Del?" He was still staring at me, assessing me. "Why didn't you push him out and kill him? Why do you need me? How can I trust that you won't kill Del or me or the both of us when this is all over? You know, to keep us from talking. And you still haven't really told me anything. What the hell is going on!"

The drunks turned toward us but dissolved into a cloud of laughter at the outburst.

"You want answers, Bernard. You deserve them and you'll have them," I said, sincere in delivery and intent. "As to your first question, I did not choose to take over Del. I was forced to flee my last host, and thus had to cast my consciousness out into the open. Del is where I came to rest. There was no choice involved. Usually a new host is carefully groomed. An opium addict would not have been anyone's choice."

Bernard nodded in reluctant acceptance of my answer.

"Del was not pushed out because… frankly, I don't know. I assume the answer lies within the circumstances of the transference or the fact that his mind was drowning in opium. In any event, it makes no difference because here we are."

Another curt nod from Bernard. He finished his coffee and slid the cup and saucer aside but kept the handle between his fingers, absently moving the cup from side to side as he thought.

"Your third question is easy to answer. There are three reasons why you're the one who is going to help me. You've proven yourself intelligent and capable. Your mind is analytical. I've taken a look inside your head and I've seen how you conduct yourself. I need someone who will think with reason and not emotion. You seem blessed with a high degree of both but what is more impressive is your ability to separate the two. You also have personal reasons to help me, which will ensure you do your best. You want to save your friend, and your own life is in danger."

"From you or this war you were talking about?" he said, his body tensing.

"Not from me. As for anonymity, I think an exception can be made in this case. If we succeed, no Mono would believe your story if you did talk. No, the danger to your life is the same danger that faces everyone in the city, the continent in fact."

"The continent?"

"Yes, for now. It will spread across oceans if left unopposed. A war is coming."

Bernard scanned the restaurant then leaned in close and switched over to a whisper. "What kind of a war?"

"One where all sides lose. Let's just say that my people, the Mentium, have lost their damned minds and are going to destroy millennia of carefully crafted systems. The world will fall into chaos. If you help me stop them I'll do what I can to restore Del and move on to a new host." I said this with confidence. In truth, I had no idea if I could bring Del back but I had a lot to accomplish and I couldn't do it alone. I needed him, so I lied to the man. "Finally, and importantly, you can help me move through the city and acquire what is needed with anonymity."

"There's that word again."

"You'll both be spared. You have my word."

"That means nothing to me."

"It soon will."

"It better," he said. "Now, the Mentium?" His short sentences were beginning to annoy.

"Yes, my kind, my society."

"I thought you said that you were Broadcasters?"

"Yes, but all Broadcasters are members of the Mentium."

"All? What if they don't want to be members?"

"When you're a Broadcaster you exist as a member of the Mentium or you don't exist."

"Christ. Who are you people? Hell, I still don't know your damn name."

"Most outside the Mentium don't."

"Try me."

"Marduk."

"The god? The one in those old carvings?"

"A history connoisseur. That name is somewhat obscure these days."

"I've been to the Louvre and have a decent memory, that's all."

"Well, god is a strong word. The influence of my kind was much more… overt in the distant past. We are more discreet now or at least we have been, which brings us to our current predicament.

My brothers and sisters wish to step into the light once again. They think that turning the monsters of old loose on the great capitals of Europe will be their ticket to glory. It's a tired old tactic that's been retired for centuries. The basic strategy is to bring death and destruction to your kind, then reintroduce themselves as gods and saviours, in which case you Monos will fall to your knees in adoration and gratitude and springboard them back into world domination."

"That is the most insane thing I think I've ever heard," said Bernard, leaning back against the padded bench.

"Insanity is correct. I was caught plotting treason to stop them and now, if I'm lucky, I'll only be entombed rather than killed."

"Entombed?"

"A procedure to trap a Broadcaster in a body until death. Once that happens, one's consciousness is recycled back into the aether and begins anew. We lose everything we ever were."

"Jesus."

"Actually no, not a Broadcaster but incredibly useful."

"Jokes? Really?"

The drunks were still making a scene. Their projected voices and disregard for the other patrons was a canker on my patience and apparently that of Bernard.

"Those Brits are obnoxious," he said. "Someone should shut them up."

"Gladly."

Again, with an embarrassing amount of effort, I cast myself into the mind of the tallest in the group where I planted a simple mental directive. I exited and watched it sprout.

The tall man retched and the full complement of his evening's cocktails and morning's food coated his friends in the booth.

Bernard, wheeled around at the sound of yells and admonishments then turned back to me. "Did you make him upchuck like that?"

"Yes. Yes, I did."

My satisfaction was dulled by the discomfort in my own bowels. Bernard looked beaten as well, which was accurate I suppose. A long span of silence ensued and the waiter used the gap in conversation to check in and apologise for the disturbance. Another coffee for Bernard and a sparkling water for me arrived while the waiter's counterparts chased the soiled pack back into the cold and set about cleaning up. We drank in silence and finished our beverages before Bernard spoke again.

"So, you promise you'll bring Del back if I help you?"

"Yes," I said with a certainty I myself lacked. I'd never restored a consciousness to a body. The idea was novel. But the fact Del remained within the mind made the process more plausible.

"Okay then, how do we move forward and what are the specifics of your cronies' plan? I was supposed to get answers, remember? I'd say you've given me half."

"The situation is far too complex and I would prefer not to talk about certain aspects in public. I have some thoughts on our next steps but I'm sure you won't like them. Let me sleep and regain some strength. Then, I promise, I'll *show* you what you need to know."

14

REDECORATION

Head to pillow, hands to sides, eyes closed, release.

Back in Del's bed, sleep overtook our still nauseous body and I descended from his dishevelled bedroom into his dishevelled mind. I stood in absolute darkness for mere milliseconds before an inner world began to coalesce before me. Del's inner world.

Before me sprawled a landscape of pavement and skyscrapers, apartments and slums, built by his experiences as he matured. It's the same for all people. Experiences are the brick and mortar of everyone's minds. Those American streets, however, were not the heart of Del's inner world. They were the roads into it and those roads were a tangled mass. Chaos. A map would do no good here.

I caught my reflection in the dirty glass of a deserted automobile. It had been quite some time since I'd seen myself as myself. Since Del's mind would be my home for the foreseeable future, I felt it only right be my true self.

The long dark beard was an old friend I had missed in these modern, clean-shaven times. My face was that of my last body, but my tanned skin stretched taut over the lean frame of a man in his twenties. Fine leather sandals adorned my feet and a dark red wool skirt wrapped my lower half. These were the trappings of Marduk the god.

One's consciousness becomes imprinted with an image of its body. In the case of a Broadcaster, it's usually a blend of their first body and their current body. For obvious reasons, I chose to use the visage of my last body. Each mental avatar is adorned with the accoutrements of their favourite incarnation as a god. We have never been gods, but we were the only gods mankind has ever known.

I wore no crown, but plenty of rich embroidery and golden jewellery. Of course, there were also my four black-feathered wings arranged like a moth's but as strong and ebon as a raven's. I had never really possessed them, but they were a favourite aspect of my chosen god-construct. This was who I projected to the people of Babel. My people.

I passed the toppled marquee in front of the impressive theatre that had been the locale for our first meeting. I hoped the core of Del's consciousness would be as well-kept as that venue. Despite evidence to the contrary, I held out hope. The core of most minds was cherished, hallowed ground.

The dirt and rot of a person's life is inescapable. It lines their mind like cigarette butts in the gutter but never takes centre stage. No, the penultimate centre of Del's mind was, unsurprising for a Chicagoan of his age, the remnants of the White City. The World's Columbian Exhibition of 1893 was a major boon for Chicago. In 1928, only two of the original buildings remained unchanged within the Olmsted-designed Jackson Park. This collection made up what could be described as Del's mental castle. He was too young to have visited during the fair, but would have spent a childhood in its beautiful carcass.

I crossed an arched bridge of fine ironwork, and made my way across a wooded island toward two monumental buildings. Their alabaster stones gleamed in the golden pre-sunset light that permeated Del's mind. I strode up to the foundation of the first building and gazed at the Art Institute of Chicago. To my right lay the Field Museum, previously known as the Palace of Fine Arts during the fair, and its green domes rose as proud pinnacles against the blue sky of Del's mind, a sky dotted with pink-tinged clouds that bled out to grey over the chaotic city that surrounded the park.

The buildings had impressed me during my visit to the fair. At the time, Ferris' wheel was much more awe invoking than these buildings but still, the architecture was commendable. I'll admit I was a bit surprised that Del could have generated such finely detailed and sophisticated constructs. For someone whose outer life was in such disarray, it was clear that he cherished and cared for this small part of his inner world as much as he did the polished guitar in his room.

Though my powers in the corporeal world were days from being at full strength, with my body asleep and my entire focus directed inside the mind, my power there was more than satisfactory to rebuild his mind into something that would suit my needs for the duration of my stay. Something organised, functional, and respectable.

I started with one brick.

Standing, calm and still, I reached toward a stone set as one of the steps of the Art Institute, yet had no need to touch it. Inside the mind, one is free to defy any and all natural laws, though many are still manifested. We are earth-bound creatures and thus, find it difficult to operate in the truly abstract.

With thought alone, I rocked the stone back and forth until it became free and hovered in front of the building where I willed it to expand. It grew ten-fold until it reached a useful size — about that of an automobile. Then I converted the monolith into iron, its rough exterior gaining a soft, smooth lustre. Still, this rectangular, ferrous prism wouldn't do. A sphere would serve better. The brick began to glow a bright, hot orange and my consciousness moulded it until all sides, all edges and points were no more. A luminous orb hung before me. A second sun in Del's sky. I held it there while it cooled. The soft chirp of sparrows echoed off the building's walls and were my sole disturbance. I could feel no rumbling beneath my feet. The only movement was that of the leaves in the relaxing breeze that circulated through this cognitive world. Del was well sequestered inside the subconscious and out of my way.

Looking skyward, my iron sphere was a solid grey once more and with slow, satisfied breaths, I began redecorating my new home.

I reached toward the orb. As I rotated my hand, the sphere spun. Drawing back my arm, I hurled the iron at the building with the force of an American baseball pitcher. It sailed through the stone facade and out the other side of the Art Institute. Dust and debris erupted from the openings, and I willed the ball to a stop then pulled it back through at a different point. The rubble exploded all around me yet it did not settle, instead dissolving into nothing.

The structure collapsed with relative ease. Its beams and bricks fizzling out of existence. Once the space was clear, it was on to the Field Museum, and the bridges and streets that led me here.

Destruction, dust, dissipation. The obliteration of Del's world. I reshaped the orb to a massive spade to dig up the earth. Next, a sturdy hammer to shatter the sky.

There is an intellectual satisfaction that comes along with creation, but there is no greater feeling than the primal surge destruction brings. The total annihilation of something by your own hands is the ultimate manifestation of personal power.

Again, my consciousness stood in darkness. Before me lay a fresh garden to sow, a blank canvas to paint, virgin land on which to build my temple. Well, almost.

There remained a single door. The blue wooden door I'd built to lock Del into the subconscious. He would likely know what I had done and he would be waiting for me.

On raven's wings, I flew over the fresh, empty blackness toward the door. Taking its handle in my palm, I hesitated. The subconscious is the place of dreams, yes, but it is also the place of nightmares — the palace of the random, an abyss where logic need never apply.

I needed to summon all my strength. Not to defend against Del, but the horrors that might have accumulated within. Del's twenty-four years of life were more than enough to gather a plethora of chaotic constructs. The opium would have only made matters worse. Del was a tortured soul, and that which tortured him would be on full display. There was work to be done, however, and so I turned the handle.

Every subconscious is unique. Some contain a serene path leading through a forest of memory and creation. Visions of reality sprouting among fantastic fictions forming a dreamscape that could dazzle the most fervent surrealist. In some, the nightmares and negativity are weak and rare. Del's subconscious was… something else entirely.

My first step through the blue door fell onto nothing and I began a free-fall amongst darkened clouds. Images flashed like lightning as I descended — a twisted cinema of Del's history both real and imagined. A first kiss burst then faded and was outshone by the rejection that followed. Another flash displayed a band in perfect unison, Del smiling and locked in the rhythm. Music rang out in the clouds like the din of a passing train. A quick glance over to Bernard revealed a shared feeling of excitement and joy. A new memory flashed. Del's hands held a letter informing him that he had been fired from the band. Torn paper and the image was gone.

My fall through the frigid clouds felt endless. My wings, useless. There was no logic. For a short time I was accompanied by a silver-winged apparition of Del who soared with grace and power. Music, blues, minor sevenths filled the air.

More flashes. A circle of boys surrounded me as I continued to plummet. Pushing and shoving, fists landing against my stomach, my face… until a teenaged Bernard pulled the alpha aside and doubled him over.

Still I fell.

Through the ghosts of drug-fueled hallucinations and the tragedies of family. A bow after an outstanding show, the embrace of a lost love, they lit the clouds around me. Creatures, a mixture of gargoyle and angel swooped down on me. Talons slashed my flesh and horrible beaks gnashed below human eyes. I writhed against their onslaught, spinning in the air until I resigned myself to their torture.

It was then that the clouds began to part, and terra firma approached. I corrected the pitch of my body and the surface below me buckled as I came to rest on one knee, a hand outstretched to brace myself. I rose and looked out on a dark, cold world.

The subconscious is fluid. It changes with one's feelings. Del wasn't feeling well. Above me the clouds boiled and continued to act like the screens of a moving picture show. The images that had played for me as I fell now covered the sky. A quilt of triumph and failure, wonder and horror. On the ground I was surrounded by ageing buildings and deserted alleys, all the same deep grey as the sky. In front of me was a single room in the middle of the cracked, filthy street. It stood alone. A cube with its front face missing. Inside, a pale boy of about twelve sat on a torn mattress strumming an out-of-tune guitar.

"Hello, Del," I said, stepping closer.

"Are you him?" he asked, looking up from the instrument but continuing his melancholic chord progression.

"Yes."

"I felt what you did up there," he said, hanging his head over his instrument. "Why? Why did you have to go and do something like that? Why is it like this?" he asked, pointing to the sky. I followed his finger to a scene of a beating against the clouds.

A deeper voice continued. "Why am I here?" Del, now a grown man, his current self, still just as bewildered.

"I meant you no harm."

"That's a damn lie!" he said, standing, the guitar falling to his feet. The words and the twang of strings echoed through the streets of his subconscious.

"No, it's not. I had no idea you would be my host. Believe me, I did not want your weak, addicted body any more than you wanted to give it up, yet it's where I came to rest. The decision was not mine to make."

"Get out! You ain't welcome here. Leave me be." He inched closer, his hands curling into fists. The images above flashed at an ever-increasing rate. A wind whipped around me and whistled through the broken windows of the buildings that towered above us.

It was pitiful. He was pitiful. I waved off his advance as if I was shooing a cat and he flew against the far wall of the singular room. My powers worked in this place but so did his. The poor wretch had no idea what he could do in the subconscious.

With a gesture, iron bars rose from the front edge of the floorboards of what was surely his childhood bedroom. Del lunged, thrusting an arm through to the shoulder.

"Hey, you can't—"

"I have need of your body and I will have it for as long as is necessary."

"But it's mine! This is my *life!*"

"And what a life you've made for yourself. You've neglected this body. You've polluted it. Let it to rot."

"I have problems, okay."

"And now those problems are mine. I've got to sort out the mess you've made of yourself just so I can function. I have to take on the responsibility you've shirked. You can thank me for that service later."

He retreated to the bed and sat, slumped in defeat. A barrage of flashes lit that broken, deserted world. Violent, depressive images. Opium dominated his realities and his fantasies. I watched as our body writhed in withdrawal in some alleyway. Next, our body lay on its back in some discount opium den. The faces of those within turned toward me and laughed. They laughed until their faces contorted. Their mouths gaped and unhinged and their laughs turned to screams. Looking down at the body, the spiked backs of dragons writhed beneath the skin. Flames shot from their mouths, opening flesh. A lesser being would have been horrified. I knew better. Opium is not psychotropic. These bizarre creations were Del's doing.

The sinister scenes faded and I turned to Del. He was standing at the bars once again.

"I can help, you know. I know myself. I can, you know, show you how I work. I can be useful to you."

"I've seen enough evidence of what you're capable of. No, you *will* stay here. You *will* do nothing, and you *will* obey me."

"But I can help! I want to help. I know what you're doing. I know your plan. I don't know how I know, I just do. I can see it. Look, I want to be useful. I'm real good with people. I understand 'em. Please let me do something. Don't keep me here."

I threw my arm forward again, doubling the bars of his new prison. He lurched back as the iron rose from the ground.

"You will do nothing. Do you understand? If you ever want this body returned to you, you will do nothing."

"But…" This time the twelve year old peered out at me with tear-filled eyes.

"I leave each host dead," I said, glaring into those eyes. "If you want to be the exception, you will do nothing. Just look at you. You stand there, a snivelling child, asking for my trust. I'm in your head, Del. I know you. I know your cravings and your failings. No, you deserve no trust from me. "

"The opium is going to eat you just like it ate me," he said, his eyes burned — literally burned — and his small body crashed against the bars, an arm, reaching for me. "You're dragon food, pal. Just you wait. Then we'll see who's weak, who's god damned pitiful. You'll see."

The boy slunk back to the bed, picking up the guitar and resuming his song. His hands shook, causing the notes of the chords to take on a vocal quality. As if someone were singing a funeral dirge. He looked up at me once more, his face swollen and red.

"Please, please don't do this," he said.

I willed the blue door to appear and it materialised high above us. I knelt and launched myself airborne. A sweep of my ebony wings bore me higher.

"Wait!" cried Del.

I hovered just above the bleak buildings that surrounded his prison, my wings slowly flapping.

"Please, just don't hurt Bernie. He's all I got and he's a good man. Just… just don't hurt him."

"Unlike you, Bernard has redeeming qualities. Don't worry, as long as he protects us, I'll return the favour. If he turns on me, I promise nothing."

The boy's mouth hung open and with a heavy thrust, I climbed skyward.

Del's dark memories and fantasies closed in, and I increased my pace as I passed each horror. The blue door opened as I approached, and I landed back into the fresh, blank world of the conscious. I wished to complete my mental temple, my ziggurat, before the body woke. It was time I took control of Del's life.

15

TRANSMISSION

My temple was nearly finished. I'd grown deeper roots into the mind, and now had ground of my own design on which to support my powers as they stabilised and strengthened. I could now act with at least a modicum of confidence in the corporeal world, aside from opium's influence.

The tarnished brass alarm clock on Del's nightstand read 12:43. My nausea from breakfast was subsiding. I rose and dressed. Bernard's door was closed but I entered and stepped to his bedside. He lay on his belly, bare athletic back exposed above the tangled sheet that covered his lower half. The glow of his healthy dark skin accented his youthful muscles. It looked as though I'd be partnered with more than a doughy musician. Another point for Bernard.

I glanced down at my pale, weak hands perched on the ends of thin, sickly arms. A withering birch, paper white and good only for breaking. Breaking wasn't an option.

"It's time."

Bernard startled. "What? Time?" He shook his head in a haze of half-sleep. "Get the hell out of here."

"More answers. It's time you see what we're up against and how we'll end it."

Bernard rolled to his back. "Come on man, get the hell out. What time is it anyway?"

"Suit yourself. You can work with me blindly."

"Okay, okay, Jesus, just give me a minute."

I left the room and took my place on the couch. The sound of drawers and hangers clamoured from within Bernard's room and he emerged wearing a jumper and a frown. He pulled a chair opposite me, and sat, covering a yawn.

"Okay, I'm here. How does this work?"

"Just breathe and relax. I'll do the work. Don't speak. Don't move. Think of this experience as if you're watching a picture show except that your eyes will be closed."

"Close my eyes? You promise you won't—"

"Bernard, please. If I wanted you harmed, you'd be harmed. If I desired your death, you'd be dead. Your continuing cooperation will ensure your safety."

"Yeah, well you don't exactly inspire confidence."

"I don't need to."

"Fine. Okay, so, close my eyes?"

"That's what I said."

"All right, there you go, closed."

His lids dropped and his breathing was steady. I leaned back into the couch, placed my hands on my thighs then entered his mind.

The Mentium, to which all Broadcasters belong, is an organisation founded three millennia ago. Its members have come and gone over the centuries but its core leadership, the Upper Echelon, has remained nearly the same since its inception. I am, was, one of the founding members.

Inside Bernard's mind, I projected my memory of the last council meeting where all members, including myself, were in attendance. The topic of discussion was the Twins' plan but I omitted the impertinent sections. Bernard needed to know enough to be of use, but no more. I was seeking to halt the Mentium, not destroy it. Some of our work was good work. Necessary work. Profitable work.

Ten ornate baroque chairs — one for each member of the Upper Echelon — were placed in a circle. Each was adorned with the same gold-embroidered, emerald fabric yet each unique in its woodwork. Versailles had been good to us while it was useful. Louis XIV, the Sun

King, had been one of Apollo's pet projects.

There were no robes or cassocks. No shrines or altars. The space was empty save for the chairs perched atop a parquet floor and framed by blank white walls. The Mentium held council within the upper floor of our temple — as regal, yet pedestrian in appearance as our host bodies. We did not always operate in shadow. Broad daylight could be much more blinding.

Bernard viewed this scene from my own perspective. It was my memory after all. Next, each member of the Upper Echelon materialised on their designated chair.

This is the Upper Echelon and these people, until proven otherwise, are our enemies. You should study their faces carefully.

As I scanned the faces of my brothers and sisters, so too did Bernard.

The persons sitting directly across the circle from you in ivory and gold are the Twins. Artemis and Apollo. Two of our most dangerous adversaries. All the Upper Echelon have wealth, power, and connections. The Twins have something more powerful. They have each other. Namely, absolute trust in one another. Something no one else in the Mentium can boast. They also have a lust for power and violence that rivals Del's hunger for opium.

The pair sat with chairs pushed close; inseparable and identical in everything including vanity and nostalgia. They refused to relinquish their former glory. In this memory, the fit, blond siblings sat with their right leg over a knee and their hands fondling the arms of their chairs. Artemis wore a sleeveless silk dress. A gold necklace spilled onto her chest, an upward-facing crescent moon hung in the middle. From her ears dangled two angular decorations carved from pale deer antler.

Her brother wore a matching ivory suit. Round, gold-rimmed glasses couldn't hide the coldness in his eyes. A gold ring in the shape of the sun adorned his left little finger.

The others within the group wore the average clothes befitting their upper-middle class covers. Aside from the Twins, we had all understood our power was most effective when masked in mediocrity. Well, the upper edge of mediocrity. We have self-respect after all.

Imagine, Bernard, that this circle is a clock. We are to the right of six, the

Twins straddle twelve. Between the Twins and myself on the right sit the following. Kali, in red with her large ivory beads, is a woman of great power, knowledge, and aggression. Ashen-haired and yellow-suited Tian, my mentor, comes next. He has asked to meet with me tomorrow and will prove to be an ally. He is followed by the analytical Ma'at who sits to your right in white. Her blue-feathered headband as proud as always.

Moving back to twelve o'clock, the redheaded man in olive tweed next to Artemis is bold, impudent Cernunnos. Next to him in blue is the noble Yemoja, worrying her bracelet of shells. The bearded man in black evening wear is the ever hospitable, ever rowdy, Radegast. Finally, to my left in emerald is Lilith, my lover and fiercest rival. She is the most dangerous of all, not only for her skill but because she knows me too well. She's been put in charge of my capture.

"Wait, so, your sweetheart is after you too? She wants you… what was it? Entombed?"

"Yes."

"So this is really bad."

I chose to move on with the demonstration.

All who sit before you keep the name of their favourite incarnation as a god or goddess. None of us ever were, and all of us have been many more. Remember, we have the power to influence and control minds. Miracles are easy to come by on any given mental plane. Miracles spur belief. Belief inspires worship. Worship brings benefits.

The meeting continued to play out in silence. I opened my eyes to check on Bernard. He was sitting still, eyes closed, mouth open, lips quivering. I often forgot how foreign and shocking these experiences are for Monos. I closed my eyes again and shifted his gaze back into my history and provided him with a montage of sorts.

For a long time, we thrived on the worship from our respective cultures and religions and our egos grew in accordance. We did not create religion. We simply refined its use.

As time wore on, we craved more power, wealth, and knowledge which we took in spades. However, we also learned some difficult lessons. At first, we ruled with our physical bodies in front of the people. We were divine kings and queens. But kings and queens can be destroyed. We independently realised it was the idea of religion that bound humanity, not a figurehead. A story repeated by many proved far more powerful than one told from my own mouth or from the mouths of those close to me.

Inspiring the common folk with suggestions and false acts, allowing them to champion our cause proved far more fruitful. We could control entire cultures with whispers. Soon each of us had multiple religions, each feeding us more power and wealth. As our complex empires grew, it didn't take long before we learned we were not alone in our powers. At first, battles were common, but we all shared the same appetites and found pooling our energies reaped the highest profits.

There was so much more I could have talked about, Coyote and his rebels, incidents with Spectres, but dwelling would not serve our purpose. Bernard now knew he was about to combat what amounted to the gods of the world. We ten were simply on top. There were about two hundred Broadcasters worldwide. Some come and others go but that number tends to stay stable. Two hundred, and we were but two. A Mono and an addict.

I let the broadcasted memory fade and sent another. The scene coalesced from a mental haze. The room was large, with high ceilings and worktables scattered throughout. Men and women laboured with bent glass, electric coils, and radio tubes. A tableau missing only its mad scientist. Izzy's strong physique stood gazing at electrical gauges.

This is Izanagi. Izzy to me. He is my protégé and belongs to a lower tier of Mentium. He's betrayed me and joined the Twins in this farce.

I couldn't stand to look at him any longer and the memory shifted, its view downward onto a tabletop. Large sheets of paper held sketches for a great machine.

These are the plans for what is essentially a radio and signal amplifier.

A hand pulled the designs away revealing a detailed map of Paris on which three points were marked. The first, the location of the Mentium's temple and my lab. Another point lay between *L'Observatoire de Paris* and *Place Denfert-Rochereau*, to the southeast of Montparnasse. The final point was at the foot of the *Champs du Mars*. Eiffel's tower. Meandering lines connected these three points, creating two sides of a triangle. A reversed L, if you will.

And this details how the system works.

A blueprint was placed over the map. Five wire-frame figures were drawn leaning against the perimeter of a tall, cylindrical apparatus. In Bernard's view, the sketch lifted off the page and became three dimensional, then fully lifelike.

The thoughts of one or more Broadcasters are fed into the radio through this apparatus.

A copper helmet covered the entirety of each head, with multiple wires leading from it to the machine.

Their thoughts are compressed by this unit and relayed through wires laid down in the tunnels of the Metro, to the second point on our map, the various chambers of the catacombs.

The image shifted to the depths of the Paris catacombs. By 1928, they had long been a tourist attraction but before that blatant disrespect, they were the final resting place for over six million. Six million bodies with six million skulls were stacked in intricate, artistic rows, and the tunnels of bones stretched throughout southern Paris. Again, I checked on Bernard. Terror quaked his body as the images of skeletal remains flashed in his mind but still he kept his eyes closed and said nothing. I was again impressed.

The skull has a greater purpose than simply housing and protecting the brain. Its unique geometry acts as a natural antenna and amplifier for one's consciousness. I developed a way to use these six million skulls as six million amplifiers to boost the Mentium's broadcasting power.

It was at that point I started altering the images Bernard was seeing. I superimposed an image of the wire network that lined the floor of the catacombs and ran underneath the stacks of skulls. It pulsed with light — a signal coming from my lab in the temple. Then the rows of stacked skulls began to glow, the false light illustrating their amplification properties.

The final step requires harnessing the amplified mental signals and broadcasting them.

A web of wires pulsed on the ceiling of the catacombs followed by a large cable leading out of the burial chambers.

Paris just so happens to have the largest and most sturdy radio antenna in the world.

The darkness of the catacombs burst into bright light within Bernard's head as I shifted his view to the grassy, tree-lined *Champs de Mars*. Above, a framework of iron loomed.

Eiffel's tower receives the signal using a third device hidden within its foundations, which relays it to the top where the signal is sent through small devices we call the tulips. Thoughts, visions, demands, once limited to a few city blocks now can be broadcast across the continent.

While our methods at controlling the world have become both more subtle and more precise, our drive for power and wealth has only intensified. Over the millennia, this growth has been steady but slow. Too slow for some. This machine will now catapult the Mentium back into the forefront of world governance. Back into popular consciousness. A reintroduction to the world. The Twins believe my radio will allow them to step out of the shadows and back onto thrones.

The gods want to return. This cannot happen.

I directed Bernard's attention to a mental narrative of my own creation. An image of the *Jardin du Luxembourg* filled with bundled people out for an afternoon stroll.

Watch please.

The image shifted back to my lab. Yemoja positioned herself within one of the broadcasting chambers. Her lithe body reclined against the plush vertical bed and Cernunnos and Tian followed suit. Each donning gleaming copper helmets.

I increased the theatrics yet again. A glowing ball of energy emerged from the machine, flew through the Metro tunnels, and spread through the burial chambers of the catacombs. The energy resonated within the skulls only to burst forth onto the cavernous ceiling. It coursed through the wire web, coalescing into one unit in one cable, ushered toward the tower. The amplified images climbed the southeast leg of the iron behemoth and were broadcast across the city from its peak.

The vision flashed back to the garden. A scream. A woman pushing a stroller hurls herself over her baby and writhes in pain. Nearby, men in suits and coats begin attacking those around them. They gnash their teeth and claw at the eyes of their victims.

"Why are they doing that?" asked Bernard.

Watch.

The image shifts. The insane men become monsters, one a grootslang, a combination of an elephant and a giant snake, and another a white haired yeti. The woman with the stroller continues to guard her child against the unrelenting blows of a frost giant's club.

The first phase of their plan involves reviving visions of the beasts of lore, the classical monsters from stories and religions. Our old tools for fear and control. The Mentium would then step in and slay the beasts they themselves had created. This theatre would go on for as long as it takes to ensure that people believed. The Twins and their allies believe the ensuing panic and deaths will force people to flock to the old gods. The world's new leaders, who have returned to save them. The Mentium will offer guidance and protection in exchange for power and absolute devotion. This is folly. As much as it pains me to say, you Monos are too smart for our old tactics. The wisest of you will question, they'll analyse, they'll revolt, and there will be war.

The image faded and I disengaged from Bernard's mind. I looked at him for over a minute before he opened his eyes.

"I... I..."

"Bernard, are you well?"

"Are you lying to me?" His voice shakes and his eyes pierce mine.

"No."

"This can't be real. This... it's..."

"I designed the machine myself. I can assure you it is quite real."

"You what?" Bernard shot up and pulled his fist back, readying himself to strike.

"Don't" I placed a small suggestion within his mind and his body froze then sank to the floor. "Bernard, I have no desire to harm you, but I can't have you harming me either. Remember, this is Del's body you would strike. It receives the damage."

Bernard climbed back into his chair and shook his head, smoothing his moustache and breathing heavy, ragged breaths. "You built this and now you want to stop it? Why? Why would you do that?"

"The device was only intended to extend our reach. It was never meant to be a means of overt control, yet that is what it became.

"They think that through the combined power of we two hundred odd Mentium, a world of two billion can be convinced of our rightful place as their masters. Even if the logic of this weren't utter nonsense, we would need time to build more machines in other locations. Izanagi thinks he can do this but I've kept information from him. The idea's all wet, man."

"Excuse me?" Bernie rocked back in surprise.

"Del… I think." My temper spiked, then a breath. "Bernard, I like my life just the way it is… or was, and refuse to go down with the ship because of their rash actions. If they succeed they'll be viewed as monsters and it will spawn war. A war many aren't likely to survive."

Bernard's expression shifted from disbelief to disgust.

"I guess we're lucky the fate of the world tied in so well with your own interests."

"A beneficial circumstance indeed."

"How much time do we have, you selfish bastard?"

"Ten days. The Twins want to coordinate their first attack with the upcoming League of Nations meeting here in Paris. They want these leaders to see their power firsthand."

"Can you stop them?"

"Yes, I believe we can."

"How?"

"We're going to kill Izanagi."

16

HUNT & GATHER

"We must be going," I said, stepping out into the cobbled street and midday air in Del's third-best suit. A dull grey affair with patches on the sleeves.

Wheels cut mired lines through the previous night's accumulation as Bernard closed the door behind us. "Must be going where?" He was bundled in a similar jacket and heavy scarf. We'd be looking even better the next day. "I told you, I'm not killing anybody."

"Bernard, calm yourself. I plan on inflicting the blow myself and that won't happen for seven days. That's two days before the Twins' plan commences. The longer we wait, the less time they have to adapt and if we fail at killing Izzy, we have one remaining day to disable my radio."

It was a simple plan but not without its challenges. At its core, it was an insurance policy. By design, Izzy and I were the only two who knew how to run my radio. No, Izzy, no Marduk, no more radio. Removing Izzy ensured my survival. In the meantime we'd prepare, meet with Tian and any other allies he'd rallied, and hone our plans, all while staying incognito.

"Okay, so what are we doing then?" asked Bernard.

"We are going on a bit of a scavenger hunt. I need to recover some items I've stowed for safekeeping as well as withdraw some much-needed funds. I have to pay you back for last night's cab and this morning's food."

"You don't need to."

"Neither did you. I am a man of my word. Except for when I'm lying, which, in this case, I'm not."

"But what about your people? They're hunting for you right?"

"Yes, but they have no way of finding me. At least not without a lot of luck. At this point, I can close my mind to other Broadcasters and they have no idea which body I've fallen into. No mind to find, no body to recognise, equals safe passage. Well, less hazardous."

"What about your lady-friend?"

"Our familiarity cuts both ways. She knows how I operate but I understand her as well. She'll likely have my home and usual haunts surveilled. I have no need to visit those locations. Secrets are key to survival within the Mentium. She'll narrow her search for bodies I'd likely choose – fit, intelligent, socially well-placed. Fortunately for us, I hadn't time to choose. Lilith will be looking for the wrong needle in this sprawling haystack of a city."

"If you say so."

The mystery of my current identity was the crux of my plan. No one would look for something valuable in the trash.

We trudged in silence through the wet snow and past pedestrians whose chilled expressions coupled well with their chilled bodies. A storm was coming. I could feel the weather change within me.

Del's familiar hunger burned in my brain, not my stomach. The cravings were growing. It was a slow burn, but a fire that I would be fighting all day. I didn't have time nor patience for the dragon that day. *Damn, you Del.*

The temperature danced either side of freezing and large, sticky flakes fell like goose feathers. That day was a selfish kind of day. A chorus of "I"s or rather *"je"*s sung from the minds of those that bustled along side us. *I'm freezing. I'm starving. I want a drink. I hate the cold. I hate these people. I just want to be at home.* It was perfect. The more people focused on themselves, the easier it was to go unnoticed.

Soon, our first stop came into view — *Gare Montparnasse*. In front of the massive train station stood a small green newsstand. What a show they must have had when that train came through its second floor wall and crashed to the street below. Was it '94 or '95? I wished I had been in town to see that.

I made my way to a bench across from the rear of the stand and sat, gesturing to Bernard to take a seat as well.

"I thought we had work to do," said Bernard, stuffing his hands into his coat pockets as he sat.

"We do and we're working now. Watch."

It was time for a test. My abilities had been strengthening steadily. With a typical transference, there is a protocol for testing powers. I was past due for another.

A thin man who was folding his crisp, newly-purchased newspaper, stopped midstride and tucked the paper under his right arm. He lifted his left arm and positioned his outstretched hand above his head on the rear wall of the newsstand as a river of people flowed behind him. His newspaper fell when he brought his other hand to his chest.

"What are you doing to him?" asked Bernard. He had followed my gaze to where the man stood.

"I'm providing us with a diversion. Do you remember the restaurant?"

"Again?"

"No, but similar."

The man was in plain sight but was being completely ignored by those who passed. His body swayed and he let out a few low groans. He wiped sweat from his brow.

"Come on," said Bernard, "this is just cruel."

I was enjoying my performance. His illness reminded me of my own — the unease flickering in my body, whispering its call. The sweet smoke of the pipe… the man gripped his chest again.

At my mental suggestion, he scurried from the newsstand and fell to the ground at the base of a nearby tree, still clutching his heart.

"Now we move," I said.

All eyes were on the cowering fellow. His fall had attracted a few of the more sympathetic Monos, and they came to his aid. The heart attack he thought he was having was in its full throes and would remain so until I no longer needed him.

The spectacle of pain creates enraptured spectators, and while the crowd was preoccupied with the unfortunate gentleman their gaze was not upon us.

"Here," I said, squatting behind the newsstand where the man first felt the pangs of artificial illness. Using my gloved hands to pry free a paving stone, I removed a wallet and a small, green velvet sack. I replaced the paver and pocketed the items.

"All that for a little bag? What's in it?"

"Come Bernard, we have more to collect." We plodded off in a northerly direction and Bernard kept looking over his shoulder to check on my marionette. I instinctually pointed in the direction of the 'dying' man and ended the performance earlier than I would have liked. *Dammit, Del.* The stranger rose to a sitting position and held his head in his hands.

"Did you have to do that to him?" Bernard rushed to catch up, breath billowing around his face.

"This time, yes. Normally I would have broadcast a simple image into the minds of those surrounding us. Maybe we'd seem invisible or look as if we were simply standing while I pried at the stone. To them it would have been as if nothing was happening. I'm still a bit too weak to manage this many people at once, so I improvised a distraction. An entertaining one at that!"

His face was still screwed up in disgust as I pulled the wallet from my pocket. We walked on and I checked its compartments for my belongings and counted the bills. Everything was as it should be. I pulled out fifty francs and handed it to him.

"No way, that's too much."

"Take it. There can be much more if you do well."

"I don't want your money. I want my friend back."

"Noted."

The leaf-sized snowflakes continued to fall as we stomped off toward our next stop. Bernard fell in behind me, stuffing the bill into his wallet. The streets were too busy to walk side by side. It was Saturday, it was frigid, and it was the middle of the day. All of those peons were out to shop or off to eat some butter-soaked food. They flooded the streets, acting as obstacles and annoyances. This was Paris.

◆ ◆ ◆

We were within a few blocks of my next drop point, the Odeon Theatre, when a shout met our ears.

"Del! Bernie! Hey, how the hell are you boys doing?"

We turned to see a chubby, middle-aged man waddling up to us. A waxed black moustache curled onto each cheek and an equally groomed goatee made a feeble attempt to elongate his round face. Every article of clothing he wore, from the beaver fur top hat, to the mink coat, boasted wealth. It also lied. The quality of the dark suit underneath was second rate at best, as was the shirt. His jewellery was one step up from costume, and the silk of his tie wasn't silk. This was a man of pretence and posturing. Someone I would brush off in any usual circumstance. This was not a usual circumstance and what's more, he knew me. Rather, he knew Del.

"Sal. Hi, it's been a while," said Bernard, reaching out to shake the man's hand. I did the same and nodded my hello, saying nothing. I could feel my body flush with the heat of anger but not my anger.

"Good to see you two. Say, how's show business treating you these days?" Sal looked back and forth between us with a slimy smile.

"It's good, Sal, real good. We've been getting steady gigs."

"Still with the same outfit?"

"Yeah, Creole Calloway runs a solid group. He's treated us well."

"Screw 'em!," blurted the faker. "The whole rhythm section of the house band at La Victoire jumped ship last night and I'm looking for replacements." The cigarette in his hand danced with his gesticulations. "What's that heel Calloway paying you boys? I'll double it." This time his gaze was set on me. I was caught off guard yet had no choice but to speak. I ransacked Del's memories and came up with the proper figure.

"Our compensation is fifteen francs, each, per night," I said. I knew as soon as the words left my mouth that I'd made a mistake.

"Listen to you with the fancy words. What do we have here? Del Chambers, star of stage and screen? Stick to the silent films, kid. You definitely aren't ready for the talkies."

I scoured Del's mind, checking for his speech patterns. I was a fool not to have practiced from the start. "Nah," I said, hoping I could recreate a believable style on the fly, "you know how it is, Sal, fancy city, fancy words. Just trying out some new things. Stretching my legs."

"Well knock it off, would ya? You sound like a dope."

"Yeah Sal, yeah, you're right." The blaggard was a fool and it felt revolting to kowtow to him, but Del would have and so must I.

"Thanks for the offer, Sal," said Bernard, steering the conversation back to the original topic. "We're happy where we are. It's steady, you know. He pays, we play. Plus, Creole's landed us a few recording gigs so we've been making pretty steady money. If things fall through, we'll definitely look you up."

"You sure, Bernie? I'd love to have a horn like yours in the pit."

"Yeah, Sal, we're sure."

"All right then, but don't say I wasn't looking out for you two."

"Wouldn't think of it, Sal," I said, noticing and tucking my clenched fists behind my back. I could not tolerate feeling Del's emotions over my own. He was lucky I agreed with his assessment of the man.

"Well if you change your mind..." He handed me his calling card. "Hot off the press. Nice, ain't they? Better than the last ones, right?" he asked, looking right at me.

"Yeah, Sal, yeah, it's a real beaut," I said, looking at gold-embossed lettering.

"Anyway, I need to get to the theatre. The damn costume girl's been jabbering on about mouldy lace or some such nonsense and the set guy keeps busting all my light bulbs. See ya, boys."

More handshakes and the fur clad clown scurried off. I turned the business card over in my hand: Salvatore Colletti, Independent Talent Agent and Freelance Stage Manager. What a buffoon.

"You gentlemen keep interesting company," I said, relaxing back into my own manner of speech. It felt like putting on a favourite smoking jacket.

"Sal's a worm but he's a good worm to know. He has connections. Plus, he helped us make our start when we got into town."

"A worm. How very fitting," I drew a long, calming breath as Del's anger cooled and faded. "Ah, almost forgot." I removed the penknife from my sock and made two slits in each of the barrel cuffs on Del's shirt.

"What the hell are you doing?"

"I'm converting this cheap shirt into something that will hold these cuff-links," I said, removing the silver watch and matching cuff-links from the velvet bag.

"Those are a bit fancy for the circles Del and I run in, don't ya think?" said Bernard, admiring the pieces.

"They are functional as well as fashionable."

"What's the function?"

"Communication."

"Miniature radios?"

I didn't bother to restrain my laughter. "No, no, not radios. Just wait and see."

"Ass."

It was off to the bank next, where I had transferred a substantial amount into one of my hidden accounts. I'd informed my usual banker, Jean-Pierre, that a friend wearing a specific watch and cuff links may come to claim the money on my behalf in the event I was unable to myself. This was a standing request. Emergency body swapping was a rare occurrence but one didn't want their savings kept from them.

"Wait here," I said to Bernard as I entered the front of Société Générale, the bank I had been with for decades. Inside, the room bustled with men in suits that made me look like a beggar. The fine wool and elegant leather shoes sent a green streak of jealousy through me. I located Jean-Pierre, showed him the jewellery, assured him this was no joke, and withdrew two thousand francs. That was more than enough to buy what we would need in the coming days. If it wasn't, I could always withdraw more. For the Mentium, especially the Upper Echelon, wealth was as sure as the rising sun. It's amazing how much one can accumulate over a few millennia.

Back outside, the watch and cuff links were returned to the green bag and we continued on foot to L'Odeon Theatre. Its columns and vaulted arches outshone its surroundings. I led Bernard to the ticket counter for the most important item of the day's hunt.

"Bonjour," I said to a freckled young man inside the small cubicle. His drooping eyes and vacant expression matched his job as well as his uniform. "I believe you have a small package an associate of mine left in your keeping."

The young man's dull face flashed with excitement then hardened and he looked at me as if I were trying to sell him spoiled meat. "Describe this associate, please."

"Oh, well Monsieur Leduc is a tall, athletically built gentleman. Well-groomed moustache with dark eyes. He said a small, heavy envelope was waiting here for me. It should be labelled with the words '*Chien Vert*' on the front and a signature over the flap. I believe the envelope was borrowed from one of your colleagues last night."

"*Oui. Un moment, monsieur.*" He turned to rummage through a deep drawer, then returned with the envelope and passed it beneath the glass. I gave him a nod of thanks and he responded with an empty outstretched hand. Of course he did. I placed a franc into that palm and turned back to Bernard.

"Leduc?" he smirked.

"Marcus Leduc."

"Subtle, aren't you?"

"Subtlety is only useful when it's necessary."

"Chien Vert?"

"A simple code word. Dogs don't come in green so the likelihood of the phrase being used by anyone else is quite low."

Hints of blue bled through the grey sky like watercolours. My mood, despite our successes, continued to darken as the cravings grew stronger.

"Find what you were looking for?" asked Bernard.

I tore open the envelope and pulled out a ring of keys. A half dozen of various sizes and shapes hung from an aged brass hoop. I gave them a reassuring jingle.

"Are you a custodian now too?" he asked.

"These are the keys to the city."

"Don't get cute. What are they for?"

"They are, indeed, the keys to various doors in this city. Keys I've collected over the years. Ease of access is important in what I do and I don't much care for asking permission. Now, let's be going."

"Aha, so when breaking and entering is in order, you skip the breaking and just enter? Why am I not surprised."

"Judge all you want, Mono," I snapped. "It's of no consequence to me."

"Whoa there, no need to be more of a pill than you already are. What's eating you, anyway?"

An errant wave of hunger flooded my body. My need for opium screaming to be heard. Then it pulled back. I dreaded the additional, similar assaults I knew would come in time. I didn't want Bernard to know they had started already. Not yet. I needed him to trust my judgment.

I paused to compose myself and noticed a gentleman who stood next to a table inside the cafe to our immediate left. His tailored tweed suit produced another flash within me. Envy. I looked down at Del's third-best suit, one that would be thrown out of most closets, then over to Bernard. His own clothing was like that of a poor but proud old man who cherished the suit he'd purchased twenty years prior.

The desire to clean up Del's act ached in my mind, surpassing the ever-present call for opium. I would ride that wave of distraction as far as I could. I hurried to the street's edge with my arm raised.

"Where are we going?" asked Bernard as he stepped to my side.

"To scratch an itch."

"You just used last night. You can't need it already, can you?"

A cab pulled up and I stepped inside, pulling the wool blanket over my legs and throwing the rest over Bernard.

"Tell me where you're taking me," said Bernard after closing his door.

"Printemps, s'il vous plaît." I said to the driver. To Bernard, I said, "shopping."

◆ ◆ ◆

We each stepped out of *Printemps* department store with two wrapped bundles, two hat boxes and two shoe boxes in our arms. I would love to say I spared no expense but alas, I had to. Still, I couldn't bear to present myself in his shabby wardrobe for one more instant.

"Again, thank you. I… *we* haven't had clothes like this since, well, really ever," said Bernard.

"I would have liked to do better. But keeping up appearances means toning down our style. It's always been that way for me when conducting business," I said, raising my hand for a taxi yet again.

"Well, I appreciate this."

"Bernard, I can no longer stand to be seen looking like Del and if you're to be with me for the foreseeable future, then I won't want you looking like a beggar either."

"Can't you just take the gratitude?"

"Stay calm and hail a cab."

"What?"

"Hail the damned cab and say nothing."

Bernard set down his hat boxes and rose a hand to the street. Twenty metres behind him, like crocodiles swimming upstream, two gargantuan men in fine suits parted the bustling crowd as they approached. Their eyes swept from person to person but hadn't locked onto us.

Listen, I said into Bernard's mind, *there are two Eunuchs walking toward us. Where there are Eunuchs, there will be an Underling close by. I need to focus on blocking both our minds. You need to get us a cab as fast as you can.*

Bernard understood and as the huge men drew closer, he stepped out into the street forcing a taxi to stop.

Be calm. Don't arouse suspicion.

He forced himself to relax and opened the taxi door as the driver loaded our things. We pulled away as the Eunuchs kept walking and searching.

"*5 Rue Mouffetard, s'il vous plaît.*" I said and the driver careened back into the busy street.

"Mouffetard? Why aren't we going home? We barely escaped those meatheads."

"We escaped and the Eunuchs were none the wiser. That's all that matters. I'm growing tired of your whining, Bernard. I took you for stouter stock."

"Lay off."

Yeah, lay off would ya, you've been harping on Bernie all damn day.

"Excuse me a moment, Bernard, I need to do a bit of thinking."

"Suit yourself."

I turned inward with voice alone to scold Del. "You must stop this."

"Stop what?"

"I've locked you away for a reason. I need you to keep quiet and leave me in peace. How have you managed to speak to me? Your anger at Sal, I felt it. How? I need it to stop. The distraction will not be tolerated."

"Look, buddy, don't know, don't care. This is still my brain and I'll do as I please."

"You'll do as you're told."

"Says who?"

"Says the man who has put you in a prison cell. Keep your comments and your petty feelings to yourself or the cell will grow more uncomfortable."

"Now wait just a—"

"Do not test me."

"Look, I ain't doing shit, man. Honest. It just is what it is and I guess my brain's just gonna do what it's gonna do."

I emerged from the mind and stayed silent for a time. Del also remained quiet. The taxi crossed the Seine onto *Île de la Cité* and as we passed Notre Dame, I deemed it time to speak again.

"We're going to see Philipe."

"Philipe?"

"He's an acquaintance of mine, a Multi-Receiver, and the best tailor in the city."

"Multi-Receiver? You mean mind reader?"

"That would be correct. His mind cannot do anything except learn about you. Don't worry, Philipe is a good man."

"Really? A friend of yours but a good man."

"No, truly. Say what you will about me, but Philipe is on the up and up. You have my word."

"I'm still trying to decide what that means."

"As you should."

Fifteen minutes later we were in front of Philipe's door with the driver unloading our wares into our waiting hands. I rang the buzzer to his flat.

"I thought you said this Philipe guy was a tailor?"

"He is. He's very exclusive. He receives enough business without needing a storefront."

Philipe, as usual, answered the door himself. The short, lean Senegalese man looked me over then shifted his gaze to Bernard. "You have the wrong address. *Au revoir.*"

"Philipe, we know where we are," I said.

He began to speak but swallowed his words. First his eyes locked on mine then shifted to Bernard, a smile spreading. I'd unblocked my mind and gave the Multi-Receiver a peek inside.

"Is it true?" he asked, not bothering to hide his laughter. "It can't be."

"We'll have plenty of time for stories while you're fitting us. We have quite a few garments that require your magic touch."

"Always glad to see my best customer but off the rack?" he said, looking at the bundles in our hands, "I thought better of you *mon ami.*"

"Time is not on our side, unfortunately. I'll be buying an entire wardrobe from you shortly, but these must be finished with haste."

"Let's discuss this upstairs," He stepped aside for us to enter.

"Let's. We just had an encounter with a few Eunuchs and the streets don't seem so friendly at the moment."

"Ah, you do have stories to tell." Philipe led the two of us up a narrow staircase to his second-floor studio. Inside there was a central worktable surrounded by over a hundred bolts of fabric. Tweeds and worsted wool and silks in every hue under the sun were heaped around the periphery of his flat. He was alone that day, which was just as well. His usual assistants weren't needed for this session.

"Set your things down anywhere you like," said Philipe. "Can I offer you gentlemen a drink?"

We set our purchases on the floor beside us and Bernard said, "I'll take a—"

"We'll take two cognacs if you don't mind and Bernard will have a Perrier as well."

Philipe swept into his kitchen and my smile was met with a scowl from Bernard.

"Stay out of my head."

"Yes, yes, fine. I'm sorry, Bernard. I'm not used to interacting with Monos on a personal level. I usually read minds as casually as one window shops along the boulevards."

"Well this shop's closed until I say otherwise. Got it?"

"I'll try to respect your wishes."

Philipe emerged with our drinks and a tape around his neck. He handed us our glasses and immediately took me by the shoulders.

"You said time was of the essence, no?"

"It is, quite."

"Well let's begin," he said. "Unwrap those mass-produced rags and let me take a look at them."

We did as instructed, and he eyed them with a snobbishness that bordered on theatrical. Bernard suppressed a laugh but not well.

"You first," he said, motioning to me. "Just look at this body. I'll need to make all new patterns. When did you say you wanted those bespoke items?"

"That will be a while. These will have to suffice for the immediate future."

"Good," he said, kneeling in front of me. "That will give you some time to fill out these clothes. When was the last time you ate? You don't look healthy."

"Just measure."

"Didn't mean to offend," he said.

The man's movements were quick and elegant. He wrote number after number on a yellow pad of paper, double-checking each measurement. He was done with me in a matter of minutes. Bernard took my place in the middle of the room.

"You're a sturdy fellow, aren't you?"

"Uh, I guess so."

"I like him," said Philipe. "A man of few words."

I didn't bother hiding my own laughter at Bernard's awkward faces while he was measured. After but a few short minutes, his agony was over.

"Right," said Philipe. "That should be all. When do you need these?"

"Tomorrow would be ideal," I said.

"Tomorrow? You must be joking."

"Tomorrow. Here," I said handing him two hundred francs. "I know you can make it happen."

"Tomorrow will be fine after all. I'll just tell my wife that I'll be in for the evening."

"Where is Sophie?"

"Out, being young in Paris. Or, to be more blunt, drinking with friends."

"Well then, that should help her in the process. We'll see you tomorrow, Philipe. Nine in the morning."

"For you, I suppose."

17

ASSESSMENT

Del's cluttered bed felt soft under my weary body. It had been a long day and I sat, legs up, trying to regain some energy. At the end of the bed stood the shoe and hat boxes I'd purchased. The organised, geometric structure was a beacon of civilization within a world of chaos.

In the corner of Del's room opposite his guitar stood a worse-for-wear phonograph. I'd cleared it of clothing and had begun playing some of Del's records — a mix of jazz and blues. The blues recordings were of particular interest to me. I appreciated the authenticity and darker tone compared to most of its jazz contemporaries. It was one discovery I'd carry with me past Del's body.

Over the slow bounce of Victoria Spivey and Lonnie Johnson's *Dope Head Blues*, I could hear Bernard shuffling about the apartment. The springs of the couch would creak, then the sound of heels on the floorboards, then the running of water in the sink followed by more footsteps. He seemed to be everywhere and nowhere. I assumed his thoughts would be the same as they had been all day — uncertainty, fear, anger, and helplessness. I could have checked but did not feel the need. He needed time to sort out the details of his new situation, something I also needed to do. I will admit I planted a minuscule suggestion in his mind to make him take his shoes off. Those damned heels just kept clicking.

I sat against the ageing brass headboard with Del's guitar across my lap. It was an intriguing piece. A totem of sorts. An idol to worship. The physical representation of his dreams.

The smooth gloss finish was buffed to a high shine. Its colour, stunning. It resembled a low fire on a cold night. The centre glowed ember orange and like a fire, the wider it spread, the more the dark swallowed its light. The outer edge was almost black and wrapped by a cream binding. Inside, unseen to many, was a device known as a Virzi Tone Producer. It acted as a second sound board and gave the Gibson L5 its signature, projecting sound. I knew that this guitar was built in 1923 and I knew that it took Del two years of saving to buy it, used.

I strummed through a few chords, accessing Del's memories and letting them guide my hands. The sound rang out clear with a gentle but thick tone. As the fingers of my left hand transitioned from one chord to the next, each digit moved in a fluid, lingering motion, giving each chord its chance to be heard before moving on.

Not bad for a thief.

Him again.

First you steal my body then you steal my skills. What an asshole.

While the sound of the guitar was pleasant, Del's voice was not. Nor was the burning need for opium. It wasn't a fire yet, still more like coals covered by layers of ash waiting to take flame. It was only a matter of time before the dragon breathed again. Or rather, I breathed the dragon.

No, I thought. *Del needs the drug. Del lost control of this body. I can break it. It's mine now.*

Good luck with that, he said. *And it ain't yours, pal.*

I'm done here. I said. He was too. I kept playing and thinking.

An inevitable confrontation with the Mentium was on its way. If I had months available to me, I would have waited until my strength returned then transferred to a more fitting host and worked to build a rebellion. Cernunnos and Yemoja would join me. I was confident that I could make them see reason. Tian's message was a gift of hope. With those three with me, I could mount a believable coup.

Lilith's desires, I couldn't comprehend. She was more wise than her actions illustrated. Her involvement, duty be damned, made no sense but it also made no difference. In the coming days, I would have to stop *all* in my way.

Accustomed as I was to doing as I pleased, laying low would prove doable but difficult. Waiting was not an activity in which I excelled. That first day as Del was a day for waiting. A day for trivial chores. To put distance between myself and my brothers and sisters. That distance would close, however, and when it did, I'd not only stop their idiotic campaign but exact a generous amount of revenge. The Twins would suffer. I would make sure of it. How? Well, revenge against immortals could be slow. And Izzy? His death would be slow and… entertaining.

Bernard's footsteps approached and he practically stomped into Del's bedroom.

"Can you play? I mean, can you play as well as Del?"

"Most of his abilities should be available to me at this point," I said, "why do you ask?"

"I need to know if you can really play. Look, play *Sweet Georgia Brown*."

I took a breath, put the guitar in position on my thigh, and began. My right foot tapped toward the foot of the bed as the lively rhythm reverberated through the room. It was happy music, the kind I usually despised, but the way Del —and I say Del because this was his skill set — navigated around the fretboard, it was like he was dancing. I dare say I was enjoying myself.

Bernard cut me off as I began the chorus. "Fine, that's fine. You've got his sound down pat," he said, then stomped back out of the room.

I hadn't paid much attention to music over the millennia. I'd dabbled. Life needs distractions when life lasts as long as mine, but I'd never set about serious study. Del had. An odd rush of satisfaction swept over me. The song had been expertly played and to be able to reproduce music with the accuracy and emotion I just had, for a fleeting moment, I'd forgotten the low, ever present pull of the opium.

Bernard's ceaseless movement was, for the moment, corralled within his own room. The sounds of his rummaging were not. I set the guitar on the bed then stared at the cracked plaster ceiling.

There was much work for the two of us to accomplish to dismantle the Mentium's 'Theatre of the Absurd'. If our attempt on Izzy's life proved unsuccessful, plan B was the same as my original plan — sabotage.

Anticipating the rejection of logic by the Twins, Izzy and I had planned to remove key, though hidden and seemingly unrelated pieces of the apparatus. As we had designed and built the machine, the rest of the Mentium could never put it right. They would have been forced work with us.

Such thoughts were pointless after Izzy's betrayal but the plan could be salvaged. You see, Izzy, unfortunately, had more self-admiration than scientific genius. That's not to say that he was a slouch. Hedging my bets on outsmarting Izzy was, to put it mildly, a risk. But I had few options at my disposal. At least I was the genius he could never be, current body be damned.

If I could not kill Izzy, we would stymie him. Rather than dismantling parts of the apparatus, Bernard and I would now go deeper. We'd go for the wiring itself. A cut here, a missing solder there, and the same result could be achieved. A bonus was that wire is easy to fix. My radio took me the better part of five years to develop. I wasn't going to destroy it.

No, after Izanagi and the Twins were dealt with, I'd use my new-found sway within the Upper Echelon to ensure the radio was only ever used for its proper purpose.

The others may have voted against me, but most tend to vote with the tide. I intended to turn that tide in my favour. Plus, once back in power, Lilith's game of predator and prey would end and we would resume our previous game of love and hate, lust and longing, and most importantly, one-upmanship. She'd need to work hard to outdo my dethroning the Twins. Doubly so to regain trust.

A small smile crossed my face. My luck for a body may have been poor but I was far from out of the game. I would have my revenge and who knew, maybe Bernard would even have his friend back. One thing was certain. Once this whole charade was over, I'd be leaving Del's worthless body for good.

The heavy thud of shoe heels approached and, much to my annoyance, Bernard once again stepped into the room, this time dressed in a smart, yet aged black suit with a red and blue striped tie.

"Bernard, don't you look put together. Going out?"

"We both are," he said, stepping over piles of clothes as he crossed the room. He pulled a black suit and an identical tie from Del's closet.

"Matching? Don't you think that's a bit… odd?"

"Get dressed," he said, throwing the clothes my way. "We have a gig tonight, remember?"

"Oh, Bernard. Do you really think that's wise?"

"You said it yourself. You need to keep up appearances. If you're trying to hide in Del, if you want the world to think you are Del, then you need to be Del. Del has a gig tonight, which means you have a gig tonight. Now get dressed and put that guitar in its case."

"What if I refuse?"

"Then Del will miss yet another gig and the show will be cancelled, again. We'll get axed, we won't get paid, which means we won't make rent, and there will be a lot of questions. Look, Del's stretched our reputations and I need to make sure we don't get blackballed. So, if you refuse, I guess I'll have to drag your ass kicking and screaming."

"But I could just pay for your—"

"Get dressed," he said, moving out into the living room.

I got to my feet and pulled off the yellow jumper. Reputation and standing in the musical circles of Paris were on the line. I understood. My pushback was more about testing Bernard's mettle and resolve. I liked what I saw.

Del's suit was lying on the bed and it was so threadbare I normally wouldn't be seen dead in it let alone by an entire audience. The thought was as revolting as my opium-starved body felt.

"Get dressed, Marduk," came Bernard's voice from the sitting room.

With a heavy sigh, I continued to disrobe.

"Oh," Bernard called from his place on the sofa. "Hey, so, I know your name, your real god name or whatever the hell you'd call it, but it's not like I can use it in public. I get that you go by Marcus Leduc and that I have to call you Del in front of people we know but when it's just us, what should I call you?"

"Those who know me call me M."

18

THE TEST

The snow glowed gold in the light of the street lamps and my feet ached through the worn leather and thin wool of Del's shoes and socks. Curls of steam escaped our mouths and dissolved into the black of the early evening as if we were enjoying rich cigars rather than suffering the frigid night air.

"Now, you need to be Del tonight. You understand, right?"

"Do you take me for a fool? I know what I need to do," I said as we stood at the side of *Boulevard de Port-Royal*, hand raised for a cab.

"This is our life. It's not just a job. Tonight's the last gig Creole's band will be playing for almost two weeks. We need to end on a high note so we get paid and so we don't get canned between now and then."

"Fine," I said as the canvas-topped motor coach pulled up beside us. The idea of performing musically for the first time in front of an audience held little appeal for me. Doing so as Del held even less. "Get in."

We hefted our cases inside and took our seats. *"Belleville, s'il vous plaît,"* said Bernard in the typical, too-friendly American tone yet with his admirable accent. The driver put a finger to his cap and pulled away from the curb. I pulled up the heavy wool blanket and tried to place half on Bernard. He declined.

"Now back to being Del," he said.

"Bernard, I understand."

"No, I mean, you really need to *be* Del. He's a character. A character people remember. Everyone says so. He's got a specific laugh. He speaks in a certain way. He plays a certain way."

"Bernard, I have it under control. Remember, I've got all his memories at my fingertips. It's just a matter of study."

"Did you study?"

"Bernard, we'll be fine."

The rumble of the Peugeot's engine blended with the crunch of the tires on ice as the car rattled through the wide streets of Paris. We crossed the Seine, a tar slick on that moonless night.

Del piped up again. *You want some help?*

No, I said to him. *If I wanted your help, I'd ask for it.*

Look buddy, there's no one better at being me than me and tonight you need to put on one hell of a show. I could learn you a thing or two about being me. Or, you know…

Or what?

Or you could let me take the wheel. Let me do what I do best. Then, after we leave the club, I'd let you take control again.

This conversation is over, Del.

Don't say I didn't try to help ya.

I focused back on reality as we swept around the roundabout where the Bastille once stood. An agitated Bernard nudged me with an elbow.

"Did you see that?"

"What?"

"I don't know. It was just spooky. I don't know."

"Describe it. I want full detail." The man was not one for theatrics, so his worry needed to be my own.

Bernard's gaze swept out the window again. A second passed and the cab stopped at a traffic light for pedestrians at the entrance to *Place de la République*. There were scores of people walking all around us. Any threat he sensed was buried in that mass.

"What is it you've seen, Bernard?"

He said nothing but kept looking. The light was still red and dozens of potential threats continued to parade around the car.

"Bernard?"

"There," he said. "Did you see that? It's like something is skipping from one person to the next."

"What?"

"There. The woman in green. See her face? See her standing there all stiff but moving her head back and forth?"

"Yes, I see"

"Now she's fine but the man with the red hat over there is doing the same thing."

This was not anything I wanted to hear.

"Lilith is doing random sweeps," I said.

"This is Lilith?"

"Sadly, yes."

Bernard froze, his face, his body, his expression of fear, all stone. All pointed at something out my own window. A woman, not a day younger than eighty glared into the cab. Her eyes fixed on my own. Her jaw was set and her shoulders dropped and pulled back. It was too much. The Mentium was but a plate of glass away from me. I was staring at a tool they hoped would be my demise. Then, with a minute twitch of the head they were gone and I waved at the octogenarian and guffawed a guffaw that should have been enshrined in some almanac.

"What... what are you doing?" Bernard stammered. "They... she... they're right there!"

"Random sweeps," I squeezed out between belly laughs. "Do you know what this means?"

"It's bad, right? They've got eyes everywhere. Why the hell are you laughing?"

"They're desperate, my good man. Desperate. Pathetic! Random sweeps aren't plan A or B. They're the last resort. Lilith must be livid. To stoop to random sweeps, if only I could taunt her in person."

"What are you talking about? So, it's all fine then? That lady's face didn't seem fine to me. What does this mean for you? For us?"

"It means that as long as we keep my identity a secret, we can go about our business. It means that if I can convincingly 'be Del', as you say, then we should be 'free as the breeze'. That's not to say we can let our guard down. Oh, no. But the desperation of this... this is the best news I've had in longer than I'd care to think about."

Bernard pressed his back against the seat and slid until his head could rest on the top. "I don't like this."

"You don't like this? Well, prepare yourself. It won't get better than this until it's all over."

"What if it never gets any better?"

"Have faith, Bernard, you're working with me."

"A murdering immortal asshole with mind control powers?"

"Absolutely."

He reached for the blanket and tugged at a section big enough to cover his legs and sat back up.

"How are those powers of yours?" he asked. "I hope you're getting stronger."

"It's a long process but I'm coming along well."

"How about the cravings? Do you need to use?"

"Need to? No. Want to? Oh yes, but the drive is manageable for the moment and I'm not about to give in to someone else's problem."

"How's Del? He's all right, isn't he?"

"He's fine, Bernard. He's tucked away safely in the subconscious. As long as I live, he lives."

"That's pretty convenient for you."

"I hope we will come to a point where you'll *want* to protect me along with Del."

"Don't hold your breath."

"You aren't the typical mindless cow most Monos are. I respect you for that."

"But I'm still a Mono. Save your respect for someone who cares. I'm here to get Del back and apparently, save the damn city."

"The scale of chaos will become much larger than that."

"Don't remind me."

I turned from him as the crowds swept past. The head-hopping Mentium continued their fruitless quest. It was a glorious feeling to see them so desperate. We came to another stop at the far end of

Place de la République and I glanced down a narrow side street. My glee came to an abrupt halt.

"*Arrêtez ici!*" I said, and tossed the blanket from my legs. The taxi pulled to the curb and I threw the door open.

"What the hell?" said Bernard, grabbing both of our instrument cases and paying the driver.

"Hurry, you need to see this."

Bernard stepped beside me with a case in each hand. "Why did we stop? We're ten blocks from the theatre."

"We stopped because we're in the middle of a test. I should have known Izzy would want to play with my toy."

"Test?"

"Look," I said, pointing down the dark, narrow street to our right. A well-dressed man, maybe forty-five years old cowered against the wall of a building, covering his head and sobbing, pleading, for something not to kill him. I opened my mind to see what he saw.

"Is he all right?"

"He's a guinea pig. It looks like Izzy's test is working."

"What test are you talking about?"

I gestured with my head at the roof opposite the quivering man.

"Holy god," said Bernard as he backpedalled, slipping on the icy sidewalk and landing arse first. The cases hit the ground and Bernard kicked and clawed his way backward toward the street.

On the rooftop in question stood the animate body of a gargoyle. Its eyes glowed like magma and its granite teeth dripped with black saliva. It moved with the deftness of an ape and eyed the victim with the imposing gaze of a viper.

"Bernard, get up. It's a figment of the imagination. Specifically, the imagination of one of my colleagues. Its exquisite detail suggests Kali. It's now our figment too. This is but a small sample of what my radio can do."

Bernard looked at me, then to the beast, then to me, then to the man, then cupped his head in his hands.

"Get up man, you'll freeze on the ground like that."

"I... I... I can't!"

"Can't what? Get up? You can, you will. You'll be fine."

"Fine? Against that?"

"That," I said pointing, "isn't real. Come on, let's leave the gargoyle to its prey and get on with salvaging Del's reputation."

"You're just going to leave him there?"

"Of course. If I intervene, I'll help them zero in on my location. Our location. We can't have that now can we?"

I gathered Del's guitar case from the icy ground and set off toward Belleville, ten steps at least. I turned to find Bernard now standing but still staring at the beast and its victim.

"Bernard, we'll be late."

19

THE GIG

Smoke, multi-coloured lights, and sound filled the narrow Chez Bricktop. The notorious Bricktop owned the club and the only thing more striking than the red hair above her tanned, freckled face was her commanding yet disarming presence. She was as big a personality as ever I'd known. It was too bad she was but a Mono. She would have been formidable within the ranks of the Mentium.

The mood in the club contrasted the swirling dread that swept Bernard's mind when he wasn't focused on playing. I'd been dipping into his mind since the encounter with the gargoyle and he'd calmed little inside, though he was a picture of professionalism to those around us.

I, on the other hand, started the night on a bit of a rocky note. I mean that literally as, I hate to admit, my nerves had gotten the better of me and I began on the wrong chord. I was not accustomed to performance before a crowd. My debut was more than a little disconcerting.

There were also my cravings for opium. The sweating had begun. Was it physiological or psychological? Either way I was soaked through in minutes.

The room was filled with the delicious smells of cocktails, wine, beer, and champagne. All made heavier with tobacco smoke. The rich scent, though nothing like opium, still poured petrol onto the fire of my need.

As one song turned into three, then four, I relaxed and channelled Del's sizable skill. My confidence in those skills became confidence in myself and I soon locked in with the band.

"Merci, thank you, thank you," said our maestro at the end of the song. The band leader, a young and handsome African American who operated under the stage name of Creole Calloway, spoke into the chrome microphone with languid words announcing each song we played as if talking about a fine meal or a work of art. The passion that coated his words had the secondary effect of seduction and at least three audience members wore the doe-eyed, slack-jawed mask of infatuation.

"*Messieurs-dames*, prepare yourselves. This next song moves like a train. Stay in those seats as you might just be knocked off your feet. Don't worry, this train is under control, my control, though just barely. Ladies and gentlemen, Jelly Roll Morton's *Doctor Jazz!*"

The music launched to life at the drop of his hand though that was the extent of his conducting. Like Louis Armstrong or King Oliver, Creole Calloway was both band leader and musician. He played coronet and announced his presence in the song with a cutting high note that cascaded down into the melody. Creole's arrangement was even more raucous than Morton's, with his coronet taking the place of the clarinet and the whole band attacking the rhythm.

As a part of the rhythm section, my focus was on the drummer. Gene Rich was his name but Bernard informed me that Del, along with the rest of the band, called him Sticky, and I should address him as such. I acquiesced.

Sticky's skill at percussion was adequate but his timing was worse than a drunk duchess during a waltz. I turned to him as his pace began to drag. Creole was not jesting at the speed of this tune, and Sticky was struggling to keep up.

Cradling Del's guitar between my right knee and right arm, my left hand bounced around the neck, chord to chord, in time with Sticky's lagging rhythm.

Del was obsessed with a hot American jazz guitarist named Eddie Lang. Lang was one of the first to see the guitar as more than a simple rhythm instrument and Del wanted nothing more than to follow people like Lang into the limelight. Bernard said it wasn't about fame for the pair, but Del wanted it, craved it deep down.

Our charismatic band leader deftly changed his demeanour from the forward-facing glee of a showman to the serious scowl of a mill foreman as he glared at Sticky. Sticky, for his part, missed the look as he was too focused on keeping up. He was a ball of sweat.

Bernard was bathed in blue stage lighting. His baritone saxophone, also a part of the rhythm section functioned as a wind version of the bass often doubling or augmenting its lines. He and the bass player, an American named Charles Wooten got along well and both played off each other like tandem ice skaters. Unfortunately, their playing was also suffering from Sticky's sluggish banging. It was then that a plan formed.

Bernard caught me looking at him and I flashed a sly smirk. His eyes widened, and I winked at him. I forced myself to focus on the music rather than my cravings. I used the music as a drug.

I turned away from Bernard as my right hand slowly began to pick up speed. It was barely perceptible at first. My downward strum sounded the strings nanoseconds before Sticky could pound the drumheads. I increased the force at which I was strumming and continued my acceleration. The band, now able to hear more of my percussive strumming began to lock into my rhythm rather than Sticky's.

The audience was wrapped by the energy of the band. I admit I was too. Listening to lively jazz was often more of a chore to me than a delight, but playing it, with other able musicians, that was something else entirely. This was a talented group. When Mr Calloway said that a train was coming, he was referring to the song but could just as easily have been referring to his musicians. The interplay of instruments was so well synced, save for poor Sticky, that he should have named his group Creole Calloway and his Locomotive rather than his New Orleans Jazz Orchestra. It was a twelve-piece outfit and the chemistry was electric. Or to solidify the analogy, steam-powered. The energy and satisfaction I was feeling bordered on euphoric. Now that I was leading them, it was sublime.

I stopped my escalation of tempo when smiles crossed more and more faces within the band. They liked the new pace and it felt right. Ella Smith, the songbird of the group, blew a kiss my way before diving into the chorus with a voice as powerful and accurate as a rifle. I don't quite know how to describe it but there is a feeling, a deep, emotional response when the music you are playing nears its potential.

Slowly, again by nanosecond increments, Sticky caught up. It was as if the synergy of the band had infected him and now he drove his kit with passion.

The room was exploding in front of me. Patrons were dancing. Bricktop herself stood by the bar clapping, her violet feather headpiece swaying to the rhythm. Hoots and cheers sprang up all around us and the tapping feet of my bandmates thundered the stage, acting like a second bass drum.

I looked back at Bernard. The fear that had begun the evening dissolved into joy and the corners of a gleeful smile spread on either side of his mouthpiece. I was smiling too. I had never been a smiler. Grins, smirks, the occasional laugh-induced curling of the mouth but never a smiler. In that moment of coordination and camaraderie, my smile could not be contained.

The song was now past halfway and I decided, for Del's sake, to push my boldness further. He wanted to stand out like Eddie Lang, and I thought it was just about time he took a step. Del had the talent, the skill, and the ambition. I could see it in his mind. He only lacked the guts. I, luckily, have those in no short supply.

My hands continued their dance, but my left hand began working double time. In between chord changes I let my fingers sound chains of notes, not unlike the walking lines of the bass. I did nothing to jeopardise the song. Music, I was growing ever more aware, was about mutual respect. The guitar wasn't the star in this band. Creole Calloway would be secure in that role for years to come, but on that night, I took the skills Del had been honing in his bedroom and shared them with the world. And the world was eating it up.

The lines I was weaving flowed within the lines singing from the other instruments, from Ms Smith's throat. Calloway spun my way.

I feared I'd made a mistake but his shocked eyes and approving nods spurred me on further.

We entered into the final chorus and as taste would dictate, I eased back on my improvisation and let the screaming high notes of Creole's coronet bring the piece to a close.

The applause was astounding. My heart pounded in my chest and my ears were filled with mass, genuine approval. There in the hot lights, the band had all turned toward me and their expressions fed me like a drug. The crowd was a drug. All of them were on their feet and applauding. All but one.

A young man, thin and tall, stood, his eyes wide, his jaw set, and his shoulders down and back. I kept him in my peripheral vision but dared not stare. His body quavered and he resumed his applause. Bricktop, now eyed the room with the same set jaw and wide eyes. My laughter was drowned out by the applause.

"Del Chambers on the guitar everybody!" said Calloway and the cheering increased. I didn't know what to do. I checked again with Bernard and he was laughing at me. The kind of laugh you give when you can't believe something just happened.

I was drinking in a cocktail of satisfaction. The adoration, coupled with the fact the Mentium had just watched me perform right under their noses, was too delicious to bear.

"All right folks, I told you that song cooked. Next up for your listening pleasure…" Creole's voice faded as I focused inward.

Deep within me, below my consciousness, I felt a vast elation. It was pride, it was excitement, it was a sense of confirmation. It was Del. I was glad for him. He was good at something after all. Damn good.

◆ ◆ ◆

"Jesus Del, where'd that come from?" asked a drunk Boneyard Dorsey, the tall, skinny New Yorker who, surprise, played trombone in Creole's outfit. His short, curled black hair glistened with the sweat of the evening. Backstage, everyone was already drunk thanks to the free bottles from Bricktop. It would seem she felt extra generous on a night when we made her patrons enjoy themselves so much.

"I'm unsure but I very much enjoyed your work tonight," I said.

"Very much enjoyed? What the hell?"

"Hey, sorry man," I said, channelling Del's method of speech. Speech is difficult to glean from memory alone. It's more intrinsic to consciousness. Del was poor and from Chicago. I'd spent time there a few decades back, so I incorporated those experiences with what I had scraped from his memory. "I'm blotto already." I gestured with my empty glass. "It's no big deal. I just thought the song ought to have been faster."

"Ab-so-lute-ly, that new tempo was swell," said Oscar, the pianist. "You really woke ol' Sticky up. Thank god." He was a big man with a thick Louisiana accent and thick Louisiana waistline.

"Well, I knew he'd lock in."

"No he wouldn't," said Oscar. I glanced over at Sticky who was drinking alone near the stage entrance and he visibly cringed at Oscar's words.

"No, man," said Boneyard reclaiming his conversation. "Not the tempo, those walking lines. Where'd you pick that up?"

"I been practicing. I like what Eddie Lang does and—"

"Lang ain't never done anything like that," he said.

"Yeah," said Bernard wrapping his arm around my shoulder, "Del's been practicing real hard. Hey fellas, I need to talk to him for a second. We'll be right back."

Bernard kept his arm in place as he walked me toward the outer door. I was still sweating and as the wet cloth pressed against my shoulders. It was the body in revolt.

"Where are we going?" I asked.

"We need to get you out of here before Owl breaks out the cocaine."

"Wise," I said, feeling more of the dragon's pull as the excitement of the evening wore off, "though, a little cocaine may go a long way to curb my cravings for the opium. They use it as treatment you know."

"Not worth it."

As we approached the door Creole called out to us. "Where you boys going? You ain't been paid yet."

We both turned. When the band leader, or anyone paying you calls, you listen.

"Hell, Creole, slipped my mind. That was some show we put on tonight," said Bernard.

"You don't know the half of it, Bernie. Bricktop booked us for a month solid starting mid-February. Plus, our take at the door was huge tonight!" Calloway reached into his pocket and handed each of us our cut. "Del, you had us hitting on all sixes there."

"Thank you, Mr Calloway," I said.

"Cut that out, would ya? Mr Calloway? Jesus, Del. Look, I oughta be thanking you. I don't know what got into you but that wasn't the little guy I hired four months back. You lit the place on fire."

"Creole," said Bernard counting his money, "I think you made a mistake and I don't want to swindle you out of your take. This is double the usual."

"That it is, Bernie, that it is. I'm feeling generous tonight. You've both earned it. Hell, all y'all are getting double!"

A unison cheer erupted as Creole circled the small, disordered room proudly paying his crew. There were crates for seats and a single sofa plus three dressing tables with mirrors.

"Let's celebrate!" said Owl. "It might be raining money tonight, but I think we oughta make it snow. Hey Del, get your ass over here."

I had taken a single step when Bernard's strong hand grabbed my shoulder. I whispered toward that hand in response.

"If Del were here, what would he do?"

Bernard grumbled something inaudible.

"Precisely. You told me yourself that I needed to *be* Del. Well, what would happen if I refused?"

"Del would just say he has people to see and go chase the dragon," he said.

"Hey Bernie," said Owl, now surrounded by most of the band, "would you quit playing wet nurse and let the boy enjoy himself? He had a hell of a night."

Bernie released my shoulder. On the dressing table next to us was a bottle of bourbon.

"Here," I said grabbing the near-full bottle and placing it in his hand, "drink up. I'll be fine and it is certainly a night for celebration."

"But someone has to keep an eye out for you."

"Not tonight, Mrs Grundy. While I'm a novice when it comes to Opium, cocaine and I have danced before. Besides, the Mentium doesn't know I'm Del. We're safe here. They've already swept the venue. We are in the proverbial clear."

"They were searching here?"

"Have fun, Bernard. You've earned a little fun."

Bernard sat as I walked over to the short side table that Owl had positioned in the middle of the room. In the centre was a small pile of white powder. Cocaine had been deemed medicine until recently. It was in children's beverages. Using a business card, I scraped out a dose for myself. I looked over to Bernard who held up the bottle and placed it to his lips. I bent my head but was stopped short by a call from Boneyard.

"Which one of you owes money?" he asked.

"What are on about?" asked Creole.

"There's a couple big ol' thugs in nice suits out front."

Bernard and I slipped out the back.

20

WALKING & TALKING

The snow had stopped and there was even a sliver of moon to light our walk home. We'd abandoned our cab at the halfway point in favour of a stroll. Our social lubrication had not only helped us settle into a continual chain of rousing conversation but also steeled us to the cold. It also steeled us to the fact that we'd just dodged Eunuchs.

"He wouldn't," I said, bouncing between Bernard and the railing along the Seine.

"He did. In fact, he pulled that shit a lot. Just because I was bigger than he was, he thought I'd always protect him."

"You do, though."

He stopped and screwed his face up in drunken thought which dissolved into resigned laughter.

"I suppose I do. Guess it's just second nature. I've been at it since I was a boy."

"But he's a grown man. Why not push him from the nest?" I felt like a booze blanket protected me from both the cold and the fire burning within.

His breath came in a large cloud that hung as he mulled his response. He looked to the moon and kept his eyes there as he spoke.

"Del's never had a shot. Not in his whole life. We're like brothers but I'm definitely the older brother. I've always been the one who's supposed to protect him."

"The world doesn't give anyone a shot. Fate is a myth. Believe me, I know. People take shots for themselves. Del took one tonight."

"No, you took one tonight. Sure, it was Del's ability but not his drive. You were the one who showed everyone what he can do. He's too weak. He's always been too weak for a lot of things. It's like he has everything he needs to make it in this world but has no idea how to use any of it." He paused. "I love him to death. He's a smart guy, especially with people. He knows how to read people. He understands them, but he has no clue how to run his own life."

We started to walk again. We both let some silence hang as we turned left down *Boulevard Saint-Michel*.

"Ah, god dammit," Bernard said, a slight echo bouncing off the buildings on the deserted street.

"What?"

"Those things I said, about Del, can he hear me? I mean, wherever you're keeping him in there, can he still see and hear and all that?"

Oh, I heard him all right. Heard him just fine.

"I don't think so," I lied and ignored Del.

"Good. I don't mean to get down on him. It's just the truth."

"Subject change," I said, because we needed one. "Is Sticky always so behind the beat?"

Bernard started to laugh then caught himself. "That wasn't nice."

"What wasn't nice"

"I shouldn't laugh. Sticky's a drunk. The fact that he only slips in tempo really means he's doing pretty well. I laugh because he's a goofy drunk. When Del and I first signed on with the Creole's outfit, Sticky kept himself together better. He lost his girl a month back and he's been a sloppy mess ever since."

"What a lost lover can do to the mind."

"Ain't that the truth. What about your lady? What's her name… Lilith. What's she like when she's not out to get you?"

The question was novel. My private life was something I kept as such. I rarely, if ever, spoke of it. In any typical situation I would have skirted the question and shifted the topic of discussion to something else. This wasn't a typical situation. Bernard was in the position of confidant and I had begun to even like the man, A rare achievement for a Mono, so I indulged his interest.

"Imagine you are on the plain in Africa."

"I've never been to Africa."

"Have you seen a lioness?"

"Yeah, at the zoo in Chicago."

"Well, Lilith is very much a lioness. You see, in a pride of lions, the male is a big, pompous beast who grows wild hair and claims he is strongest. And yes, he is bigger and yes, has more muscle, but the lioness, oh, she is cunning. She is the one who hunts. She is the one who coordinates the others in the pride. She is the one who lets the male think he's on top while she controls all from a place of feigned subservience. Lilith is a lioness to her core."

"She seems like quite the lady. Why won't she help you?"

"Oh," I said, fighting depressed laughter, "as I said, a lioness hunts. I'm currently Lilith's quarry."

"But you two love each other, right?"

"Love is a small concept. We share a bond that has lasted thousands of years."

"Does she really want you dead?"

"Possibly. Likely not. She wants me caught and she'll want me punished. She wants to do her duty and to win this round."

"I don't understand"

"I wouldn't expect you to. We are bonded to each other but we've never been on the same team, as it were. Competition defines us. I'm down and so she'll kick me. I just hope she does not kick me in the head."

We took another left onto *Rue Cujas*. The bite of the evening was somehow permeating both my jacket and the alcohol. Home was ten minutes away and we would have tea and beds soon.

"There's something that's been confusing me about your people, the Mentium," said Bernard, there were a few additional s's on the word something, indicating that his inebriation was still holding strong.

"Ask away. I do have a little experience with them."

"In your, what did you call it, the top ten?"

I had to laugh. I quite liked that moniker. "I think you mean 'Upper Echelon'."

"Yeah, the Upper Echelon, you've got women and people from all over the world, right?"

"Well, I suppose we do. At least from the Old World. I am considered Middle Eastern as is Lilith, also a woman. The Twins are European though one is a woman. Tian is Chinese though he's covered most of Asia in his time. Yemoja, African from below the Sahara and a woman. Kali, Indian and a woman, what's your point?"

Bernard stopped walking underneath the illuminated expanse of the Pantheon and gave me a strange look. It was as if his thoughts were coalescing in his mind right in front of me. He clearly didn't like what was materializing. Drunk philosophising at its finest.

"History," he said. "Every part of it. What about all the people that have been stepped on over the years? There's been so much oppression. So much hate and pain. All of those types of people are part of the Mentium yet you all just let that happen?"

"Bernard," I said, patting him on the shoulder, "you are quite spectacular for a Mono. That is an extremely good question. Unfortunately, I doubt that you'll like the answer."

He tensed, and it was as if the cold night air had sucked away any warmth between us.

"The Mentium are a self-serving lot aren't we, Bernard? To put it simply, when half the population controls everything, there's only half the population to control. Now start creating power imbalances within that half, and our life was made much easier.

Northern European men have done more than their fair share of walking over others in the past thousand years, to an insidious degree, but before that it was the Mediterraneans, the Steppe, and North African people stepping on them. The Chinese have stepped on plenty of people in their region."

He set down his saxophone case and rubbed his neck.

"The Arabic peoples stepped all over the peoples within a vast territory. The Mongols, the empires of the Americas, the Egyptians, I could go on. We Broadcasters seek efficiency for our own systems, that's all. And we care little for others, especially Monos like yourself."

He was nodding but I doubted it was in agreement.

"We nudge. We don't dictate and we don't rebuild. It's that fact that drives our current quest. Stepping into the light will destroy our empire. It's better to leave Monos to their own devices and continue to collect. We've been doing so, more or less, since the crusades. Hell, even longer in some cases."

"I had almost forgotten what an absolute bastard you are, you deluded, evil, son of a bitch."

Though his new, foul mood wouldn't penetrate the positivity given to me by the booze and my stellar night, I understood the root of his frustration. Would he ever grasp our position? Did it matter?

"Bernard, don't get that way. 'Don't be sore' as Del would say. Your anger will change nothing, though you are more than right to feel it. Understand that there are things in this world that Monos aren't supposed to know. I felt you could handle the truth. Was I wrong?"

"If you expected me to accept any group of people manipulating the lives of others for their own gain, then I suppose you were wrong."

"Fair enough."

"Tell me again why I'm helping someone as disgusting as you?"

"Well..."

He turned from me and again looked to the moon before stammering and backing away from the colossal building beside us.

"What is it?" I asked, searching the domed roof of the Pantheon. I opened my mind and needed no answer.

Above us, circling the pinnacle of the Pantheon were two gryphons. Their fore-talons slashing at each other while their beaked mouths hissed and clacked in vicious gnashing. Feathers floated toward us as the creatures continued to land blows against one another. The lion's tail of the smaller gryphon was bleeding profusely as it tried to pull it from the other's dripping maw.

"That's why you're helping me." I pointed up to yet another of Izzy's tests. "These monsters will bring ruin to us all unless we stop them."

He glared into my eyes, then up at the sparring beasts. He stared long and hard and winced as the rear claws of both animals screeched against the metal rooftop.

Bernard put two fists to his eyes. "Fine," he said throwing his hands down, grabbing his saxophone and marching on into the night. The snow-covered streets heard nothing but the crunch of our footsteps.

21

DREAMS

My head swam as I stripped off my concert clothes. Bernard disappeared into his bedroom as soon as we arrived. This was fine since there would be nothing more of import to discuss.

The chaos of Del's room only fuelled my feelings of unease and disorientation. The night had been filled with adrenaline, my belly with alcohol, and my body with the smouldering need for more opium. My body ached for sleep but my mind ignored those pleas.

Chin deep under the duvet, I squeezed my bloodshot and burning eyes shut and tried to focus the cacophony of questions, plans, and assessments that echoed between my ears. Sleep came in fits and starts but it came, and when it did I dreamt of the life I'd just lost and lives I had lived.

◆ ◆ ◆

The smell of sun-baked grass and lake water filled my lungs. Hard, sharp wood pressed into my back: a hot hand in mine.

I lay against the bow in the large rowboat Lilith and I shared. The sun beat down on us as we floated between the islands of *Lac Inférieur* near the eastern edge of the Bois de Boulogne. The trees were too far from the water to provide any shade, so my pale boater hat had to do the job.

"Darling, how can you stand to lay like that?" Lilith wore white linen pants that flowed to her bare feet. A sage blouse opened to the heat under her collar, all below a rose-hued straw affair of her own. I reached out but was kicked away.

"That has never been successful."

"Someday, a tickle shall grace those hooves."

"Hooves? That's a fine thing to say coming from my snake dragon."

"I'm not the one who's a demon."

"Self-styled. Remember that."

"How could I forget."

The lake was thick with watercraft but we'd found a small refuge between the islands.

This was a dream spawned of memory, five years earlier, maybe more, but certainly after my radio had gone into operation.

Lilith reached for the oars and gently turned us, keeping us in the channel and away from the Monos. Days like this brought on so many thoughts of joy, love, and lust that it was about all a Broadcaster could do to stomach it. Mostly we tuned out their Mono drivel but curiosity always won out and that curiosity always disappointed.

"Let's play, shall we?" asked Lilith, still gripping the oars in her strong, summer-tanned hands.

"Play? Okay, I'm game. What do you have in mind?"

She turned us parallel to the channel and with unison strokes, sent us sliding out into the lake.

"I've been craving a game of Cause and Effect."

That piqued my interest. As she tucked our oars to the side, I sat up and we faced the centre of the boat to survey the most area.

"Who goes first?" I asked.

She leaned in and gave me a slow kiss then pushed me away. "Me," she said. "I won last time."

"As usual, but I'm feeling particularly cunning today."

"Spare me. The only thing you ever feel around me is horny."

"Just make your move, demon."

She gnashed her teeth at me through a poppy-red smile then began scouting the throngs of happy people for one to use.

Cause and Effect was a game of chance.

"There," she said, pointing a slender finger toward a man, also in a straw boater hat. "The dunce will lose balance and the wife will grip with both hands."

"Both hands?"

"Both."

Lilith planted a suggestion into the man's head. Something discreet. Lift a foot. Shift your weight. Something so base and natural as to be imperceptible to the victim. That was the 'cause' portion of the game. It was the only aspect one had control over. Each player's move. The gamble and payoff came from predicting the effect.

She broadcast, the man shifted, the wife gripped the sides of their boat with both hands. One point Lilith.

"Hardly a worthy play, my love," I said.

"Then show me what you've got, darling."

Keeping my eyes, ears, and mind open, I bounced from one head to another, getting whiffs of personality and competence. Drunks were always a favourite and I came upon the perfect wine-soaked pawn.

"That one," I said pointing to a rotund gentleman in his seventies. He sat on a blanket in front of a group of boys playing football, and flanked by two groups of twenty-somethings being far too boisterous and self-important for anyone's tastes. The old man was busy exchanging one bottle of red for another.

"The old man will pull the cork with too much force, sending the wine to his right and onto Little Miss Sundress and his cork hand will swing back into the passing boy's shoulder, sending the child to the ground."

"Going for double points, are we?" She fanned herself with her hat.

"How else am I going to win?"

"Best mind your timing, darling."

Too true. My first suggestion planted was simply for the man to stop once the corkscrew was fully inserted. The old man obliged with a blank stare out to the water's edge. I studied the group of boys kicking the ball around, readying my next suggestion. The rules of the game only allowed me into the mind of one person at a time, so I waited.

A tall boy came careening toward the old man's blanket after a stray ball. In an instant another suggestion was placed. The old man tugged at the cork, it sprang from the bottle, and his elbow flew backward toward the unknowing teen. The wine bottle sailed to the right and the contents sloshed onto Little Miss Sundress. The corked hand did not land. The boy bent for his ball and returned to the others unscathed. The old man made his mortified apologies to the young woman. The sundress was as ruined as the wearer's day, and I sighed at my demi-defeat.

"Only one point!" said Lilith with an excited clap.

"We're still tied."

"Not for long, darling. My turn."

She wasted no time. Her black hair glistened beneath her hat as she hunted for a target.

"Anything interesting?"

Her gaze paused, a squint, then her smile broke into laughter.

"What?"

"They're going in!" she said.

"Who?"

"Watch!"

"Wait," I said trying to see her target. "That's not how…"

She didn't wait. Instead she pointed out across the water to a small dock where a middle-aged man was fishing next to a group of schoolgirls soaking their feet.

"What?" I asked again, then it all happened. The man yanked his line from the water as if he'd felt a bite. That was the suggestion. The still-baited hook cleared the water's surface and arced behind the fisherman, coming to rest in the auburn curls of one of the girls. She let out a shriek and stood, trying to free the wet, dead worm that wrapped the hook from her locks. Her two friends tried to help but the panicked victim was all elbows and hips and twisting. Her arm connected with the jaw of friend number one who in turn reached for friend two in order to steady herself. Friend two was not prepared and both tipped off the dock and into the lake with the dramatic scream unique to girls between eight and sixteen.

The splash was high and drenched two overdressed boaters, in ivory and gold, who had been sitting idle near the dock. They both yelled and both stood, but not in unison. The action of their pumping legs as they tried to steady the boat tipped an edge under the water. The angry pair joined the girls for a swim.

"Was that...?" I asked.

"Who else?"

Every person on the shore nearest the unwitting swimmers stared up at the sky. Every single one. That went for the boaters on the lake as well, except for Lilith and I. My view swept from the disquieting scene to the capsized boat where Apollo and Artemis marched toward the shore from the murk.

I burst out laughing and Lilith added her own giggle to our mocking chorus.

The Twins were too far away for us to hear their words and we were certainly not going to open our minds to them, but the grunts and growls carried across the water and made sweet music.

Lilith leaned back against the boat and put a hand on her still contracting stomach. "I do so hate those two."

"They're despicable," I agreed.

"But... they're Mentium and they're our family."

"Family cannot be chosen. They were."

"We can't always be expected to make perfect decisions, love."

◆ ◆ ◆

Hot, sulphuric water splashed my face and filled my laughing mouth.

"You're cute when you're frustrated," she said, sliding across the steaming hot spring toward me where I sat on the marble seat. She wrapped her naked arms around me while the rest of her did the same.

Aquae Helveticae, now Baden, Switzerland, once a northern outpost of the Roman empire. Then, in 200AD, it was but a small thermal refuge from the onslaught of the Germanic barbarians. Cernunnos and Radegast had yet to be brought into our ranks and they were putting up a hell of a fight.

"Those bastards will fall," I squeezed her hips. "Their dominions are too scattered, too fractious to prevail. The might of the Mentium, and of Rome, will crush them."

She kissed me and put a cup to my lips. How I miss lead-sweetened wine.

"My love, you do not understand chaos."

"Chaos? What is there to understand? Chaos is disorder and disorder brings failure."

Lilith *tsked* and pushed away from me, coming to rest across the rectangular marble bath. Everything inside was white marble, from the statue of a woman with an endlessly pouring amphora, to the walls bathed in the glow of candles, to the vaulted doorway where two Thracian servants awaited command.

Despite the centuries spanned in this vision, my love looked as she looked in 1928. We Mentium have had so many faces, we tend to only hold onto what's current. The body is but a vessel, after all.

"Chaos," she continued, "is a distraction. It can be a disguise. Above all, it can be a weapon. One whose blade we've felt all to keenly."

"And how are these unwashed simpletons wielding such a weapon?"

She sipped at her wine and gazed at me with a smile that challenged and mocked.

"Don't do this," I said.

"Come now, I know you won't refuse a puzzle."

"Just make your point so we can go back to enjoying our bath."

"Don't concede before you've begun."

I looked toward the pair of Thracian women standing at the doorway and entered them. They began to wave their white robes in slow, flapping motions, fanning our bodies.

"Coward," she said and spit a stream of wine across the water at me.

"Come here and explain your genius, love. You know you're dying to share."

Like a python, she slid across the water and came to rest straddling my thighs.

"Cernunnos and Radegast have one enemy," she said. "Us."

"No, both Rome and the Mentium are their enemies."

"We are Rome, love. That makes one unified enemy. One army, one manner of operating, one way of thinking. We, on the other hand, have hundreds of foes. These two northern gods have village, after warlord, after culture, after fighting technique to command. The war cannot hope to be won through battle."

Wine trickled down my chin as laughter trickled across my lips.

"Darling, then why have we been grinding against these Germans for untold years? The Twins seems to prefer this method. So too, the others."

"Success and pride, my dear. A battle is not a war and collecting victory only makes defeat more sour. We are a prideful and boastful lot. It's time we let the northern gods win this battle for us."

"And how do you propose we do that?"

She bent to kiss me again. First my lips then my forehead then my neck. Her lips came to rest at my ear.

"I'm going to propose that they join us."

I pushed her off of me and sat up on the edge of the stone pool. "You're going to what?"

She stood in the middle of the water, steam rising from her shoulders.

"I'm going to meet with them. I'm going to explain what the Mentium is and how we operate. I'm going to paint a picture of our luxury and power, then I'm going to ask them to join us."

"This is absurd!" my words bounced off every hard surface. "Lilith, they're savages!"

"They are already part of us. Our kind exist as a part of the Mentium or they don't exist. I will explain that as well."

"We don't need them."

"Rome is dying M. It's crumbling and has been for centuries. Small cracks are turning into fissures. Think of the opportunities these two "savages" can bring. The wealth, the resources, the land. Our dominion does not have to be Rome's dominion. It can be more. It is more. It's always been more."

I sat back down in the water. She did not. "I don't like this, and the Twins will hate you for it."

"I will do what's right for the Mentium. All of you be damned." She strode through the water and as her wake broke against my chest, the servants at the door began to wrap her body.

"It's a mistake."

She turned only her head. "The mistake is not to seize opportunity. You may be too much a fool to see it but once I've spied my prey, it's mine."

"What you speak of, if it works, will take an incredible amount of time. Too much time."

"Time will set things right," she said, and she left me.

◆ ◆ ◆

"She left me," I whispered as I sat up in Del's bed. My whole body felt heavy. Lilith had left me then as she did now. The difference was, she was right that night in the bath. Cernunnos and Radegast became two of my most trusted — if trust exists — of all my brothers and sisters.

She was right then, but what of now? Could I have been wrong? Could I have made some terrible oversight? No. No, she'd followed the Twins, people she despised, people she mistrusted, and left me to fend for myself. No, it was more. She was actively working against me.

I could feel her growing distant in the weeks before my demise. It wasn't the first time and I assumed it to be another of a thousand irritations we'd given one another. I assumed wrong and now my love had turned her back on me. I needed her. I needed Lilith.

I rubbed my new, thin face and rested against the corroded brass headboard. The clock read 5.12am. The need for opium glowed brighter and I feared it would take flame soon.

There would be no more sleep for me that night. The need for the drug and for my love would burn on. How could one sleep through such agony?

She left me and I her.

She made a choice, a dire one. But I'd made a choice too.

We would have to live with our choices.

We might have to die defending them.

SUNDAY

8TH JANUARY

1928

22

MONTMARTRE

"The fit is amazing, Philipe. Thank you," said Bernard as he adjusted the lapels of his new ash-grey jacket in front of the mirror. The room was filled with the smell of clean, dyed wool. The craftsman smiled and took a short bow. I sat in the corner wanting, needing. The dragon breathed within me and it burned.

"M," Bernard said with hesitation. "Thank you as well. You didn't have to do this."

"Yes I did. We couldn't spend one more day in those rags."

We'd worn only the bare minimum of clothing to pick up our new suits and I'd told Bernard to choose his most worn items as we'd be throwing them out.

"Philipe," I said, already putting a new coat over a crisp, perfectly fitted, slate-grey tweed suit. "We need to leave the other suits here until this afternoon. We have errands to attend to in the coming hours."

"Of course, M."

"You work miracles, Philipe," said Bernard, "real miracles."

"Skilled hands and a keen eye."

Bernard stepped to his side and gave him a pat on the back. "Whatever it is, you're an artist."

"This one understands my genius," said Philipe, his smile the only thing further from modest than his statement.

"Please, Bernard, his prices will double if you keep that up. Besides, you haven't yet seen his genius. These were mere adjustments. His bespoke—"

"As if price matters to you," said Philipe. He began organizing suits and shirts.

"It may, soon enough."

"Is the situation really that bad?" Philipe turned from his work.

"Have you seen today's paper?" asked Bernard as he picked up the folded periodical and handed it to Philipe, whose mouth opened as soon as the newspaper did.

"Gryphons? In Paris? Izanagi must be out of his mind," said Philipe, putting the paper aside.

"It's the whole damned lot of them. The gryphons came from the Twins, no doubt."

"Not everyone, though," said Bernard.

"True. I meet with Tian this afternoon and I cannot express what a relief that will be. We'll bring each other up to speed on the current situation and I'll learn of the resources and manpower he has available to him. Today is the day we begin taking back the Mentium." My enthusiasm rushed through me but evaporated like kerosene in a flame.

"I hope you're right, M," said Philipe. "For all of our sakes. Forgive me but it sounds a bit like you're counting chickens."

"Tian is no chicken. He is the only Broadcaster I can trust. I know he won't betray me."

The other two men said nothing.

"The situation is under control," I continued. "Granted, it's less than ideal but at least for you, Philipe, it's nothing you should worry about. Just keep on your toes for the next week or so while we end this charade."

"Well, come back soon so I can get you two into *my* suits. I don't like fixing that commercial drivel."

I'm keeping these suits once you're out of me. Bernie too, said Del from his cell in the subconscious.

What use would I have for such tiny garments? You need to stop this interrupting before I come down there and remove your mouth entirely.

I'd like to see ya try.

"Of course," I said to Philipe. "Soon. I promise."

I gave Bernard a nod and he picked up his new black Homburg with an orange and green feather.

Look at that fancy guy with his life all together, said Del.

Be grateful you have a friend at all, you buffoon. Stop yammering on.

"Philipe, it's been an honour as usual," I said taking his hand and forcing the civility he deserved.

"Take care of yourself, and him," he said, pointing at Bernard. "And Bernie, you watch over this one too."

Bernard shook his hand as well but said nothing.

From Philipe's studio, we set off into the world as new, sharp-looking men with much to do. Of course, as our luck seemed to have it, our march toward business only lasted a few icy blocks.

"Bernie! Del, would ya look at you two! Where the hell did you get the dough to put on the Ritz like that?" The man was in an energised state and rocked back and forth as if his feet hurt.

I knew better than to speak to Sal first and Bernard knew better than to let me.

"Business has been good," said Bernard. "And we were getting pretty threadbare."

"That's a load of baloney. Those are some nice duds. Too nice. You boys gotta be better with your money."

I swear to god if that dumb fucker opens his trap one more time, I'm gonna feed him a knuckle sandwich so big he'll be smelling my armpit!

At that, I couldn't help but enter Bernard's mind. The memories of multiple instances of Sal swindling them flashed before me and my anger grew along with Bernard's and Del's. This time I did speak. Carefully. "Lay off, Sal," I said, playing my best Del. "It's our cabbage to spend."

"You spend like a couple of saps."

"Nah, we ain't saps. Not no more. We got wise to you, Sal. We know what ya did. What ya been doing all along. We know ya pocketed some of what ya owed us. We'd a been able to shine up a lot sooner if it weren't for you."

Bernard put a hand on my shoulder. "What Del means to say is—"

"Del's a god damned ingrate is what he is," said Sal stepping in close. He was a short, fat man so I met him as eye-to-eye as his belly would allow.

"Can't be ungrateful for being taken for a ride, can ya?" I said, centimetres from his face.

"That's it. I'm done," said Sal, throwing up his hands and stepping back. "Don't you two worry. I won't be coming 'round. No, sir, old Sal ain't your pal no more."

"Come on, Sal," said Bernard.

"No Bernie, and don't come crawlin' to me when you're out on your ear, starvin' and homeless. At least you got these fancy duds to keep you warm."

"Sal," Bernard said, pleading only out of politeness.

Sal chomped the cigar between his yellow teeth. "I don't have to take this off you two schmucks," he said and began to stomp off.

I couldn't help myself. I popped in, planted a seed, and the braggart tripped over his own feet, coming down hard — first on his knees, then his face.

He rolled like a bottle then caught himself. Blood had already begun to spread down his trouser legs.

"Let's get outta here, Bernie," I said still playing Del. "We've got places to be."

Nice acting job Mr Barrymore, said Del as we hurried off. *Couldn't have said it better if I tried.*

◆ ◆ ◆

The opium cravings were the only cravings I felt but it was food this body needed. Bernard savoured the warmth of a *cassoulet* and I struggled to eat a small *pot-au-feu*. We each enjoyed a heavy red wine and that was easier to stomach. The small cafe smelled of onion, cheese, and the must of wet wool coats heated by the coal-warmed air.

As we settled into our meals, I studied a green door positioned down a narrow street across from the window table where we sat. This was *9 Rue Aristide Bruant*. This was Izzy's front door.

"This isn't smart," said Bernard.

"It couldn't be more simple. We eat and wait," I said, watching the street and the people passing for any signs of random sweeps. Luck may have been tipping in our favour. "When the time is right, very unfriendly men will leave Izzy's apartment and we'll slip inside and copy his calendar."

"So we sit here and wait for who knows how long until these thugs of yours decide to leave? What if your buddy is home?"

"No, he's not home. He's always working. As for the Eunuchs guarding his flat, their decision to leave will be made for them. Just not by me. To enter their minds will give away our location. We're waiting for someone else. Now, finish your food and leave the strategy to me."

"Wait," he said, stirring his beans, "you explained before that you pick up consciousness like a radio signal, but you always talk about going into someone else's head. Which is it?"

"Now? You need to know now?"

"All we have is time, right?"

"Fine, fair enough." A heavy breath left my nose. "The quick answer is both. It is simply the limitation of metaphor. We don't snatch the signal out of thin air but rather from the head itself. Think of the brain and skull as a small antenna."

"Just stop," he said. "It was confusing enough before."

We continued to eat in silence, or rather the silence of a bustling eatery, and I searched *Avenue des Abbesses*, which ran perpendicular to *Rue Aristide Bruant*, for a suitable rabbit. As I did so, I managed to finish my stew and called for a second bottle of wine. I had resorted to using alcohol to curb my opium cravings and dull the persistent headache that had joined my constant sweats. It wasn't working but I couldn't give in to Del's yearnings just yet.

As I put more wine to my lips I noticed, through the bottom of the glass, a blob about half the size of an adult bobbing down the street toward us. I rapped on the window and the boy, no more than twelve, glanced up from the snow-covered sidewalk. I waved him into the cafe and he obliged. Using francs to do the waving may have helped.

"*Monsieur*?" the boy asked.

"A kid?" asked Bernie, equally annoyed and concerned. "What's he for?"

"English?" asked the boy with a spirited grin. "I speak English. A very little bit but I speak. Mon oncle, he's—"

"Good for you." I passed the boy five francs. "But French is fine," I said, switching into his native tongue. "Now, I have fifty more francs waiting for someone who can do me a small favour."

"Fifty?" he asked in a whisper, a thousand-yard stare crossing his face. "What favour?"

I leaned in close and whispered, "My ex-wife's brothers are currently in my apartment. I left a small wooden coffer on the mantle above the fireplace. The coffer is very dear to me, but my brothers-in-law would never let me have it. It's been just the nastiest divorce."

The boy made the sign of the cross.

"What are you saying to him?" asked Bernard. "You're talking too fast. I can't keep up."

"If you would be so kind as to retrieve the box for me," I said, pulling out the francs and an empty envelope from my inner jacket pocket, "then these fifty francs will be waiting for you behind the counter here. What's your name, boy?"

"Thierry."

"Wonderful," I said as I wrote his name on the envelope and sealed the money inside. I then waived the waiter over to our table while Bernard stared at me with so much contempt it was as if he were a nun who had caught me writing left-handed.

"What are you saying to him?" he asked. "Leave the kid alone, M. Leave him be."

Leave him be, M. This isn't right and you know it.

I ignored them both and kept a kind gaze on the boy.

"*L'envelope est pour le garçon*," I said as I put the envelope in the waiter's thin, delicate hand along with ten additional francs. "Please guard this for the boy until he returns. I'm sure that nothing will happen to the envelope or its contents. I'll be checking later to see that all goes as planned." I wouldn't be.

"Of course. It's safe with me, monsieur."

"*Parfait. Merci.*" I said, and the waiter scurried off behind the counter. He hid the envelope behind the dustiest bottles in the bar. I appreciated the tactic.

I turned once again to the boy and passed him a key I'd copied a year earlier after Izzy had changed his locks. "So, here is a key. Open the door with care and move quickly but quietly. The box will be on the mantle to the right in the sitting room. It's made of a dark wood and will be the only one you see. Once you enter, run to it, take it, and run out. If you're caught, these men will keep you until someone comes to claim you. I'm sure whoever does claim you will not want such a headache and I'm sure you do not want to suffer the company of these men. Do you think you are up for the challenge?"

"*Oui.* I do it," he said, again flexing his English.

"*Parfait. Merci et bonne chance.*"

The boy shot out of the brasserie, key in hand, and charged into the building.

"What the hell was that?" asked Bernie, grabbing my wrist across the table. I did not like his tone.

"That was what we were waiting for. Our rabbit."

"Rabbit?"

"Our distraction."

"What do you mean distraction? Wait… you son of a bitch. You sent him in there as…"

I held up my hand. "Bernard, I need to concentrate."

I entered the boy's mind and guided him up the steps of Izzy's apartment building. The green carpet felt unfamiliar under Thierry's light feet. Two levels below his flat, I made the boy fumble with the keys. An alarm bell if you will. His body then crept higher and when he reached the door, he slid the key into the lock and turned the handle as if it were his own home.

Light filled the boy's eyes as the generous windows of Izzy's apartment entered his view. Three large Eunuchs sat around the opulent sitting room.

"M, stop it, he's just a kid. Damn it. Stop."

"Enough!" I said, pulling away from the boy to deal with Bernard.

"I'm not going to sit here while—"

Shouts loud enough to be heard from inside the café had us both turn our heads. Our little rabbit, beaten and bloodied, fled Izzy's building followed by the hounds. The three mindless, gargantuan men were well dressed, well trained, and lethal. The boy was empty-handed, of course. Bernard's next admonishments caught in his throat at the sight of the fleeing child, and I placed payment for our meals over our check.

"Off we go, Bernard. We haven't much time," I said, reaching for my hat and coat with my hand, while intrusive empathy compelled my mind to reach out for Thierry's to suggest an escape route.

"When you next see the boy, give him the envelope whether he asks for it or not," I told the waiter, passing him another ten francs as I made for the door. He gave an eager nod. I paused for a moment and entered his mind. He would give the money to the child.

The sounds of shouting continued but grew more distant. The young lad was quick; I had hoped as much. We looked much like rabbits ourselves as we scampered through the soiled slush and pawed our way inside the building. The staircase was deserted but still I paused, listening. There was nothing but the errant sound of a radio pouring from within an upper-floor apartment. The coast was clear, and I sprinted up the stairs. My lungs burned from the exertion and I cursed Del with each step. The green carpet still felt foreign under Del's slight weight.

The door to the apartment was open and I set about ripping the place apart. This served two purposes. First, it would make it seem like a robbery. Second, it felt so good to destroy part of his life, even if it was trivial.

"What are you doing?" asked Bernard, checking and rechecking the doorway.

Books and furniture were scattered like autumn leaves by the time I'd finished. I pulled the key from the door and placed it in my pocket, then walked to the rolltop desk.

"Are we still alone?" I asked.

"Yeah, but hurry."

I tore a piece of yellow lined paper from a pad and pulled Izzy's leather-bound calendar from its place in the desk. Izzy was a creature of habit and ritual. He'd be where this said he'd be. I turned to January 9th— tomorrow— and began to write. Tuesday, Wednesday, Thursday, all the way to the following Monday — the day when the Twins planned to launch their assault on civilization. I folded the paper and hastily put it in my chest pocket.

Looking up, Bernard stood in the archway near the main door. Behind him loomed three more Eunuchs.

"Bernard!" I shouted, but it was too late. One of the automatons had him by the collar and another began to pummel him about the ribs. He threw fists, and an all-out brawl ensued.

"Bernard, relax!" I shouted, pulling one last item from the desk.

"Relax?"

"Yes, drop! Now!"

His body crumpled and as it did, I raised the gun but fear squeezed my throat.

Del, enough!

I sent a bullet at the skull of each of Bernard's attackers. The first shot sailed through a cheek. The recoil sent my twiggish arm up and back and the gun just missed my face. I grabbed the handle of the Colt 1911 with both hands, corrected, and the second shot caught the outer edge of the second Eunuch's skull and the third Eunuch's jaw ate the final .45 caliber bullet. Bad shots but effective enough. The concussions echoed through the building and out into the streets, sending our ears to ringing.

I am a highly-skilled marksman but Del's shaky, flimsy hands fouled my aim.

Are they hurt? I don't want to hurt nobody. Are they dead? M, did I just kill people? I just... I just—

You almost got Bernard killed! Now quiet!

"Get up!" I screamed to Bernard.

"Huh?" he asked, shaking his head. He regained his feet, picking at his ringing ears.

I grabbed one of the dead men by the left hand. His sleeve slid up revealing a small symbol, the size of a cherry, branded into the skin of his inner wrist. An eye. The pupil, a thick, round, raised scar. A decagonal iris surrounded it, each side representing a member of the Upper Echelon.

"What did you do?"

"I simplified our situation. Now, come look at this." I shook the bare wrist at him. "This is the symbol of the Mentium. Remember it. This man, all of these men, are Eunuchs."

"Yeah, Eunuchs. The ones you've been talking about? A they real Eunuchs?" asked Bernard with a stunned expression

"No, no, they're physically whole. It's their minds that have been castrated. They're Monos like you but are constantly under Mentium orders."

"Thank god."

"You're welcome. Now, we must leave before more arrive. I cannot afford to be discovered in this new body and you cannot be seen with me."

"Won't they be able to read your mind or something?" asked Bernard, panic in his voice as he took in the scene like a starving man takes in food. And like the starving man, the more he consumed the worse he felt. "Won't they already know it's you?"

I grabbed Bernard by the sleeve with gun in hand and the yellow paper in pocket. As we descended the stairwell again, I tucked the firearm into the pocket of my heavy wool coat. "They're Monos. They can't sense me. Even if another Broadcaster arrives with them, I can mask my consciousness. I've been doing so for over a day now. If we're seen though, they'll know that you and this body are somehow working for me which is just as bad. If I am captured…"

We emerged into the late morning light and we marched away from the apartment, away from the brasserie and onto quiet *Rue Veron* where two elderly women walked with the day's provisions and panicked looks. A still-shaking Bernard had a spray of blood from the Eunuchs drawn across his chest like a spotted red sash.

I led us east, straight toward the basement of *L'Église de St-Jean-de-Montmartre*. It just so happened I had a key.

Inside, we crossed the cavernous storage room past stacked chairs and decorations that lay in wait for the next holiday. Really, the next big payday for the Mentium. I pulled Bernard into a closet on the far wall containing the robes for the choir. We sat below the swaying fabric.

"I, I can't do this, M. I can't."

"You did fine, Bernard"

"I can't. You gotta get into a new body. Let's find you someone else and you can give me Del back. This is… I don't think…"

"You did fine, you'll do fine, and I'm staying right where I am, unfortunately. It will likely be a week at minimum before I can attempt to leave this body. I would gladly give up Del if it were possible but it's not."

I reached into my jacket pocket and removed Del's small steel flask. A lukewarm, rotgut whisky sloshed inside as I handed it to Bernard. He nodded and drank. I couldn't tell if his head or hand was shaking more but by sip number four, he'd calmed.

"Did you get what you needed?" asked Bernard, struggling to see me in the weak light that permeated the closet through the hole where its knob should be. His face had come away unscathed from the fight, but he rubbed his ribs. I hoped it was a minor injury.

"I did indeed," I said patting the paper through my jackets. Now we could track the bastard and I wanted to watch the life leave his eyes almost as much as I wanted opium.

23

CHICAGO?

L'Église de St-Jean-de-Montmartre was a beautiful Catholic church completed in 1904 and built in the Art Nouveau style. While the building was new, the choir robes were well past their prime and the scent of old sweat and new mould hung over our heads as we sat in the dark closet. All I wanted in my lungs was the earthy musk of the drug. We'd been sitting, waiting, for at least thirty minutes and it felt like hours.

"Del hates tight spaces. Claustrophobic. I used to wrap him in a blanket when we were little, just to mess with him," he said, his voice still a bit shaky from the nerves.

"Charming. What a good friend."

"I'm the best friend Del has." He wouldn't look at me.

"I know you are, Bernard. So does he. I have his memories. Remember."

"Yeah, I remember."

Silence fell, again. Most of our time in that mouldy closet was spent in silence save for the occasional shuffling of legs. I had never been inside such a slight body and I was learning there were some positives. I was much more comfortable than Bernard who was a head taller and twice as thick.

"How much longer do we need to sit here?"

"I'd say we've suffered enough. Can I buy you a whisky? Between our success and my meeting with Tian this afternoon, we have reason enough to celebrate," I said.

"No, I think I've had enough." he shook the dregs within the flask. "And did you forget about the blood?"

The spatter had dried and at a distance could have looked like spilled port.

"A cab home, then a shower, a change of clothes, and a bottle. I'll buy."

"If I don't have a choice…"

"Consider it doctor's orders. I was a physician once, in Venice."

"Lead on doctor."

◆ ◆ ◆

We sat across from each other at the kitchen table. Del and Bernard had scurried home with it one night after they found it on the street. One leg was broken and a stack of books did their best to level the top. It was an amusing memory.

"Tell me, Bernard, what was Del's childhood like?" I asked as I poured him a glass.

"That's direct. I thought you had all of his memories anyway."

"I do but I want your perspective."

"Why?"

"Humour me."

"No."

I put my hands on my knees and rubbed them through the crisp new fabric of another suit. I couldn't believe I'd bloodied the other jacket already. My sweating had lapsed but I knew it would return. My head still ached.

Del and Bernard's apartment was decrepit in a plethora of ways, but it was clean and warm, almost too warm, and my legs had begun to itch as the sweat formed. The smell of old coffee and old grease was a balanced blend of revolting and comforting.

"I have Del's memories, but all are framed by his perception of himself, for good or ill. What I don't have is the perception of others. It's often more honest and less judgmental."

"So you want my take on my best friend and you think that's supposed to be more accurate?"

"You'd be surprised."

He tipped his glass of whisky back and forth, watching the amber liquid coat its clear walls.

"Can he hear me?"

"I don't know. I don't think so but to be honest I haven't asked him."

"But earlier you said…"

I shrugged and sipped at a glass of Laphroaig. The peated scotch was a vast improvement over the flask and the alcohol cut some of the edge from the opium pangs. A dull knife still stabs, however.

"He's okay in there, right?" asked Bernard. At first, I thought he was making an awkward amount of eye contact, then realised he was searching for Del within.

"Yes, Bernard. He's safe."

He rubbed his face. A well-polished, though humble silver ring sat proudly on his little finger.

"That's a fine ring. Your father would be proud of the care you pay to it."

"Get out of my head, would ya?" He finished his glass then stood.

"It's habit."

"Well, stay out."

"I'll try. I promise." I filled his glass again. "Please, tell me about Del. The more I understand the man, the easier it will be to work with him and his body. And you. His reaction to the violence earlier was a bit... intense, and something about his reaction smelled of trauma. I need to know what to expect from him as we move forward. I need to understand how he'll react when the time comes to deal with Izzy."

Bernard stared at me, judging my words. "His reaction makes some sense," he finally said. He picked up his glass but did not sit. "Your reasons do too."

"So?"

"So," he continued, "Del had it bad growing up. I mean real bad. His mom was a sweetheart, but after Del's real father died when he was five, she was a mess. His stepdad, Paul, was slimy as hell. He'd be sweet as pie if he needed something but cross him…" Bernard leaned against the countertop. "You know what? No," he said. "Come on, you already know this stuff."

"How did your family come to know Del's?"

Bernard began to pace their minuscule kitchen. "Del and I lived on the same block. We'd been playing together since we were small. Del's dad, his real dad, worked with mine at the post office. After he died, Del's mom never recovered. Del spent a lot of time with my family. After his stepdad came on the scene, my mom and pop practically adopted him. He spent the night all the time and Mom was always feeding him. We were his shelter."

A sadness grew within that was not mine.

"How did his family take it?" I asked, blocking Del's emotion.

Bernard folded his arms. A long sigh. A rub of the head. Pain. "His stepdad didn't much like us, didn't think it was right that Del spent time with us. That was the one thing Agnes, Del's mom, kept her spine over. Del was always allowed to come over and we were always welcome at their place. That didn't go over well with Paul so my parents just stopped visiting."

"It must have been difficult dealing with someone like that up north in Chicago."

"It's always difficult, but it wasn't anything new. It's not like it was all sunshine in Chicago. Far from it. That's half the reason I left. America is tough whether you're living up north or down south. The south just doesn't bother to hide it. Chinese, Japanese, the Indians, we all get it a little different but it's all the same. The French aren't perfect either, just look at what they have Josephine Baker doing. A banana dance? Come on. But they respect our music and it's done on our terms. She might be playing savage but she's draining those French wallets while she's doing it and they love her for it."

"It doesn't sound all that different."

"Oh, it's different. I mean, we get to be people here rather than a problem."

"I'm sorry."

"Are you, now? You and your people are in charge, right?" Bernard placed both hands on the edge of the kitchen sink with an absent stare toward the drain. "You've been pulling the strings all this time. The way I see it, it's all your doing anyway."

"No, not our doing. We set up the framework for society but as I said before, we've been letting you Monos run your own show for over a thousand years. We just provide a push in this direction or that depending on what benefit can be gained."

"No push away from slavery and racism, huh?"

"No. Some Mentium nudged but a push was not possible, for many reasons."

"Bullshit, these problems are a lot older than a thousand years." Bernard sat once again. "Don't try to tell me they're not, and don't tell me you couldn't have done something. That you couldn't do something now."

Minutes passed. We sat drinking as the red second hand on the Bakelite clock ticked on. In the silence all I had was my cravings and when I couldn't take it, I asked my next question.

"Would you tell me the story of your journey to Paris?"

"Why?"

"Please?"

"Fine."

He sat back, crossing his arms over his chest. "So Del's mother died when he was sixteen. Tuberculosis. His stepdad dove deeper into the bottle after Agnes passed. He made Del drop out of school and start working to pay rent and keep them in food and whatever clothes they could afford. Paul had lost his job at the bakery and just spent his days drinking away Del's paycheck. That went on for years even after prohibition got voted in."

Bernard crossed his fingers behind his head and let out a slow breath. "By the time we were twenty-one we had both gotten into music pretty heavily. We were playing in a local band and even making some cash. Del's stepdad didn't like that either. Said it was the devil's music. Del kept his new guitar at my parents' place. He was afraid Paul would hawk it for booze money but he never got the chance. A few months after Del bought the thing, Paul tripped down the stairs of the front porch and landed on the bottle he was carrying. A shard got him in the neck."

"That seems like a win."

"That's a wicked thing to say… but you're not wrong. No one was too broken up about Paul's death, least of all Del. When Del's mom passed she'd left him some of his real dad's stuff but Paul never told him about it. It was in a safety deposit box. Evidently Paul couldn't get into it because, aside from a couple of watches and his dad's wedding ring, there was still five hundred dollars in cash. We used that to come here."

"So Del paid?"

"Yeah, I owe him a big debt."

"It seems like he owes you substantially more."

"Well, I'm not keeping score. We're all each other's got. It's not right to keep a tally."

"You're a better man than he is."

Don't I know it.

"Anyway," he said peering out the kitchen window, "we didn't move overseas right away. My dad got a new job working for the post office out in Portland, Oregon. It was a big step for him, but I wasn't about to move out west. I'd barely been outside Chicago let alone across the country. Plus, word was the Klan was surging in Oregon. Sure, I could have moved north and started playing in Seattle. They have a good scene up there but that's the only scene. Del had nothing left and with my family moving, neither did I. Then I got beat."

"Beat?"

"Yeah, I'd been talking to a woman I recognised from the neighbourhood one night after a show. Two college boys didn't like that, and they jumped me in the alley. Del can't stand it when people get beat, since he got it from his stepdad so much. Anyway, he tried to step in but just managed to take a few to the ribs before we both ran. The next morning he was sitting on the couch in our apartment — we'd been living together for a few months — and he laid out two tickets on the coffee table. Boat tickets. We packed the best clothes we had and our instruments, and we left the next day."

I poured a finger each into our glasses and walked over to the couch.

Any comfort the kitchen chair had afforded was a distant memory and Del's sharp, unpadded coccyx ached.

"Thank you, Bernard, that was enlightening."

"How?"

"Your relationship is illogical. Del's an anchor you should cut loose. I now understand why you don't."

"Don't say that."

"And, I now understand Del's aversion to violence. I can work with him on that."

"I'm so glad to have been of service."

"Tell me about this Sal," I said, folding my thin leg under me as I settled into the couch.

"Come on man, just read my mind. I'm tired of talking. And after that show you put on this morning, Sal is the last person I want to talk about." He took his place on the damask chair I'd tied him to the day before.

"I can read your thoughts but the words you choose to speak are more telling."

"Jesus, fine. You want to know about Sal? Well, he's scum. Scum that helped us get established in the local scene. Del and I struggled for a couple months when we got here. Bread's cheap but we still lost some weight. Sal heard us playing with this small-time outfit in a dive in Belleville. He knew a guy who knew a guy who liked us, and we sat in for a few nights with his house band at the time. Sal got us another gig across town in Montparnasse. A guy named Pierre saw us there, liked us and we played with his group for six months. We've been working steady since."

"Why all the hate for the man?" I'd already gotten my answer but again, his words told more.

"We agreed to give him a percentage of our pay from our first gig. We agreed on ten percent and he took fifty. Fifty percent of eight different gigs. He tried to pull the same shit in Montparnasse but couldn't because the band leader paid us directly. We gave him his ten percent but he complained like a son of a gun."

"So, an upright citizen, then. I assume you parted ways after his second attempt to cheat you."

"Yeah, well, when Pierre got caught sleeping with the venue owner's daughter, we were out on our asses again. Sal got wind of it and set us up again with our current gig. For a fee of course, and one that didn't stay fixed. He's been great for our careers but hell on our wallets."

"And now you two are here."

"We're here," he said, waving at the room.

Lemon-tinged light streamed in through the frosted windows and fell across the living room between us. The clock on the wall read five minutes to one. I had a train to catch.

"Bernard, I've got to be going." I said, standing and stepping toward the coat rack.

"Tian?" he asked.

"Yes, and hopefully to find reinforcements. Now, I'd like for you to stop by Philipe's later on and pick up the rest of our clothing then meet me back here."

"How long will you be?"

"I don't know."

24

THE TRAIN

Under the palatial, sloped glass roof of *Gare du Nord*, the air hung with the soot of engine after engine as they came and went, ferrying the masses around the country. Whistles, chatter, and the rapid pounding of late feet sprinting toward departing trains rang off every surface. It especially rang inside my aching head. The dragon had evolved from simply breathing a low fire to inflicting actual pain. My insides were twisting and my muscles ached but I couldn't let the drug win. Not yet.

I was one of hundreds, hidden in plain sight. As it had been during the entire day thus far. There were no vacant faces, no swivelling heads. It appeared Lilith had given up the random sweeps. If only she would come to her senses about the rest.

With my head down, Del's small body made weaving through the throngs that much easier. I used the clamour of the crowd to check in with Del and explain the necessity of his cooperation.

I need you to please keep quiet until my business has concluded, I said. *These are important meetings and I need my wits about me. The cravings are bad enough and I cannot have you interfering.*

Don't worry, pal, I get it. The more they help, the faster I get you outta me.

Precisely.

A little advice though.

I don't want it.

Distract yourself. Look, I know you gotta be in top form around your buddies but in between, when you're alone, keep your mind off your guts and how much you want to smoke. Whistle, sing a song, recite poetry, I don't care what. Trust me, it'll help.

Just remember our agreement and let me handle things my way.

I reached quai three with time to spare but milled about just outside the door to my carriage. If I was going to end up a sitting duck, at least I had some control over my ability to fly if need be.

My thoughts went to my mentor. I was so close to Tian and his aide and guidance that I almost forgot my pain. I thought of his note the night of my loss, the cleverness of the use of our drinking song — Ambush on Ten Sides — and I began to hum it to myself in a hushed tone. As usual, I butchered the complex song.

While I knew I could be stepping to my doom, I also knew Tian would not let that happen. Tian was my real father. He would not let me down.

The final whistle sounded its raspy call and I patted the gun in my right overcoat pocket. I trusted Tian with all my being but even he can't guarantee complete safety. A deep breath, a nod to myself, and I boarded the train. It was time for answers. It would be good to see his face again. I needed to.

The train jerked into motion beneath my feet and I steadied both my body and my nerves as I checked for my seat. The elegant wood-panelled car had a central isle with plush navy seats lining each set of windows. Small tables, draped in white linen, lay between each set of paired chairs. I counted as I walked, and as my seat neared my heart sank. An ocean blue turban hat crested the back of the chair opposite mine. I knew that hat and the woman wearing it. She was not Tian.

"Yemoja." I took her blue-gloved hand and opened my mind to her as I took my seat. If this were an ambush, I had already lost. Where was Tian? Why was she here? Had I fallen into Lilith's trap? The questions spun free until I caught myself. She was in my head and heard them all.

Yemoja sat as still as stone in her teal dress and navy overcoat, and her eyes were as cold as a falcon's.

It's me, I said to her mind.

Her red lips curled, and a blue glove rose to meet them. *Excuse me,*

M, she said without moving those lips. *I… I just had no idea that this would be the you we would meet today.*

We?

The red velvet curtains swayed along with our bodies as the train switched tracks. The crystal light fixtures tinkled like wind chimes. The silver and seashell brooch at the centre of the turban twinkled in the midday light.

Yes, we three.

Come to bring me in, have you? Where's Tian?

I was scanning her mind for answers, but she was filtering what I could sense. This was Yemoja after all. She was anything if not careful and I was still weak. I couldn't break in if I tried. It was difficult to remember it hadn't even been forty-eight hours since I had died.

No, we are here to listen and decide.

Here to listen? Come now, that ship has sailed, hasn't it? You've had months to hear me out. I thought you had. Now, where is Tian? I want to speak with him. Stop stalling.

Her mouth lost its curl and her shoulders sagged. She closed her mind completely and turned her sharp chin toward the icy world outside the window. She bit her lip.

The world around me blurred and I sucked in slow breaths through my nose as tears welled. I waste little time with emotion but in that moment, I let it saturate my being. I didn't think I could feel worse than I already did that day, but somehow the ache in that moment felt as though I would be crushed to dust.

"How?" I asked, aloud but as a whisper.

Yemoja shook her head and placed a hand on mine. She was kind. Fierce when provoked, practical in business, but kind. She always had been but I'd rarely taken the time to notice. Now that compassion was right in front of me.

M, she thought, *I don't think…*

"How?" My words shook with my ragged breathing.

She sat back, her hand worrying at the strings of pearls around her neck, her eyes still focused on the frozen world outside. *It was the night of your death. The Twins called a meeting. We had all heard the news as soon as your body was found but it was one in the morning before everyone arrived, everyone but you of course. And Ma'at who hasn't been seen. Do you know what's become of her?*

No. I said, mentally once again.

I don't know why she fled but I envy her foresight, she sighed. *Before entering the council chamber, Tian handed we three our train tickets, he'd managed to force a ticket agent to sell them after-hours. He must have had an idea of what the meeting meant. The Twins were livid, especially Apollo. He was unhinged. He marched around the council room waving a knife like an idiot and throwing out accusations of treason and conspiracy. Everyone, even Artemis sat back in their chairs and let him rant. It was silent save for him. We hoped he would wear himself out. Tian… lost his patience.*

My eyes continued their cycle of tear, blur, blink, and I could feel myself shaking. This was rage, not the cravings. *Go on, please.*

M…

Go on.

All right. Tian stood from his chair and walked to the middle of the ring. He spoke in his soft yet firm way and told Apollo exactly what he thought of their plan, their actions, and their competence. Apollo asked who he was to judge, and Tian's response was 'who better?'

And…

And Apollo stabbed him through the top of his skull. It was brutal, M. It was deep. It wasn't entombment. Yes, it was, but he didn't, couldn't survive. And with the knife in there…

He couldn't escape that body.

I'd lost my mentor. My friend, my father, I'd lost him. Truly, irrevocably lost.

My head was pounding with my heartbeat and I was grinding my teeth so hard my jaw popped.

Yemoja placed her hand on my knee. "M, we're here because we need to know what you have planned."

"You want to know if fighting is worth it."

"Yes."

"Coward."

She scoffed. "Come. It's time to see the others, and remember, Tian called this meeting. We're only seeing it through."

She rose and I followed, clearing the tears with the sleeve of my new suit. At the far end of our first class carriage stood a four-seat booth. Yemoja slid the door open and two audible gasps escaped the mouths of the men sitting before me.

Cernunnos' teeth clamped onto a polished antler pipe that smoked underneath his red moustache. His bright green eyes stared wide above his olive tweed suit. His shock at seeing what I'd become held him frozen. Radegast on the other hand, settled back into his beer with a short chuckle and an incredulous shake of the head.

Yemoja closed the door then took a seat next to the window, and I next to her.

Cernunnos turned over his pipe and knocked the ashes from it, still staring. "You've got to be kidding me," he said. "That body isn't quite up to your usual standards, M."

I was still shaking but the look on his face was trying its damnedest to lighten my mood. Radegast noticed the shaking and reached inside his black jacket, pulled out a flask, and slid it my way.

"Told him, eh?" he said, looking to Yemoja.

"He wanted to know."

"Fair enough," said Radegast. "It's a damn shame."

Trustworthy wasn't an accurate word for Radegast but neither was evil. Unpredictable would be the proper term. He, like all of us, had been many gods to many peoples but the persona of Radegast the "dear guest" of Slavic tradition continued to be his favourite.

"Drink up," he said, and I did.

"Why did Tian call this meeting? How long had this been planned?"

The three looked at each other, none knowing who should speak.

"Say something, dammit." I was losing control in a variety of ways.

"Tian came to us, individually, two days before your death," Cernunnos said finally. "He said that you were hiding something from him and that he knew it had something to do with the Twins' efforts to use your machine. He wanted to know where we stood and the three of us, as you can tell, all shared the same feelings."

"My feelings," I said, trying my best to drink from Radegast's flask. My head continued to pound; any medication was welcome. Welcome, but not as wanted as the opium. The memories, Del's memories of its smell, the warmth of it in his lungs, that warmth spreading through the body, it was so delicious and vivid. I wanted it. Not just Del, not just his body, *I* wanted it. I took another long pull hoping to douse the dragon's flames.

"Maybe," said Radegast, "but feelings and action are two different beasts and it's your strategy that interests us most."

"If you are against the Twins, as is clear, then why the need for discussion and decision? Let's join together now. A united front against the Twins. There's power there."

"Not enough, "said Yemoja. "The situation is worse than even you feared. Izanagi," The name felt like glass shards in my head; "has rallied many of the Underlings to their cause. This is a power grab not only for the Twins, but for those below. Any front we can muster will be eclipsed by their numbers."

The news was devastating.

"M," she continued, "we want to help if we can, but *only* if we can. We will not make things worse."

"It seems like your votes as of late have made things worse. You all voted for this plan. You all voted against me even though you profess not to support them. Which is it?"

"There was no vote, M," said Cernunnos. "The Mentium is no longer a democracy. The Twins rule now. Direct confrontation killed Tian. If that can happen to him, what of us?"

I didn't answer.

"What's your plan, M?" asked Radegast, stroking his groomed black beard. "Give us a reason to help."

I took another pull from his flask and studied their faces. I didn't like what I was seeing.

"It's two-fold," I said. "In my original plan with Izzy, we each chose select points in the wiring of the radio to sever. Neither of us knew which points the other had chosen. If my primary plan fails, then I'll continue with my sabotage. It will at least slow them down. It will give us time."

"And what exactly is your primary plan?" asked Yemoja.

"I'm going to kill Izzy. He and I are the only ones who know how to run the radio. Killing that bastard cripples all their plans and is an insurance policy for my life. No me, no radio."

The three looked at each other, I could tell they were discussing this mentally. The two men returned to their pipe and beer respectively and Yemoja turned to me.

"You have nothing more planned?"

"We need nothing more. Yemoja please," I hated the desperation in my voice. "Please help me end this."

"It's too much of a risk," she said.

"Risk? You won't risk to stop our destruction? To stop the world from imploding into war?" I asked.

"No, we won't," said Cernunnos, chewing his empty pipe. "And you shouldn't either. We all have funds in reserve, lifetimes' worth, as do you. That's plenty of time to re-establish a cash flow."

"And that's not a risk? You can't guarantee that you'll re-establish anything. You can't guarantee there will be any systems left to use."

"That gamble is not nearly the risk you've chosen to take," said Yemoja. "If we turn against the Twins and fail, we lose everything, including our lives. If the Twins succeed now, they will still fail. We know their plan is doomed. There is no need to convince us of that. Where we need convincing, is whether it is most beneficial to fight or flee and let them end themselves."

"We fight. Of course we fight," I said, I couldn't bring myself to look at them. The tips of my fingers were white against the metal flask in my hands. "Think of everything we've built. Centuries, more than two thousand years of careful, painstaking planning and execution to build our empire. You'll sit here and let the Twins destroy it?"

Radegast held up a hand and finished his beer, setting the goblet aside. "It's already gone. Tian's gone. The Upper Echelon is divided and the Underlings have chosen a side. It's over, M. Killing Izanagi, breaking your toy, it won't stop what's already started."

"You're right. Sides have been drawn" I said, mustering as much calm as I could. "We are on the same side. You've said so yourself. Help me do this. Help me take the Twins' heads and we can take back our Mentium."

"Join forces?" asked Cernunnos. "M, that's only we four Upper Echelon against another four, plus Izanagi and the Underlings. Those are bad odds."

"Four? Let me guess, Kali is with them."

"Of course," said Radegast. "And Ma'at is in the wind. No one as seen her since that last meeting. She had the good sense to leave swiftly. I say we should too. The Twins have Lilith running the show, M. You know her better than anyone. You have to see there's no winning this time."

"That's it then? You're going to abandon me, abandon the Mentium."

"Like I said, the Mentium is already destroyed." Radegast adjusted his white silk scarf, a flag of surrender. "Don't you see? How do we come back from this? And look at you, you really expect us to place our faith in you? You look sick, M. You're weak. You're sweating."

"He's addicted," said Yemoja, "I read him when he first arrived. Opium."

"M," said Cernunnos, "I'm so sorry."

I didn't answer. I simply sat and waited for excuses.

"This is insane, M, you must see that," Cernunnos said. "Come with us, let us get you a new host, and we'll let this play out. Maybe in a century we can pick up the pieces."

"Yemoja, what say you," I asked. Maybe I couldn't convince them all, but one, two?

She shook her head.

"Radegast?"

"Don't take us for fools. You know what the answer is, M. Now, what's yours? Will you come with us?"

I searched the train with my mind, reaching for the train engineer. I found him but when I tried to make him stop the train, nothing. I was still so weak. He couldn't have been more than fifty metres away.

"No," I said. "No, I won't be coming with you. I won't crawl under a rock and let my life's work be destroyed by two infants and the idiots who follow them. If you'll excuse me."

"Where are you going?" asked Cernunnos, partially rising from his seat.

"M," said Yemoja, placing a hand on my arm, "if you succeed, we'll return."

"I might not want you to."

I pulled open the door and slammed it shut then marched through the car toward the engine. My head and heart pounding in unison, the muscles in my neck and face tight as rage and desperation settled into my bones. I wished I couldn't believe their selfishness, their cowardice, but I could. Yet that hurt was nothing compared to the loss of Tian.

Hey there, buddy, let's slow down and take a breath or two.

I ignored him and passed from the first-class car into the baggage-filled fourgon. A steward stopped his organising and approached me. This time proximity wasn't a factor.

"*Monsieur, arrêtez, s'il vous plaît,*" he said holding up a hand. I entered his mind and his hand curled into a fist then slammed into his face, once, twice, sending droplets of blood against the valises around him. He lost consciousness before I passed.

Everything felt like it was on fire: my head, my body, my cravings, my emotions, all in flames. At the end of the fourgon, I placed my forehead against the door and again searched for the engineer. He was there, a metre away, and I told him to stop that damned train.

He threw the brake so hard that I was pressed against the door. The banshee's squeal of steel on steel was deafening as the train slowed and a cascade of baggage drummed around me, but I kept the engineer's hand on the brake until the train had come to a stop.

I kicked aside a pile of leather cases, threw open the loading door and hopped out of the train. I didn't look back. I didn't listen for their mental words. I kept my mind closed and marched through a snowy, dead mustard field toward the blurred outline of a small town. Voices called out to me and a series of sloppy footfalls approached. I kept walking.

"*Monsieur, monsieur, arrêtez! Arrêtez!*" said the closest, a conductor. He reached for my shoulder but instead I made him stop. I made him drop to his knees, and I made him lie face down in the snow, mouth open. The second pursuer, wisely, stopped to help the man up. I made him resist.

Motorcars were passing as I approached the edge of the field. I continued my steps until they took me into the centre of the street. A pale yellow Renault with a black canvas top slammed on its breaks and I strode up to it.

"You idiot!" cried the driver stepping from his vehicle and over toward me. I entered his mind too and he stepped aside, waving me onward with his arm. I sat behind the wheel and he closed my door for me with a silent bow.

My weak hands wrung the steering wheel as if it were the necks of the Twins. My need, my rage, my despair. I was molten.

"*Monsieur?*" asked the driver. Who still stood next to the car. I made him slap himself for speaking then I made him run off into the snow and strip naked.

You need to calm down, M. Just ease up a bit, said Del in a soothing internal voice.

Enough.

I'm just trying to help. I know what it's like to lose control.

I said enough, Enough! ENOUGH!

I slammed my fist into the wheel over and over until the throbbing was halfway to my elbow. I cradled the damaged limb and as it lay across my chest, the crackle of paper sounded from my jacket pocket. I took out the folded yellow paper and as I read, a dark determination grew beneath my tears.

The engine roared as I sped away, pulling the collar of my coat tight to my neck. The road was a muddy scar in that white world, and again the snow was falling. Again, I had lost something precious to me. Again, I was at the mercy of others. Again, I was betrayed. I wanted control. I needed it. If I had any hope of stopping this madness, I had to regain control.

25

SNAKE IN THE HOLE

An anaemic January sun sank below the rooftops, painting heavy grey clouds in the pale red of fevered cheeks. The yellow motorcar idled on a small side street in Montparnasse. A street above the catacombs.

Pedestrians went about their meaningless lives, crossing in front of my position. I chose at random and an old man walked up to my door.

"To the station and back until I return." These were the only words I needed. I stepped out and the man took my place, then drove off. The car would be there when I returned, or he'd be arrested for my theft. Either was a benefit.

With my collar turned up to the cold, I joined the plebeian throngs and began walking along *Avenue du Maine*. Everything was an irritant. The voices, the crunching snow, the smells. My focus was deplorable but I willed myself to go on. I opened my mind and began to hunt.

I know you're here. You've always been so predictable. I knew you'd be fretting over my creation.

There was no reply. I turned down another street.

You're pathetic. Grovelling before the Twins for their scraps. You would betray me for the promises of liars.

Still nothing. I emerged onto another busy street, and before me stood four Eunuchs at our preferred entrance to the catacombs. I was close. I turned ninety degrees and marched away from them. My head was spinning, and while trying work out the layout of the bone-filled limestone quarry beneath my feet, I found myself cycling between tasks.

You're nothing but a jealous nursemaid, desperate to raise my child as your own. You ungrateful bastard. You swine. I should have seen your betrayal coming. I should have seen the flaw in your character. How naive I've been.

Quite, said Izzy. There he was. Not before me on the street but below.

I've come for you, apprentice, I said, searching through the pavers for his location under my feet.

Unwise. I do hope you've counted my Eunuchs.

They don't matter. I know you'd never give up a chance to kick me when I'm down. Closer. He was closer but he stopped broadcasting to me.

The heads of the Monos in my area began sweeping motions with vacant eyes. The bastard was looking for me. One mind after another, darting from one end of the block to next. The screeching of motorcars breaking, shouts from onlookers. His distracted puppets were focused on finding me, not on traffic.

There was a minor entrance to the catacombs one block west of my position. With calm determination, I turned and took out my keys to the city. A click of the lock and I began my descent. I'd find him first.

Why? I asked, opening my mind once again. *What could have possessed you?*

Personal gain, power, a change of pace, what answer would you have of me? he said through the aether.

Whether from my burgeoning withdrawal, my despair, my rage, my guilt, all of it, I didn't know but I found myself shaking and it was all I could do not to scream.

I want the person whom I once deemed my equal in intellect to explain himself. Explain his logic. The tunnels were black as death but I dared not use a light or flame. Instead, I ran my hand along the creases and crevices of the skull-lined passageways and listened for movement.

Your equal? What good are lies, M? You've never treated me as anything other than your whipping boy. I've done your bidding for centuries but no more. I'm taking control of my destiny.

By betraying me? By taking what's mine?

As much as I can get my hands on.

Typical! Rather than work for your gains you steal them.

I've worked for centuries for my gains and you've kept me down. I deserve this. This is my time.

A rock skittered in the distance. The shuffling of feet on the rough cavern floor. Oh, yes, I was close.

I crept on. A bend to the right and at the end of this new passageway, light. Dim, electric light. Izzy.

Where are your Eunuchs, coward? I thought to him as I crouched and moved on. My head was pounding.

I'm taking you up on your proposition. I want to be the one to throw you at Lilith's feet. Nothing pleases me more than to please her.

Do not speak her name.

She speaks mine now.

I ignored the childish jab and grasped at my overcoat pocket with my shaking hand. The hard outline of Izzy's fate sat at the ready.

You still haven't explained yourself, Izzy. How can you join with the Twins? They killed Tian. Izzy they killed him. You loved him too. How can you stand by them?

I paused in his silence, not wanting to announce my presence.

The Twins are our future, M. Tian was the past.

With each syllable I moved into position around the last corner from where he paced. I knew that area well. It was one of many small laboratories within the chambers.

Through the eye socket of a skull that faced me and the broken occipital lobe that faced Izzy, I got my first glimpse of his last minutes. His knuckles were white on the handle of a large pair of pliers. He bounced it, checking its weight and utility. My tool was stronger.

We've been in the shadows for too long. The Great War was proof of that. These Monos are cattle. Mindless and weak. The world needs us to do our duty, not to leech off our past. The world needs us to act. I've chosen to act.

And what of Tian? His blood is on your hands, Izzy.

I held my breath as I pulled the gun. I used both hands, but both shook so I placed the muzzle into the eye socket and pressed down against the mossy bones to steady myself.

The old man died because he couldn't accept the future.

I squeezed the trigger. Bone fragments peppered my face. I fell back, regained my footing, and ran. Izzy's footfalls were close behind.

"Another failure, M!" he bellowed.

I swung my arm around and sent two more rounds toward him but buried them into bones instead.

"You won't die like Tian, M. I'm going to make sure you suffer."

Another bullet and another bone. I was twisting and turning with abandon. The darkened tunnels were impossible to navigate, and my body bounced form wall to wall as I sprinted through the hopeless abyss. I couldn't let myself fail again. *Would* not fail again.

I stopped running and pressed my back against the bodies of dead men and women. I held the gun out with both hands and waited. Two steps, four, close enough. I pulled the trigger.

I saw nothing but heard Izzy cry out as his body scraped along the cavern floor. My bullet had landed true. I hadn't failed. I'd avenged myself and Tian.

The iron smell of blood hit my nose and satisfaction spread across the chaos of my mind. Then his grunts and the shuffling of his feet stripped that all away.

"My arm! You shot my arm."

I pocketed the gun and propelled myself through the black. My feet pounded the stone and splashed through condensation puddles. My lungs ached and my legs felt as though they would give out. Instead it was the tunnel itself that reached its end.

"No, no, fuck, fuck, fuck."

An iron gate. I reached for my keys yet again but I knew it was hopeless. I couldn't see a thing. Izzy was coming.

You're little!

What?

You're little, jackass, said Del. Del! *Use it. Squeeze through the bars.*

I had to turn my head sideways but I managed to wiggle through. I put my hat back on my head and resisted all temptation to look that traitor in the face. If only I had one more bullet.

But I'd failed yet again. This body had failed me yet again. Everything had gone wrong yet again. If I were to be seen by Izzy... seen.

I backed away from the door. Too far for any aspect of my person to be deciphered. I waited for him to come.

"Blast it!" he said and slammed a palm against the gate.

"I'm here," I said, lowering my voice.

"Don't worry, M," he said, panting. "I won't kill you for this. No, you won't die. I'm going to wake up every morning and wheel your entombed body out into this new world we're creating. Every day I'm going to show you just how wrong you've been."

"I'll remember that, Izzy. I'll remember."

26

THE MADAME

"So why are we in Pigalle?" asked Bernard as we exited the yellow Renault.

"Things have changed and we need to see a friend," I said, leaving the keys inside. This was as far as I'd take the stolen motorcar.

"What's changed? Who's this friend?"

"The Madame."

"The Madame? So I take it your meeting didn't go well."

"No."

My body could have melted the world with just a touch. I'd calmed my rage but the despair and the call of the dragon swallowed me whole.

I led us through the sooty slush and red lights, past chilled prostitutes and shivering paupers, toward the salon. The fact that we were mere blocks from where I became Del did not sit well in my mind. Nothing sat well. Focus was impossible. I was pouring sweat and my entire body ached.

We walked past scores of shuttered windows in silence, Bernard just at my heels. At the curve of what was but a glorified alley, Madame Vivienne's claret door called out from the pale snow and pale stone that surrounded it.

Above the door, the typical blue tile building number that adorned most residences in Paris was enlarged — a discreet way to denote the type of business held within. I rapped on the door using the appropriate pattern and waited for her doorman and all-around muscle, Jacques, that hulking bastard, to open up. I was tired of waiting, I was tired of the cold and I was tired of the damned shaking that racked my body.

The sky reddened further as we stood, freezing, outside Vivienne's very private, very elite, very lucrative business. We weren't here to make deposits. I needed to make a withdrawal and to plead a favour.

My knuckles rapped again, and this time Jacques emerged and folded his ape arms over his ape chest. The monolithic Frenchman wore pressed white shirt sleeves and a tight-fitting tweed vest. He scowled down at me and out at Bernard then barked a snide laugh and turned to close the door again.

I had no time for his insolence and before his hand reached the knob, he paused mid-step, moved aside and held the door open for us.

"Better," I replied and slipped a franc into the pocket of his vest. The brute hated it when I tipped him.

"Did you make him do that? Of course you did. He's going to be mad, right?" asked Bernard as we entered.

Inside that nondescript door stretched a dusky world of elegance. The area surrounding the twisting walnut staircase was decorated with dark, rich wood wainscoting topped with deep red brocade wallpaper. Brass oil burning sconces cast limited light giving every item an amber aura.

"Of course," I said, "Now, up we go."

We tramped up the wooden staircase past the first floor. A short hallway matching the decoration of the ground floor stretched out before us with three doors on either side. All were closed but sound emanated from each.

"I've never been in a creep joint before," said a sheepish Bernard.

"It's like being in any other building except that here, there is more amusement and often more regret."

As we ascended past the second floor, two nude women stood in the hallway discussing a book about which they held differing views. Bernard's eyes went to the floor as soon as they came into view.

"*Bonsoir, messieurs.* Would you like—"

"*Non. Non, merci madame. Désolé.*" The words tumbled from Bernard's mouth. The women responded with a giggle and we finished our climb.

The third floor reflected the same decor as the previous levels. I knew this floor well and marched up to the final door on the right. I didn't bother to knock.

"Viv, hello, sorry to burst in but I'm having some difficulties."

Madame Vivienne stood from behind a massive carved walnut desk. An emerald leather writing pad lay beneath the sleeves of her Edwardian dress, also in emerald. The grey of her pinned hair was the only allusion to her more than seventy years of life. Her body was as fit and her mind as sharp as a woman half her age. My memory often drifted back to a time when she was half her age. She was still magnificent.

I opened my mind and she recognised me.

"What the hell happened to you? You look terrible."

"It's complicated."

"M, I don't want you here. There are rumours and from the look of that awful body you're in, I'm guessing the rumours are true." She gave me a cold stare, which melted when she noticed my companion. "Bernie, may I call you Bernie? Please, have a seat." She motioned him toward a sofa, the same red as the walls.

"How… thanks," he said, accepting the offer. "How did you know my name? M, how did she know it was you?"

"It's obvious. She's a Multi-Receiver," I snapped. I had no patience for anything in that moment. "Her powers lie between mine and your own. She can read your thoughts and memories but can't project into the mind."

"You Mentium and your terminology. Make up your mind already. What was I called before? A reader? A seer?"

"Bilingual. The old language analogy is obsolete."

"Charming. Now, what is going on? Word has it that the Upper Echelon want you captured."

"We had a bit of a falling out."

"Don't play with me, M. You came to me. You asked me to look after your papers. I didn't know just how far I was sticking my neck out for you. That favour puts me in the middle of whatever mess you've made. I need to know what I've gotten myself into."

I rolled my eyes and took a seat next to Bernard, placing Del's derby on my knee. "Come now, Viv, I've always been trouble."

"Cut the cute, M. I'm in no mood."

Nor was I, but a lighter mood would feel better than the one I'd been trapped in since the train.

"Here, I'm open," I said, opening only the necessary parts of my mind. "Take a look for yourself."

I brought Vivienne up to speed on what was happening. She focused on my memories and thoughts while I turned to Bernard, who somehow managed to look even more uncomfortable than he did in front of the nude women. He was staring at us as if we were ghouls.

"I'm never going to get used to this," he muttered.

"No, you likely won't," I said.

Vivienne broke in. "Christ M, you can't be serious. Eight days?"

"Well at this point it's really more like seven."

"And they… they were just going to… wait, wait…" she said, tipping her head and staring past us. Her blank expression twisted with anger. "Stay here."

She shot up from her desk. Her high leather boot heels drummed on the hardwood floor as she bolted into the hallway where she called out, *"Jacques, premier étage, maintenant!"*

Of course I didn't stay. What would be the gain in that? Plus, watching Vivienne work was sure to brighten my mood. I grabbed Bernard by the arm and pulled him to his feet. By the time we reached the first floor, Jacques was holding a naked, flabby, middle-aged man against the wall by his throat. His eyes bulged and his tongue protruded from his mouth as if it could somehow catch the air for which his lungs begged.

Vivienne had a hand on the bare shoulder of a petite, enraged woman but her mind was on the choking man. The prostitute's dark hair was wet with perspiration and red welts had begun to rise on her cheeks. Matching welts appeared on her arms and bare hips. I could tell right away that we were in for a wonderful show.

"You can let him go now, Jacques," said Vivienne, never breaking eye contact with her pudgy client.

The man sputtered and gasped as air filled his lungs once more.

Jacques had let go, but still stood at arm's length from the idiot. After a few deep inhalations, the man began to spew the obvious and inevitable. After all, Madame Vivienne served a clientele with wealth and power matched only by their egos.

"You'll pay dearly for this," he spat. "I have connections, I'll have you shut down. You'll all be out on the street in a week. If only you knew who I was you'd—"

"But I do," said Vivienne in a voice that would be terrifying if I didn't find it to be so invigorating. "I do know who you are Lord Humphrey Brixton. I'm sure the British consulate will be more than interested in discussing the details of an assault committed by one of their diplomats. Or maybe Beatrix. That is your wife's name, or maybe a daughter? No, that's Clara. I'm sure Clara will be more than happy to hear of her strong papa beating a woman for sport."

The man's face twisted so much that I burst out laughing. It felt so good to be distracted from my own anguish. The squishy fool quivered like a slice of flan. It was nice to see someone else shake for a change.

I turned to Bernard but he was not sharing in my mirth. His fists were balled and his face was stone. At least we shared a feeling of disdain for the buffoon.

"You… no… I was promised anonymity. I was promised—"

"You harm one of my artisanes and you dare speak of kept promises? Here is a promise, Lord Humphrey. One you can rest assured will be fulfilled. I won't inform your employer, you have a family to provide for after all. Your wife, however, will hear of this, a letter I think. It will be rumour of course, but rumour erodes trust. Trust you will not gain back. And I think a letter for Clara as well. She'll learn just how much of a pig her Papa truly is."

"No! Dear God, please…" said the man and every hole in his face rained down on him. Tears, mucus, pitiful.

"And if I ever smell your stink within ten blocks of this house again… I assure you that Jacques is as good at hiding things as he is at silencing them."

The man would have pissed himself had he been wearing pants.

Instead he pissed Jacques' pants. The ogre looked at his madame and she gave him a nod, fighting back a grin. He gripped the offending manhood and dragged the now screaming man back into the room where he had assaulted the artisane, who spit in his face as he passed.

"May I?" asked the woman.

"Of course, but remember where to hit," said Vivienne, and the woman followed the two men inside. She closed the door and a second beating began though none of the bruises would show above the lord's starched collar the next day.

I was all smiles but an unease soaked my chest and pulsed with each fleshy thud. I chose to place my fingers to my ears to soothe Del's trauma and relieve myself of his dread.

Without asking, I slipped into Bernard's mind to glean his reaction to all of this. There was no joy, none, but a satisfaction surfaced that solidified Bernard's usefulness to me. For Bernard, violence was tolerated when directed at the deserving. That attitude would do just fine. Despite Del's emotions, I was having so much fun I had almost forgotten about my need. Almost.

The dark-haired woman emerged again, her knuckles red.

"Gentlemen," said Vivienne as the artisane stepped to her side, "if you'll be so kind as to meet me in my office, I'll be along shortly," she said as she led the woman toward the stairwell. Muffled thuds continued to resonate within the closed room behind them.

"Of course, Madame. Take your time. Do you need help?" asked Bernard.

"No dear, thank you. We'll be fine. There's liquor behind my desk. Please, help yourself."

We retired to her office where Bernard again took a seat on the red sofa. He was angry. Angry about one thing. Not government takeovers, not fake gods, or even the theft of his best friend. In that moment his anger boiled over the flabby man and what he had done.

"A drink perhaps?" I asked, pouring myself another cognac. I was struggling to keep myself together.

"Scotch, neat, if it's there."

"There we go," I said, pouring him a double of Dalmore. Who was I kidding? A triple. "I've been waiting for you to cut loose."

"I'm calming down, not cutting loose."

"That peacock really has you riled up, doesn't he?"

"My whole life I've dealt with people like him thinking they were born better than everyone else. Then… then he beats on someone half his size, a woman… I'd like to…"

"By all means. I'm sure Jacques would love a break by this point. Don't get me wrong, he enjoys his work. I mean, really enjoys it. My old body was on the receiving end a time or two. For different reasons mind you, but I'm sure he'd be more than happy to let you take a few whacks."

"No, not my style. I'll defend myself and I'll defend someone who needs defending but this fight's over. He's getting what he deserves. Defence and punishment aren't the same thing. I'm no punisher."

"I know. I admire that."

"Do you?"

"Here," I handed him the glass. "Drink up."

The door opened as he took his first sip. Vivienne strode to the left wall of her office. There, she removed a small key from behind a painting which she took to her desk, unlocked the large lower drawer, and hefted a thick notebook onto the leather writing pad. The notebook contained all my research and designs, the blueprints for the entire system. Our bible as it were. The tome that would help destroy it.

"Here. Take it. That's why you're here, isn't it?"

"Yes, partly," I said taking the book. I placed two hundred francs where it once lay. "Vivienne, I wouldn't involve you if I didn't have to."

"Christ, M, you know you can't lie to me. I'll help if I can. Just don't do something stupid and get yourself or any of us…" she glanced at Bernard, "hurt in the process."

"That happened earlier."

"What happened earlier?" asked Bernard.

"Everything is ruined. Our plans, everything."

"What are you talking about?"

"My meeting on the train. I met with four other Upper Echelon.

Tian's been killed and they refuse to help. I chose to act. I went to the catacombs and tried to kill Izzy."

"You what? That's Del's body you're in," said Bernard, standing pointing his finger at me. "That's his body you risked. Not yours."

"Yes, yes, fine. I do not need you to lecture me right now. I'm trying to put pieces back together. I'm trying to regain some damned control."

I downed my cognac. My hand was shaking so badly I dropped the glass.

"M, what's wrong with you? You look like hell," said Vivienne.

"That's the other reason I'm here."

Bernard shifted his weight and looked into my eyes.

"This body is opium addicted. It muddies things too much. I can't think. I can't work. I had Izzy dead to rights but this shaking… I need to take back control."

She hurried around the desk to where I was standing, removed my hat, and felt my forehead.

"M, feed it," she said, stroking my hair. "You don't have time to kick an addiction like that. Feed it then come down and get to work. You'll be in much better shape if you do."

"No, I want this gone. I know you have some experience."

"No, M. You can't possibly do this. Not this quickly."

"I'll do it with or without your help. I have to try."

She returned to her chair and chewed a nail.

"You can't be serious," said Bernard. "Del's tried this already. It's hell. He couldn't take it."

"I don't care what he could or couldn't take. I'm going to solve this problem even if he couldn't."

"Do you really think you can pull this off?" asked Bernard. "If you really think you can manage it, you'd be fixing Del as well.

You don't have a shot in hell, buddy. You're just going to make us both feel like absolute shit. Don't even bother.

Del, you know nothing of determination.

"There's no convincing you otherwise, is there?" asked Vivienne.

"There's not."

She stared at my drug-sick body and sighed.

"All right."

Jacques re-entered the room, rubbing his fists.

"Jacques, has Lord Brixton, been taken care of?"

The brute gave a curt nod.

"Excellent. Be a dear and bring the motorcar around. We're taking these two gentlemen to the country house."

27

DESCENT INTO HELL

The four of us stood huddled around a heavy black door at the back of Vivienne's ancestral home. It was a modest stone and thatch structure, but the cellar was deep and had at least one room with a door. That was important.

"You sure about this?" asked Bernard.

"I just want it over with."

Bernard held two empty buckets stacked into themselves; Vivienne, an oil lamp and a brass key for the door; Jacques held two large pitchers of water, and I held my stomach. The pain in my bowels — a new present from the dragon— grew by the minute. The taste of bile tainted the back of my throat.

The lock clicked.

The door opened.

"Do you think you'll be warm enough?" asked Vivienne, leading us through the darkened kitchen. She only visited in summer and there were no neighbours in the vicinity.

Another necessity.

"Warmth is the least of my worries."

"I'll bring him a blanket once we get him settled," said Bernard.

"All right, if you will all follow me."

We fell in behind Vivienne as she led us downward into the dark. The stone on which the house was built is a soft limestone. It is easy to work and easy to remove, so many homes have at least one if not multiple basements. Vivienne's farmhouse had two separate levels.

The iron stairwell into those pits wore a sweaty black coat of paint blotched with scabs of rust. The handrail was a thick jute rope that ran through iron rings, pounded into the soft stone walls.

The first basement opened to our right. Crates of canned food and bottles of wine were stacked neatly against the walls. They were joined by excess furniture, boxes of candles, and other miscellaneous items. The mixing smells turned my already fragile stomach and I pushed into Jacques' back to hurry him onward. The smell was wasn't pleasant and grew less so once I added a little of my own fragrance.

"I apologise." I could feel my ashen face flush.

"Get used to it," said Bernard. "When Del tried this, well, the gas gets real bad."

At the bottom of the stairwell was a final room. It had another heavy, black iron door with a small window, crossed with iron bars. Vivienne again used her key and we all stepped inside. I walked to the far wall and knelt, feeling a cramp and wrapping my stomach with both arms.

The bare stone room was empty save for a single drain in the floor. It was cold inside but more from the damp and dark than from the depth.

"What was this room used for, again?" I asked.

"Wine, beer, other expensive stores. The drain is there to help with moisture run off."

"Well I guess I'll be the first to put it to use."

"No, you'll be the fifth."

"Fifth?" asked Bernard as he separated the two buckets he'd been carrying and placed them on the floor.

"A few customers needed a place to think about the expectations of being a guest in my establishment and two of my artisanes have had their own troubles with opium."

"So you're putting me in your torture cell? You could have told me, Viv."

"It will be torture for you no matter where you are, my dear."

"Fine. I'll be fine," I said, still doubled over and rocking and shaking against the wall. "Just leave me then and let me get to it."

Jacques set the two pitchers of water next to the door and Vivienne placed the oil lamp next to them.

"Jacques," she said in the matronly tone she always used with him, "could you be a dear and fetch a cot and side table for M?"

Jacques gave his signature short nod and retreated from the room.

"Madame?" asked Bernard.

"Please, Bernie, call me Vivienne. There's no need for formality."

"All right, Vivienne, would it be possible for me to stay here while M goes through the process?"

"You don't have to," I said. "I'll come out all right."

"It's Del I'm here for. Not you."

"He'll be fine."

"Of course you can stay. I'll have Jacques make up a room for you upstairs and we'll come by in the morning to bring some food."

"That would be great. Can I give you some money?"

"Bernie, no, I can—"

"I'll pay," I said, reaching in my pants and throwing my wallet at them. "I should pay."

Vivienne picked up the wallet and tucked it into her handbag.

Bernard stood with his arms crossed, his forehead knitted. "I'm going to come by every few hours until you come out of this thing," he said. "You better not do anything to hurt Del."

"We're both going to suffer but I assure you, I won't do any additional harm. There would be no reason for it."

"Good." He turned to Vivienne. "Is there anything specific I should be doing for him? You said you've done this before."

"There isn't much we can do except wait and try to keep him as comfortable as we can."

Jacques' heavy footsteps pounded down the iron stairwell. A rolling cot slipped through the doorway followed by the big man. He unfolded the bed in the far-left corner of the room and disappeared again.

My insides burned with an ache I could barely comprehend. I'd known pain, but the way in which this leached from my stomach into my chest, my head, my extremities… it felt as if something had ruptured.

"Leave me," I said, "I need time to myself. This will require meditation and patience."

"It's going to require a lot more than that," said Bernard. He stepped over to me and extended his hand. "Take care of yourself, all right?"

"I will," I said, taking it.

He pulled me up from the floor and guided me to the bed. "You can do this. You're stronger than Del."

"I know that. Now leave me in peace. All of you, leave."

Bernard shot a knowing look at Vivienne and I hated that he knew more about what was to come than I. As a man of science, I should have been versed on the topic but I'd never considered it necessary reading. The plight of the weak rarely secured my interest.

"Wait," I said and began stripping off my new suit and shirt. "Take these, I don't want them ruined." I knew enough to realise the danger my clothing was in. Now down to my union suit, I handed the garments, all but Del's watch, to Bernard and sat back down on the bed. "Bernard, one last thing, please. No matter what I say, no matter how much I plead, do not let me out. I have to see this through."

"Yeah, okay, M. Okay."

Jacques came back inside holding a wool blanket and a small wooden table as Bernard passed him to make his exit. The two men acknowledged each other with a shared nod. The brute threw the blanket over me. That silent bastard could have just handed it over. I wrapped myself in its rough warmth and wriggled backward. I again caught myself rocking.

Vivienne's ape positioned the side table he'd been tasked with fetching next to the cot and retreated to the doorway. Vivienne bent, ever graceful in her movements, to retrieve the oil lamp. She sat on the edge of the cot, setting the lamp on the side table.

"M, do you understand what you're getting yourself into?"

"I do," I lied.

"This isn't some puzzle to crack or mechanism to build. This is deconstruction."

"I know what it is. I love destruction."

"No," she said, placing a hand over both of mine as they held the blanket under my chin, "deconstruction not destruction. The challenge in something like this is preserving yourself while removing the rest. This is what an exorcism would be like if they were real."

"An apt metaphor," I said, placing one of my hands over hers. "I appreciate everything you're doing for me."

"I'll be by to check on you in the morning."

"Viv, please, I don't want you to come down here. Bernard will bring me my meals, my water. I'll come to you when I'm ready."

"Are you sure?"

"From what I understand," which was regrettably little, "I won't be in any sort of state to receive compan..." My guts contracted and it took all the strength I had to keep their contents in.

Vivienne stood and backed up, both from fear and instinct.

"M, are you okay?"

"Leave, please."

"M?"

"Lock the door!"

She did, and the heavy thud of the door was not as heavy as the click of the key. It was, however, necessary. This was a problem I couldn't be allowed to escape.

I threw the blanket off of me and hurried to the other side of the room where my bucket awaited. As the cold metal pressed against my collarbone and my abdominal muscles nearly imploded, I let the first of what would be many pathetic whimpers escape my throat.

Here we go tough guy. You asked for it, sighed Del.

I was locked in with only myself, Del, and our mutual enemy, the dragon, and we were about to set about tearing each other apart.

MONDAY

9TH JANUARY

1928

28

A FRESH CIRCLE

Dragon fire seared my insides and a cramp so strong that it bent me in half comprised yet another volley in the battle for Del's body in this fresh circle of hell.

Bile burst from an otherwise empty stomach and painted the bottom of the bucket with foul acid. I could only imagine the colour in the dim light of my subterranean abode. The dry heaving that followed felt like blows from a pugilist and only once they subsided could I lay my face on the cold ground. The chill against my skin a momentary comfort.

When the chill became an ache, I rose, bucket in hand, and crawled on my knees to the drain where I emptied it like I'd emptied my stomach. I left it there and returned to the bed where I cocooned myself in the wool blanket. I lay naked, foetal, and staring at the dancing light of the oil lamp. The movement of the flame was mesmerizing just like that of an opium lamp. That simple memory ended my momentary reprieve and made my cravings swell.

The cramps continued their slow march, radiating out from my core. By four in the morning, the muscles in my limbs were beginning to lock and release at random. My bowels, however, had become an assembly line for the foulest liquid one's body can produce. The rate of production was unsafe. Inside, withdrawal acted as the plant foreman. One who should be fired for the stresses he was putting on the machinery.

I had long since soiled my union suit. There was no dignity left to preserve after that and my naked body brought far less shame.

The air was fouled with the scent of the hours of filth I had been emptying down the drain. Up and out, down and out, both at the same time, it did not matter. The muscles that governed the contractions within were swollen and burned like legs burn after a hard run. My addicted body demanded that I purge everything. My mind was convinced there was nothing left to purge but the unthinking mechanism of stomach and intestine has no ears, no brain, no sympathy. It wants what it wants and continues to force action despite a lack of outcome.

The buckets, whose dedicated uses quickly became gospel to avoid any cross contamination, had taken more abuse than any brasserie toilet takes on a given night.

Keeping myself clean was an instant struggle. Nakedness was easiest not least because my perception of temperature had lost all meaning.

"M," said a distant voice from outside the heavy metal door. My name was followed by the gasping and coughing of two people. A man and a woman.

"Viv," I said, scrambling to the bed and pulling the blanket over my pathetic body. "I told you not to come."

"I brought you more water," she said, as if it were explanation enough.

"I've got some food for you," said Bernard, stepping slowly into the room with a hand over his mouth and nose. "You need food. Del needs food. You've been upchucking all night. It's just some rice porridge. It'll be easy on your guts."

I bit down on the blanket. The mere thought of anything entering my body induced the light flutters that warn of an imminent eruption.

"No, Bernard, please no. I… I appreciate the thought but I… can't."

"You need to eat," he said.

"I can't. Please don't make me. Not now. I promise I'll try in a few hours. Just please, leave me."

Bernard did not respond.

I could feel my ragged breathing as my aching chest muscles expanded over my bones, which also ached. Just three pipes, Del knew that just three small pills could cure the pain. I wanted it. I wanted it but I wanted to kill the dragon more.

"M, can I come in?" Vivienne's soft coo from outside the room sent a fear that she might discover me in this state.

"Viv, please, you don't want to see this."

"But you must need water. Would it be okay if I slide some inside?"

"Viv, please, just please leave me."

"What if Bernie just puts the water inside next to the door? Bernie, would you mind?"

"No, I don't mind."

"I can't drink any water," I pleaded.

"M, take the water. You need it. Del needs it," said Bernard. There was no room for debate.

"Okay, just set it down there and leave. Okay?"

"Okay."

The iron hinges rang with the low thrum of an eastern monk's chant. A short pause followed, then the call of the key ended the meditation. Through a tight squint in the dim light of the oil lamp, I found two empty wine bottles that had been repurposed as water pitchers.

This is where I gave up. It's where I always give up, said Del.

Because you're weak.

Maybe, but you'll give up too. You ain't got no hope against this.

I do.

I crawled over to the bottles and took one in my hand. Its weight felt enormous. I didn't want the water. I hated the water. I hated them for bringing it to me but the scientist in me knew I had to drink. The logician in me knew they were right.

I tipped the bottle to my lips and let a little slide over my white, coated tongue. It felt cool in my throat and soothing to my stomach.

A short minute passed before I retched. I groped for the bucket but left a trail on my way there. A few strings of hot bile dripped from my lips. The smell as I waited for the last of it to settle into the bucket brought on yet another round of dry heaving. I knew it would eventually pass. All of it would pass and I would be free from the opium. I'd suffered before. Battles, imprisonment, torture, they were nothing new. They were, in fact, old memories but I could cope with this too.

29

DANTE KNEW NOTHING

Dante knew nothing.

The damnation he painted was just that, a painting. A canvas on which to splash pain and suffering in all shades of red and grey. My pain, my suffering, there naked on Vivienne's cot — the cot I'd destroyed with my innards — that pain was absolute. It was visceral and eviscerating.

I was a writhing bag of rats. My limbs moved constantly like some sort of perverse automaton. Every pause, a cramp, every cramp, a groan, every groan a reminder that I was trapped inside that body.

Del had gone silent and I was glad for that small peace.

I'd stretch each locked muscle to soothe the cramp only to feel the opposing muscle lock. My senses were on fire. The mattress was pumice against my skin. I could feel my aching bones articulate. My heartbeat, the engine of my sorrow. The drum that drove the rowers across the river Styx. I was sure I was dying.

All I could do was move. So much so that I could not move. I was in motion but stationary. Bound to the bed but free to flail.

My mind tried to find escape. Thoughts of Tian and his fate, Lilith and her betrayal, the Twins and their hubris all were readily at hand, but they only added a new dimension to my agony.

"Let me out! Please, just a few pipes. It's too much. A few pipes and I'll try again. It's too much. It's too much!"

No one came. No response. My solitude was an eternity. Solitude.

All I wanted was solitude and yet I reviled it. Solitude hid my disgusting state but it drove a depression that was consuming me whole. I was alone. No, Vivienne was here, but she wasn't of my kind. She wasn't Lilith.

"Bernard! Anyone! Let me out!"

I rolled over and attempted to stand. Sharp electric pain flashed. Every orifice was acid-burned and filthy and just wanted to stay still. I couldn't stay still. All I could do was hurt. All I could do was trade pain for pain and watch insanity, like a wolf beyond the firelight, lick its lips.

I managed to stand. No, pace. I looked like a bird as my leg muscles locked and jerked. My hand went to my stomach as another contraction tried to empty my empty stomach. The frequency was far less. The limb cramps had taken up the task of torture.

My quadriceps contracted so hard I fell, slamming an elbow against the damp limestone floor. That sent a cascade of cramps running through my body.

"Kill me, please god, please, have mercy. Kill me, please!"

The words were followed with sobs that broke into a grotesque laughter. I was a god, praying to a god that didn't exist.

I pushed myself back against the side of the cot, my head draped over the thin mattress. I focused on my breathing and escaped into the brain.

My eyes opened onto my mental kingdom but it was not right. My sandstone throne scraped like the mattress. My body, my mental avatar still writhed and everything still ached. I stood and leapt into the air. My ebony wings flapped, pushing me high into the black expanse above but they too contracted violently and I was falling, only to come to rest in the ground floor of what would have been a merchant's home.

The subconscious. Could I escape there? I shuffled through the streets dragging my contorted wings behind me. The blue door was in sight but as it drew closer, my yelling grew louder. I knew the body would be screaming in pain, screaming for help, screaming for the drug, but as I fell to my knees in front of that blue door, it was clear Del was howling from within. Even he wasn't pardoned from this fate.

I bellowed and pounded my fist against the ground in front of that blue door but when I opened my eyes, I was back in the dark room underneath Vivienne's farmhouse. I was yelling and frantic and I was shaking again. I was so cold.

Back in the bed I tried to wrap myself in the blanket but my motion did nothing but kick it away.

"Please! Please. No more. No, no more."

The door opened and Bernard stepped through. His face contorted and he gagged at the smell and the sights within the room.

He was carrying half a baguette and a cup of onion soup. He set both next to the previous food, none of which I'd touched.

"Bernie. Bernie, please, you have to let me out. Or, or just bring me a pipe and a few pills just let me ease out of this, just for a little while."

"Del?" Hope and panic twisted his face.

"No, no I'm sorry, I'm… it's me, please, Bernard, please…"

He backed out of the room, keeping his eyes on me, eyes that wore the heaviness of one watching a loved one die.

"Don't go, please, don't."

As he closed the door, cotton flashed white from inside his ears. He didn't want to hear my visceral, animal noises any more than I wanted to loose them.

I threw myself at the door and clawed at the cold metal. More screams, more sobs, more salty tears tainting my mouth.

In desperation I tried pulling away from the mind like I had the night I woke in Del's body. But like Excalibur in the stone, so was I bound.

TUESDAY

10TH JANUARY

1928

30

NOTHING LEFT TO GIVE

Raw.

Every sense, every nerve, every thought, every inch of skin on my body was raw. I huddled near the door in the corner of that devastated room, too disgusted with the state of the mattress to go near it. The wool blanket had somehow survived the brunt of the assault but still smelled foul. It was warm though, and my naked body was numb with cold.

I was prepared for the process to shift from the physical to the mental. I could not have prepared myself for how much worse that evolution was.

The dragon, by then, had burrowed deeper, leaving the body to rot and bringing chaos to the brain — an organised chaos that somehow held focus. Opium. I was drowning and it was my oxygen. I was falling and it was my salvation. I was dying and it was my cure. I was locked away from it and I would die in that room. I was sure of it.

And what did it matter? Tian was dead. Yemoja, Cernunnos, the others, they'd run like cowards. Izzy. Lilith. Why did she abandon me? Why did she forsake me? Why couldn't she see this wasn't a game?

With a skeletal hand, the skin already the colour of aged bone, I hooked the edge of the plate holding all the food I hadn't eaten and slid it toward me. None of it was palatable but my nausea was gone and so too was my energy.

I picked button-sized pieces from the baguette and forced them down. Nothing moved except my hand to my mouth, and time.

I took water after the bread and continued to force-feed myself. A chicken leg came next, its greasy skin and rich meat threatened to make the retching start once again. I stopped after that.

Memories of opium dominated my mind. Del's memories. The smell of it, flowers and burnt maple syrup, the feeling of warm vapor filling the lungs, the calm, the sweet calm, I've never wanted anything more.

I wanted it. Needed it. I was pathetic. I was Del. I'd lost. I'd lost so much and I lost this battle too. I was finished. I was as ruined as this body, as this room. I was filth. I couldn't beat it because I couldn't get it out of my head. The longing, the need.

It wasn't my head though. It was Del's. Del's memories, Del's need.

I slammed to the ground inside the mind, right in front of the blue door. I gripped its brass handle and threw it open then plunged back through the twisting grey clouds of the subconscious.

My wings were back to working order and I streaked past all the horrors still on display, all of them opium-related and all of them intense.

My wings acted as a parachute and I glided up to the bars that held Del inside his childhood bedroom. I gripped those bars with both weak hands. Hands that had never been weak.

"Del! Stop this. I know it's you sending me all those memories. All those experiences. I can't do anything if you won't stop sabotaging my work."

He charged up to the bars and put his face close to mine.

"The only thing I've been doing is suffering right along with you. We're sharing this body, remember? It's the drug. It brings on the memories, the cravings, all of this shit. It's the drug."

He was right and I felt ashamed for even being there. My mind was so twisted, so broken.

"We need it, M," said Del. "We have to have it. You know we can't take this."

I was a caged lion, pacing the bars but I was the one who was free. Rage radiated from me like the light of the sun. I kicked and punched at the buildings around us. Brick and mortar bursting into clouds of dust and stone.

"M, get us the opium," he said. "We can't do this anymore. We won't.

I won't and you won't. We have to fix this. We have get better. We have to get well. I can't take it. We can't take it. We can't take it!"

I continued my rampage. Windows smashed, motorcars overturned, I screamed into the sky.

"M!"

I turned to him. He stared at me with a hungry scowl, an all consuming need, a mandate.

"Get. It. Now."

I exploded back into the physical world, throwing the blanket aside and rolling to my knees in front of the door.

"We need it!" I screamed, pounding the black metal door with both fists. "Give it to us! Let us out! Let us out!"

"No, I can't," said a voice from above and I skittered back on my hands and heels. Two eyes glinted in the light of the oil lamp.

"Damn you!" I lunged at the door, throwing my shoulder into it. My body crumpled at the pain.

"M, you told us not to let you out until you'd beaten it." Bernard's voice. His sad, caring voice. I wanted to slit the throat it came from.

"Let us out and get some damned opium. We can't take it anymore. We give up, I give up! Just let us out."

"I can't."

"Damn you, Bernard!" I stood and threw the other shoulder into the door and let rage propel a torrent of fists. "Damn you to whatever hell you hold."

"M, you're hurting yourself. You're hurting Del. You have to stop."

The idea came in a flash.

"Hurting myself. Yes, yes I am. I've found my way out, Bernard, I've found Del's too, and it will be on your head!"

I dropped to my knees and groped for the chicken bone. I snapped off one knuckle with some hidden store of strength and scraped the cracked end across the ground in a few vicious motions.

"What are you doing?" Bernard was frantic. "M?"

I stood straight and tall and filthy and naked and held the jagged bone to my neck.

"I'm leaving this room right now. Either through that door or with this bone. We can't do it anymore. We're getting out."

"Vivienne! Jacques!" his voice was distant. One set of footfalls echoed away, time passed, too much time, then three returned.

"Get us out of here!" I kept the bone in place.

The clicking of keys and grinding of hinges sent a wave of elation through me, then a torrent of water sent me to the floor. Jacques stood over me, hose in hand, and swept the jet over me. I tried to escape it but was stopped by the rear wall.

The bone was gone, lost in the fall, and my mind finally let go of the opium long enough to focus on not drowning as the stream of water crossed my face, my torso, my genitals, my face.

"Gentle," I could hear Bernard plead over the spatter of the hose. "That body isn't his. Don't punish Del because of M. Gentle."

◆ ◆ ◆

"Drink this, quickly," said Vivienne as she tipped a small glass of wine to my lips. My tongue flexed at the unexpected bitterness. I was dressed now. After the hosing, Bernard had carried me upstairs in a clean blanket, dried me, and put me in fresh underwear. My elation at being out of the room did little to ease my rage. I was a bull, let out into the sun, seeking my red cape: opium.

"It's laudanum," she said as I coughed. "I have nothing to smoke but this will help for now."

Laudanum, the wonder drug of the Victorian age. A blend of alcohol and opium tincture that possessed the chemicals my body needed. I didn't care.

"I need opium. O-P-I-U-M," I said, then downed the rest of the glass, wiping the laced wine from my lips.

"And you'll have it. I know a place. This is only temporary," she said, leaving the room.

And it was. The opiates within the laudanum passed into my blood stream within minutes. All the while, Bernard watched me from the corner of the bedroom, his arms crossed tightly over his chest.

"Bernard, I—"

"You failed."

"Are you angry with me? Disappointed?"

He sat on the opposite edge of the bed from me. "Angry? No. Disappointed? Maybe a little. Of course I hoped you'd lick that habit but I'm not surprised you didn't. It's probably for the best anyway."

The laudanum continued to settle but its effects were not strong enough.

"For the best?"

Bernard rose and grabbed for my clothes. He tossed the loose bundle in my lap.

"Yeah. It's a good thing when arrogant bastards like you get taken down a peg. It helps you realise you might not have as much control as you think."

"Don't talk to me about control. This whole business has been out of control."

"Look, you've got three people all here to help. Take it. Let us help."

"Get dressed, M," called Vivienne from the other room. "We've got to get you to Monsieur Khamdao."

31

THE DEN

Jacques came to a stop in front of a slender door on a street so narrow, I had difficulty opening the door to Vivienne's motorcar. Bernard, Vivienne, and Jacques stayed seated.

"M, take this," said Vivienne, handing me her calling card. "Give this to Monsieur Khamdao and he'll take very good care of you."

"Why won't you stay and speak with him yourself?"

She smiled her coy, wonderful smile. "Monsieur Khamdao owes me more than one favour. That doesn't mean he likes me."

"Ah."

"Good luck and get yourself right. Have Monsieur Khamdao ring me and we'll be by to pick you up when you're ready."

"M, take care of that body," said Bernard.

"I'm trying."

The trio left me in the snow at a door which led to the most exclusive opium den in the city. Del would have lost his mind had he not already lost it to me.

The dragon was clawing at my brain, begging to be fed even after a taste of the laudanum. I was more than eager to oblige. Defeated, embarrassed, but eager.

Like the madame's door, the slender brown door was plain and bore no marks to indicate what lay inside. I knocked twice and a diminutive Laotian man emerged. He looked well past eighty with a long white goatee and a short, round cap over even shorter white hair. He eyed my haggard body with suspicion to which I returned a strained smile.

Is he going to let us in? asked Del.

The old man said nothing while looking me up and down then he shook his head.

No, no, no.

When he turned to go back inside, I tapped his shoulder, which drew ire. He spun on his toes and his body tensed. Everything about him from the furrow of his brow to the set of his jaw proclaimed that he was more than ready to teach any lesson that was necessary. I needed none and wanted none.

"Madame Vivienne sends her regards and promised I'd be well cared for," I said, fighting the urge to storm the room in search of relief. I handed him her calling card with a quaking hand. He gave it a brief inspection then handed it back.

"Does she?" he asked, again taking in my ill complexion and Del's frail body. "This is a promise I can keep as long as it is one you can pay for."

I withdrew one hundred francs from my wallet. More than enough to get me through multiple evenings let alone that night. His eyes followed the bills as I gave them a small wave. He was neither eager nor impressed but with a nod and admirable restraint, he withdrew a reasonable number of notes from the collection in my hand and stood aside, guiding me into his *cave des rêves*.

Inside was a small bar, three tables with no patrons, and a stone stairwell leading downward. The old man again waved me onward.

Here we go, here we go.

The spiralling staircase made one full turn and I emerged into the vaulted limestone basement of the building. About twenty elaborately woven mats, maybe more, lay scattered around the cavernous space, their bright colours blotted out by the creams and blacks of fine silk pyjamas that sprawled across them. These silks were filled with the shells of wealthy men. And there were women too. The curve-clinging fabric made them look like sleeping cats. Their eyes, if they were open at all, were vacant, but all wore something of a smile. Peering out into the haze of floral smoke set my mouth to watering like a dog waiting for his scraps.

The amount of wasted time, energy, and life that filled this room was disgusting. I was disgusting. I was better than this but Del wasn't. He was all but panting at the sights and smells. After my ordeal, the body would get what it wanted. Instead of ridding myself of Del's curse, it would have to be factored into my schemes. Despicable.

Monsieur Khamdao led me to a changing room and I exchanged my clothes for a set of those cream silk smoking pyjamas. I rearranged my belongings into the interior pockets of my suit before disrobing. I did not want the nimble fingers of staff taking advantage of me while I drifted into oblivion.

A final gesture from the old man told me where my mat was to be and I sat, cross legged, next to two men who paid no attention to my arrival.

A young 'pipe boy' hurried over and placed a wooden tray on the floor next to me. On it lay a long wood and brass pipe with a small bowl perched near one end. An ornate pill box sat next to it. Inside lay the dark, sticky substance we longed for.

That's about ten pipes' worth, said Del. *Oh, that's the sweet stuff. I ain't never had nothing this good. Tell the kid to get cooking already.*

A small oil lamp burned in the middle of the tray and next to that lay a long, narrow scraper and the other instruments necessary for dragon chasing.

The pipe boy held up the pill box and said, "Fook Lung."

No shit? That's top stuff. Vivienne wasn't kiddin'. This place is swanky.

The name meant 'abundant luck'. Oh, how I needed some.

I reclined on my mat, propping myself up on an elbow. The boy loaded the pipe with one of the sticky, pre-rolled pills that had been made from the finest chandu. He handed the pipe to me and began demonstrating the procedure.

Oh yeah, okay, now put your mouth…

I know what to do, Del. Just shut up and take your medicine.

I waved the boy off and he sat back on his heels.

I leaned the bowl of the pipe near the flame. The dark substance began to heat, then smoke, and when the first whitish curls rose, I inhaled with a fervour that bordered on embarrassing.

Unlike the laudanum, the effects of opium are slow to take hold. One does not simply smoke one pipe. The dragon feeds in courses. I had the pipe reloaded and reloaded until I'd run out. Eleven pipes in total. The boy was skilled and had more than earned his pay.

I rolled to my back and stretched out on the mat after the final pipe. My hunger for the drug had been satiated and the accompanying maladies that pained my body were gone, replaced by a soft, warm feeling that flushed through me. This had an extreme calming effect on me. When I say me I mean we. The dragon held us both in its claws just as it had when we tried to break free from the prison it built for us.

My focus drifted to the ceiling, studying the nuance of the cracks between the stones. The play of lamplight over the myriad textures of wall and carpet and stone and body produced a deep fascination. Minute, overlooked details sprang forth and demanded scrutiny.

I adjusted my position and the sliding of silk on skin was divine. I began to scratch slow circles over my back and chest and waves of pleasure swept over me like August on a Mediterranean shore.

There on my back, I swung my limbs about in languid motions. This opium, the purest Del had ever experienced, did not distort one's coordination like the dross Del could usually afford. It did not call for sleep but energised instead.

My examination of the ceiling cracks, nearly Arabic in their geometry, became interrupted by thoughts on ending the Mentium's plot.

Any ideas had while inebriated were sure to be folly but I couldn't help myself. The intricacies of the problem were fascinating. I smiled at the marvel of engineering I'd managed to create and at the irony that I would have to break what I'd built. Disabling the radio was now an imperative rather than a mere option. But how? The original portions of the device? New? When? The challenge was delicious and distracted from my true reality.

I continued to grin like a fool and float on my chemical cloud as I drifted between daydream and drug den.

The dragon's lullabies were silenced by a clamour that erupted upstairs. Monsieur Khamdao's voice began to protest before stopping mid-sentence. A cacophony of footfalls tumbled down the stairwell and three gargantuan thugs thundered toward me. I pondered what might be their trouble.

The strong men stepped over the scattered bodies in the room as if they weren't there. Three sets of cold, dead eyes remained locked on me even as they backhanded the pipe boy at my side, sending him on top of a nearby patron who was drawing on a pipe.

As they pulled my body to its feet, my eyes fell to the exposed wrist of the man who had me by the collar, the sign of the Mentium was branded there. Eunuchs. I did not resist. Behind them, Kukulkan smiled at me.

Who are they? asked Del in a slow, languid voice.

I was in no state to do anything but feel some small seed of anger at myself for what amounted to leaving the door unlocked. I'd let down my mental blocks as the opium took hold and the Mentium had sensed my consciousness. They sent their goons. I'd all but turned myself in. The realisation made me laugh out loud. What a fool I was. How blind the opium had made me. Third eye indeed.

32

LILITH

A slap woke me from my slumber. One of many brief blackouts since I'd been taken. The sting was dulled by the drug, but I could still sense the sentiment behind it. Lilith was enjoying herself. Of course she was.

"We found you, you poor, pitiful creature. What terrible luck you've had, my dear. That body… just disgraceful. And the least you could have done was come dressed. Those pyjamas are not becoming on you."

"Spare me," I said as I pulled with weak arms at the silk ropes that secured me to my chair. And it was indeed *my* chair, my seat within the council room for the Upper Echelon. The chandelier that hung in the middle of our circle was the only light and it revealed all other chairs were empty but two: my chair and the one next to it. "Lilith, I'm sure you've been practising your victory speech in a mirror all day but I'm sorry to say that I'm in no mood to listen."

Another slap came fast and hard and I had no time to react. Her enamelled nails, a red that approached black, tore skin as they passed but pain was distant. I was still dragon-bound. Inside I fought to regain composure and control. On the outside, my body was wrapped in the euphoria it had been so desperate to attain. I won't lie, this was a benefit for more than just pain relief. Staying calm would send Lilith into a froth, which was always a treat to behold. We lived to tug each others' strings, and that night I wanted her to be my harp. This was my swan song after all.

Lilith was a woman of action but her true prowess lay in strategy. She was a tactician. *The* tactician as far as the Mentium were concerned. To her detriment, her cunning was not matched by her self-control. Her outbursts of rage or lust or excitement were as captivating as a stage production and I often amused myself by provoking such reactions.

"You'll listen to every word that falls from these lips," she said, her bobbed, obsidian curls bouncing with fury.

They were amazing lips, familiar, dangerous. That night they wore scarlet, which paired exquisitely with her chestnut eyes. The paleness of her skin had been something of a recent departure compared to the olive sported by her historical choice in hosts. She'd worn this new sun-frightened skin for a mere two centuries-worth of bodies. All since our move north.

"You're mine now, Marduk," she said, those lips curling into a wry grin. "Everything you are is in my hands. I've already bested you. Should I play or punish?"

"How far you've fallen, love. So why not both, darling? That is your typical want, is it not?"

"Alas," she said, grabbing me by the small lapels of my pyjama top, "your questioning must come first."

"I would expect no less."

"And I've been tasked with your entombment."

"Entombment is it?" I tried to stay focused on the conversation. The drug was adamant, demanding I relax and drift off to sleep. I could not oblige. "Got the Twins to agree to that, did you?"

"I follow protocol."

"You do their bidding."

Another hard slap.

I started to laugh and as I did the dragon's coils squeezed my brain. I lost control and began to cackle. The sound was surprising. Though Del's body was slight, this laugh was powerful.

In my haze I had almost overlooked the figure standing at a distance in the dim wash of the chandelier's new electric glow. He held one arm with the other.

"Izzy?" I said through lung-bursting guffaws. My diaphragm was beginning to ache. "You silly bastard. You… ha ha ha! You damn snake!

SSSSSSS! It's Lilith who has all the venom, though. You'll only ever be an errand boy. Errand boy!"

Izanagi stepped next to Lilith, placing his good hand on her shoulder. She placed her own over his and smiled, though her eyes never left mine.

"Ha, ha! This is too delicious." Tears streamed as my exhausted chest heaved with more laughter. "A love triangle. Oh, you bad boy. You've stolen my girl away. What *ever* will I do? Idiot. You think you're the first? You think we're… exclusive?! If it's jealousy you want then I'm afraid you've made," my laughter rolled, "made a terrible mistake. All I can offer you is my sympathies. She treads on hearts with heavy heels."

"Traitorous scum!" This time it was Izzy who struck me. A fist. My head snapped to the side and the taste of salted iron filled my mouth. He'd cured my laughing fit.

"Ill played Izzy," I said, spitting blood on his linen sling. "Ill played. Striking a bound man? And one so small and weak? I shall remember that." I stared up at him and spit more blood onto his pants. "Just as I will always remember your betrayal."

"Well then, I'm glad that 'always' for you is but a few more hours," he said with a smugness he hadn't earned. "I should thank you for providing a vacancy within the Upper Echelon. I think I might look good in that chair."

"*Tsk tsk*, Izzy, such deplorable character. Where are your scruples? Really Lilith, I don't understand what you see in him."

"I see him in me from time to time," she said, still ignoring him. Still with eyes locked on mine.

"Truth! Do you hear that, Izzy?" I said, shifting my gaze to his ordinary looking face sitting on top of his ordinary looking body. "Just like in the laboratory. You're only good for ten minutes of work at a time."

"Lilith, please," he said, looking wounded and lost. "I thought—"

"That, my dear, is your problem. I think it best you stick with bedding, brooding and science. Why don't you run along and pout. I'll come cheer you up in a few minutes."

"But…"

"Do you hear yourself?" she asked, now looking into his eyes, making her disgust plain. "Apparently, there is much work before I've made a man of you."

My laughter returned but I kept it in check the best I could as my former assistant skulked from the room. Lilith turned to me with a coy smile, how I loved that smile, then straddled my thighs, wrapping her arms around my neck.

"You know this is checkmate, don't you?" she said with soft words next to my ear, one hand to stroke my hair.

"You know this is lunacy," I said, enjoying her hand. "The world has changed. The Monos are different. They'll never accept us as gods. Not again. Stepping into this vacuum the Twins intend to produce will paint targets on all our backs. They won't be seeking guidance but vengeance. This is not the way. You have to see that."

"What I see," she said, placing a hand on my chest and pushing herself back to standing, "is a man who has lost everything. Your body, gone. Your position, gone. Your credibility, gone. Your dignity… and for what?"

"To keep this damned boat afloat."

"The Twins have taken care of that. You could have been part of it all."

"I'll never understand what's happened you, Lilith. Never."

"We'll be performing the entombment when the others arrive," she said.

"Others? Who? Kali? That makes four of you. I know Yemoja, Cernunnos, and Radegast have fled. I'm told Ma'at as well."

She did not bristle at that. She stood as stone and she studied my face.

"There are new members on the council to witness your punishment," she said. "You have a few hours to prepare yourself. Try not to cry."

"I wouldn't think of it. I have to deny you some satisfaction. I trust you'll miss me."

"All the satisfaction I require lies in catching you, not in losing you."

"You didn't lose me. I left. It was my choice."

"A choice we all must live with."

My love bent in close. Her soft lips grazed mine and I took in every sensation of her. One last time. She again pushed off my chest and turned to leave.

"Lilith…"

"Goodbye my little snake-dragon."

She left with a confident swagger. Too confident. She would mourn me as I would her.

33

BOUND

Under the lone, dim light of the room, I sat in solitude, sorting the few options I had available, or at least attempting to. The fog of opium was still thick in my mind and between the urges to sleep and the unjustified euphoria, it was difficult to grasp the seriousness of my predicament. I was to be entombed. The serious punishment inflicted on a member of the Mentium.

M, said Del, *you gotta figure a way outta this. It's not just you getting trapped in here.*

Del, they have us. Even if we were to escape, they've seen us. If it weren't for changing into these pyjamas, they'd know who you are. Kukulkan might have gleaned that information when he found me. I think it best to start resigning yourself to fate. You should have been killed when I entered you. Consider these past few days a gift.

A gift? M, get it together, buddy. We gotta do something.

I'd seen the procedure done many times. I'd performed it myself, many times. The irony was not lost on me. I would remain bound, though an additional rope would secure my neck, and my head would be pulled back and strapped down. A device, little more than a striking surface at one end and a short blade at the other would be pressed to my forehead.

A hammer would strike the device and the blade would penetrate the skull, damaging the brain and thus my ability to operate it. I would be trapped within with no means of escape. The body would live. Basic functions would remain, but cognition would cease.

I would be as Del is now; I would join Del as a prisoner, and we would both be witnesses to the Mentium's destruction. They'd make me watch. They would want to gloat.

Don't give up on us, M. This isn't just about you, remember. The whole goddammed globe is in danger.

At least I'd have the last laugh, or thoughts of laughter as the world burned around them. They were bringing themselves war not power. The Monos would no longer suffer public tyranny.

Such topics weren't interesting enough to fight the drug-induced sleep my body screamed for. I released the negative thoughts and slipped away.

34

CONFUSION

"Marduk…. Marduk. Wake up you swine," whispered a biting yet soft voice. It was deep but gentle as rough hands shook me. Looking up, a hulking Eunuch stood rigid, an expression even more hollow than usual hung like a wooden mask.

"What is it? Come on, Mr Personality, are you here to beat me or bore me?" I asked, the opium smiling at him like an idiot. "Know that I am far too inebriated to care."

The Eunuch said nothing, instead he removed an envelope from his inner breast pocket and placed it on my lap. On its face, two short messages were scrawled in a cryptic hand.

- Run, you have an ally.

- Find your new friend and leave his home.

He then circled behind me and began untying my ropes. When my hands were free, I took up the envelope and turned it. Over the sealed flap was a third message in the same script.

- Do not open until sober.

When the ties at my ankles were undone, I rose and the Eunuch stepped back three paces. Still wearing the wooden expression.

"What do you want? What?" I asked. "Who is this from? Who sent you?"

The behemoth again reached inside his jacket, this time exposing a knife which he pointed at my face. White knuckles gripped the hilt and the knife was close enough to smell the well-oiled blade. I tried to anticipate his next move but focus was impossible while in the grip of the drug. The big man's chest filled with air and I readied myself for his strike.

"Run!"

His voice hit me instead and as I stood, motionless, he drove the knife into his neck.

My breath caught in my throat as blood left his. I was frozen and frantic until I managed to free myself of Del's pathetic horror. I stuffed the envelope into the chest pocket of my silk pyjamas as I sprinted away from the spurting Eunuch. The stark white room moved as if it were a cabin on a steamer, though I knew I was the only one experiencing the motion of the waves.

The open door rushed toward me but as one foot extended through it, both hands gripped the frame. In front of me stretched a hallway lined with three more Eunuchs on each side. Each turned to me, knives extended. I stepped forward and as I passed each pair, the knives were plunged into their necks as well.

My bloodied escape continued until I reached the street where a taxi waited.

"*Monsieur Leduc?*" asked the driver.

"*Uh, oui… oui.*"

The driver said nothing and opened the door for me. He ran to the driver-side door and sped away from the Temple of the Mentium.

"Where would you like to go?"

"Montparnasse… Le Dingo," I said, not wanting to reveal Bernard's address. I could walk from there.

WEDNESDAY

11TH JANUARY

1928

35

DESPERATE TIMES

"Pack. Now. One bag. Only what's necessary. And don't forget the new suits," I said, stomping through the front door and into the sitting room were Bernard sat with his elbows on his knees, rubbing his hands and looking worried. It was just on midnight. Bernard truly was Del's surrogate parent. Depressing, even while dragon chasing.

"Just sit down, calm down, and sober up," he said, standing, still rubbing his hands. "You're too zozzled to think straight, that's all."

I thrust the envelope at his chest and went into Del's room to gather my own provisions, kicking piles of dirty clothes out of my way as I entered. The effort threw me off balance, which was already questionable, and I cursed Del under my breath.

Bernard followed me into the room, staring at the envelope. "What happened to you?"

"I was enjoying a pipe or twelve and was taken by Eunuchs."

"Taken? How did they find you?" he asked "Do they know about me? Vivienne didn't rat us out, did she?"

"No, not Vivienne. Don't even suggest that."

I threw a suitcase onto the bed and spread it open. "It was the opium. It… you remember how I block my mind from others? I was careless. I let my guard down as I smoked and Kukulkan found me and took me to Lilith. And yes, they do know about you and this place, hence my insistence on packing."

"What's in the envelope?"

"It's sealed, isn't it? How could I possibly know? Open it."

"But it says you should be sober first."

"You're sober. Read the damned letter."

Bernard ran a finger under the flap and pulled out a single sheet of paper. It was type-written and contained only a short message that Bernard started reading silently.

"Out loud, Bernard. Come on, man. Hurry!"

Jesus. Cut him some slack, M.

He looked up at me, then at the page once more before he began.

"Plans have changed. Incubi still inflict chaos in the streets

but at the summit, the heads of the heads will roll as well.

Monos will be monsters, murderers, and messengers.

The Twins and those that follow, saviours, protectors, gods for a new age.

New leaders to replace the dead. This is folly and the outcome, a fantasy.

You have an ally."

He again glanced up and then back to the page, shaking his head. "What the hell?"

"Later. Let me think," I said, my mind dissecting the bad poetry. The brain-haze was thinner but I could not yet grasp its full extent. All I could do was circle the room like a fool, grabbing at clothing, putting on my new, tawny suit. The only new suit that remained.

Bernard left, and I could hear the sounds of clothing falling into a valise. I continued myself and scoured Del's bedroom for anything that looked clean and wearable. When finished, I found Bernard ready to leave, his valise lay at his feet.

Don't leave my guitar behind. Or Bernie's sax. "Ah, our instruments," I said to Bernard.

"Right," he said, and we both retreated to our rooms to collect them. Back at the door, I put on my hat, always a derby, and a heavy jacket.

"Where are we going to go?" he asked, placing his own hat on his head.

"To ask more favours."

◆ ◆ ◆

"I need a drink," said Vivienne as I lay on the couch in her office, fighting the last of the opium. Bernard sat across from her, and Jacques stood at the door, arms folded. She poured herself a cognac and leaned back in her leather chair. "You got all this from some riddle?"

"No, not a riddle though the note was oddly cryptic," I said. "My new *ally* seems to be getting a kick out of making me work for their information, however, the message is simple when you understand the symbolism. The plan has changed. That line is clear."

"Why the flowery language, M? That seems so strange," asked Bernard.

"It's a common tactic for hiding one's identity. No chance of using phrases common to the writer."

"They went a bit overboard, right?"

"I won't say I'm enjoying it."

"Okay," said Vivienne, her arms folded, "but what of the lines about heads and monsters?" she took a long sip of cognac.

"Their original plan, well, the plan that drove me to treason, was to essentially stage a scene from Revelations in the streets. Mass hallucination. Then, the old gods would step in to slay the monsters who slayed the friends and family of those who survived. The fools. Rather than a hostile takeover, they think they'll be handed the keys. The idea is that it doesn't matter whether the sheep like their shepherds, they need them for protection."

"I thought you said these would be hallucinations. How can that kill?"

"Because in addition to the phoenixes and giant golems, these hallucinations will turn Mono against Mono."

"Say that again," said Vivienne.

"The lines from the note. It's all there. 'Incubi will inflict chaos in the streets. Monos will be monsters, murderers, messengers. The monsters, the murderers, are the citizens of the city. The populace will rip each other apart. People will appear as creatures to each other and Paris is just the start. The original plan called for other cities in Europe to be hit in rapid succession after the initial Paris attack. I doubt that's changed. My radio has more than enough power."

"That's just so insane," said Vivienne.

"Which is why I defected," I said, the wooden beams that crossed Vivienne's ceiling had engrossing textures, the deep brown of the wood was velvet in the dim light of the room. It was all chemical distraction, I had to stay focused. "An ethereal attack that disappears into the void will only inspire confusion which in turn inspires questions. Dangerous questions for those who are after blind faith. The Twins must realise this now. My departure must have spurred them to rethink their strategy. No, more likely, Lilith made them take note."

Bernard poured himself a cognac and sipped too much. After a ragged bout of coughing, he spat out a question. "Okay, so what is the new plan? I assume the line about heads refers to the changes."

I sat up and reached for my glass of Talisker. "Exactly. They're sticking with the salvation angle but are adding some additional targeted carnage."

"Which is?" asked Vivienne.

"The League of Nations meeting. The note said, 'at the summit, the heads of the heads will roll.' That must refer to the heads of state attending the League of Nations meeting. They were originally only meant to witness the Twins' stepping in as heroes. Now they're getting rid of what is essentially their competition. They'll probably have Churchill seeing Wilhelm Marx as some vampire and putting the leg of a chair through his chest. The meeting room will be a slaughterhouse. And the free world will be left adrift. This had to be Lilith's doing. It's precise and will be more effective than the sideshow the Twins had planned."

"That still seems pretty reckless," said Bernard.

"Oh, it is, very, but it's not without some merit. Monos crave leadership. Without it, they're lost. No presidents, no chancellors, means even more chaos. A chaos the Twins will gladly remedy with their own rule."

"And you think breaking their toy is going to stop them?" asked Vivienne.

The room fell silent as the reality of the situation settled in.

"It's the only option we have left. They've seen me. I can't get close anymore."

From the start I had only wanted time. At first, time to convince, then time to shift power away from the Twins. Now, what good would time do?

Finally Bernard broke the silence. "This is too much. I… what the hell am I doing here? We can't fix this."

I looked at the man and at Vivienne and tried to ready my rebukes. Their fear wasn't at all helpful. As I searched my mind for the words I instead found the truth they'd beaten me to. We could not stop this. Damaging the machine only postponed the inevitable.

"M, say something. Please," said Bernard.

"We're gonna be fine, buddy. You'll see, we'll—" I threw a hand over my mouth, cutting Del off.

"Del?" Bernie perked up.

"Yes, Del, damn it all." The whisky burned like my irritation as I emptied my glass. "We're outmatched. I… I don't know. I don't know what we do. Everything I've done has failed."

"What about this new ally?" asked Viv.

"We have no guarantee as to what role they'll take. Even if it's active, two Mentium, a Multi, and a couple Monos are no match for the power the Twins wield with their army and my radio. It may turn out to be a ruse. We can place no trust in this 'ally'. Not yet. To match the Twins' power we'd need…" The thought was so absurd, I laughed at myself for even thinking it. "Well, no, what we need doesn't exist."

Again the room fell silent. Jacques stood like stone and wore a matching expression. Bernard looked beaten and depressed. Vivienne, however, her mind was racing. She kept that mind closed to me, but her face was easy enough to read. She was angry, scared, and puzzling over something.

My muscles ached from my recent captivity. I rubbed my neck and wrists and continued to study Vivienne.

Finally, with difficulty, she spoke. "Say you did have the power you needed, what would you do?"

"Well," I said, "it's not about electricity. If we had enough Multis or Broadcasters to hide our presence as we worked, we may still salvage our sabotage plan, weak as it may be. Even with my powers at full strength, I couldn't achieve anything close to that."

"I see," she said, closing her eyes.

"Viv? What is it?" I asked.

She took a long breath. "I think I know someone who can help but I need you to swear to me, M," she said with a wet, terrified stare. "Swear to me that you won't hurt her."

"Viv?" I asked, incredulous about the coming answer. "Someone? What exactly are you saying?"

"What's going on? Who are you two talking about?" asked Bernard, splashing a little cognac as he looked between the two of us.

"You can't be serious," I said, coming out of my seat. "Viv, I trusted you."

"M, you've said it yourself. We're desperate. Everything has failed. There is no other choice. I wouldn't have said a word if I didn't believe that."

There I stood, a failure. A failure at diplomacy, at treason, sabotage, murder, a failure to even convince my love that I was right.

Vivienne downed the remainder of her drink. "Swear it!"

I gaped like some brained fish. A Spectre had lived. Hidden from our sight. Impossible yet reality.

"I... I swear it. Viv? How old? How long?" I asked, forming the words carefully. Trying and failing to mask my shock.

A mix of anger, fear, and worry swirled within Vivienne's pained face. Her mind was closed tight but her thoughts were still on display, as were mine. Betrayal and astonishment among them.

"Eve is twenty-three." Vivienne said.

"Eve? You've named it?"

"That 'it' is a human being, M, you insufferable ass. Just like we all are."

"Insufferable?" I said, my own anger flaring. "You harbour this dangerous creature for twenty-odd years, years you spent calling yourself my friend, and you talk to me about insufferable?"

Bernard broke in. "Dangerous creature? But's she's human?"

"A Spectre, Bernard. Viv's got a damned Spectre."

"And Spectres are people," said Vivienne with the snarl of a mother bear. "She was born of one of my artisanes. I sensed her power within the first week. She was strong even then. Knowing what your kind does to people like her," she said, pointing a perfectly crafted sneer at me. "I had the child sent to another friend, one who would know how to train her to use her powers and to defend herself."

"Train her? Who?" I asked, but the answer materialised in my mind. "Coyote? You sent her to Coyote, didn't you? You know him?"

"A friend of a friend."

My fists went to my forehead.

"How could you do that?"

"M, I love you despite the Mentium not because of it. You know how much I hate them. This isn't new. Is it really a stretch to think I'd also have friends on the other side?"

"Other side? What other side?" asked Bernard. "What the hell are you all taking about?" His confusion was annoying.

"I'll explain it later."

"M, what other side?"

"Later!"

"M," said Vivienne, coming around the desk and placing a hand on my arm, calming me in that subtle way with which she had so much skill. "She's in London."

"London? For how long? How have we never sensed her presence? We have Mentium there."

"She's powerful, M. More than you could know. London has been her home for two years now but she's often in other cities."

"Why, pray tell, is that?"

Vivienne hesitated. "The Reformed keep her busy but I don't know what she does."

I felt as if I would burst all over the rug.

"A Spectre working with the Reformed and you expect me to trust her?"

"No, I expect you to put your faith in the only hope we have. You have to trust *my* trust in her."

I wanted to throw my glass at the wall. Throwing it at Jacques would have been even better. "I do trust you Viv, despite the betrayal."

"Don't get righteous with me. Don't you *dare*."

Bernard had taken a seat again and was focused on anything but the two of us. I couldn't blame him. The fighting was useless to continue.

"Well," I said, reclaiming my own seat. "How trained is she? What are her abilities?"

"I'd need to let her explain. Right now, I just need to know whether or not you want her help."

I stared at the floor. Never in my wildest dreams did I think we would end up here. I looked at Jacques and his smug smile taunted me. It was meant to taunt me. He was a Mono. His mind screamed with unrestrained glee at my current predicament, relishing my pain.

"Contact her. Set up a meeting."

36

A TAXI TO VENICE

The next day was a day for waiting and a day for hiding. I wanted none of it. It was also an inescapable day for thought. So, I chose to partake in a pure diet of thought and hoped it would make the waiting and hiding less insufferable.

I rose at dawn, though sleep had come hard and in fits. I dressed, wrapping my shoulders with a heavy wool overcoat and finishing with Del's derby.

I placed a short note outside Bernard's door informing him that I had gone out, would be hidden and protected and not to become concerned until the afternoon. He, of course, would become worried immediately but at least he'd know I'd departed of my own volition.

Out in the morning light. I found a waiting taxi.

"La Seine s'il vous plaît," I said as I sat and closed the door.

"Where on the Seine?"

"Along it," I replied, "First the right bank then the left." I handed the driver one hundred francs, "Until I say stop."

Being locked within Del was prison enough and after my predicament with Lilith and that of Vivienne's country basement, confinement was not at all palatable. I could hide while mobile just as easily as indoors and the solitude of a taxi felt right.

The first circling of the river was spent looking for any random sweeps like those that had been ordered by the Mentium days before. All clear.

By the second time we crossed in front of the tower, the snow at its feet reflected the peach hues of morning and I finally let my mind drift into thought, and thought turned to memory.

◆ ◆ ◆

The sound of inky water lapped at the Venetian foundations outside our window. Chilled, damp air coursed across my powder-coated neck. My mask, an angled Bauta, held a humid, wine-scented mist to my face.

Above me in the near-dark, her ragged breaths echoed against stone walls, her jade eyes, the only feature visible from under her Volto.

A single candle lit her room, the glow was enough to watch her satin and lace writhe against me. Enough to see her high white wig quiver.

It was enough to see her.

My gloved hands groped at her bodice as her breasts strained close to my face, layers deep. Her skirts, an avalanche of cloth, threatened me with suffocation and kept her softness as speculation. I pulled at her arms, her hips, seeking a closeness that was impossible within our fabric cages. Frustration burned within me but it could not compete with the crucible between us.

There had been no fire in the room when we entered from the masquerade, only the February night air, yet we found warmth.

Together we burned. Together we tended our own small, intense fire. Its flames licked at me as she hammered. A blacksmith in satin.

"Lilith…"

"Shhh," she hissed, and placed a silken finger under the sharp pointed chin of my mask and over my lips.

She arched harder, driving her hips into mine and let the finger slip into my mouth. It tasted bitter but it smelled of her, so I bit gently and breathed deeply.

She pulled the finger away then gripped my throat, leaning in close.

"You'll be punished for that," she whispered, though the garnet lips of her mask remained unmoved.

The other hand joined in the game and our pyre flared as her fingers flexed.

"You've been awful tonight," she said, the expression in her eyes more than compensating for the dead shell that covered her face.

"Have I?" I strained.

"You'll pay."

"I'd love to."

Fists drummed on the door behind us. Lilith slid from me with a growl. My abdomen clenched at the detachment, as if I'd been struck.

"*Un momento*," she said, smoothing her skirts and adjusting her white wig.

I tied the laces at my groin and rose to light more candles. Another volley of door-thunder echoed through the room.

"Sit," said Lilith, motioning toward the small table that held a game board. I sat.

"Hello," she said as she opened the door to Izzy, the long nose of his Pulcinella waving as he scanned the room.

"Hello, Lilith. I'm sorry to disturb you both."

"Just a game of Ur," she said, "but we're quite invested, what is the problem?"

Izzy stepped inside, quite uninvited, and gave me a nod. I crossed my legs, reclaiming a modicum of modesty.

"There's been a discovery."

"What discovery?" I asked. I had no time for any games other than the one he'd interrupted.

"A Spectre. Near San Zulian."

"Curse this night!" I said, standing and straightening my costume. "You're sure?"

"Take us," said Lilith.

Izzy led us through the bustling halls of our temple near the *Basilica dei Santi Giovanni e Paolo* in north central Venice. The building was filled with Mentium dressed in their Carnivale finest. We were nearing the end of our centuries-long stay in Venice but in 1642, we were still very much happy with our location.

"Quickly," said Izzy, "the Twins are waiting."

Radegast stood near the wine, dressed in vines with a cornucopia atop his broad head. He was discussing Descartes' recent publication, *Meditationes de Prima Philosophia* with Yemoja.

"Come," I called out to them as we passed.

"Where?"

"A Spectre. Here, in Venice."

Yemoja set her wine down and followed, holding her skirt high.

"I'll stay here, thank you," said Radegast. "The red of wine is the only red I wish to see tonight."

The Twins, in matching gold, smiled from under their Colombinas as they stood near the door. Izzy, Lilith, Yemoja, and I huddled around them on the black and white stone landing.

"Are we all ready to go hunting?" asked Apollo.

"This is a serious matter," said Yemoja.

"We know," said Artemis, drawing a dagger from beneath her dress. "There's a weed in our garden."

"A weed that could poison us all," said Yemoja. "Remember that."

The night air bit even through our costumes. We were a stampede as we twisted through the dark, wet streets of Venice. After the last of uncountable bridges we stood, breathless, in the square before the white stone of San Zulian.

Our circle turned inward, and active eyes swept dead masks for reassurance.

"Do you feel it?" asked Lilith.

"I do," said Apollo. "The wretch is there."

He pointed to a modest second-floor apartment to the left of the church.

"How old?" asked Lilith.

"Young, very young," said Izzy. "This should be easy."

"It is never easy," said Artemis.

"Look at us," said Lilith. "These masks. We are a pack of monsters, come to kill a child."

"The child is the monster," said Apollo. "One that would see us destroyed."

"Enough," said Yemoja. "Let us do what is necessary."

Lilith assessed the building and issued orders. The six of us then walked toward the door to the building housing the Spectre. Izzy stood guard at the door, waiting to alter the reality of anyone passing by. No one, aside from we six, would remember what transpired that night.

Inside, the rest of our group crept up the stairs until we reached the small, wooden landing outside their apartment.

"Remember, the youngest are the most unpredictable," I said. "Act calm and make slow movements."

"I'll take care of the neighbours," said Artemis. She leaned back against the wall and closed her eyes. To the others in the building, that crisp, February night was nothing but serene.

The remaining four of us stood silently for a moment, clarifying in our minds what was inside and what our tasks would be.

"Do we all understand our roles?" I asked.

"No," said Apollo. "I want this one. You can have the next, M."

"By all means."

"After you," said Yemoja, and Apollo shouldered through the locked door. Lilith and I charged in after him, going straight for the master bedroom as he and Yemoja made for the child's room.

The parents, wrapped under heavy blankets, had just opened their eyes when we entered their minds. The two stood at our command and walked into the living space.

"Do you have them?" I asked Lilith.

"Yes, go," she said, then directed the parents into the kitchen where she made each take up a knife.

I stepped toward the children's room. It was quiet but the kitchen was not. The sputtering of slit throats carried through the apartment.

"What's happening?" whispered Artemis from the landing.

As I turned toward her, chaos erupted behind me.

"Look out!" cried Lilith, as Yemoja and Apollo ran, blank faced, past me and out of the apartment. They left a trail of blood behind them.

"It must be awake." I said.

Lilith responded with a wave of her hand and we both crept toward the child. We each pressed our backs either side of the door and I peered inside.

Standing like stone in the middle of the room was a girl of five. Her eyes were cold and her face, frozen. She was a snake about to strike but she was not the Spectre.

Not her, I broadcasted to Lilith. *The cradle.*

She shook her head and pulled a knife from her boot then stepped in front of the door. The girl attacked Lilith with primordial roar.

Lilith's blade did its job and I stepped over to the to baby to do mine.

He was wailing and his toothless gums glistened in the moonlight. I reached for my own knife but as his screams intensified, my body buckled and I bent into knots on the floor.

"Lilith!" I called, grunting as my rib cage compressed against my thighs.

I watched her feet as she ran then lunged. Her skirts brushed my face as the screaming stopped and my body relaxed.

"It's done," she said.

Outside, we found Izzy and Artemis trying to help Yemoja and Apollo regain their composure. Apollo was sitting on the ground and had his knife sticking out of his shoulder. It was his left shoulder; he'd done it to himself.

Behind them, a brigade of Underlings marched across the bridge toward us.

"The baby?" I asked, stepping into their cabal.

"Yes, the power, was…" said Yemoja, hand on her hips as she heaved for air, "I have no words."

"Will we never be rid of these monsters?" asked Artemis, stooping to help her brother. "I do not enjoy feeling like prey."

The group of Underlings gathered around us, and their leader, the Filipino god Bathala, stepped forward.

"Burn it," said Apollo, shaking with pain and rage.

"That's messy brother," said Artemis, wrapping an arm around him. "The neighbours. That would be too many bodies."

He pushed her off and sneered up at Bathala.

"Burn it to the ground, Underling. Now!"

Bathala nodded and his team walked toward the building.

"I think we should go," said Izzy.

"No, I want to see that demon burn," said Apollo. Artemis helped him to his feet and again cradled his wounded body.

Izzy, Yemoja, Lilith and I set out to find wine. The piteous deed was done but the party still pulsed. Our moods had need of cheering.

37

DISCUSSIONS

"Don't do that again," said Bernard as I tipped the taxi driver in front of Vivienne's establishment.

"I was perfectly safe."

"You were captured and almost killed not fifteen hours ago."

"Not killed, entombed, that's different."

"M," said Vivienne, "just shut up and get inside."

She was angry. It wasn't the anger that begged for levity, so I demurred.

I went for the kitchen. While the opium ensured I was never hungry for anything but it, I still tried to consume what I could. I started a pot of coffee and poured a generous amount of cream into a large cup.

"M," said Bernard. "That's Del's body you're risking. I'm here to make sure that body is taken care of. I'll lock you up myself if I have to."

"Please, warden, don't."

"M, enough," said Viv. "What were you doing anyway? Why go out?"

The percolator began to bubble on the gas range.

"Two days, Viv," I said, trying to temper my frustration. "I was locked in that basement for two days. I've been bound to this body for five. I was tied up last night. The last thing I want to do is stay holed up here."

"It's better than being entombed," she said.

"Yes." She wasn't wrong. "It is, but I have as much chance of being seen through a window here as I do the window of a moving taxi."

"That's a bullshit argument and you know it," said Bernard.

"I'm sober right now. I can block my mind."

"But they know your face, Del's face," said Bernard, sitting at the long table in the kitchen.

"They do. You're correct. But a skinny brown-haired man under a big hat in a Parisian taxi doesn't exactly stand out."

"M," said Vivienne, "if you're going to stay here, you need to stay here. If you run off alone again, leave for good."

"Viv…"

"No, I'm not going to risk my artisanes, my business, Jacques, or myself just so you can stroll alone."

"Fair point."

The percolator was boiling steadily now.

I used a rag to grip the metal handle and poured the hot liquid into my cup of cream. I took down a second cup. "Bernard?"

He gave a curt nod but said nothing. I filled it, then handed it over.

"Viv?" I asked.

She stared at me as if she could not believe my gall. What did she expect? That I'd be stammering my apologies? She should have known better.

"No," she said, "but Jacques may want one."

"Well, there are cups in the cabinet, I'm going upstairs. Vivienne, can I speak with you in private?"

Jacques grumbled past me as I walked, cup in hand, up to Vivienne's office.

"This is reckless, M," she said as we rounded the first floor.

"Reckless? Yes, but what about harbouring a Spectre?"

"I can send her a telegram and tell her to stay in London if you'd prefer."

"Viv, how can we trust her?"

"I know her, M."

"Do you? How old was she when you sent her to America?"

We crested the stairs and went into her office. She closed the door. "She was three years old."

"And how many times in the last twenty years have you seen the girl?"

Vivienne took a seat at her desk and I took my place on her couch.

"I don't know, ten times perhaps."

"We're trusting our entire future to a woman who you've talked to ten measly times. A woman who has every right to want to see the Mentium burn. That's what you're asking of me."

"I'm not asking a thing, M. I'm giving you an option. What choice do we have? Again, I can send the telegram."

"No," I said, standing with my coffee, "no, just answer me one thing."

"Yes?"

"Will she help us? Truly help us? Or will she watch us burn?"

"She will help me, M. I know she will. She trusts me. The Twins' plan puts me in danger not just you. I need her help. Non-Mentium need her help. She will help us."

"I need to lie down, Viv."

◆ ◆ ◆

Howdy, Marduk.

The voice came from behind me. I sat on my pale stone throne, my hands worrying at the heads of serpents carved into the fronts of the armrests. My mental palace was complete. A city of sandstone stretched before me, surrounded by black. A deep blackness. The black of nothing. I like an organised and uncluttered head.

"Del," I responded, "I have no time for games. I've more pressing matters to devote my mind to."

Aw, does the poor schmuck have problems? Del's disembodied voice continued. This was just another annoyance in an already trying time. *It can't be as bad as being locked inside your own god-damned head by some egg who thinks he can just take what he wants.*

"Leave me, Del."

You've sure fouled up this plan of yours. If I were you—

"You. Are. Not."

I stood and began descending the steps of my ziggurat. I could smell the flowers from my hanging gardens, which, in reality, had only ever been planted terraces.

Yeah, sure, I get it, he continued, *I've got a problem. But I ain't no junkie, okay. I ain't a criminal. I pay for what I get. I've worked hard all my life. Just because I have a problem, that don't erase all the years of learnin' I've had.*

"And what does that equate to?" I said with the sharpness of a spear. "Twenty-four years of learning? Learning what?"

Learnin' that guys like you always think they're the smartest in the room. Guys like you spend so much time, so much energy trying to stay ahead of the game that they don't notice the small stuff.

"And what small stuff have I missed, my oh-so careful detective of the diminutive?"

The voice stopped.

"Too shy to offer your expertise, Del? Hmm?"

Silence. "This is supposed to be your little strategy session, right? Or would you rather pout?"

Del's voice boomed again in my mental sky. *Why don't ya talk it out for yourself? Maybe you'll see what you've missed. I'll let ya know if ya found it.*

"Don't patronise me, prisoner."

I'm not so trapped. I'm not so free either but when a guy like you builds a cage, all those right angles leave a lot of space in between. Creatives like me, we know what to do with space. We operate with curves and squiggles. You're stone and I'm fluid. Fluid knows how to get around.

"The stone weathers the storm, Del."

Not forever! And what's a storm, smart guy? Water. Liquid. Now quit stalling and start talking. The faster you get this right, the faster I get my body back.

I wasn't accustomed to taking orders. Especially not from someone as plebeian as Del. He was right, however. I needed to regain control of my situation. Especially with this Eve on her way.

"Fine," I said, making my annoyance at Del's intrusion plain for my own sake if not for his. "Where should I begin?"

Why don't you come down here and talk to me face to face.

"So first, what's got ya so bent out of shape," he said as I stood in front of his barred bedroom.

"This girl Vivienne has sent for. She shouldn't exist. Involving her is just short of insane." Frustration drove me to pace.

"Well ain't it good news that she does exist? We don't really have other options, right?"

"No, we don't. That's what worries me. There's a reason she's the only one who exists."

"She's going to be pissed at you when you meet her."

"Keen observation, detective. This meeting may never happen. It's up to her to attend. Even if it does take place, nothing may come of it. It most likely will prove fruitless."

"You don't think she'll help?"

"No, she won't help me. Absolutely not. I'll be lucky if she never tries to kill me. Our only hope is that the girl's trust in Vivienne and fondness for all things non-Mentium is enough to convince her."

He sat up and crossed legs. "Okay, so how can she help? How does she fit into your plan?"

"She is the plan. At least she's the core. Disabling the radio is still a priority. Everything falls apart for the Twins if my radio won't work."

"So what exactly will Eve do?"

"I would hope that she would immobilise our enemies as we move to disable the radio."

"Again with the disabling. M, are you stupid? Details, the small stuff. Think about what you have."

"I have nothing, Del. I've lost my body, my place in the Mentium, my lover, everything."

"Don't be so damned grand. Things. You have things. Fine, look," Del said, leaning back on his arms. "I'll spell it out for you. You have the designs, the plans, the measurements to build the radio. You have the most powerful mind you've ever seen coming here, tomorrow. Put that together."

The dawning of the idea was embarrassingly slow. "Build a second signal generator and tap into the system. Let Eve counteract what the Twins do, if we can't disable the machine first. They'll be left impotent. Brilliant."

"Who's brilliant?"

"Del, I have to go and begin planning."

"Schmuck."

THÜRSDAY

12ᵀᴴ JANÜARY

1928

38

PÈRE LACHAISE

I have seen more than my fair share of death, its rites, and the remnants of both. But the cemetery of *Père Lachaise* haunts you with more than its spirits.

It was like a garden, in a way. Even in January, the green of moss adorned the dark stone tombs and concrete gravestones. Life among the dead. The tombs were like limbless trees and we weaved our way through the forest of the dead to meet her.

Bernard, Vivienne, Jacques, and I marched under a menacing grey sky. The real trees within the cemetery possessed limbs that looked like the hands of corpses, reaching to pluck us up and snuff us out. The snow-coated the branches like decaying flesh on bone. It was the perfect kind of day to meet a woman who should, by all counts, be dead.

"How big is this place?" asked Bernard, tightening his burgundy scarf against the biting air that swirled around us.

"Have you never been here, Bernie?" asked Vivienne, stepping closer to him in an elegant stride.

"Never been much for cemeteries. I like to leave the dead in peace."

"And now that you're here, what do think?"

"This place reminds me of one of those fly trap plants. It feels dangerous and you can see that it is, but it's beautiful and draws you in anyway. Once you're there, it wants to keep you."

Jacques stepped on a twig hidden beneath the snow and the resulting crack gave Bernard a start. Vivienne patted his hand.

"Well put. But remember, death is about patience. It comes for us all, but it cannot take us until it's our time. Death, like the fly trap, must be triggered into action. Until then, it remains a passive flower."

"I'll remember that."

"Oh, would you two stop playing poet," I said as we came to yet another crossroads. The dragon was scratching at me yet again.

In truth, *Père Lachaise* was more a city than a forest. Streets and pathways crisscrossed its surface in a manner befitting Dædalus' labyrinth. "Are we close?"

You are. Sixty paces to the right. Twelve left. Then stop... and do not move.

"Did you all hear that?" asked Bernard.

"None of us heard anything," I said. "That was in our minds. All of our minds. She's close." My mind had been closed but somehow, she got in. An ill start.

Vivienne made the right turn and quickened her pace, holding up her skirt to make room for her footfalls. Her black leather boots clicked against the stones and she called back, "Let's not keep my sweet Evie waiting."

Jacques caught up with his mistress and we two followed suit. I spent years goading that man for sport but to be fair, there were few humans who ever did their job more dutifully and with more precision than Jacques.

After the final twelve paces, we came to rest near the tomb of Molière. High mausoleums surrounded us and between the pawing trees, the looming tombs and the oppressive sky, a feeling of claustrophobia settled over us.

Don't move and don't speak, said a woman's voice.

How are you doing this? I asked. *How are you in my mind?*

Marduk, I'm a 'Spectre'. You have no idea of what I can do.

From behind, the creak of a time-battered wrought iron door rang out. We turned in unison to see a petite woman with hair the colour of cedar wood step from her position within a tomb. She wore a heavy purple overcoat and a matching cloche on her head. A bright red scarf wrapped her neck. Her face was stone and her eyes were fixed on me.

"Evie!" said Vivienne rushing the young woman. Her demeanour softened as Vivienne's arms wrapped her.

"Auntie Viv! It has been too long." Eve squeezed Viv for a second hug. "I should be visiting you more often now that I'm close."

"You are close," I said, "and hidden. Why?"

"You don't get to ask any questions yet. And Don't think me a fool."

"I beg your pardon."

"I know what this is about you piece of shit. I'm only here because Auntie Viv asked. If you want my help, you'll keep your trap shut until I'm done with my own questions."

"Fair enough."

She was full of fire. I liked her immediately. I feared her, there was no doubt of that, but I liked her. When in the company of a predator, its ability to destroy you makes it no less impressive.

Our group stood in a circle in the middle of the small cobblestone walk. Our breath rose in puffs of small cloud. A ring of train engines idly steaming away. The clean smell of the snow mixed with the musk of moss and earth and I greedily took in its fragrance. Nature provides the best perfumes.

"Hello miss, it's good to meet you," said Bernard extending his hand. "You're American?"

"Please, call me Eve, and yes I'm American. At least, that's where I was raised." She was warm but untrusting as she shook his hand. Like a business meeting more than a social call, which was exactly what this was.

"So," I said, restraining my impatience, "you mentioned questions and I am eager to provide answers."

"Are you?" she asked, the social niceties draining from her. "Fine. First question. Will you try to kill me once you're done using me?"

"Evie," said Vivienne, "that's not—"

"I know, Auntie, it's not you I mistrust. What you would never do is very different from what his kind would 'never' do. So, will you try to kill me?"

I couldn't contain my smile. I really liked her. Right to the points of contention. Blunt. Efficient. "No, I won't. I make no promises for the future but for the time being, you are perfectly safe and, assuming we all survive the coming task, you'll be allowed to walk free."

"Allowed. How generous of you. Remember that I said try. Also remember that I was raised by your kind. I know you inside and out, Marduk. Your allowance isn't necessary."

"I fear no one, child."

"Coyote said as much."

"So it's true then. That traitorous bastard really did raise you."

"He did, as did others. You have no idea how strong they've grown."

"And frankly, I don't care at this point. What I care about is accomplishing our goal. Now, ask those questions."

Eve stepped forward across our little chat circle. Vivienne reached for her and Bernard took a step back. She stopped inches from my face, a feat achievable only due to Del's short stature.

"I don't ask. I take." She dove into my mind with a force I'd never before felt. I was at her whim as if I were a simple Mono. I loathed the feeling. Helplessness is a disgusting thing and I'd had more than I could stomach in the preceding days.

I turned inward myself, standing atop my newly-constructed mental ziggurat. I looked to the horizon in all directions. The black sky was barren, the sweeping sands were desolate. I peered behind every palm and through the streets of the markets below. She was nowhere and everywhere. I could sense her presence, feel her reading memories and studying me but could not see her. She was a ghost.

I felt odd sensations flash within me then she appeared, inches from me, her eyes locked on mine.

"Disgusting," she said, then vanished.

The process lasted seconds. Her power was immense. She withdrew, and I followed her back into the real world.

"Not interested," she said and turned to Vivienne, giving her a tight hug and another to Jacques.

"But Eve, just hear us out," said Vivienne.

Eve shook Bernard's hand once again, then turned to me. "This radio, the one you built with your own hands, it will destroy the Mentium," she said, the words rolling atop a stifled laugh. "You really expect me to help you stop them from committing group suicide? I'd rather sit back and watch you scum burn. The Twins are even more careless than Coyote described. Honestly, I hope your plan fails miserably."

"Evie, wait. This is important," said Vivienne, reaching toward Eve.

"Auntie, this is a waste of time. I'm not sure why you thought I'd help but I won't. I won't help a butcher like him."

"But what about the rest of us? There are innocent people who are going to get hurt. A lot of people will die."

"The death of the Mentium is more important."

She turned and stalked off into the sea of stone. Vivienne opened her mouth to speak but instead lowered her head.

"M, I'm sorry. I thought..." Vivienne looked both shocked and saddened. We needed Eve. We all knew it.

"Vivienne, please, it's not your fault. Expecting a Spectre to assist a member of the Mentium had little chance of success. I..."

Bernard stomped forward and trudged headlong into the tombs. He was going after Eve.

"Bernie, she's not the type to change her mind," said Vivienne but he paid no attention. He only increased his pace.

"Oh, this should be good." I said. "Wait here."

I left Vivienne and Jacques and began darting tomb to tomb but gave that up as Bernard never once looked back. His focus was forward.

"What do you want?" asked Eve. Her voice carried, disturbing one of the resident ravens that picked at the ground for grubs and worms.

I wanted to enter Bernard's mind to watch the interaction but assumed Eve would detect me. So I squatted behind a headstone to listen.

"Miss, please. You have to help. This is about more than M and his cronies."

"It's Eve, and this is all about them. It's always about them."

"No, please, hear me out."

"There's nothing to hear. Look, you seem like a decent guy. Just let it all go. There's nothing you can do."

"I have to do something. M's inside my best friend and apparently my whole world is about to turn sour so, yeah, I have to do something."

The freezing rain intensified, soaking through my jacket.

"Look, it's cold," she said, "I've got to go."

"Please, Eve, just hear me out. This is important. Look, I'm freezing too. How about I buy us some coffee. Give me a few minutes. We talk, we warm up, and you make your decision then. Sound fair?"

"I already know what's happening. I don't need an explanation."

"Okay, then let me add some context."

"Context and coffee," she said. "I'll take some coffee."

I reached out with my mind and sent word back to Vivienne telling her I was going to be longer than expected and to meet me back at her place.

"Do you want my help?" she asked through the aether.

"No, I think Bernard might just be our best hope."

39

CAFÉ

I followed them to a small cafe opposite the western wall of *Père Lachaise* though I stayed inside the cemetery, huddled inside an unlocked tomb. The sleet fell even harder and I pulled my knees in close to my chest, hands tucked into my jacket and chin buried in my scarf.

Now that I was comfortable, I searched for someone within the cafe to use as spy. A lone man sat, pen in hand, writing in a notebook with a cooling *chocolat chaud* on the table in front of him.

He was positioned behind Eve at a shallow angle. The pair had taken off their jackets and Eve's heavy jumper and thick wool skirt, both beige, flared a pang of jealousy within my freezing body.

He's gonna do it, ya know, said Del.

"I hope for all our sakes, you're right."

From my vantage point inside the writer's head I could see Bernard ordering his drink but Eve's face was obscured. It would have to do.

"Eve, look, I understand why you don't trust him. You have every right not to," said Bernard once the waiter left them.

"You don't understand. Do you know what it's like to be hunted just for being who you are?"

"No, not hunted, but I do know what it's like to be born into a world that looks at you as different. As dangerous. I do know how that feels."

"Shit, okay," she said, looking out the large plate window and playing with the end of her necklace, a simple gold chain with an opal as a charm.

"Sorry. Look, even if I wanted to help, it wouldn't make any sense. I've spent my entire life dreaming about the collapse of the Mentium. Why would I want to do anything to stop that from happening? What they're planning is crazy. They'll be the hunted ones. They'll be the victims of their own hubris. That's a very satisfying end if you ask me."

"There's more at stake than that. You have to know that. The war that M talks about, the one that's going to bring down the Mentium, well, a lot of us Monos that are going to die in that war. This plan of theirs, killing off heads of state, that's going to throw everyone for a loop. Sure, we may come out on top but what kind of life will we have afterward? If this plan succeeds, it's going to be more than the Mentium who crumble, the world will crumble. Society will crumble."

"A society built by the Mentium, manipulated by the Mentium, and controlled by the Mentium. Why preserve that?"

"Because a house, even if it's broken, can be fixed."

"Isn't it easier to just build a new house?"

"Only if everyone works together to build it. Think about the world we live in. Do you really see that happening? A junk roof over your head is better than nothing."

Their drinks came, café crème for both, and Eve took a long, slow sip. Bernard stirred in his sugar and stared into the steaming cup.

The silence hung until Eve finally spoke. "Tell me, why are you involved in this? You're a regular person. No abilities. No ties to any of this. Why are you working with him?"

"My friend is in there."

"In where?"

"In M, I mean Del. Look, the body that M is using, that's my best friend, Del. The thing is, Del is still inside too. He wasn't kicked out or whatever happens when they take someone over. M jumped out of his old body and just ended up in Del. It wasn't his choice. He found out that Del was somehow still there. M has him stored away in his subconscious. He says it's to keep him safe but I'm not sure I buy it. Please. If nothing else, help me get my friend back. He didn't deserve to lose himself. Please help."

"Bernie, I..."

"Wait, you were just in his head. Did you see Del? Is he all right?"

"I don't know. I didn't go into the subconscious. I'm sorry. I had no idea."

"I need my friend back. At first, helping M was the only way to make that happen. If the Mentium catch M, they catch Del too. But it's more than that now. If the Mentium's plan goes through, we may all end up dead anyway. We need to save each other. Like you said, they're done for either way. I'm fighting to make sure the rest of us don't lose as well."

Both took another long sip.

"And I'd be doing what exactly?" she asked.

"It depends on what happens. Mostly we need you for protection. M, also wants to build you a machine of your own so you can stop whatever the Twins do."

"He'll put me into his radio to stop them?"

"If it comes to that."

Eve looked to her coffee, tapping one finger on its side. She followed this with a shift of position in her chair, a look up at the ceiling and finally the faintest curl of her mouth. I couldn't believe what I was seeing. Bernard had done it. Even before she spoke, her body language gave her away.

Attaboy! See? Told ya he'd do it, said Del as our body swelled with pride. This time, we shared the emotion.

"Okay, Bernie, okay. But make no mistake. I'm not doing this for Marduk. I'm doing it because you're right. This is about more than the Mentium."

40

WHISPERS

After Bernard's victory in the café, I chose to walk back to Vivienne's. The brisk winter wind bit at my face as I trudged down *Boulevard de Belleville*. There is precious little I would enjoy less than working with a person who not only had the power to end me, but also reason to.

She was, however, a necessity. Trustworthy? That was an entirely different question. I defaulted to Vivienne's wisdom on that front. Still, despite it all, I did very much like Eve's spirit.

Adult versions of Spectres were not entirely new to me. We had discovered one individual in the remote foothills of the *Pyrénées* at the turn of the last millennium. The illiterate brute had run Cernunnos through with a scythe, and had tried to rip me from my body and fling my own consciousness into the aether. If not for Lilith's skill with a crossbow, none of us would have survived.

All of that chaos and injury was wrought by the power of one untrained, unrestrained ogre. Eve was none of those things.

Thanks to the Reformed, she was fully aware of her own abilities. Aware and trained and skilled in their use. We'd never dealt with anyone like her and there I was recruiting her to battle my own brethren. The thought chilled me, but I had no recourse.

I continued my frigid walk but detoured to *Parc de Belleville* where I took up residence on a wet, though snow-free bench, wrapping my scarf over my nose and pulling my hat low. Only my eyes were exposed and my mind was blocked. I was alone.

Patches of grass had emerged from the melting blanket of snow, a fitting allegory for the changing minds of the Monos. How could the Mentium not see? The Monos were reaching a point of enlightenment that far surpassed the so-named era. This awakening ran deep. The scepticism that was so easily controlled in the past now swept the populace like a virus. The plague of knowledge was infecting even the lowliest of classes. Gods? No, we would be tyrants insulting their intelligence.

The frontal assault proposed by the Twins was foolhardy. A flanking manoeuvre at the Monos' fears and insecurities was the far better option. It was the option that worked, and it was the option my radio was intended to strengthen.

Above the bulk of my scarf, I noticed a boy of fourteen or fifteen walking toward me. He sat beside me on the bench without asking.

"Good day, Marduk." he said, his eyes fixed on mine.

"Ah, a proxy. Very good," I said. There was no need to show the unease that gripped me. Speaking through random intermediaries was a common Mentium tactic and it appeared that I had been found. "With whom do I have the pleasure of speaking? Friend or foe?"

"If I were foe, there'd be no use for a disguise, would there?" the person in the boy said. "Tell me, was my letter plain enough to understand?"

"Quite, though the style was a bit dramatic. The mass hysteria via mass hallucination goes on as planned with the addition of governmental murders. Do I have that right?"

"You do."

"The ignorance and arrogance are staggering."

"That's why I am with you."

"Are you? If you were truly with me, you'd give me more than a letter and an escape. How do I know you aren't just toying with me?"

"I'm not toying with you, Marduk. I'm allowing your strategy, whatever it may be, to play out while I work on my own. A two-pronged attack."

"Why the subterfuge? Why not join with me? We can still move forward with both strategies. Who are you?"

"I know you, Marduk, and you know me. I know your skills and I know you can be a bit hasty. Revealing myself now is foolhardy. I have too much work yet to do, though, I have no doubt we will succeed in the end."

"Thank you for the ego stroking but what I really need is information."

"I'll give you what I can, when I can. No more, no less. This is a dangerous game we're playing."

"This is no game," I said, glaring into the placid, unaffected face of the boy. "This is our livelihood we are talking about. Our way of life."

"That's dead. You must see that. There's no turning back. The crack in the Mentium is irreparable. There's been a hole in our boat and we've been bailing water for a long time. It's now a fissure. Our boat needs dry dock, an overhaul. When we succeed, a restructuring will be necessary. One we can achieve together."

"Together?"

"Of course. We are on the same side, Marduk. We haven't faced a challenge of this importance in ages. Relish it."

"That's an interesting take."

"It's the proper outlook. Melancholia is unproductive. The life of immortals is so difficult to excite. This is exciting. I'll contact you soon."

"That's it? No new information?"

The boy stood and strode off toward the wrought iron gate of the park. I stood as well but did not follow. Whoever this friend was, they not only knew me, but knew whose body I was in and with the information they had access to, they were certainly of the Upper Echelon.

Ma'at was in the wind. She had the most freedom to move but returning to the temple would prove dangerous for her. My associates from the train were gone but what does gone mean when you have the time and means to travel anywhere? Or could it be Tian? I'd managed a transference under duress. Could he have been fast enough?

No, Tian was gone, I had to accept that just as I had to accept the aid of this so-called ally, whoever they may be.

41

NEW ACCOMMODATIONS

Through Jacques' eyes, I saw the door to Madame Vivienne's salon grow close. Eve and Bernard walked ahead. We'd already made one additional trip to Del and Bernard's apartment to retrieve a few forgotten items. Aided by Eve of course. Her mental-blocking abilities were both astounding and useful. Jacques gathered our things undetected. Once we returned, Bernard and Jacques had volunteered to help Eve move her things from her hotel. They had returned to the salon more heavily burdened then I would have thought.

Our girl didn't seem the flapper type; her hair was past her shoulders and her style was far from avant-garde, but two steamer trunks was quite a haul for such a petite woman.

I descended the spiral walnut staircase from my new room on the third floor near Vivienne's office. Bernard had settled into the room across from mine. As I passed each floor, the muted sounds of convivial business leaked beneath closed doors and the decidedly unmuted chatter of silk-robed businesswomen met my ears. They weren't sure how our presence would affect profits.

My feet hit the main floor and I placed a few drops of laudanum under my tongue. It did little for my wants but dulled my needs. The trio entered and the click of Vivienne's boots echoed down the stairs followed by her voice.

"Oh, Evie, it's so good to have you back in this house."

"Auntie, I was just here in August."

August. My utter irritation was impossible to contain.

You can be irritated all you want, said Eve into my mind. *Your opinions don't bother me in the least.*

Our two luggage handlers set her trunks down and Jacques closed the front door to both the cold and any prying eyes. Bernard untied his burgundy scarf and wiped sweat from his brow.

"I know it was only August," said Vivienne, "but that doesn't mean I have to like our time apart."

"I was in America for fourteen years."

"Too long. These last two years have been so nice."

I still couldn't believe my ears. One thinks they know their friends…

"How many times have you seen her? You said it had only ever been ten times."

"Enough," said Eve. "You'd have hunted me down and slit my throat. Do you really think she would have told you? I wouldn't have taken you for an idiot." Her sharp American accent added a staccato to each word that felt like a finger poking my chest.

"Touché, young one."

"Spare me, man-child."

Oh, she's a keeper, M. I gotta say, I'm lookin' forward to watching you two work together.

Shut up, Del.

"I believe you are referring to this particular body. Remember, I've lived longer than the words you spit at me."

"Can we go?" she asked.

"Of course. You're on the top floor near my office and chambers."

By that, she meant in the room next to Bernard.

"Gentlemen, if you'd be so kind as to bring the trunks…"

The ladies started up the stairs. I turned to Bernard and Jacques with a smirk.

"After you, gentlemen."

"Why don't you give it a shot, M. I don't mind," said Bernard with a touch of venom. Jacques just glared at me with his usual silent hate.

I think I detected a few added wrinkles on his furrowed brow.

"Alas, dear Bernard. As you have pointed out many times, I'm in Del's body and therefore must take care of it as if it were my own." I flexed Del's thin arms. "I don't think these are trunk worthy."

"Fine," he said and lifted the steamer with an exaggerated grunt. Both hands straining at the handles. Jacques picked his up and placed it under one arm and the three of us ascended.

To my absolute delight, Bernard's bashfulness had not diminished. As we passed each floor his gaze was on nothing but the top of the trunk in front of him. Vivienne's artisanes liked Bernard. He was a genuine fellow who was both respectful and kind, but being shy and a bit prudish, the women took to a brand of subtle teasing that can only be achieved by the fairer sex. Watching this game was a delight.

I stepped close to Bernard, who was sandwiched between Jacques and myself as we climbed. Floor two held Simone, a sinfully funny artisane who relished in teasing Bernard almost as much as I enjoyed watching her do it. This time as we passed, she turned with the grace of an expert dancer and called out to Bernard. As her body twisted, I noticed her hand gently tug at the lower hem of her robe. One small breast said hello as the silk slid to the side.

"Hiya Bernie, didn't know you were so strong."

Bernard looked over then snapped his gaze back to the trunk. "Uh, thank you. Thanks. It's not that heavy."

Poor guy needs to lighten up. Been sayin' it for years.

On that, Del, we can agree.

We continued our ascent and as we rounded the corner, I shot Simone a knowing wink that garnered a broad smile and wink in return.

"Over here, Evie. This will be your room," said Vivienne from above. By the time we reached the upper floor, the women had already retreated to Vivienne's office. Jacques and Bernard continued into Eve's new room, and I marched straight toward the bar in Viv's office.

"So," I said, pouring myself a generous glass of Lagavulin, "you're here. I appreciate that."

"You're frightened of me," she said in response.

"Naturally, though I'm intrigued as well. I haven't come across an adult of your variety in quite some time."

"M, honestly, 'your variety'? Don't you have one of those silly new Mentium names for Evie's kind?" asked Vivienne.

"No. There's no need since—"

"Why update the name of murdered children, right? Calling us Spectres is as accurate as it gets," spat Eve.

"Yes, correct."

Vivienne stood from her desk and her blank face was a poster of the awkward air in the room. She took a place next to me at the bar, pouring herself a cognac. "Anything for you, Evie?"

"Lagavulin, neat, if you have it."

"A woman after my own heart."

"Jesus, you don't stop? I'm here to do a job. Just because you benefit doesn't mean I'm on your side."

Viv handed the drink to Eve and elbowed me before picking up her own.

"M, sit down if you must stay, otherwise let us catch up in peace."

"Oh, no, I'd love to stay. I'd like to attempt some of those questions I wasn't able to ask at *Père Lachaise*."

"I'll allow it." Oh, how she loved to bare her teeth. I ignored the barbs, growing tired of her game.

"So, let's begin with something simple," I said. "Where did Coyote raise you? I know it was in the US but I'm curious as to what area."

"Oh, look at the detective trying to be cunning. First of all, I'd never tell you where he is, or any members of the Reformed for that matter. Second, it would do you no good even if I did. We move around a lot. I have good memories from all over but I've never had a home to speak of."

"Well you've always had a family. I hope you know that," said Vivienne.

"I do, Auntie. I do."

"Very well, how about another? How have you been spending your time in Europe? Is that a fair question?"

She took a short sip of her whisky and leaned back into the couch.

"No, but I'll answer. I've been in and around Europe for the past five years. The first three years were spent moving around the continent though I've settled into London as of late."

"And whereabouts have you journeyed?"

"I've been around. Think of it as a grand tour of the capitals of Europe. London has been one of my longer stays."

"Why so many moves?"

"Practice. I came with clothes, and some personal stuff but not much else. Becoming self-sufficient was the main theme of my trip. Coyote wanted me to make a life for myself before coming back into the fold."

"Trip? So you plan on going back then?"

"Of course, once I feel my task is complete."

"And that task?"

What's with the third degree, M? Ease up would ya? You might spook her. Good.

"Self-sufficiency, like I said. I've learned to get by on my own. Now I'm just honing the craft."

"Self-sufficiency? Ha! The lure of power affects your kind as well as mine. I'm assuming some forms of criminality are paramount in your strategy for self preservation?"

"Yep. A lady has to eat."

"And kill?"

"M, what kind of a question is that?" asked Vivienne, stepping away from the bar to join Eve on the couch.

"A valid one, I think. Lives may be lost in the coming conflict and we may need to take some of those lives. I need to know how Eve chooses to wield her powers."

"Well, if the question is 'have I killed' then the answer is yes. If the question is, 'will I kill who you tell me to?' then the answer is maybe. I kill who I need to kill. I'll figure that out on my own."

"You know, in order for this to succeed, we need to work as a team."

She rolled her eyes. "I'm well aware of that but I gotta wonder whether you have any experience with teamwork."

"I've worked within the Mentium for—"

"That's just it," she said, waving her glass at me, "you've worked within the Mentium not with them. All you selfish bastards have your own agendas. Your little social club is only there to serve your individual goals. Money and power are the glues that bind. That's not teamwork, that's survival."

"That's quite the generalisation. So, the Reformed, ex-Mentium let's not forget, taught you teamwork?"

"Yes."

"Laughable."

"M, enough. Evie has barely had a chance to sit since she arrived. Give us some time to settle in. Please?"

Had to push it didn't ya, M, said Del.

No, but I did. Yet another loss of control.

"Of course, Viv. There will be a meeting in one hour."

42

BRASS TACKS

"Blow it up. Just blow the damned thing up!" said Bernard in a tone that oozed with disgust. Off a duck's back and all that, but the insinuation stung more than it should have.

He's right, M. Blow it to smithereens, said Del

"Seriously M, he's right," said Viv, sitting at her large walnut desk. The rest of us were scattered around her office as if there was some repulsive force keeping us at a maximum distance. Her words stung too. I didn't want to hear any of it.

"It's by far the best option. It eliminates the possibility of—"

"It eliminates years of work! No. I won't destroy my radio. Remember, all of you, we are not out to ruin the Mentium. The Twins are doing a bang-up job of that on their own. We are simply here to remove them and of course, preserve normalcy for the rest of you."

"You selfish bastard," said Eve. Her disdain dripped like candle wax.

"Yes, excellent observation. Perfect deduction. Have you been reading Christie?"

"Stop it!" Bernard's voice boomed with authority. Had he been able to muster a voice like that with Del? "We need to get this ironed out. We only have four days until they unleash this thing. M, tell us again just what the hell this new plan of theirs is."

I walked past him to the bar and poured more than a double, Laphroaig this time. I dosed myself with a long sip then turned back toward the group. "Very well. I'll make this plain. Their plan hasn't changed. There are simply additional elements that I hadn't anticipated."

"Why not?" asked Eve.

"Because, child, I had more respect for my kind. I didn't realise how deluded the Twins truly were. The others, those that remain plus an army of Underlings, seem to be just as drunk on the idea of this return to form. But this won't make them gods again. No more than a Dane donning an iron helm becomes a Viking."

"M, their plan, it's essentially visions causing murder?" prompted Viv.

"Yes. Step one, the original strategy, was to broadcast visions of classical monsters and demons into the heads of the populace via my radio. Along with those artificial visions, people would see each other as demons and lash out to protect themselves. This makes real carnage, thus substantiating the existence of these fictional monsters. The event was scheduled for the same date as the League of Nations meeting so that heads of state would be on hand to not only view the devastation but also witness the salvation by gods first-hand. Now, they plan to use the same tactic meant for pedestrians on those very heads of state, causing them to kill each other and thus, decapitating dozens of countries. They believe the power vacuum will make their takeover even easier, which greatly underestimates the logic of the people."

"Thanks for the vote of confidence," said Bernard. "This is just nuts."

"It very much is. These next steps are clearly an attempt to add credence to the need for the gods to return. I'm assuming this latest addition is Lilith's work, though I find it a trifle beneath her abilities."

"Speaking of your lady dearest," said Eve. "What do we do with her?"

"Leave Lilith to me."

"I'd rather not. Conflict of interest, don't ya think?"

"You will not touch her," I said.

Jacques stood next to Eve where she sat, one leg tucked beneath her on the couch. The brute said nothing, of course, but he watched my every move.

"Give me some credit," I said. "She won't go unpunished I can assure you."

"No, you can't."

"It's not up for debate."

"Nor is the fact you're compromised. You worry about trusting me? You're clearly more of a liability than I am."

She ain't wrong, buddy. You're pretty twisted up about all this.

I'm fine.

Vivienne clapped. "Let's get back to the matter at hand. We're not supposed to be fighting each other."

Bernard poured himself another drink. A logical move. My people, the Persians of old, would debate a topic once drunk and once sober to ensure a sound course of action. Our limited time would only allow this one evening, so drunk deliberation it was.

"So," said Bernard, "you say that people are going to start seeing things, like that gargoyle and the gryphons we saw? What else can we expect?"

"I can't predict their projections but it's safe to assume that something like a kraken emerging from the Seine and dragons raining fire from the sky will be involved. It will certainly contain that sort of fairy-tale drama. The monsters will, in general, be recognisable to the population. That recognition is important. Our minds jump straight to fear when the monsters are known. Familiar fears have always been the most useful."

"And how is that supposed to make us accept them as gods?" asked Vivienne.

"The knight that slays the dragon gets the love of the princess and the respect of the kingdom. Remember, there's yet another reason why familiarity is key. The monsters they'll employ have been described as real by the religions of the masses for centuries, millennia in some cases. In the beginning, these monsters were real. At least in their minds. We used to broadcast that drivel all the time. It was our bread and butter. Disbelievers will repent in a heartbeat if demons come for them now. At least until they stop to think. Which will take longer than you'd hope."

The room grew silent. I took up residence in the overstuffed armchair across from Eve and Bernard. I threw a leg over the arm and swirled the scotch in my glass.

"This mess has me drinking more than I'd like," said Bernard, looking into another glass of red wine.

"Switch to stronger stuff. You'll feel numb faster," I said.

"So," said Viv as she stepped around her desk for her own top-off, "how do we stop them, M?"

"That is the question. Our two-part plan still seems to be the best course of action. Disable the radio, our old plan B, will now be our primary objective. That can't happen until the night before the League of Nations meeting. We need them to be delayed for as long as possible. In the meantime, our new plan B is to build a small secondary chamber for Eve. If we can't stop them from using my radio, then we have to stop them while they're using it."

"So let me get this straight," said Eve. "I'm on guard duty while you break the radio. If that won't work, you hook me up and I disrupt their transmissions."

"Something like that. You'll be in charge of counteracting anything they broadcast. I think you will be more than up to the task."

"So, tit for tat," she said, going for the decanter. Everyone in the room had been taking turns at the bar.

"Essentially. At least until the rest of us can get to my lab and subdue them. Then, it will be up to you to put things right."

"I like it," she said.

"You do?" asked Viv.

"Sure, it's about time this schmuck realised just what I can do. Should be a piece of cake."

"Now I'm worried," I said.

"Don't be. So, what's next?"

The heroine angle delighted Eve and there was no way I was going to slow this new-found momentum by pulling her head from the clouds. It would be anything but a piece of cake. Even for her.

"What about the rest of us?" asked Bernard. "And what about this ally you have in the Mentium?"

"Our ally contacted me this morning on my walk back from *Père Lachaise.* They promise aid but refuse to be forthright about what the aid will consist of and how that aid will come."

"They're playing with you," said Eve.

"Yes."

"You people are disgusting."

"Noted. Now, we cannot count on specific help from our ally. We move forward as if no help will come and adjust once it arrives."

Bernard sat forward on the sofa. "Okay, so your plan leaves yourself, me, Vivienne, and Jacques without roles after the initial sabotage. What do we do?"

"You will be helping Eve," I said. "Jacques and I will be entering the Temple of the Mentium and Vivienne will be our eyes and ears, or more accurately, Eve's eyes and ears above ground. Our second signal generator will be in the catacombs. Viv will keep you informed of who's coming for you. "

"You have to be joking," said Bernard.

"He's not," said Eve, staring into her cup and again swirling its contents.

"It's not a bad plan," said Vivienne. "I'll have to find the proper vantage point."

"There's a cafe with excellent coffee and better cognac very near the site where I wish to build. I think you'll be comfortable."

"I have to say, I'm actually excited," Viv said.

"So, when do we start?" asked Eve.

"Tomorrow morning, my dear. The Twins are the root of evil within the Mentium. Removing them will be sweet. You couldn't ask for a better chance for vengeance."

"My life's about more than vengeance, though I won't lie, it'll feel good to see those bastards squirm."

"Remember, I want them incapacitated, not killed."

"Just like your radio and your Lilith?"

"Just like my radio but not Lilith. The Twins will be entombed, by my own hand if I can help it, and I'll care for their bodies for the rest of those lives. I want to be present for that suffering."

"Bernard headed for the window. "We're sitting here talking about murder and torture as if it were something normal. You realise that, don't you?" He was glowering down at the snow-covered sidewalk.

"It's normal for us," said Eve before I could add my own rebuttal. "The act is as quick and as easy as you make it. It's living with the act that's the challenge."

"Challenge? That's it? It's just some challenge?"

"No, not really. Not anymore."

FRIDAY

13TH JANUARY

1928

43

RECONNAISSANCE

"You sure we're supposed to be here?" asked Bernard as he, Eve, and I stood outside a nondescript iron door in a nondescript wall made from the pale stone for which Paris is known.

"Of course we aren't, but who's going to stop us? No one is guarding the door and it's six in the morning."

"What about your Mentium buddies? Doesn't that Izzy guy know about this entrance?"

I rifled through my collection of keys and smirked.

"Izzy likes to think he knows all but I've only ever fed him half rations. It rarely behooves a person to divulge all their secrets. As far as Izanagi is concerned, there are exactly eight entrances to the catacombs." I found the correct key and, with effort shook it into the rusted lock. A little more effort and a satisfying click, and the door was unlocked.

"Eight? How many are there really?"

"I've found twenty-three but I'd wager the number is much higher."

"That's unbelievable."

"Bernard, have you ever been into the catacombs?"

"No. I mean, you showed them to me back at our place but never in real life."

"Well, I have a feeling the word 'unbelievable' is going to be your phrase du jour. Now, in we go." I pulled open the heavy door and we three stepped into the dark.

Aside from studying our future workspace, Eve had the additional task of playing bodyguard. She took on the responsibility of keeping Bernard's mind closed to others and masking our faces in the minds of passersby. It would have been tiring for me but Eve insisted it was simple.

Bernard reached into the shoulder satchel he carried and handed out three electric torches. The trio of beams swung through the dank, dusty air.

"How deep does this go?" asked Eve.

"About one hundred-odd steps."

As we descended a rough stairwell cut out of the limestone, the echoes of distant drips fought with those of our footsteps. The steady hiss our breathing was cut by the incessant calling of rodents — a strange music within those expansive subterranean halls.

When we reached the bottom, a new sound echoed off the walls. Bernard's gasp caught in his throat as his light swept across the wall and he caught his first glimpse of the tenants.

"Those are…"

"Yes. Those are the bones." I shone my own light on the wall. "Just like in the visions."

The word 'wall' is a bit of a misnomer. The pathways leading throughout the catacombs were lined with pillars. Between these pillars were stacks of bones. These stacks were carefully built, often geometric, even artistic in design. The exterior face consisted of mostly femurs and skulls in stripes, shapes, and patterns. The skulls were what brought us there.

Eve gaped as well, as our torches swept across the remains of hundreds. There were more than six million in total within those retired mine shafts.

"You've not been here either," I said.

"No," she said, studying a moss-eaten skull.

"This way."

I led them further into the quarry-turned-mass-tomb. My light stayed steady on the ground ahead while Bernard swung his about, taking in the scene. It was good. I needed him sharp before we set about our task.

Unfortunately, my own head had begun its tailspin toward uselessness. My last taste of opium was but a memory and, depressingly, I would have to appease the dragon soon if I was to function.

"Stop."

Bernard started a bit at my voice but collected himself and added his light to mine as I checked the map. Eve surveyed our location with her own light.

"You both realise it's Friday the thirteenth, don't you?" said Bernard, pointing the torch at us.

"Get that out of my eyes," I said.

"You're not superstitious are you Bernie?" asked Eve.

"No, I'm not superstitious, but what are the odds?"

"There." I pointed toward the crossroads ahead. "We need to go left. There should be a gasoline generator twenty paces down. That's our first destination. That's where we'll build."

I sent Bernard on ahead and let some distance grow between us. His light was still swinging wildly and the rapidity of his gait betrayed his fear. Being the kind soul that I am, I reached down and picked up a few stones.

"Stop that," whispered Eve.

I sent one sailing to the left. It skittered across the top of a row of skulls and Bernard's torch darted toward the sound.

"Is somebody down here?" he asked.

"No, no, it was probably a rat."

I sent another rock, again to the left. This time a bit closer to him.

"Jesus, M, do you hear that? Someone's down here with us. Eve, do you sense anyone?"

"Calm yourself, man. You sound like a schoolboy."

Come on man. Lay off would ya?

"It's fine, Bernie. We're alone," said Eve, slapping the remaining rocks from my right hand. I had two more in my left.

M, cut it out. He's got the heebie-jeebies.

Let me have my fun. He's going to experience much worse before all is said and done. I'll stop, I promise. Just one more volley.

As we approached our worksite, I threw one of the remaining rocks against the pile of bones directly to his left. He turned, exposing his back to me and I lobbed the final stone between his shoulder blades. He spun so fast his torch dropped.

Jesus, M, come on.

"What was that? What was that!?" Bernard swatted at his back.

My laughter rolled out. I couldn't contain it. Big, scared adults were pure comedy. What wasn't comedy was how quickly the cravings were coming back. I should have taken more laudanum.

"You asshole."

"Guilty as charged."

"Leave me be. I don't like it down here."

"Just wait," I said, sweeping the scene with my light until I located the generator.

"Wait for what?"

I started the machine and a string of lightbulbs lit the surrounding area. The sheer scale of death was fully illuminated and Bernard's face was a sight to behold. After the initial shock he leaned against a stone column and rubbed the back of his neck.

"Remind me never to die," he said.

"Don't die."

"Thanks."

I waved him over to me and took out the notebook Vivienne had been keeping for me. Eve took a place over my other shoulder. I turned to a section labelled 'schematics'.

"This," I said, "is a junction box for the wiring in the catacombs. There are hundreds down here but this one is important. It's one of the first ten in the series. It's also one of the first that was installed, and it's been tested multiple times."

"So?" asked Eve.

"So, Izzy will have no need to be in this particular chamber. We'll be free to build, in theory."

"In theory?" she asked.

"Well, if anyone gets near, I'm sure you'll let us know."

"I'm not some alarm."

"Well, bark then."

"Now I know how my folks felt when Del and I went at it," said Bernard. "You two need to cut it out."

"Right you are, Bernard. Eve is being juvenile. Let's try to find that junction box." Her glare was priceless.

"I don't see anything," said Bernard, "just the lights and the generator."

"Precisely. The cables running from the main signal generator in Montmartre to the catacombs and again from the catacombs to the tower are large, but so are most of the other cables in the metro tunnels. That's one of the reasons we chose to route our wire though them. To hide them in plain sight."

"Okay, I follow but what does that have to do with the wires here?"

"Excellent question. The large cables are simply a collection of smaller wires. Rather than running the same bulky cable throughout these caverns, we used triple filaments and wove webs. Painted to blend in, of course."

"And the junction box links one web to another?"

"Yes. Step one of our plan will be to disable a number of these junction boxes."

"What number?"

"Five."

"Is that it?" asked Eve.

"Yes. There are five within the network that, once disabled, will route the entire signal though only a small number of webs, thus shorting the system."

"Too much water and the dam bursts," said Bernard.

"Precisely."

"Okay," Eve said, searching the ceiling for the junction box. "Where is this thing?"

"Come with me."

To our right was a low point in the bone wall. I jumped up to a sitting position on the edge, the ball joints of femurs digging into my thin thighs, then turned and began to crawl toward the back wall, the actual stone wall.

"You've got to be kidding me," Bernard said.

"They're dead. They can't hurt you."

"I don't even walk over people's graves let alone crawl all over their bones."

"There's a first time for everything. Now get up here so I can show you what to do. Both of you."

Like a cat in the snow, Bernard gingerly crawled back to where I lay on my side. The sound of knees popping and fabric rustling gently echoed through the tunnels. Eve beat him by several seconds. If only there had been some way to preserve the faces he was making.

"This," I said, pointing to a tar-coated object about the size of a tobacco tin, "is a junction box." I opened its lid and exposed a small bundle of wires painted charcoal grey. "Do you see the connector in the middle?"

"Yeah, should I pull it apart?" asked Eve.

"No."

"No? When?"

"Never. This one needs to remain intact. This is our build site. We'll need to do more hiking in order to find the boxes we want, and that hiking happens Sunday. Remember, we need to wait until the last possible minute."

Bernard rolled onto his back and stared up at the junction box. "Okay but what if they do go through with it? Do we really have enough time to build a new, what'd you call it, signal generator?"

"It has to be enough time. Tomorrow is going to be a long day."

"And if we build this thing," said Bernard, "The Mentium won't be able to detect it?"

"All of the gauges for the radio are located in my lab at the temple. This is downstream. The only thing that will register will be a small power surge when we do our test. We'll have to keep the test small, but I assume Eve will have no problem scaling up when the time comes."

"I can do that. Now, can we get off these dead people?"

44

EVE

The booth at *Le Dôme* was cosy and our lunch was fine, at least I assumed it was fine. I'd ordered onion soup, hoping that some sustenance would make it past the dragon and provide some nourishment. The constipation had returned, and I had no appetite for anything.

It was a luxury to even be out of Vivienne's establishment. I had Eve to thank for that. She not only kept an eye on who may be around but also kept us disguised. She could alter the perception of our faces in other people's minds. It was a feat a Broadcaster could only manage for themselves. While it felt good to be out again, Eve's babysitting tainted the experience.

"You need to eat," said Bernard, sawing at his entrecôte.

"I know that."

"Try harder. Look, I had to do this with Del too. It's more in your head than your body. Just force it down."

"Don't presume to talk to me about goings-on within the mind."

Eve swallowed the forkful of canard she'd been chewing. "Do you ever stop being so dramatic? He's got a mind too, you know. He can have thoughts about how it works just as easily as you."

I managed two spoonfuls of soup and some wine as the meal continued. Bernard and Eve were discussing the banality of everyday life, or rather, banal things they enjoyed in their everyday lives. A Chaplin film, that dreadful bullfight novel from a few years prior, American music, it all seemed endless.

Le Dôme was known for catering to American and British expats and the music playing reflected that. Armstrong's 'Savoy Blues' rang out across the open wood-panelled room.

It was an enjoyable song, not too happy and upbeat, but the cravings had come on strong since that morning and everything dug at my mind.

"Please," I said, leaving my spoon submerged in the soup, "can you two stop yammering on and finish your meals? We've a lot still to do today."

Eve scowled and emptied her gin martini then turned her body toward Bernard, making the slight against me plain. "You know what, Bernie? We have a lot to do. Why don't we get a wiggle on?"

"That sounds like a plan," said Bernard, smiling at the insult.

"Petty," I said, rising and heading toward the counter to pay while they stepped out into that bright afternoon to hail a taxi.

The car rumbled out into the street, narrowly missing another taxi, sending it careening around other vehicles.

"Bernard," I asked, "would you make sure we arrive at Vivienne's? Eve and I need to have a meeting."

"We what?" asked Eve.

"A meeting? Here?" asked Bernard.

"No, here," I said, pointing to my temple.

"Why?" asked Eve.

"Because we need to settle some things."

"Fine."

I did not wait for Bernard's agreement and Eve and I both retreated into my mind.

◆ ◆ ◆

I opened my eyes onto my Babylon from atop my ziggurat. Eve had already arrived and was standing at the foot of the stairs leading to my throne. She appeared exactly the same as she did in the physical world. She'd forgone her outerwear, standing in that day's jumper and skirt ensemble.

"That's quite the get-up you have on, M. I didn't realise it was

Carnevale. Isn't that still a few weeks away?"

"You lack imagination," I said. "And experience. One does get so bored as the centuries go by. We're allowed to make ourselves here. Why not enjoy the crafting?"

"I am who I am. I like this version of me just fine."

"We'll speak again after a few dozen transferences."

"Doubtful."

I stood and began to descend the stairwell, tucking my wings behind me.

"And why would that be?"

"I'm not leaving this body. It's my home and I'm staying put."

My leather sandals slapped against the sandstone steps and echoed through my empty city as did my laughter.

"Walk with me." I said as I passed her.

"Where are we going?"

"Nowhere, I just don't feel like staying stationary."

The two of us started down the main market street in Babylon. I picked a fresh fig from a stall, teeming with fruit. All the storefronts displayed their wares for me. Any item I could desire lay down one of my streets. I need only take what I wanted but what I wanted was opium. The cravings were worsening. I fought the drive to be trite. I had to seem congenial in the face of Eve.

"Try one."

Eve chose a dried plum and nipped at its edge.

"I asked you here to extend an olive branch as it were."

"I like olives."

"Good, try those. The bright green ones."

She followed my pointing finger toward a wooded pot with a mound of herbed and oiled olives. She took one, chewed the flesh from the pit and threw the pit aside.

"Talk, M. I'm not hungry enough for imaginary snacking."

"This way." I turned down a small side street and pushed open a fabric door that led into a room that should not have existed. The ceiling was high and the stone floor was too pale. Then there were the skulls and bones.

"Is this…"

"It's the chamber where we will build our new signal generator. Look."

I pointed off into the far corner and closed the door behind us.

"That, is what we're building."

The exterior of the apparatus did not gleam in the dark of the cavern. It lacked the polished brass of the original. This was a crude device. One large pylon, ringed in green glass, rose from its top. Two small chambers were built into its rectangular iron frame. The only speck of glamour within this machine were the copper helmets.

Eve ran a finger down the side of one.

"So I put this on?"

"Yes, go ahead and enter the chamber if you like. A walk-through might be wise."

Eve stepped inside and leaned back against the sofa cushion that had been secured inside. There would be no time for customisation.

"Now, don the helmet and grip the handles at your sides."

Eve did as instructed. "Why can't I see? Can't you add some eye holes?"

"No. We found we achieved better performance with unbroken construction."

"I suppose that will have to do," she said and removed the helmet.

"What about our run-through?"

She paused and cocked her head for a moment. "I got it."

"Got what?"

"The procedure. I just read your memories. Now, if there's nothing else, I'd like to get back to the real world."

"There is something else."

"Oh, god, what?"

I walked over to her. She was still resting against the chamber's cushion. "I require a promise before we move forward. First an answer, then a promise."

"Now you're expecting promises. Do you really—"

"Please. Only two."

She grumbled and stepped out of the device. "What do you want."

I locked eyes with her because I couldn't get inside that mind for the truth. "Can you do what you say you can? Can you perform when the time comes?"

"Yeah, unlike your kind, I'm no liar. My *performance* will be copacetic."

"Good," I said, still reading her eyes. "Now, I want your word that you won't kill Lilith, Izzy, or the Twins. I want to be the one to dole out punishment. I feel I've earned that right."

"Why should I promise that?"

"No reason. There is no reason you should, but please do. Vivienne trusts me to do what's right. Please, trust her trust and let me."

Eve considered this for a moment, tapping her fingers at her hips. "Fine. But only those four. The rest receive whatever's necessary."

"The key word being 'necessary.'"

"What about this ally of yours?"

"If they haven't revealed themselves by then, well, that will be their mistake."

"Ruthless," she said looking around at our finished work. "All right, you have my word. Can we go now?"

"Thank you."

◆ ◆ ◆

Bernard did a fine job making sure the taxi driver took a direct route. The motorcar pulled up in front of Vivienne's salon and Jacques stood outside at the door. He wore nothing but his shirtsleeves and the ever-present tweed vest. His gorilla arm held an envelope and his face, a frown.

"Are you okay, Jacques?" asked Bernard as he stepped from the taxi.

The big man nodded. As I emerged, he handed me the note and then turned back inside.

"What's it say?" asked Eve, peering over my shoulder.

I pushed inside leaving the two to follow as I fingered under the flap and removed the note. It was a half sheet with an even shorter message.

"What's it say, M? What's happened?" asked Bernard, hanging his hat and jacket by the door.

"Well, it's another damned riddle," I said. The dragon had me in no mood for puzzles.

"Read it," said Eve.

"You've got the letter?" asked Vivienne, coming down the stairs toward us. "Jacques said an elderly gentleman delivered it."

"Yes, yes, the letter," I said with an addict's irritation. "Here it is. It says…" I disliked the words before I could speak them.

"Out with it," said Eve.

"Dark clouds fill the council room. Dark words, the ears of their faithful. Dark deeds are to come. Even darker creatures. Keep your dear ones close."

I threw the paper into the fire and flung my jacket off on the sofa in the sitting room.

"Dark deeds? So something's brewing," said Bernard.

"Yes, something is most certainly brewing but our ally-cat is not done throwing we mice around. I cannot tell if we're toys or prey."

The group gathered around me as I paced until I had nothing left to do but put fists to hips and stew in my own frustration.

"So, what's our play?" asked Eve.

"I say we sit tight until morning," said Bernard. His fists mimicked my own.

"No," I said, retrieving my jacket. "We go shopping."

"Shopping? You can't be serious," said Vivienne.

"I am. We don't have time to wait on ghosts that may never materialise. We build to completion tomorrow. I intend to keep on schedule. Jacques! Come! We need your brawn."

"I'm coming with you," said Bernard, taking up his own jacket.

"Fine. Eve, you come too. Viv, are you all right here?"

She signalled to me and I opened my mind.

Are you sure this is wise? she asked.

It has to be. We have no other choices. At this point, preparation must come before safety.

45

CONSIDERATIONS

My room was simple in its opulence. The paper on the wall was the same red damask that coated the whole of the interior of Vivienne's establishment. The furniture, a deep walnut of high quality but simple design. The smell of damp wood, well-laundered bed linens, and Lysol permeated the air around me. Despite its new assignment, that room, like most others, was intended for business.

It was about time I began some business of my own. On the bedside table lay a smoking kit. Lamp and pipe and little box of black tar balls that would satisfy the body that held me. Vivienne had called in yet another favour to Monsieur Khamdao. He also returned my suit. The laudanum was but a bandage and this, a suture.

I knew that I'd smoke until the opium was gone, until I was gone, then the cycle would begin again as the chemicals coursed, and guided me toward bliss, only to fade into the same longing I'd felt since I'd first become Del.

I had to force myself to wait. This was not the place, but I did have another option.

Eve had offered to watch my mind in case my guard fell while smoking as it did in Khamdao's den. Allowing her free rein inside my head while under the opium's spell, was intolerable. As luck would have it, she had gone out for the evening.

I could feel Del's coping mechanisms rising within me. My feet tapped against imaginary ground as my reason fought our need. I began to rock just as Del always rocked. My whole body, *our* whole body was trembling, which was compounded by my frustration. Finally, I stood and placed the instruments of my pacification into a brown leather satchel.

"Vivienne," I said, knocking as I entered her office, "may I to borrow Jacques for a few hours? I have some business to attend to and I have need of his skills."

"Hours? Jacques? Why, I… yes, of course, but…" her expression grew solemn. "M, you don't have to leave to… I could message Eve, and should could…"

I stepped close to her and took her hand then squeezed it twice. She recognised our silent signal and entered my mind where she found the answers to her questions.

"I understand, M. That's considerate of you. This is a refreshing turn. Del must be rubbing off on you."

"Have your fun, Viv."

"You're sure this is a good idea?"

"It will be fine."

"Jacques, dear," she called, and the brute lumbered out of her office. "Could you please escort M out for the evening? He'll be needing a bodyguard."

Jacques' lips did not move but the scorn and annoyance that dripped from his bearded face was priceless and I couldn't restrain my laughter. This only added to his annoyance and thus a pleasant feedback loop was born.

"Thank you, Viv. I shall return medicated and ready to work," I said as I hurried toward the spiral staircase where I paused and turned toward my knight in silent armour.

"I'll have Simone fetch more Laudanum," added Vivienne. "The less you have to smoke the better."

"Agreed."

"Do look after him, Jacques. He'll be more vulnerable than he leads on."

Jacques frowned and looked away. He gave a single curt nod and met me at the top step.

"Thank you," I said to Vivienne.

"Thank him."

◆ ◆ ◆

Starlight dazzled in the dry, crisp winter air as we walked along the Seine. We strolled under several pale stone bridges until we reached a service door I knew to be severely underlit and neglected. The Seine oozed its usual dank smell even in the cold as I flipped through the multitude of chiming brass keys.

Jacques stood sentinel next to me, scanning the stone path for signs of trouble. We were alone but this did nothing to ease his alert and angry demeanour. The door opened with the lazy protestations of rusted hinges and I stepped inside the room, little more than a closet, and sat cross-legged on a plush mat facing the door. I groped for the small copper oil lamp to my right and lit it.

Jacques turned to me and his irritated expression turned to one of confusion. The mat on which I sat was clean and covered by a pair of pillows, a navy blue, wool blanket, and a neatly folded quilt in shades of green. Books lined three interior walls, mostly scientific journals and philosophical treatises though there was the occasional penny dreadful. Bottles of wine, scotch, and water filled the lowest shelf on each wall. From time to time, I required an escape. This was essentially my isolation chamber.

Jacques placed a hand on either side of the doorframe and heaved one enormous shoe inside before coming to a sudden halt. My space was not designed for two. Pushing my cravings aside, I slipped inside his mind and planted his instructions for the evening. With calm, dead eyes, he stepped back out into the night, closed the iron door, and stood with his back to it. Vivienne's request that he keep me safe would have sufficed but adding some artificial devotion was in order. Besides, good old Jacques could hardly hate me more than he already did.

I lay back against the pillows, covered myself with the quilt, and stared up at the dark door in the dim oil light. The opium called but something nagged at my mind. *Fool.* I called to Jacques to open the door once more, not bothering to enter his mind.

The door squealed on its hinges and I threw the blanket at Jacques' still blank face. He wrapped his shoulders as I released his mind. The man would do his job without any commands from me. I knew this, that's why I'd requested his assistance.

"Close it," I said, and he did so. I turned the key in the lock from the inside, sealing myself in.

That was a kind thing you just did.

No, not kind. Decent maybe. If that man freezes, he won't be much protection.

Just take the compliment, would ya?

Let's begin shall we?

No footsteps passed as I smoked. At least none that registered. The heavy, floral perfume of opium vapor filled the confined space and seeped into my quilt, sleeping mat, and books. That scent would serve as a lingering sign of my current plight and Del's shame. I lay back after packing my fourth pipe and turned onto one side. I placed the black substance over the flame and began another round of slow, deep inhalations. I was fully merged with Del's body at that point in time. In truth I had been since the third day. I could no longer pull my consciousness away as the body was satiated by, and suffered from, the drug.

After the box was empty and the pipe drained, the dragon had me fully wrapped in its warm, soothing scales. With my eyes closed, I sank again into the mind. Back into an image of myself that I could be proud of. I was done being Del for the time being, but I still had business with him. Awkward business. I had decided, in as much as an inebriated mind can decide, to have a conversation. A conversation I'd been putting off. One that this body needed to have. One that it could only have with itself.

My eyes opened onto the lush expanse of the mental rendering of my Babylon. A rendering that saw my city as it was, a flourishing oasis, not the dried waste it had become. From my throne the black, star-filled sky fell to meet the land in all directions. I flashed a chemical smile toward all that I'd created and a joy set in as if I could see myself being proud of myself. I laughed out loud at the thought and I hated Del for having a body that made me act the fool.

Above me, the stars that formed the constellation Draco began to intensify and shift. Soon that dragon was slithering across the black dome overhead. Taunting me? Watching me? I couldn't tell.

At a distance stood the blue door. I didn't want to enter but as reluctant as I was to admit, I needed Del's help. For all the disdain and scorn I held for the man, Del possessed an expertise I lacked. A skill I needed to learn if I was to be worth a damn in the fight against the Twins, Lilith, Izzy, and the rest.

I stood and swayed lazily then a simple jump sent my mental avatar airborne and my four raven wings carried me over the empty streets of Babylon, my tunic fluttering in an imagined breeze.

My Babylon was empty of people as it always was, but the streets were filled with all the details of the city in the prime of its life. Baskets of figs, crates of pomegranates, and man-sized clay jars of olive oil lined the market streets. Carts filled with flatbreads and fine fabrics, housewares and hand tools. It was as alive as I ever let my dead city be. A monument to memory. No one was allowed in my monument but me. There were never any residents, only the occasional guest.

I came to an unsteady rest in front of the blue door. The air around me felt warmer than usual but not unpleasant, and smelled of the surrounding market streets. It was a soft blanket, swaddling me like a babe.

Taking the tarnished brass knob in my hand, I turned it and pushed, falling forward and taking wing yet again. As I hurtled through the dark clouds of Del's subconscious, the painful images that danced and flashed on and in the lightning-infested cumulus were now accompanied by scenes of children at play, and lively gigs in packed jazz bars. I was pleased to see the change. An angry captive was an annoying captive.

He didn't look up as I landed with unsteady feet on the street of his birth. He acknowledged me with a simple nod.

The same damp, sooty smell remained but the pervasive bouquet of opium smoke seeped in. I couldn't tell if it was being generated by his mind or my own, or simply the olfactory senses pushing the scent throughout our shared consciousness.

"Del, my dear boy. I assume you're comfortable."

He kept his gaze on the floor but the tensing of his hands betrayed any restraint he attempted.

"Oh yeah, sure, nothing better than being confined like a crook in a cell. Nothing better than sitting here, looking up at the sky and seeing every cockamamie thing that's ever run through my head. I'm just a bug in a god damned rug in here."

The flashes above my head grew in intensity and I noticed the ratio of pleasant to dark imagery was turning darker by the second. A memory of a summer swim with his stepfather who used his hand to send playful splashes at the boy turned into a severe beating by a different hand. My opium-soothed mind didn't know how to process the images or Del's mood.

"I get your point. What do you need? Entertainment?"

The small man looked at me with distrust. The same look a zoo animal gives its keeper. "Entertainment? Hell yeah I need entertainment. It's been days in here with nothing but my thoughts. I can't handle that. I've never liked what's in my head. I need some fuckin' distraction."

"What kind of distraction."

Del screwed up his mouth as he thought. "A phonograph would be nice," he said as he slid his thumbs absently under his suspenders, his tight look of thought dissolving into a weak smile. "Yeah, a Victrola, with a bunch of records with Eddie Lang playing on 'em."

The device appeared at his bedside and the song *Wild Cat* began to play. The rhythm of the song bounced and pulled my lips into a languid smile despite its merry tone. The interplay of Joe Venuti's lyrical violin with Lang's subtle yet driving guitar was nuanced and delightful. Sitting in as Del at the gig brought on a new appreciation for jazz.

"And some new strings for this hunk of junk." He thumbed toward the cheap, almost toy guitar sitting on the bed beside him. "Can I get some strings?" His guitar was missing two.

"No, I think not," I said dismissively, wrapped in the warmth of the drug and focusing in on the lovely music.

"Why not? Just do your genie thing and conjure some up. A Victrola but no strings? Bullshit." He paused.

"Del?"

"There we go." Del's voice began to slow and soften, the opium had made its way to him as well. "Took it long enough. Now, how about some strings."

"You do it."

"Me?"

"It's your subconscious," I said, waving him off. "Do what you like." I held up a finger, waiting for Lang's walking bass line to turn to solo.

Del scoffed then lifted the guitar from his bed. It was an old, battered parlour guitar. It had been his first. He held it with both hands and concentrated on the blank spaces were the missing strings had been. He concentrated on the gaps for a few seconds, squinting in the way all who rarely focus do, and two new strings took their place. Wonder crossed his face but was quickly wiped away by more concentration. Soon, an entire set of brand new strings adorned the worn guitar.

"Why stop there?" I asked, now with my head bobbing and foot tapping, but it was unnecessary as Del was again concentrating on the guitar. Seconds later, his beloved Gibson L5 appeared in his hands. Its beautiful amber burst and shining chrome hardware gleamed as much as they could in the dismal light of his subconscious. Del was a quick study. I was impressed, but of course hid that fact.

"How am I able to do this?" he asked, still staring at his beloved.

"How do you go about creating something in the real world? How do you create your music?"

"I don't know. I just think about what would be good, or what fits, then play it."

"That's all you're doing here," I sauntered to the bars that separated us, gripping them for stability. "How have you been able to harass me this entire time? Because you wanted to. The mind is a world of energy. There's no matter to forge into the items we want. No chemistry or biology needed to create the creatures and people we want. Here, all we do is manipulate energy."

"That's incredible."

"It's science. Or at least as much science as we've been able to apply. There's still much that's a mystery, even to us."

"A mystery? Come on, this stuff is your thing, right?"

"It is 'our thing' but spare me your incredulity. Would you have an answer for me if I asked you to state the frequency of an open A string?"

"No, but scientists could."

"All right, but could they tell me how old a mountain is?"

"I guess not."

"Not yet. The universe is full of the unknown but that doesn't mean it is unknowable. It just takes time, technology, and thought. I've seen it happen thousands of times over thousands of years. The journey toward understanding doesn't come with a map or a fixed distance to travel."

"Fair enough, I guess," he said, placing the guitar back on the bed. He stood and came to the bars. "Now, why are you here?"

"I...," I turned my back to him. I balked at asking, then let the question fall from my mouth as I would a sigh. "I need your help."

46

ADVICE FROM A FRIEND

"My help? You told me you'd never need my help. You told me I had nothing to contribute. My help? Ha!" he said, then continued with more subtle, unrestrained giggles. The drug was growing stronger.

"Well, I was wrong. I need your help with the opium."

Del sat back on his bed and perched the guitar on his thigh. His hand moved through a progression of chords on its neck, working through a song without strumming. He said nothing for a moment, considering what I'd said. A look of relaxation fought with the frown brought on by my request.

"What about it?" he said finally. "You put the paste in the pipe and smoke. I've watched you do it. You're obviously zozzled right now, so it looks like you've worked out the nuts and bolts."

I straightened my posture and widened my stance to increase balance. A hollow attempt a composure.

"Besides, you're immortal or whatever you are. You've lived a lot of lifetimes in a lot of places. I'm sure you've had plenty of mind-altering experiences over the years."

"Some," I admitted, a few memories flashing faintly in my opium haze, "even with opium though no experience has been quite so… potent. In the old days, we'd eat opium as a pain-relieving measure but smoking it is a different beast entirely."

"Yeah, a dragon."

"A particularly persuasive and debilitating dragon," I agreed.

Del continued to work through chord after chord on the Gibson's neck, not looking at me anymore. "I think you'll manage and frankly, I ain't in the mood for being your dope coach."

"No, you don't understand. I need help controlling it. Controlling the cravings, Controlling myself once I've smoked. You have experience in that."

Del burst out laughing and lay down on the bed where he put his hands behind his head and stared up at the ceiling. The mirth subsided with his laughter and his demeanour sank in spite of the drug's effects. In fact, the space around us dimmed.

"There is no controlling it," he said, still staring at the ceiling. "The opium is like the ocean. Sometimes you're on top and ride the waves but you can't control 'em. You just try your best to stay in your boat and out of the water. A lot of the time you fall overboard and end up swimming."

"I understand. That's what I need help with. How do I swim?"

Del sat up again and rubbed his neck.

"I screwed up. Don't think of it like swimming. It's drowning is what it is. But not like drowning. You don't feel like you're dying. You feel like you're becoming a part of the ocean. It flows and moves and you move with it. The water is so warm and calming you just float there like a bath. All you can do is hold on to yourself and hope you don't dissolve."

"That's very Hans Christian Anderson of you, but please," I said, the opium blanket felt heavy around me and my knees wanted to buckle. I gripped the bars of Del's prison with added effort. "There has to be something I can do to work through this."

"Might be. Be sure to let me know once you've figured it out. I've never found it."

The music from Del's phonograph stopped, leaving an excessive amount of popping and hissing escaping from its brass horn. Then, Ravel's *Prélude à la Nuit* crept into our ears. Its dark strings echoing the sinking mood.

"It doesn't sound like either of you boys are trying very hard," said a voice that echoed off the dying buildings that lined the streets of Del's subconscious.

Lilith.

"Look at our quarry," said the voice of another, "huddling in his mind like a rabbit in a den. And he has a friend. I want to skin them both."

Artemis.

The women stepped out from behind the corner of a shuttered butcher shop. Both appeared as their typical, personal mental projections. Artemis wore her golden Grecian armour. An ivory tunic flowed underneath. Lilith was draped with the long earthen green linen tunic she had preferred since ancient times. Then, one's dress was even more of an indicator of wealth and power than now. Ever cunning and practical, dressing like a peasant allowed her to be among them and control them at less of a distance and thus with more power. Her hair, now long and flowing over one shoulder retained its raven hue.

Both women, despite reverting to historic, favoured dress maintained the facial features of their current body, which again was typical. Also typical were the flourishes allowed in the mental realm such as my black wings. Lilith sported the eyes of a serpent and sharp, violent teeth. Artemis allowed her skin to flush gold or go pale alabaster depending on her mood. She was a gleaming gold on that night. Both stood wrapped in an aura that was surely provided by the dragon coursing through me. Air between us shifted like heat off the desert sands except it wasn't heat. The drug was coming on strong. The volume of Lilith's music, even more so. Was I causing it? Or her?

"What has become of the great mind of the Mentium? Our scientist?" asked Artemis. "Even your mental self is weak. Look at you, weaving and grovelling to a Mono."

"Opium," answered Lilith. "His mind and body are coursing with it. He's fully merged. He can't escape it."

"Excellent deduction, my dear. Have you been practicing?" I struggled to keep my senses about me and my panic at bay. "I don't remember inviting the two of you in."

"The drug must be why the fool left his mind wide open to us," said

Artemis with triumph. Ignoring my words.

"Yes." Lilith never took her eyes from mine and certainly did not pet Artemis' ego for such an obvious answer. "It is the same as before."

I pressed my back to the mental metal that held Del and gripped two of the bars. The muscles in my arms clenched as I held myself as upright and still as possible, but my knees buckled and only the friction of my wings on the iron kept me off the floor.

"Let's end this now," said Artemis, stepping forward and drawing her golden sword.

"Calm yourself you twit," said Lilith, shaking her head at Artemis. "He will be taken alive and he will face our justice. You know this."

The precursory tremors of a tantrum shook Artemis as I felt the precursory tremors of laughter in me. I also felt a hand tap my shoulder from behind.

"Are they?" asked Del, his eyes wide but jaw set. He too was swaying on his feet.

"Were there not enough clues? Come on man," I said turning my head toward him.

"So which one is your lady friend?"

"Dammit, Del."

I turned back to our unwanted guests and Artemis had her back to me, discussing the situation and clearly not happy with Lilith's decision-making.

"We want him gone. He must be killed before the—"

"And so he shall, but after he faces justice. He is one of us."

"He gave up that right when he betrayed us."

"He is of the Mentium. He is of the Upper Echelon. I won't tolerate another Tian incident. He will meet with our justice but will suffer no other attacks. I will personally entomb anyone who attempts to rush his fate. Do you understand?"

"This is foolish."

The buildings around us started moving. Dripping and oozing like hot butter. The charcoal of the sky was turning lavender and the tarmac, a pale periwinkle. Was it the drug?

The wrought iron fire escape of the building above the bickering Artemis and my stoic Lilith drooped away from the brick wall and swayed above their heads. My laugh split a crack in their discussion and the two turned toward me.

"Unless all Mentium protocol has disintegrated since my departure," I said with all the sobriety and snark I could muster, "I believe my dear Lilith's command is absolute in the field, is it not? She is, after all our Field Marshall."

"It is," agreed Lilith. "Artemis, send in the Eunuchs."

"In here?" I asked, honestly and shamefully confused.

"No, you idiot," she said, "they'll deal with that French ogre at the door then we'll bring you home."

"We'll stop you!" shouted Del. He, too, was holding himself up on the bars.

Artemis smiled and removed the golden bow from her shoulder. She nocked an arrow and drew it back with her lean, powerful arm.

"M, step aside. I'll do you the favour of evicting the previous tenant. What a pest he must have been."

The whole room shuddered, just once, but it was enough to bring Del and me to the floor and cause the women to catch their balance. I thought it was the dragon. I was wrong. It was a different fire breather.

"Get out," said a voice as cold and hard as a glacier. I knew that voice as well. It was my voice, but I did not speak. Once I understood who had, my anger flared along with relief.

Lilith steadied herself and scanned the still-wilting landscape for the origin of the command. Artemis drew back her bow again.

"Out!" roared Eve through my mouth and she made my arms stretch out in front of me. At the motion, the bodies of my fellow Mentium doubled over and flew backward as if they had been struck in the abdomen by twin cannonballs. Their arms and legs flailed in front of them as they disappeared into the lilac sky of Del's subconscious.

"Stay here," I screamed to Del as I knelt on unsure legs. The irony of the statement was lost on me at the time. I leapt and flapped my great wings in awkward strokes, sending myself back into the land of the conscious then back into the physical world.

The cloud of my breath hung in the cold air that my opium-warmed body could not feel. Outside, the muted sounds of fists falling against flesh and air being forced out of lungs rang out despite the heavy door. I crawled to the handle and turned the key. Opening the door but a thumbs width, I bore witness to Jacques being pummelled by no fewer than five Eunuchs. Each took turns landing blows as Jacques' body bounced around the circle they had formed. He threw wild, uncoordinated punches in desperate attempts to defend himself.

I reached out, trying desperately to break into any of their minds but I knew it would prove fruitless. The beasts were not under my control and until their minds were released, all I could do was watch, helpless, as blood poured from Jacques' mouth and nose.

"Leave him be." I blurted. "Stop this."

A single Eunuch broke formation and walked to the edge of the stone path along the river. The coal-black waters of the Seine coursed below. Another followed suit and Jacques' body collapsed in the space they'd made. The remaining three joined their brethren, all staring into the river below. I looked back to Jacques who had lost consciousness.

The sound of a splash followed by flailing echoed off the stone walls that lined the river. The first was followed by four more as each Eunuch dove head-first into the water for a fatal mid-winter swim.

Someone in a purple overcoat rushed forward and stooped over Jacques, placing a hand over his mouth to check for breathing. I pushed the door open, wide enough to crawl out onto stones that should have felt more frigid than they did. Opium was like chemical goose down. So warm and cosy. I scooted across the stones for a look at the valiant sack of muscle that had defended me. Jacques did not look comfy or cosy.

Eve wheeled from her kneeling position and back-handed me across the face without a word spoken.

"You…" I stammered, "you had no right. You had no right to be in my head and you have no right to hit me."

Still she said nothing. The sound of casual footsteps clapped against the sidewalk at street level above us. Eve looked up and the steps stopped. They then reversed themselves and moved toward the stairs next to the nearest bridge. Two young, fit men walked with a somnambulant gait toward our position.

"What are you doing?" I asked, still prone on the stone walkway.

Again, there were no words only a she-wolf's glare as if I had attacked her pack.

The first young man to reach our group lifted Jacques with great effort. The second stopped next to me, his arms reaching round my back and under my knees.

"Get your mitts off of me, you…" the words trailed off as did the little remaining ability I possessed to control my body. This was Eve's doing more than the drug. Saliva fell from my slack mouth as I was carried along the river and up to street level. The men waited until Eve could hail a cab then they stuffed us in the back seat.

The motorcar sped away and I stared at Eve. We passed our looks of hatred back and forth as if in a tennis match. I wanted desperately to unload my anger on the child but my tongue was bound. The dragon confused my words and Eve had made me unable to speak them.

For the remainder of the trip I sank back into the subconscious with my-opium soaked companion. Jacques was still passed out and my staring contest with Eve grew tiresome.

"You should be thankful you know," said Del as I again approached his childhood bedroom.

"Thankful? She broke into my mind, *our* mind without consent. That's a violation."

"You do that to people every day," said Del, sitting on his bed and rubbing his hair.

"Of course, but it's different."

"How?"

"I don't pretend to be good. I'm an insidious, invidious bastard and I relish it. I don't ever play the part of the righteous. She talks as if she's so different from us but then she uses minds just as we do."

"She saved our lives."

"So what?"

"So," said Eve, instantly appearing between Del and myself, "you should be kissing my feet, you selfish son of a bitch."

"Insulting a woman who's been dead longer than the insult's existed, isn't going to wound, child."

"Thank you, miss," said Del, ruining the mood.

She tossed a look of scorn at him over her shoulder then turned her eyes back on me.

"The junkie has more manners than you and he's only had a couple decades to learn them. Thousands of years and you still can't accept help."

"You broke into my head."

"I'm done with this."

She vanished and her absence left Del staring at me from behind the bars of his room.

"You need to play nice, M," he said.

"What are you talking about?" I folded my wings around my body and lowered myself to the ground. "What pearl of wisdom does the opium fiend have for me now?"

He walked back over to the bed and again picked up his guitar. He didn't play, he just held it.

"She hates you and you're terrified of her—"

"I am not terrified."

"Of course you are. It's plain to see. I ain't no sap so stop pretending. Besides, you should be. She could kick your ass without even batting an eyelash."

"Thanks for the confidence."

"Look, you gotta fix this negativity that's going around. It's no way to work. The band can't jive until everyone is playing the same song. You understand?"

"Should I?"

Del set his guitar on the bed and started pacing the room.

"You gotta stop this shit. It's crackers. You two are spending so much time working against each other when you're supposed to be trying to stop these bastards so you can get the fuck out of my body and give me my life back."

I lowered myself again to a supine state. The clouds of Del's subconscious swirled, still tinted in lavender. I was helpless lying there. I was useless and worthless. We had less than three days. Then, either the Mentium would touch off the demise of both themselves and that of the Monos' civilization, or we'd stop them. There I was, trapped in my own mind and ravaged by the juice of a fairly unattractive flower. I let my head rock back and forth until I found a comfortable position, then relaxed my body.

"You're right, Del. I need out of you."

47

AFTERMATH

The heavy walnut door to Vivienne's salon was thrust open and for a moment, Jacques and I were left out in the cold as Eve stormed inside. Bernard soon came rushing out with Vivienne. Eve trailed and fumed. Vivienne and Bernard pulled Jacques from the taxi and helped the big man, who had come to but was far from lucid, toward the warmth of Vivienne's sitting room.

A group of Artisanes, led by Simone, flooded through the door and rushed Jacques inside. Two women were enough to carry my frail body in after him. It wasn't the heat of the large sitting room that engulfed me but rather the dry air and smoky smell of the massive fireplace. Its fireback glowing from a night of flames. The air engulfed me, as did a feeling that felt foreign to my mind and sour in my stomach, despite the euphoria of the drug. I felt guilt.

The two women set me on the couch next to the fire then rushed to tend to Jacques, and why not? While the brute had no sense of humour and hated me thoroughly, he was a master of his craft, which was to care for and protect the women who were now returning the favour. He'd more than earned it. I'd earned and expected the treatment I received.

I scooted my small body into a more comfortable position and placed a satin pillow underneath my neck. The wood panelling on the ceiling sprang to life in opium-tinted detail. I was so enthralled with the right angles and wood grain that I almost didn't hear the pounding of boot heels as Eve thundered down the stairwell and out the front door.

The cold wind her exit generated swirled around me and a second swirl was sent by Bernard charging after her. Both cyclones raged, only to be beaten into submission by the fireplace. Vivienne's decidedly more gracious footsteps followed down the stairs and my study of the woodwork was interrupted by her hand on my brow.

"You are a bastard. You know that, right?" she said, stroking my head.

"I know. But this scenario is exactly why I left. Consider my actions a sacrifice of Jacques to save the rest of you."

"Benevolence is new for you, so I don't expect perfection. That doesn't change the fact that you knew what would happen to him."

The ceiling began to spin as if I was lying on Del's gramophone. The motion made me uneasy but satisfied in my unease.

"I did not know for certain, and of course I didn't wish it."

Vivienne in her infinite wisdom said nothing and simply continued her comforting. My head was now in her lap.

"Viv, what am I doing?"

"You're enjoying opium, dear."

"No, what am I doing challenging the Mentium? I've sacrificed so much to stop this lunacy but have I suffered my own in the process?"

"No, you've taken a stand. And it may have started as self-preservation but it's become more. You must see that. Your kind are about to plunge all of us, Monos, Multis and Broadcasters, into chaos. Did I get those silly new names right?"

"You did indeed."

"You're attempting to prevent that, M. You don't have to be a noble man to do something noble."

"I'm an asshole, Viv."

"You are, but you've been my asshole for fifty years."

"Viv, you know that Lilith and I—"

"Stop talking you fool. Don't make this about lust. It hasn't been about lust for years. We were friends who fucked then stopped and continued being friends. I love you, dear, but I never loved you and you never loved me and that was enough for us both."

Vivienne had powers beyond her powers. An uncanny ability to cut through falsehoods and lay reality bare. She not only made you accept that reality but convinced you that it was okay. It was a rare gift. One that did not come from the aether but from her knowledge of the human experience. From her temperance and grace. It defined her and it made me love her.

"Viv, thank you." I said and took her hand in mine, squeezing it twice. She entered my mind where I, as best I could in my opium haze, opened myself up to her. I laid my feelings bare.

A moment passed then, her reply. "Time for bed I think."

She wore the smiling mask of a worried mother as she stroked my hair a few more times before clapping and turning toward the stairs.

Four hands groped at my body, only to hoist me onto their shoulders. My feet skipped against the dark walnut steps and, in the end, dangled off the edge of the bed where I had been laid. The kindest of the two women removed my shoes and readjusted my legs before covering me with a blanket and blowing out the oil lamp that illuminated the room.

SATURDAY

14TH JANUARY

1928

48

A MORNING CHAT

Breakfast the following morning consisted of croissants served with butter, jam, and admonishments.

"You could have told us you know," said Bernard, licking the croissant flakes off his fingers. He'd gotten in late but managed to convince Eve to stay the course so his mood was better than could be expected.

"What good would it have done? I did tell Viv."

He sipped some coffee and leaned back on the couch opposite Vivienne and me, looking at Jacques, who sat in a chair next to the fire with a swollen, purple face. Our breakfast was situated on the coffee table that lay between us in the ground floor sitting room. The artisanes were busy at breakfast in the main dining hall. It was too loud and the subject matter too private to discuss in their presence.

"Well M, to start, if you'd been caught, we'd know you were taken and didn't just run off."

"I would never—"

"Yes, you would, M. You've done it before," said Vivienne, swirling a spoon in her tea. "It's one of your old sayings. 'Sometimes retreat is advancement.' Don't turn our concerns around on us. You can't beg for trust. Not after the life you've led."

A click and a thud rang out opposite the fire as Eve shouldered her way back inside. The snow had intensified, and she slammed the heavy door behind her as if the cold were a beast biting at her heels. The frigid air swept over the rest of us carrying with it the earthy smells of wool, leather, and cedar that collectively made up Eve's bouquet.

She marched over and sat next to Bernard, pouring herself a coffee before sitting back as Bernard had done. Her glare seemed as though it was formed by the ice outside.

A silence fell and we continued our contest. Eyes locked and jaws set. In my peripheral vision I could see Bernard and Viv beginning to squirm. I remained steadfast. The effects of the drug were nearly gone, my need satiated. I was back in control and relished the chance to use it.

Eve broke our stare and scoffed. "Not even a thank you. Typical Mentium scum."

"You proved useful. But do you really think I should thank you for invading my mind without invitation? My subconscious, even. You've done that far too often already."

"You mean the prison where you keep Del?"

"Prison?" said Bernard. His shock flaring to anger faster than gunpowder over a flame. "What the hell is she talking about? What prison?"

"He's got your friend locked behind bars in an awful little room in some depressing dark neighbourhood. Chicago from the looks of it. It's dirty and cold and frankly, creepy. Everything dead or decaying."

Bernard's brow was so tightly stitched that I could have cracked a walnut between his eyebrows. "Get him out, M. Let him out of there, now."

Now there's an idea, said Del.

"I can't do that, Bernard."

"You can and you will."

Attaboy.

I upended my coffee cup and swallowed hard. I then stood and stepped in front of the fire. Jacques flared his nose at me until it reminded him that it was broken, and slack returned to his face.

"First of all," I said, "Del is in *his* subconscious and yes, I put him there, but only two items in that entire realm are of my design."

"The bars?" asked Bernard.

"Yes, the bars and the Victrola by his bedside. The room is his childhood bedroom and the *creepy* area as you so eloquently put it,

Eve, is the neighbourhood in which he resided. Your old neighbourhood, Bernard, though, I doubt you'd recognise it. In Del's subconscious, the place has been tainted by dark memories and thus takes a dark tone."

"Our neighbourhood wasn't nice but wasn't hell either. Why is his so dark?"

"Ask him. Well, next time you can. It's his subconscious. His rules. The rules in that realm flow from emotion as often as logic. It's formed by his feelings toward his memories."

"Fine, but why lock him up?"

"For his own good. He has no experience dealing with the inside of a mind and I can't deal with him knocking about while I have work to do."

Bernard said nothing. No one said anything. The fire crackled and the spoons clicked against porcelain, but words were absent until Eve erupted.

"Aren't you going to say something? He's treating your best friend like a criminal. The only crime Del's committed was getting in his way."

"He's not wrong," was Bernard's reply.

Aw, come on Bernie!

"Yes, he is. He's Mentium. He's wrong."

"No," said Bernard, staring into an empty cup. "Del doesn't do well with stress and confusion. He's also a curious little bugger. I hate it, but M's right to keep Del locked up."

"You can't be serious," said Eve.

"I am. I don't expect you to understand because you don't know Del, but I understand what M's doing."

"Then you're as much a bastard as him."

"I guess so."

And you can fuck right off, old pal.

Vivienne set her tea down and crossed her hands over her lap. She gave Eve a look in silence and the two women sat, focused on each other but no words escaped their lips. Vivienne's expression darkened and Eve's grew angry.

"No, Auntie, no. His *problem* is going to get us captured or killed or worse. He's risking us all for a fix. He can't just hold off for a few more days. Feeling good is worth more than success. Why am I even here? Why are you all following him? Leave them all to rot."

"You're wrong, Eve," said Bernard. "I'm sorry but you've got it wrong."

"Do I? Well, enlighten me, Bernard."

"It's Bernie, and maybe I need to."

"I'm all ears."

Bernard sat back against the couch and took a deep breath. "Eve, M couldn't wait. If he did, he'd be worthless. You heard about him trying to quit. You know how that turned out. He's got to use to function. That shit drives a person like its driving a car. It didn't matter what had to be done, Del would get the opium he needed. That's Del's body and it's making M have to do the same thing."

Eve crossed her legs. Her arms were already wrapped tight on her chest. I appreciated his added context. He could have let his anger silence him but chose to side with logic. I was glad I hadn't killed the man.

"We need him to get this contraption built. We need him to run it. We need him, Eve. We need him able to think straight."

"I won't be smoking anymore," I said, drawing all eyes.

"What?" said Vivienne.

"Laudanum. I should have purchased a barrel of the stuff. Vivienne, did you get a new supply?"

"I did but will it be enough?"

"It will have to do. I'll be on a strict dosing regimen for the remainder of our mission."

"So you'll be constantly scrooched the entire time?" asked Eve. "Wonderful."

"More like just having an edge, I think," said Bernard.

"Right. I'll be using small, consistent doses, many times a day. This will be medication not meditation. I want my mind as clear as possible. It won't stop my cravings like smoking would, but it will keep my body and mind functioning."

"So we just follow Blotto Bill's lead," said Eve, "and hope we can get this thing built in time to essentially go to war. You all realise that, right? This will be a battle."

"Yeah," said Bernard. "But it's one we have to fight. I'd rather fight in the first battle than wait for the world to crumble. The battles after that will be a lot harder to win, and a lot more bloody."

"Well," she said, "There'll be plenty of blood during this round. None of us are going to come out of this clean."

49

THE BUILD

"Softer please," I said to Jacques as he hammered. The bear had refused to rest, even at the behest of his madame. His eye and cheek bore a swollen, aubergine bruise and he leaned slightly to favour the bruised ribs he'd suffered while protecting me. I made myself a promise, not to harass the man until our task was complete.

Our dreary, putrid corner of the catacombs dripped with our condensed breath. Jacques, myself, Eve, and Bernard each toiled at a task.

From my jacket pocket, I removed a small brown glass vile of Laudanum and placed two drops underneath my tongue. The bitterness threatened to turn my mouth to stone. Two drops made for a light dose but I was still experimenting.

"Bernard, have you patched into the junction box?" I asked.

"Almost," he called, lying flat on his back atop a two-by-ten metre stack of bones. I could see his arms working from my position at our makeshift lab table.

"The connections must be free from grime. Are they clean?"

"Yeah, yeah, I got it," he dug a heel into the bones to adjust his position but sent a scapula skittering. A few grunts and puffs then, "There. Got it."

Jacques had volunteered to do the heavy lifting and the welding. A surprising and helpful skill. He continued to force appreciation from me.

Our shopping spree the prior day consisted more of compensated stealing than actual shopping. The skills Eve professed to have learned during her time on the continent were on display.

In a 'rented' van driven by Jacques, we drove shop to shop collecting the necessary supplies and tools. We fell into a rhythm if you will. Eve would charm then instruct the proprietors to give us what we needed, Bernard and Jacques would move said goods, and I would pay for what we took. This had been at Bernard's request, much to the confusion and annoyance of both Eve and myself, but the man had morals and he knew I could afford to pay.

Vivienne was practicing for her upcoming role as scout. By practicing, I mean drinking mulled wine and reading Colette at our designated café and checking in with me from time to time to comment on what a lovely crisp day it was.

I stood hunched over my notebook and the larger binder full of schematics. The build had been going smoothly. Jacques was nearly finished with the chamber frame and it would soon be my turn to labour. I would be in charge of the wiring and Bernard would assist.

Eve busied herself with attaching parts to the chamber. This was, however, not her assigned duty. Our location was strategic because it would not be checked by the Mentium and it was distant enough from the main hub within the catacombs, that our work should go unnoticed — *should* being the operative term. Her real role was to scan the dark, skull-laden passages around us for unwanted minds. If she found them, she was to make sure they never noticed us.

"What next?" asked Eve, removing the vinyl record from our 'purchased' phonograph. "Is it your turn to pick, Bernie?"

The idea of having a Victrola down here had been a collaboration between Bernard and Eve. It was also a way for Eve to show off. It created even more sound for Eve to erase from outsiders' minds, but she swore it would be no additional work. I chose my battles with Eve, and the music lifted everyone's spirits, including my own.

"No," he said, "it's M's choice this time."

I turned to Bernard as he slithered down off of the bones. "Did you bring the Blind Lemon Jefferson?" A new favourite of mine from Del's collection.

"Yeah, it's under the Victrola. Looks like Del keeps rubbing off on you."

"The man has good taste in music."

Eve put the record on. With a subtle scratch, *Booster Blues* reverberated gently off the cavernous walls and my body moved to the beat. These were Del's movements but I enjoyed them. I'd come to appreciate American blues from time spent in Del's room with his records. It did not lack for feel or power, but its energy wasn't frenetic like the dance jazz played in clubs and cafés. When I listened, I could feel Del's enthusiasm for the music foster my own.

"Eve, could you come here for a moment?"

She joined me at the table, placing both hands down. "Is this going to work?" she asked, studying the piles of drawings and notes scattered before us.

"It will."

"You think you'll be finished by tonight?"

"Yes. At this point, the build is more akin to building a model. There's no creation or experimentation. We only have to put the parts together."

"I haven't forgotten you know?"

"Forgotten what?"

"That this radio you built was evil from day one. Just because you wanted to be subtle, doesn't mean your intentions were good."

"No," I admitted, "but they were no worse than before. The only increase in power I sought was in speed and efficiency. It was supposed to be business as usual."

"Well your usual business is bad business."

"Maybe, but it has been our business for a very long time and I had no intention of upsetting the balance we'd struck."

"How noble."

At the edge of our table lay a long iron rod beaded with green glass insulators. I handed it to Eve.

"Be a dear and mount that, would you?"

"Sure thing, Mr Big Cheese," she said. "Hey Bernie, wanna give me a hand?"

"Yeah, just a second," he said, wiping his hands on a soiled rag and tossing it aside.

Jacques made two final welds, and Bernard took the bottom end of the insulator pylon and guided it over the attachment bolts. Eve climbed a ladder and steadied the top.

"Lower," said Bernard.

"How's that?" said Eve.

"Right, lower, lower,"

"There?"

"Perfect."

Bernard began tightening the nuts around their respective bolts and Eve stepped next to him where she put a hand on his back.

"Everything Jake?"

"Yeah," he said, tightening the last one, "just fine."

Of course it was fine. By the start of our build, the pair had finally allowed themselves to start flirting. It was, of course, very inappropriate and inopportune. We had other matters on which to focus.

"Eve, Jacques," I said. "If you'd be so kind, I'd like for you to start placing the cushions, handles, and standing platform. Bernard, you'll assist me with the wiring."

"Let's get going then," said Eve, giving Bernard a pat on the shoulder before moving off with Jacques. The negativity between Eve and Bernard had fully subsided. All that tension had centred on Del and me. I was sorry for that. Bernard enjoyed his time with her, and he needed a bright spot in his life. We all did.

For me, nothing would be brighter than snuffing out the Twins. No, not snuffing out. I had greater plans for them.

50

AN EVENING MEAL

"Could you pass the wine?" asked Eve at the end of the long table in Vivienne's grand dining room. I obliged then went back to my work. We'd finished the signal generator save for the copper helmet needed to capture and focus Eve's transmissions. It is amazing what can be accomplished when simply building rather than creating. In lieu of eating, I was busy finishing the last of the wiring within.

We had arrived late and thus were eating alone. A group of five at a table for sixteen. My laudanum dosing regime was coming along well. I stuck with two drops at a time, varying the frequency of doses as needed. At dinner, I'd switched to dosing my glass rather than placing the foul tincture under my tongue.

Music had continued to be a comfort throughout the day and true to her word, Eve had kept our work party a private affair. No Mentium had come within earshot and Eve only had to deal with two city workers. Here at the table, the caramel-voiced Bessie Smith was busy informing us of her opinion on the opinions of others.

"You all had quite an achievement today," said Vivienne.

"They were wonderful," I said, focusing on a frustrating connection at the crown of the helmet.

A silence fell, leaving only Ms Smith's voice to reverberate off the red damask walls.

"What?" I asked. "What's happened?"

"Did you just compliment us?" asked Bernard,

"I suppose I did. Yes. You all deserve a bit of acknowledgement. You performed admirably, followed my instructions well, and worked independently, without the need for constant mentorship. We moved quickly and I'm grateful."

"Simone," said Vivienne and the graceful, dark-haired artisane came into the room. It was her night for dinner duty. She wore a flowing, pale-yellow sheer dress, covering all but leaving nothing hidden. "Please, bring us more wine. M has reached a milestone in his life."

"Of course," said Simone moving toward the kitchen door and past Bernard, who's eyes became transfixed on his plate.

"Why Bernie," said Eve, swatting at his bicep, "I didn't take you for a Mrs Grundy."

"I'm no prude, I just…"

"You're sweet," finished Vivienne.

"And silly," said Eve.

Bernard flushed and Eve laughed.

"Lighten up, lookin's free in a place like this," she said. "Hell, I can't keep my eyes to myself."

Simone returned with two bottles of red and showed the labels to Viv.

"Both, I think," she said, then seeing our eager faces said, "two more of the same actually."

The mood in the room was as light as it had ever been. Genuine laughter and genuine smiles were being cast about like ticker tape at a parade. Vivienne kept the wine flowing and despite my stomach, I drank. I smiled and I laughed too. Jacques laughed but it hurt him. Smiling irritated his bruised face.

"I want to say something," I said standing and raising my glass. The room quieted.

"That man," I pointed to Jacques, "I hate that man."

The smiles faded.

"But I have to give credit where credit is due. I have never met one so loyal or so diligent at his work than Jacques. I owe him, and Eve of course, my current freedom. We owe him for bringing his skills to today's endeavour, and we need him for the coming trials. Thank you, Jacques." I took a drink as the other four exchanged confused smiles. It hadn't sounded that awkward had it?

You really know how to tug the old heart strings don't ya? said Del.

I'm not well practiced.

You did fine.

The unblemished portion of Jacques' face turned a soft pink, one that contrasted nicely with his bruises. He raised his own glass and gave me a nod. His lips, neutral, which I took for a smile.

We went back to drinking and talking, and I finished with the helmet. We'd planned a test of our new signal generator at midnight. The thought being that anyone up past midnight on a Saturday night, well Sunday morning, would have alcohol or something stronger to blame for anything they saw.

Eve reached for the helmet. "Let me see that."

I slipped the helm over her light ginger hair. The glinting copper matched.

"Like a glove," she said with a muted voice. "I still wish I could see out, though."

"That's pretty good, M," said Bernard as he reached over and gave the helmet a wiggle.

"Knock it off Bernie," said Eve.

"Aw, come on," he said, gently rapping his knuckles on the side. His entire body froze by the third tap.

"Whoa, whoa," said Eve, removing both the helmet and the suggestion she'd put in Bernard's mind. "Bernie, I'm so sorry. It, it was instinct."

"It's all right," he said shaking his head and laughing.

He was laughing.

I wasn't.

What other instincts might present themselves?

51

OUR TEST

"Over there. Connect those two wires." My voice bounced off the bones.

"Where?" asked Bernard, searching the floor.

"There, by the archway."

He found them and snapped them together. "Now what?"

There was no music. This was an important event.

"The switch," I said, pointing to a large, red throw switch at the base of the signal generator. "Pull that up."

He did and the apparatus sprang to life. Its iron frame glowed with amber signal lights. A central bulb illuminated the empty chamber. The puce velvet of the sofa cushion on its back panel somehow managed to look even worse under the golden light.

It was just the three of us that night. Vivienne had convinced Jacques to get some rest and we all fought against his protestations. He relented but not before we'd gotten an additional bottle of wine in him.

Eve sat reading from my notebook. I'd scribbled down a script of sorts. It was more like stage direction. I'd decided to let Del help with its creation. He had enjoyed his work. She was shaking her head.

"Is there a problem?"

"This is ridiculous."

"What portion?"

"All of it."

Aw, she's no fun, said Del.

"It can't be that bad, can it? Bernard said, meeting us at the central table.

"Make said beast chase victim with ball peen hammer? Beast must be over two metres tall but must have hands no bigger than a doll? You have to be kidding?"

What does she know? That's gold right there. Put that in the movies and you'd make a mint.

"I'm not."

Eve and Bernard looked at each other and rolled with laughter.

"How the hell am I supposed to come up with this baloney?"

"Be creative," I said, snatching the notebook away. "This is a test, remember? Our machine isn't the only thing being tested. We need to make sure you can create accurate images."

"Are you doubting me?"

"No, just the interface. It has to be flawless. You'll need to neutralise anything Izzy and the Twins manage to broadcast. Any weakness here may mean that some effects will remain."

"You have to promise to show me what you come up with. After the test of course," said Bernard.

"Oh, I'll show you, just while you're sleeping so you wet the bed."

"Har, har."

"Can we get back to it?" I asked.

"Fine," said Eve, "but why the silliness?"

"It's a way to measure accuracy. If we include out of place, easy to spot details, we can determine how accurate we are. Plus, Del really wants to see his work in action."

"You gave Del a shot?" asked Bernard.

I shrugged, "We'll see how it goes. Now, that chamber over there is the signal generator the rest of the radio simply amplifies and sends that signal. The quality of the initial signal is paramount."

"Okay, okay, I get it. What's left to do?"

"Prepare for the test," I said.

"Hot damn, this is exciting isn't it?" asked Bernard as he shot over to the apparatus.

"It is indeed. If we've managed this, which I think we have, then we actually have a chance against the Twins."

"Well, get your ass up there, M," said Eve, backing into the chamber. The copper helmet was connected and sat at the ready above her head.

"Bernard, please, could you get my paperwork in order for me? Don't put it away, in case there's a problem."

"Yeah, M, no problem. Just let us know when you're in position."

"Right, off I go. Eve, can you cover me?"

"Of course, now get."

I took off down one of the passageways in the catacombs. This was exciting, and I truly was excited. The build had gone masterfully, better than I would have hoped.

My quick gait turned into a jog then back into a quick gait. I might have been excited but Del's body couldn't keep pace.

The beam from my torch bounced along the skeletal walls as I snaked my way through the catacombs. My chosen exit was a service hatch into a tunnel of the Paris Metro.

I raced along the black walls of the tunnel. Black from both a lack of light and from brake dust. The light from an oncoming train shone in my eyes. This was not London, however, and I pressed my back against the dirty wall. The metal box on rails rattled past, square windows flashing like frames from a moving picture. My jacket flapped around me in the cold draft and when it passed, I dashed to the next platform then surfaced into the night.

"Eve?" I asked mentally as I took up my position along *Boulevard Saint-Jacques*, an apt tribute, all things considered.

The street was empty but I noticed a dimly-lit window above me. A figure moved across the glass and I stopped.

"I've found our test subject," I thought to Eve. I hadn't the power to find her at this distance, but I knew she would be listening for me.

This is it. She better not clam up, said Del.

"I won't, Del," she thought back.

Oh, shit she can hear me.

"Of course I can. Now remind me how to direct this thing."

"Just do exactly as you would normally do. Reach out with your mind and find me, then search for another waking mind. It should be the man above me. Then just broadcast to us both. The radio will take care of the rest."

I left my mind open to Eve and watched the window from the snowy street below.

"There you are," she said in my mind.

"Good, now find him."

I stood as patiently as I could, waiting for something to happen. I did not have to wait long.

"*Non, non, s'il vous plaît!*"

It was glorious. I could see the beast snap to life through the window. The height, the hands, the hammer, they were all there and so much more. Eve did not give herself enough creative credit. The chartreuse beast snarled at the man with mucus-soaked fangs and glossy eyes of absolute black.

Well if that ain't just the berries. Look at her go!

The man, in his union suit underwear, ran circles around his sitting room as the baby-handed beast gave chase. Through my laughter, I told Eve to stop and the image disappeared. The only sounds on that desolate street were the test subject's gasps and my chuckles.

◆ ◆ ◆

"How'd it look?" asked Bernard as I approached the signal generator.

"Eve, well done."

She was out of the chamber and sitting next the neat stack of paperwork on the table. She gave a calm nod but the swing of her legs betrayed her glee.

"We are officially ahead of schedule. We've got about thirty-six hours until the Twins act. Tomorrow night, we'll begin our surgical demolition."

"Just say cutting wires," said Eve.

"Where's the flair in that?"

Bernard hopped up on the central table, his legs dangling below him. "I gotta say, M, it was a little anticlimactic."

"Not at all from my end."

Tell him how good I did, M. Tell him.

"I get that, but where was the glow?"

"The glow?"

Yeah, from the skulls. I didn't see any of the energy light up the skulls."

Eve could not restrain her giggle.

"Oh, I'm sorry Bernard, The demonstration I broadcasted to you was a bit… illustrated. The lights were for demonstrative effect only."

Bernard rubbed his neck. "Don't I look the fool."

"Not at all. You look like someone who needs to help us celebrate."

Eve hopped from the table. "Finally, something we agree on."

You didn't tell him.

"Oh," I said. "We shouldn't forget Del's creative contribution."

"Forget?" Bernard ruffled my hair as if giving Del a pat on the back. "Only Del could come up with something wild enough to give Eve a run for her money."

"Bernie, there was no running involved, maybe a stroll," said Eve.

"Yeah, well it's nice to have Del in this with us."

Ah hell. I didn't know he was gonna get sappy.

We powered down all the components and left the catacombs. The feelings of victory and camaraderie felt foreign after all the failures and betrayals I'd suffered of late but toasting an achievement was standard practise for me.

I procured a bottle of Moët from a nearby café using only a little manipulation, and Bernard popped the cork before we climbed into our taxi.

We all drank eagerly on the ride back to Vivienne's and I was left hefting the empty bottle as we exited the taxi at *Place Pigalle*. It was well past one in the morning but the area teemed with pleasure seekers. Snow was falling again, confetti in the neon lights.

Bernard had pointed out as much and we all felt it a perfect end to a successful night.

As we began to cross *Boulevard de Clichy*, Bernard frowned, twisting his nose at the air. "What's that smell? Fire?"

"No…" whispered Eve, and she sprinted away from us, her purple coat trailing behind her.

I stretched with my mind and sensed what Eve had. "Viv!"

Bernard set off after her without hesitation and I tried my best to follow.

52

THE FIRE

The smell of smoke intensified as we neared Vivienne's building. Turning the corner onto her street, the heat and the scale of the devastation was immediate. The pale stone of the five-story building had become an oven. Paint bubbled, flames groped at the night from the windows and smoke billowed from the roof and open front door like a hell spirit.

Three fire trucks stood in the melting snow and scores of *sapeurs* worked to treat the artisanes scattered throughout the street. They'd been given blankets but couldn't stay out in the elements much longer in their meagre dress.

As I neared, Bernard had his hands clasped on top of his Homburg. Eve was gone.

"Is everyone all right? Jacques? Vivienne?" I asked, using the last of my leg strength to sprint up to him.

"I don't know. Eve stopped right here and by the time I caught up with her, she took off again. This is bad, M. This is really bad."

"I know." I searched mind to mind, trying to find them. Trying to find Vivienne. Eve was searching too, seemingly everywhere at once.

"I can't find them," I said. "What do we do, Bernard? I can't find them."

Bernard scanned the scene. His eyes, wet with worry, glistened in the firelight. It would have been beautiful at any other time. Not then. The firefighters had fled the building and were working from the outside.

"We help," he said, squeezing my shoulder and leading me toward the nearest *sapeur.*

I want to help, said Del. *What can I do? Lemme do something.*

Del, I understand but please, just let me think. Keeping our head clear will be help enough.

"Couvertures?" asked Bernard, *"pour les dames?"*

The *sapeur* reached into the back of his vehicle and handed each of us a stack of simple wool blankets.

Most of the women had congregated a block from the burning structure. Most of them had wrapped shoulders but their bare legs were still exposed to the night.

"Here," said Bernard to the first group of artisanes we found, "Double up. Like a towel on the bottom."

"Bernard, we have to find them," I said. "I have to find her."

"M, just keep yourself busy. Just stay busy and let them do their jobs."

We made two more trips back to the *sapeur* and as we handed out the last of the blankets. Bernard knelt to talk, and I returned toward the fire. The heat stung my face but the heat inside burned hotter. This wasn't accidental. I was sure of that.

"M!" said Bernard grabbing my arm, "Listen."

A cacophony of coughing echoed off the buildings around us. To our right, Eve led three hunched, hacking people down the down the dark, adjacent street. Simone and Jacques each had one of Vivienne's arms, and Eve kept the coat she'd draped across Vivienne's shoulders from falling to the wet ground.

"Viv!"

I rushed to her, putting my own arms under hers. Trying to take over the burden from the others, trying to take Viv in my arms. Her limp weight was too much for Del's body and Jacques caught us as my knees began to buckle. I backed away in shame and fear.

"Is she well?" I asked. "Tell me, is she okay?"

"She's alive," said Eve, taking a blanket from Bernard and wrapping Vivienne in its warmth.

Simone had run to the *sapeurs* and two of the men came running back with her. Vivienne sat in the snow against the cold wall, hacking her lungs to pieces, trying to clear the smoke. Jacques, squatted low, despite his bruised ribs, and cradled her hand. Simone took the other one once she arrived. Both had to let go to allow the professionals to do their work.

"Who?" I asked.

"Who do you think?" said Eve.

"There were three," said Simone. "A blonde woman, a blonde man, and an Indian woman. They just charged in. Jacques was in bed, but I don't think he could have done anything."

My stomach boiled.

"They called for you," she said. "When we told them you weren't there, something happened to us. They made us all kneel in front of the fireplace in the sitting room. Vivienne and Jacques came down the stairs like corpses. We were like dolls. We had voices in our heads, and we did whatever they said. The woman in red, the Indian woman, she made Vivienne reach into the fire…

I stared at her hand. The *sapeurs* were wrapping it in gauze but the damage was plain.

"She made Vivienne throw a burning log onto the carpet and we all had to watch. We just knelt there and watched. Once the flames were high enough, the blond man made Gabrielle stand and said, 'Tell Marduk that the hiding is over. Tell him that everything is finished. He's finished. His little rebellion is finished, and that his radio is finished. He cannot stop us.' Then he made her go outside and they left us kneeling, watching the fire. Celine screamed because the fire was so close she was getting burned, then, for some reason we could move again. All of us. We could hear someone speaking to us. A woman but she wasn't there. She told us to get out and Jacques and I ran to Vivienne. She was shaking from the burn. By the time we got her up, our way was blocked."

All eyes were on Simone, all faces stone.

"The smoke was thick, and we were having trouble seeing and breathing but then the voice was in my head again. She told me to remember the cellar and, like a picture show, I could see our way out. The cellar has an exit on the other side of the building. We carried Vivienne down then out. We put her hand in the snow to try to soothe the burn then Eve found us."

I hugged her. I reached out and took Simone in my arms and squeezed. That is not what I do but I did it.

"You saved her," I said. "You cannot know my gratitude."

Simone teared up. "It's no great thing. I had help."

"Oh, but it is," I said.

Jacques had gone back to looking after Vivienne but Bernard and Eve paced like cats. Bernard's jaw was set so tightly that I feared broken teeth. Eve... Eve boiled.

"*Pardon,*" called a voice from above.

An elderly woman leaned from a window three floors above us. She held something but let it drop as soon as our eyes met.

It was paper and it floated amongst the snowflakes as it fell. Bernard lunged to catch it and read it as soon as it hit his hands. He pressed it into my chest just as quickly.

"Read it. Aloud," said Eve.

I smoothed the paper. " It says, 'I'm sorry. I didn't know this was planned. I've done what I could. Stay vigilant, stay safe, stay hidden. Wait for my message. Do not give in and trust that time will set things right'."

"That's it?" asked Eve, pressing her gloved fists to her forehead.

"That's it. But it's something," I said.

"Something?"

"It's evidence. Our ally took an active role this time."

"If they were our ally, they would have stopped this. They would have never let this happen to Auntie Viv."

"They should have stopped it," I said, "if they'd known. They say they didn't."

That was the wrong thing to say. Eve stormed off toward the ambulance that was to take Vivienne to the hospital. Jacques and Simone joined them.

"What do we do?" asked Bernard.

I took in the scene. Fourteen freezing women and Vivienne burned. I burned.

They had gone too far. This was unnecessary and uncalled for and they would pay.

I read the paper in my hand once again. This ally was useless. They'd allowed Vivienne to be hurt and I needed to know why.

M, I know you're mad, but Bernie and the ladies need you, said Del.

I studied the note. The handwriting, the words. This wasn't masked in prose. This wasn't careful, discreet. This was hurried.

M, snap out of it.

"Just let me think!" I said to Del, but it was Bernard who jumped.

"M, I just need to know what to do," said Bernard.

I read through the note over and over. It was familiar. I knew that handwriting. The words. I knew those words. 'Time will set things right'. Her words! Her.

"Here," I said, reaching for my wallet and shoving two hundred francs into Bernard's hand. "Get these women to a hotel, get them fed, and tell everyone to rally at Philipe's by morning."

"Where are you going?" he asked, as I turned and bolted. "M?"

SUNDAY

15TH JANUARY

1928

53

AN EDUCATED GUESS

The click of the door handle echoed through the darkened stillness of the apartment. A darkness cleaved by a blade of light as the door opened. A stillness shattered by her footsteps. I did not move save for tracing the upholstery tacks of her armchair with my fingers.

The door closed, renewing the dark and fanning her perfume toward me, mixing it with the smell of spent incense. Just enough streetlight bleeding into the apartment to see her reach for the light switch. It was then I opened my mind.

"M," thought Lilith, "I—"

"Leave them off," I said aloud and she pulled her hand back. "Turn, but don't move."

She did as I asked and the spectral light in the room cast her shocked face in sepia hues. She was dressed as a woman dressed as a man, a popular trend. Her wide trousers, blazer, wool vest, shirt, and tie hung below her bobbed black curls and the feminine angles of her made up face. No light reached me where I sat. Everything about me was dark.

"I'm a desperate man, Lilith."

"I know."

"I almost lost one of my closest friends tonight."

"I know."

My grip tightened on the arms of the chair and I re-crossed my legs. She stayed still.

"I need answers and I need you to answer clearly."

She stepped back, resting against a seventeenth-century Italian credenza, her hands hooked over its gold-leafed edge. I knew it well, as I did every inch of her home. Lilith decorated like a Spartan king. Everything was of the finest quality and everything had a purpose. She spared no expense when items were a necessity. That credenza had a purpose.

"It's here," I said and raised the pearl-handled revolver I'd taken from the top drawer.

"M, tell me what this is about so I know how to proceed. You owe me that."

"Either I owe you everything or nothing."

I tossed the gun at her feet. My chest heaved and I gripped the chair once more. "If I'm wrong, and you aren't the one who's been writing these letters, if you're not the one who let me go, then just kill me and be done with it. This game ends right here."

She did not move. She did not take her eyes off of me.

"Lilith, this is my endgame. I've lost everything, I've endangered someone I love and I'm hoping that someone else I love has been with me all along. I'm here, right in front of you, hoping that I have made the right decision. I need this to be the right decision."

"M, just—"

"Be with me or kill me, dammit!"

She picked up the gun and her dark eyes burned into mine as she moved toward me. She stopped when her knees touched mine and she put a second hand on the gun.

"I'm a fool," I said, closing my eyes.

The sound of scraping metal met my ears, but it was softer than that of a hammer being pulled back. The weight of a small object landed against my thigh. Then another. I opened my eyes to see Lilith empty the last four bullets from the gun.

"I'm with you, love," she said and I pulled her into my lap and wept.

54

EXPLANATIONS

"What were you thinking?" I asked, trying my damndest to keep calm. Refusing to move from my seat in the corner of the darkened room. "I lost my body to the Twins, Tian—Tian lost his life and you just stood by playing this game."

"This game," she said now sitting on the plush green carpet and leaning against the credenza, "has been the only thing between you and capture. This game is the only thing keeping you from ruining everything."

"Ruining everything? You want to talk about ruin? Look at me. Look at what I've become. And Tian? Tian is gone! Where were you when Apollo put a blade to him? Where were you?!"

"I was there," she said, her tone was low "I couldn't stop his death, but it damn well solidified what I already knew would be my course of action."

"Which was?"

"Get close. As close as possible. I'd already started weeks before when Izzy came to me."

"He did *what?*"

She rolled her head against the marquetry and gazed off into the black of the room.

"He told me what you had planned and that he believed you were overreacting. He thought you were wrong."

"Right, okay." The revelation stung. "So then you, what exactly?"

"I told him not to speak to anyone else and to trust you. Then, naturally, I had him followed, and as his turn toward the Twins became more and more obvious — and it was obvious M, even if you couldn't see it — I moved closer."

"You started sleeping with him."

"That's as close as one can get, isn't it? I thought I might as well enjoy myself before destroying that Judas. You can't blame me; his current body is gorgeous."

"Fair point," I said, and it was a fair point. If there has been one ill we've managed to cure over these past few millennia, it was jealousy. "But it wasn't close enough, was it? And here we are."

"I swear to you, M, I had no idea what was going to happen that night. He hadn't mentioned anything about betraying you. I thought there was still time to affect some change."

"Go on."

"Once all hell broke loose, I had a choice to make. I could work with you on the outside or work for you on the inside. I chose to burrow deeper."

My seat felt wrong. I'd been locked in position in that chair for too long and needed air. I parted the curtains and opened the window out onto the Seine. The cold and the lapping of icy water crept into the apartment.

"And how exactly would aligning yourself with the Twins help me?" I asked.

"Time, pressure, everything."

"I don't follow."

"The search you idiot."

"The search?"

"After I sensed you near the opera, I had you followed. You tried to hide but it didn't take long to notice the one person standing still with his eyes closed."

"Well played." I'm a fool.

"At first I had you followed by Kukulkan. When he knew you were heading to Tian's apartment, he relieved the Underling who had been watching the place and made sure your little distraction worked."

"Give me some credit, love."

"Credit when credit's due, darling."

Lilith was never one to dole out praise.

"Then," she continued, "once I learned how well that cretin Sal knew your new body, I made him my spy."

"That explains the sore feet and deteriorating state."

"M, this entire time, I've kept the Eunuchs and Underlings searching for you in every part of the city where Sal told me you weren't. It wasn't perfect but it let you carry on doing whatever it is you're doing. I'll need full details of whatever scheme you've cooked up so we can adjust to our new circumstances."

"Of course. Speaking of new circumstances. I need to know, who other than Kukulkan do you have working for you? Yemoja, Cernunnos, and Radegast said they were leaving but was it a ploy?"

"Not to my knowledge. What about Ma'at? Have you heard anything from her?"

I had to chuckle. She'd seemingly been the smartest of us all. "No one's seen her, and I doubt we will for a good long while."

Lilith stood and walked over to me, placing a hand on my hip and looking out over my shoulder. "I have Kukulkan, a handful of other loyal Underlings and a few Eunuchs."

"Well, that's not much."

She stepped beside me and looked into my eyes. "We have whatever newfound power you've come upon."

"What?" Power was the least accurate descriptor for me.

"These new abilities. Artemis and I were blasted out of your head, remember. I don't know what's happened to you but that was impressive. Is it the drugs? Maybe there's more to the little man in that little body than meets the eye. Has he been a Multi all along?"

She didn't know about Eve, which was by design so at least we'd been successful in that regard.

"Here," I said, both out loud and into the brain, "I'll let you two have a little conversation. It's about time he did some real work. Del, you have a visitor."

Lilith perked up. "You're letting me inside."

"Yes, but give me just one minute."

I sank into the mind and straight into the subconscious. The sky was lighter and less turbulent then even my last visit. The streets, cleaner.

Del was lounging against the gigantic pillows that topped the king-sized bed at the centre of an imagined Ritz-Carlton suite. The prison bars still made up the front wall of the room but he was becoming more flexible within his mind. He'd added twin parlour palms at the foot of the bed and a crystal chandelier above it all. Of course his Gibson L5 lay across his belly.

"I'm going to do what now?" he asked without getting up.

"You've said you wanted to do more to help the cause, correct?" I asked, stepping to the iron bars.

"Sure." He set the guitar down and stood.

"Well now is your chance. You're going to do some storytelling."

"To Lilith?"

"Yes."

"And I'm going to tell her what exactly?"

I started backing away.

"About you and your life, what happened when she was kicked out of our head. You'll explain that you're just a Mono and that I don't have any extra powers."

"And," he said, gripping the iron, "I'm going to explain what Eve is and what she's been up to. Is that it?"

"Very perceptive."

"You little chicken-shit."

I gave him a bow "Lilith? Come in please."

She materialised in her green linen and curled black hair, now down to the middle of her back.

"Take it away Del," I said and returned to the physical world.

55

A MEETING OF THE MINDS

"This is stupid, M," Lilith said into my mind. To the cab driver who steered us ever closer to Philipe's apartment, we were stone silent and staring out opposite windows. It was a black morning. The snow fell in sheets, making the windows glow white in the new light. The darkness was inside us.

To the driver, it was just another lover's spat and he would ignore it like he had all others before it. If he only knew the magnitude of this 'spat'.

"This is stupid and you are stupid. Maybe I should have just let the Twins have you and taken care of this myself."

"Vivienne trusts her. The only reason she is even helping us is because of Viv. Now that she's been hurt, Eve will be more focused than ever."

"Focused? Unhinged is more like it. M, you've made a mistake."

"No, you're just afraid."

"I am not afraid."

"Yes you are, and so am I. I have been since I met her but I've kept that fear deep inside. There's no reason to let it cloud our judgement."

"That's rich. Keep telling yourself you're not clouded."

I climbed out of the taxi and onto the icy street. Lilith stepped next to me. We both felt our own unique brand of dread.

"Shall we?" I asked, and reached for the buzzer. I never made it.

Every muscle in my body went into spasm. I couldn't see Lilith beside me but from her grunts, I assumed her body was locked as well.

"Traitor," said Eve into our minds.

"No, now Eve, listen. Lilith is on our side."

"She's Mentium and she's going to die. You can watch."

My head turned toward my love. She was fighting against Eve, but it was futile.

"Don't, Eve. Take her thoughts. Take them and see for yourself."

Lilith's nostrils flared but I'd take her anger over her death any day.

A few pedestrians shuffled past us, not noticing a thing. Eve was in total control of the entire situation, probably for blocks in every direction.

Hey, kiddo, said Del. *He ain't shittin' ya. Lilith is the real deal. C'mon now.*

"Eve?" I asked. "Eve, have you done it?"

The click of the door sounded in my right ear. It swung open and both our bodies moved forward in stiff motions. We passed a frightened and confused Philipe as Eve forced our bodies up the stairs and into the apartment.

Eve leaned against the far window, dark against the daylight.

"On your knees."

Lilith's hands shot up behind her head and she sank to her knees. Philipe had closed the door but stood as stone.

"Eve stop!" I said then my own body copied Lilith's. The impact of my kneecaps hitting the hard ground sent electric shocks through my body.

"You let them hurt her! You let them and I'm going to end you." Eve made Lilith stand, hands still behind her head, and walk closer.

"I didn't know. Eve, I'm here to help. I mean you no harm."

"Liar. You knew where we were. You sent the notes."

"Yes, but I never told the Twins where you were, I was playing them. Read my thoughts!"

"That's the problem with you Mentium, this isn't a game. Life isn't to be played with."

I strained to speak, my mouth, unresponsive, Eve, in complete control of every part of me.

"Please, I'm here to help, I've always been here to help."

"Stop lying to me," she said, and Lilith's muscles contracted. She wailed.

"Stop it! Stop this shit right now goddammit!" said Del, but through our body's mouth. "I'm not a brain but even I know we need this lady. Eve, just take a fucking breath and think for a minute. This is wrong. You gotta know it is."

"Do I?"

"Sure you do. Be angry. You should be, but she's not a good place to start. Those Twins, this Izzy guy, they come first. Just for now. Take care of them first."

Eve's muscles relaxed and so did Lilith's. She fell to her side against the red carpet. My own body regained mobility and my first instinct was to punch Del in the mouth. Alas, it was my mouth too. How dare he even suggest that she continue past Izzy and the Twins?

The damned truth of it was, his approach was well conceived. He told Eve what she needed to hear. Del, despite all his flaws, was a man of honour and I'd grown to at least trust his intentions.

"Del?" asked Bernie, moving toward my body.

"For now, buddy. Just for now. Someone's gotta talk some damn sense into her or she might have us all pushing daisies."

"I'm not going to kill you," said Eve, slumping against the glass.

"That's good. Real good," said Del, "Now just chit-chat with these two and be civil. We've got work to do, am I right, M?"

<h1 style="text-align:center">56</h1>

<h2 style="text-align:center">REVELATIONS & REVISIONS</h2>

What came next was planning. We all huddled around Philipe's worktable. All but Eve, Philipe and Sophie. I'd given the couple money for an extended vacation in exchange for his apartment keys and the promise they wouldn't divulge their destination and wouldn't return for weeks. Eve chose to brood at the window.

We laid out our current strategy of sabotage and our secret chamber. The Field Marshall didn't approve.

"So you're just getting rid of my plans?" I asked.

"Not entirely," Lilith said. "The extra chamber was a stroke of genius, love, and we can always fall back to it if need be but at this point we need finality, and sabotage isn't going to cut it. You forget that with each passing day, support for the Twins is growing amongst the Underlings. They've always been so hungry for power and this is the best shot they've ever had to acquire it."

Lilith had waited an hour for the dust to clear and for the couple to pack and leave before she ordered us to the table. Eve had protested, Lilith had 'explained' her qualifications as a military leader, and Eve relented.

"Fine," I said, looking around the table. Jacques and Bernard were content to let Lilith, Eve, and I duke it out. "I assume you have some alternative?"

"I do, in fact."

"Oh, really, and how long have you had this plan?" asked Eve.

"It came to me after you tried to kill me."

"Well," I said, moving to the fabric-strewn sofa, "Do tell."

She sat beside me and the others turned toward her.

"You're going to crash a party."

"A party?" asked Bernard.

Eve cut in. "And where will you be?"

"I'm on the guest list. The Twins are throwing an 'Opening Gala' for their world domination. It starts at nine in Eiffel's Apartment."

"Unbelievable," I said. "A party? In Eiffel's apartment?"

"They want you humiliated. What better way than to one-up your celebration?"

"How exactly are we going to waltz into a party for the Mentium?" asked Bernard. Jacques refilled his coffee and moved to the next empty cup. "They've seen M, they've seen Jacques, that only leaves Eve and myself."

"She wants me to mask your faces from the others," said Eve. "That's not a problem."

"Please stay out of my head, dear," said Lilith.

Eve narrowed her eyes.

"Eve's right," said Lilith. "To everyone else, you'll just be the night's entertainment."

"I don't follow," I said.

"You're all musicians. The Twins will be delighted that I've hired a live band for their soiree."

"The orchestration is all wrong," said Bernard. "Not to rain on your parade, but a guitar and a bari sax is not a very pleasant duo."

"I see where she's going," I said. "I'll swap guitar for bass. I know Del's dabbled."

Dabbled? We'll be just fine and you know it.

"Jacques plays piano," said Eve, softening her tone. "Don't let him tell you he's anything but brilliant."

Jacques shrugged.

Bernie is a hell of a singer. Put him out front.

"Del, has just informed me that Bernard has quite the voice."

"Whoa no. I'm not playing frontman." Bernie shook his head like a child avoiding food. "And besides, unless Eve plays, we don't have a drummer."

Lilith gave me a wink. "Leave that to me."

57

PARTY CRASHERS

"Toot, toot, Tootsie, Goodbye. Toot toot Tootsie, don't cry…"

Bernard sang the words in a rich, warm tone. The back of his black tux — one of several we had 'rented', despite it being a Sunday — swayed as the small party carried on before us.

The angular room of iron girders and patterned wallpaper was lit with candles whose light danced with the cut glassware in the hands of my Mentium brothers and sisters. A hulking Eunuch bartender slung champagne, whisky and gin in the far corner of the tiny space as others offered silver trays of finger food to the elegant, arrogant partygoers. The trays and thus, the air, reeked of garlic and cheeses.

I grit my teeth and thumped along with the energetic beat. I hated this song. It had borne me into Del's body and into an opium hell. I hoped it would lead me out of this mess.

"Kiss me Tootsie and then, do it over again…"

Sal, of all people, sat pressed against the ornate wall striking a stripped-down drum set with expert brush strokes. Sal, for all his offenses, was a much better drummer than Sticky.

He had been Lilith's eyes for days. She'd picked up on his drum experience from reading his mind. She'd also picked up on his deplorable character. At my behest she made sure his drumming was the only skill left to him. Sal the drumming Eunuch.

361

"When somebody says goodbye to me, I'm as sad as I can be…"

The gala was still getting started and its similarity to my own party there in Eiffel's tower-top apartment was both insulting and hilarious. It was yet another example of the Twins using something of mine for their own purposes.

"He seemed to take a lot of pleasure, saying goodbye to his treasure…"

The Twins and Lilith were the only Mentium I knew by name. Kali and Izzy were yet to attend. The other dozen or so guests were Underlings I'd neglected to remember.

Jacques was phenomenal. Lilith had Eunuchs heft a small upright piano into Eiffel's apartment and Jacques' touch was as nuanced as his manner was blunt. He had a collection of women, and a few men, leaning on the back of the instrument watching him work.

One of those men was Kukulkan. The man who had been at Tian's home, who had me pulled from the opium den, who was Lilith's right hand and, that night, our puppet master.

He stood by that piano, in his black satin tuxedo and tapped his snake-skinned boot while pretending to control our actions. A band of outsiders was never allowed to perform unchecked.

While Kukulkan pretended, Eve was at work from across the Seine inside the *Jardins du Trocadéro*. She altered our appearance to all in attendance and they were none the wiser. No Broadcaster would think to worry about the influence of a Spectre because to them, there weren't any.

"Thank you, we'll be right back," said Bernard at the conclusion of that hateful song, our tenth of the evening. Del's fingers were not used to the hefty strings of the upright bass we'd been playing and the tips of each ached. I removed the small brown glass bottle from my pocket and placed a few drops of laudanum under my tongue. Just enough to keep my cravings from being a distraction.

The room was abuzz with energy and other sorts of distractions. My attention fell toward my love. She was chatting with the Twins near the far window, stunning in a floor-length, emerald-sequined gown. Her black hair pressed down by a delicate ruby-studded tiara.

I wanted to stare but that night's bass player could not, so I let my eyes drift, always sweeping across her.

Their words vanished in the din of the crowd but the trio's body language was positive and relaxed until Artemis reached out for Lilith's arm and pulled her in close. After a few whispered words, Lilith looked at Apollo with excitement then back to Artemis. The bastards were beaming about something. She squeezed both their hands and excused herself from the conversation. As she turned away and made her way toward us, her face melted into concern.

She weaved and swayed through the tightly packed space, setting her empty coupé of champagne down as she moved. Her perfume, spicy and floral, drifted toward me as she passed and stood close to Kukulkan.

"We have a problem," she said to Kukulkan and thus to us all. "The Twins ordered Kali and Izanagi to stay back at the lab. They're going to perform a demonstration like it's a damned fireworks show."

"Not good," said Kukulkan. He had a flare for understatement.

Kali produced the most vivid visions of all Upper Echelon. With Izzy's expertise, who knew what horrors they'd unleash on the city. Even if brief, even if contained and late into the evening, word would get out. This was reckless.

"What do we do?" asked Bernard. "We need them here. Do we abort?"

"No," said Lilith. "We have to be patient. They're set to arrive after the demonstration. We'll delay until then, kill all four, and offer the Underlings our ultimatum."

Lilith had, despite my protests, convinced the group of the efficacy of killing the Twins, Izzy, and Kali. It would have to do for revenge, but I wanted so badly to fill the coming years with their suffering.

I don't like this, said Eve into all our heads.

"Just stick to the plan and all will be well," Lilith said, and strode off toward a new group of Underlings.

"Another song would be good, boys," said Kukulkan, tipping his feathered hat toward the Twins who were none too pleased at the length of our silence.

Jacques jumped into a solo version of Gershwin's *Rhapsody in Blue,* and the mentally castrated Sal and I settled into his playing, adding accompaniment when appropriate.

"I'll just keep an eye on the Twins," said Bernard. The song had no vocals.

Bernard took his position next to Kukulkan. "Stand rigid," he told Bernard. "I keep my puppets on tight strings."

Bernard stood tall and Jacques breathed life into the party. His fingers danced and his timing ebbed and flowed for maximum effect. I had no idea of his skill and I couldn't help but watch as he played.

Just watch what we're doing here, boss, said Del. *Jacques ain't going anywhere.*

I turned back toward Sal who kept perfect time but whose face held no expression.

This is silly. said Eve. *Why don't we strike now? We have the Twins. Just because Izanagi and Kali aren't here doesn't mean that's a bad thing. We just have two fewer threats to deal with. I say now's as...*

Jacques played on. The notes crescendoed then cascaded toward a deep chord.

"Eve? Are you okay?" asked Bernard. We all turned toward Lilith who was back with the Twins. Hand gestures, feigned ignorance, anger, raised voices.

"Tell them to start now," roared Apollo. The room went silent. "Start broadcasting now. We can't wait. We're under attack."

It was over before any of us knew what had happened.

"The band, they're different," said Artemis, "That bass player..."

Lilith reached through the slit of her dress and pulled a snub-nosed revolver.

"Traitor!" said Artemis and she grabbed at Lilith's hands. The room, chaos.

"Get to the elevator now. Both of you." I said to Bernard and Jacques. "I can't protect all our minds. Go!"

They did as they were told and that left me in a room with Lilith and Kukulkan. Sal, oblivious, played on as a mass of Underlings surged toward me. I planted my feet but was pulled backward by

Kukulkan's strong hand. The red feather in his Homburg streaked past my face and gunfire erupted.

The Underlings scattered and a second round tore into the ground at Artemis' feet. Mental powers mean nothing to blocked minds, meaning weapons still had use amongst Broadcasters.

"You're done. Do you here me, Underling? Done." Apollo tugged at his sister and Lilith rolled grabbing at her legs.

"Look out!" I cried, but Kukulkan's arm was wrapped by a lithe Underling. Fists fell. Blood. Kukulkan reeled and his foe pressed until a bullet opened the enemy's skull.

"Follow them!" Lilith was up and charging toward the elevators. The Twins were gone, so were most of the Underlings, and so was the elevator.

The three of us reached out for Eve. None of us could sense her. The elevator was our only way down. Lilith and Kukulkan culled the remaining Underlings with their remaining bullets while we waited the excruciating moments for the elevator car to return. Sal, who was still banging his drums, received a final bang from Lilith.

The two threw their empty guns aside when the elevator finally came. The calm in the box as we descended was so out of place. There was no speech, verbal, mental or otherwise. Bernard and Jacques were down there somewhere. Eve? The Twins? Who knew? The three of us practically vibrated with nervous energy and we stood there bottling it for what we knew was to come. The car came to a stop, the doors opened, and we prepared to uncork those bottles.

A half dozen Underlings stood scattered around the second floor of the tower. All staring right at us.

"Hold and fold?" I asked.

"What else," said Kukulkan as he and Lilith lunged at our attackers. I stayed behind near the elevator and studied the minds of each foe.

Lilith landed the first blow and her victim lost just enough focus to allow me access to her mind. I forced her body to freeze long enough for Lilith to lay the woman out.

Lilith and Kukulkan kicked, elbowed, and punched and I in turn, jumped from dazed mind to dazed mind until we'd cleared the second floor.

The elevator doors again closed, again there was silence, but when we arrived on the first floor, it was empty.

"I don't want to know what we're going to find down there," said Kukulkan as we ran toward the final elevator.

"Just focus, soldier," said Lilith, calling the last car.

As we descended the northwest leg of the tower, we could see a group of Underlings and Eunuchs through the glass of the elevator. They were gathered in the snow around a pile of bodies. Some sitting, others on their sides, all bound. Our enemies' faces tracked the elevator until we came to rest.

We stepped out onto terra firma to meet a wall of opposition. Between the legs of the Eunuchs and Underlings, Bernard and Jacques lay beaten and bound. Eve was there too, blacked out. Or was she moving?

"Stand aside, all of you," said Lilith.

"We don't take your orders anymore." One Underling stepped forward. I couldn't remember his name, which was just as well.

"Then take my warning," I said. This was the ultimatum that was supposed to come after the Twins' deaths. "You have one choice left to you. You can choose the path of the Twins and die along with them and our beloved Mentium. You can help them destroy all we've built. Or, you can join us, you can help us stop them and you can help us mend our broken order. What say you?"

The Eunuchs stood sentinel, snow collecting on their wide shoulders, awaiting orders from their Underling masters. The Underlings only stared and sneered.

The Underling who has spoken took another step toward us, but only one. He froze in place. We all froze.

A small, solitary figure rolled to its side behind the line of Underlings and Eunuchs. A single Eunuch pulled a knife from its place on his belt an turned away from us. The knife scraped against fibres and the huge man stepped to the side. Eve emerged, knife in hand, from the hole he'd made, unbound, and from the look in her eyes, unhinged.

Holy shit, said Del.

She marched up to us and stared into Lilith's eyes. The bound bodies began to move. A second Eunuch cut the bonds of Bernard, Jacques and our four other Underling allies. The Eunuch then returned to his place in the line as did the first. Eve's silence was deafening and I kept my eyes trained on her. Our secret weapon, my gamble.

The small woman adjusted her purple overcoat and walked back toward the line of our enemies, pointing at them with the knife.

I turned to look at Bernard whose glistening eyes reflected the knowledge of what was coming, the understanding that he could do nothing, and the disappointment of discovering a companion was not what they seem.

Eve started at the end farthest from us. She grabbed a lean, muscled woman by the shoulder and thrust the knife up and under her ribs. In, up, twist. The woman dropped as her agonised wail filled the winter air. Next came a short, stocky man. Eve again placed her hand on his shoulder, then pulled it back, instead handing the knife to him. She turned with a smirk. As she trod toward us, he opened his belly like a samurai, dropped to his knees, and held the knife up to next person. This continued, one by one.

"Where are they?" she asked over the death rattles behind her.

"Jacques," said Bernard, his eyes fixed on the man. "You're changing. Eve are you doing this? M?"

Vivienne's enforcer was dumbfounded as we all watched it happen. His hands gnarled into long-clawed monstrosities, his mouth stretched into a salivating muzzle. A tail…

Above us, giant bats filled the sky, their shrieks splitting the snowy night. Beyond them, fireballs leapt up from city streets. It could only be a dragon.

"It's begun," said Lilith.

Eve growled and blocked it all from our minds. Jacques was Jacques again and so too the city, But the world…

"We need to go," said Eve. "Now!"

58

THE STREETS

Jacques kept the car at fast but even pace. Despite the heavy snow, we kept the top open and our minds open to the horrors around us. While Eve made sure we all looked like ourselves in the eyes of each other, we needed to understand what was happening. Eve needed to see what she had to set right.

Our motor car held Jacques, Eve, Lilith, Bernard, and myself. Kukulkan drove a second with the four other loyal Underlings. Our caravan snaked through the streets of Paris and around monsters of every fashion.

"What is Kali thinking?" asked Lilith. "We're in Paris, these should all be Western European visions."

No one answered, but I'd wager that she was using the confusion and panic to have a little fun.

"Is that a pterodactyl?" Bernard's voice was solid but his eyes were wide. The beast soared through the dense falling snow on broad, leathery wings.

"Kongamato," said Lilith. "From the Congo basin but yes, essentially a pterodactyl."

At least it had been. The streets below were showered with its blood as a European dragon snapped the kongamato's neck in its jaws.

The streets were a far darker scene than I had feared. Kali, inside my signal generator, was a true master. People were spilling out of their homes though none looked like people. All of them knew they were themselves, but in others they saw demons and they brutalised each other in mass self-defence. The sounds of screams, gunshots, and breaking glass came from all around. They clawed and pushed and bit and punched at each other. Their fear too deep to hear that the screams from the demons attacking them sounded much like their own. The details of Kali's visions were so visceral, deadly and above all, believable.

"Nephilim!" said Lilith as she pointed toward the heart of the city. The heads of three giants swayed above the buildings with wild dark hair and thick beards. They took turns thrusting their grey spears into the air then down into some terrified mind.

Agonised screams broke our collective stare and Jacques swerved to miss fresh horrors that were in our path, but of course weren't.

"Allghoi Khorkhoi," I said, "Mongolian death worms."

The cobra-sized worms wiggled from the sewers. The hooks at the end of each fire-red body segment clawed at the snowy cobbles as they scattered. A couple cowered and writhed against a store front, screaming as the worms soaked them with their famed acid.

"Faster Jacques, please!" said Bernard, looking at the big man but seeing a corpse. "Can we help them? What can we do?"

"All we can do is finish this," I said.

Eve leaned against the window, studying the chaos. Study was good. Undoing these nightmares would take much effort, even for a Spectre.

Putrid smoke rose from manhole covers and coalesced into two massive jinn. Their muscled arms swiped at us as we passed. Eve was silent and calm, letting the arms sweep a mere metre from her head. She was angry. I hoped that was also good.

We sped on, huddling together against the wind and snow and cold. We crossed the river under the water spray of a colossal serpent, the Amazonian Yacumama, which froze in the frigid air and pelted us with ice pellets.

Street after street, the carnage grew. The sky was filled with all manner of flying beasts. Bodies, real bodies, lay over red snow.

"Faster, Jacques, we have to stop this," yelled Bernard.

Something thundered ahead of us. A pillar crushed the pavement as we approached the Champs-Élysées only it became clear it was no pillar.

Erawan, the massive three-headed Elephant of Thai lore thundered down the street. Jacques tried to stop but our tires slid in the snow. We spun beneath the imaginary monstrosity only to right ourselves and continue on. Onward toward them.

"Damn it," said Lilith as our motorcar slowed on a narrow street near *Gare Saint-Lazare*. Before us, a mob of people, maybe fifteen, brawled in the middle of an intersection. Jacques honked the horn and revved the engine but it only served to draw the wretched creatures toward us.

"Watch out!" cried Bernard as a woman launched her body onto the hood of the vehicle.

Eve yelled into the night and stood on her seat, gripping the windscreen for support.

"Move!"

The bloodied people ran to the building walls on either side of the street, some with broken legs, others cradled their arms. They hurled themselves against the bricks and kept marching, pressing their faces into the cold stone.

"Drive, Jacques," she said.

He nodded. He was terrified. It was the first time I'd seen the man show fear. It wasn't for the nightmares in the streets. He feared Eve. We all did.

Within minutes, we'd reached Montmartre. The tower glowed to our right as we climbed higher, showing itself and disappearing again as the buildings rolled by. Nothing about it had any trace of menace. Its amber search light swept the snowy air in slow circles, oblivious to the torture it was inflicting.

Below the tower, eight massive black tentacles groped at the night from under the murky depths of the Seine. There had been a kraken after all. A prediction I was not happy to claim. Above us, clouds of screaming bats slowly changed to flocks of harpies. A buffalo-headed mahishasura shifted to the bull-headed minotaur. The people around us became more refined though still terrifying.

"The Twins," said Lilith, "they've taken over."

The temple of the Mentium grew larger in the windscreen and so too did a bright red figure against the winter white. Kali stood ready before the main door to temple. She was not alone. Nor, were we.

Jacques stopped the motorcar fifty metres from the Temple door. Three more cars stopped behind us. Our cavalry had arrived.

We stepped from the vehicle and gathered in a semicircle. Kukulkan tipped his hat to Kali with a smirk.

Kali licked at her lips. "Lilith, you traitorous bitch. I'm going to have your head. Marduk, I'll grind that pathetic body into the ground."

"So she's the one," said Eve and she started to walk forward.

"Now!" cried Kali and her Mentium hoard rushed us. Eve ignored them, keeping her eyes on Kali, who stepped out to meet her.

Jacques and Bernard wielded blunt instruments. Bernard, a tire iron, Jacques, a wrench. Aim for heads, they'd been told.

The two waves of combatants crashed together to the chorus of Monos screaming all around us. Our own yells joined the song. This was wrong. Eve wasn't stopping them.

Blows came in fits and starts as we battled with both mind and body. Physical blows opened minds to attack as focus was broken.

Bernard and Jacques fought back-to-back, circling, though the pummelling they received was brutal.

"There!" I forced a body to freeze. Bernard swung his wrench and ended the threat before being forced to swing the tool at his own leg.

"Again," I called, holding the attacker and Bernard swung. After the blow, his free hand reached for a gun dropped by his victim, and I turned to seek another foe.

"M!" he yelled.

The gun was pressed under his own chin. How could I have been so stupid as to not warn him?

Time seemed to slow, in the scrum that boiled around us, I couldn't find the mind responsible. I reached toward Bernard unable to do anything else.

Jacques leapt, gripping the gun as it fired. The bullet grazed across Bernard's cheek. Jacques landed flat on his bruised ribs and he rolled onto his back, groping at the damaged bones. Bernard sank to his knees, one hand moving to his cheek and the other his ringing ears.

The gunshot echoed and with each repeat, more of our enemies paused.

"Come on," said Eve, standing over a quivering, mutilated Kali.

"Eve," said Bernard. "Jesus, Eve, what did you do?"

Kali's stomach had been opened and an eye lay at her feet. A knife protruded from her head where an entombment would take place. All the wounds, self-inflicted.

Eve said nothing and stepped through the temple door.

Kukulkan and the Underling man known as Karora made a move to help Jacques but he waved them off. He'd managed to push himself up against a wall.

Our group, now down to five including Lilith, Eve, Bernard, Kukulkan, and myself, walked around Kali's convulsing body. I couldn't stand to look at Eve's handiwork.

As I entered the amber light of our temple foyer, a shot rang out from behind.

"Bernie, no," said Lilith, as he dropped his gun next to a now-still Kali.

"It wasn't right," he said, shock wracking his body. "That wasn't right. I couldn't leave another person like that."

"Bernard," I said, "you are a good man. Now, pull yourself together. We need to find Eve."

59

THE TEMPLE

"Stay close," I said to Bernard as Lilith led us through the labyrinth of stairwells and passageways that made up the Temple. No route was straightforward. Up to go down, right to go left. The Mentium owned the entire block, each building linked from within and we would be traversing them all to reach my laboratory.

I hoped we'd find Eve along the way. We needed to help her get her head straight so she could set our world right.

"There will be more Underlings and Eunuchs," said Lilith.

"How many?" asked Bernard, still shaken from his gift of mercy.

"Plenty," said Kukulkan. "But most are scattered around the city. The Twins wanted detailed reports about their big broadcast. We're lucky they sent them out, they've called in dozens of Underlings from all over the world."

"They just wanted a bigger audience," I said, leading the group up the stairwell along the custard-yellow walls.

"You got it," he said.

Once everyone was on the first landing, Lilith gathered us together. "It will be close- quarters combat until we reach the lab. M, your body's useless in a fight. You'll take up the rear and try to get into any minds you can. Karora, cover his back."

"Insults is it," I said.

"Reality, love." Having the banter back felt like the dragon had me in its grip. So delicious and so inappropriate. Verbal sparring with Lilith always excited me.

"I'll lead," she continued. "Kukulkan, you'll follow me and Bernie, you're behind him."

"Okay, what should I do?" asked Bernard, shaking his limbs, both trying to pump himself up for the task and shake away his first kill.

"You can start by throwing that gun away," she said. "We don't need a repeat of that street scene, do we?"

He tossed the gun over the railing. "So, just my fists then?"

Kukulkan kicked at the balusters of the railing. Two broke off at the floor and he pried them free, handing both to Bernard. "There, just swing them hard."

Bernard clacked them together. "Got it."

"Let's move," said Lilith, and we continued at a jog.

It wasn't long before my lungs were burning. My legs as well. I blocked out the pain and kept pace, reaching forward with my mind.

"Three, second door!" I called.

Lilith was all knees and elbows, placed with surgical precision. Kukulkan was a brawler, fast on his feet and even quicker to strike. He could have been a champion featherweight. It took Bernard no time to get used to his improvised weapons. One by one the mental blocks of our foes slipped, and we jumped inside their minds. The temple was crawling with hostile Mentium. We needed to even the sides which meant we needed most of them gone. "Run to Versailles," I told them, and each ran down the hallway past me. Simple, time consuming, and in that weather, deadly.

"Well played, my love," said Lilith.

Our strategy was efficient. We encountered no fewer than six additional groups. We suffered bruises but they suffered leg cramps as all of them began their marathon run.

"There," I said, pointing forward. "That open door."

Our jog turned to a sprint and the glow of the doorway came ever more into focus as did Apollo, his hands on his hips like some sort of hero.

"It's done, M, you've lost," said Apollo.

We four squinted at the contrast of light from the dim hallway. Kukulkan was first through and as his snakeskin boot landed on the top step of the short iron stairwell into my lab, Apollo's eyes drifted to the left, to where the control panels lay, to where Izzy most certainly lay in wait.

The sound of a throw switch met our ears as Kukulkan was already crumbling from the electric shock he'd received. Izzy had booby trapped my lab, the bastard. "Where is Eve?" I said to anyone. "We need her, now."

"We can't wait," said Bernard as he charged past us.

"What are you doing?" I screamed.

He leapt through the doorway as Izzy pulled the switch again, but the airborne Bernard wasn't grounded. He landed with an awkward roll and popped up to give Apollo a swipe across the face with a baluster. The other he threw at Izzy, who wailed as it struck his injured arm.

Lilith and I used the distraction to enter the room.

The game was on.

Bernard had wrestled Apollo to the ground and knelt on top of him, driving a fist into his face. Apollo was a strong man but so, too was Bernard, and he'd reached his limit that day. Apollo was his catharsis and I tried my damnedest to block Bernard's mind to allow the session to continue.

"Get off of him," roared Artemis, throwing off her copper helmet and springing from the signal generator, leaving two Underlings to continue broadcasting. Lilith was already on her way to meet her. Izzy reached Apollo first and kicked Bernard in the back, sending him tumbling.

I used the distraction to take my place amongst the control panels of my radio. Voltage gauges, glass vacuum tubes, brass knobs, everything polished for my triumph, a triumph the Twins had tried to steal, a triumph they had bastardised, a triumph Izzy had sold for my seat on the Upper Echelon.

"Behind you," boomed Bernard, but Izzy's knuckles landed above my ear, his fists falling in violent waves. He'd forgone his sling to inflict more damage, more revenge.

"You will not take this from me, M."

"Izzy, pl…" I could feel my consciousness slipping back into the mind as the concussive blows rattled the brain.

"You've shit on me for too long, M. I'm not going to take it. This is my time!"

The light dimmed in my eyes and I was falling. Falling into the mind. I turned to my belly and my Babylon rushed up toward me. My home. Would it be forever?

The ground approached quickly but something else approached faster. A figure, small, grey, Del!

I landed in a cloud of yellow dust and turned back toward the sky. I could feel it as the thin bones of Del's hand broke against Izzy's jaw. The pain seared. I could feel Izzy's ribs crack against Del's narrow knee.

Del pushed away from Izzy and groped for the copper laboratory still, perched atop a nearby work desk, a still full of conductive liquid. Izzy in turn reached for Del as did I.

Del, I screamed from within. *No, hold onto it!*

The still was slipping from his fingers and he attempted to throw it. As his arms swung forward, those same fingers flexed and instead it crashed to the floor in front of the panel.

I could feel Izzy's hand cross our cheek and Del came falling back into the mind as our body crashed to the lab floor.

I jumped, my wings digging at the air until I reached a falling Del, taking him in my arms and gliding back to my throne. "Del, how?"

"I don't know. You were hurt. You needed help. I, I had to help."

"Del, I…"

The muted sound of Lilith's voice rang inside the mind. "M, love, come back, M,"

"Go," said Del.

6O.

THE RECKONING

"I'm here," were my first waking words. Izzy lay next to me, a broken baluster across his head. Both Mentium within the signal generator remained there, stabbed through the chest by Lilith. Kukulkan was dead. Eve was still missing. Bernard stood with a knife at his throat. Artemis held that knife and Apollo sneered.

"The world has seen our visions, M," he said. "It's done."

"Once, Apollo. You've done it once. I'm going to make sure that it's the only chance you have."

"You don't get to make threats," said Artemis, gripping Bernard tighter. "Leave us, or he dies. Those are your options. We direct you, Underling."

Lilith fumed next to me. Her eyes darted around the room, analysing the space, looking for weapons, strategising, and then shaking away the dread when our situation was confirmed.

I reached into Bernard's mind.

"M," he asked, "What should I do. Just tell me what to do."

"What they ask, Bernard, whatever they ask. At this moment, we have no options."

I pulled out of his mind. There was no discussion to have.

"Leave us, and never return," said Artemis.

"No sister, I want blood."

"I'll show you all the blood you can stomach," said Lilith, stepping toward them, which only served to draw the first drop from Bernard's neck.

"I'm sick of this," Artemis released Bernard only to kick at the back of his leg and grip his hair as he fell to his knees. She held the knife out, ready to strike.

"Get Del out of here, M," said Bernard. "Get him somewhere safe. Get a new body. Fight then. Just get Del the hell out of here."

Artemis smiled at that. Then at me, letting the look linger and burn. The smile then drifted to her brother as she squared her arm to strike.

The Greek devil lifted the knife, gave me a wink, then with a shriek, pushed the knife into her own skull, at the perfect point to entomb someone, and just deep enough.

Bernard staggered to his feet. Apollo stood as stone and behind him stood Eve, motionless, letting her mind do the work. Apollo sobbed and his only motions were the tears that slid over his golden skin. Where had she been? It didn't matter. We still needed her.

Eve grabbed Apollo by his ivory lapels, and stared into his eyes, eyes that went wide, then blank. He, too, a heap on the floor.

"Help me fix this mess," said Eve, her face stone.

We three said nothing.

"Get me hooked up. Now!"

Lilith guided her over to the empty chamber where Artemis had been. Bernard placed the copper helmet over her head.

At the control board, I asked, "Are you ready?"

"Do it."

I turned the radio back on, and Eve's mind was broadcast over the entire city. Her hands flexed at the handles as she focused on her task. Lilith, Bernard, and I made our way to the window. The dragon circling the city dissolved into the falling snow, the giants shrank away to nothing, and the Monos woke from their nightmare.

The screaming and cries from outside stopped at once, leaving only the sound of shuffling feet. Monos in pyjamas trudged along the sidewalk, no doubt on a somnambulant march back to bed. Still, the bodies of the dead lay strewn across the icy ground.

The visions were gone, the populace, docile.

"The bodies?" I asked, still looking out at the world the Twins had scarred.

"A suicide cult," Eve said. "It's messy but it's a workable explanation."

"That's good, well played," I said.

"I think so."

I turned to find Eve standing behind me, out of the chamber. Her work was done but she wasn't smiling. Lilith lay on the floor, eyes wide.

"You gave me your word!" I said, taking Lilith in my arms.

"Eve, what have you done?" asked Bernard.

"What was necessary. The Mentium needed to pay for their sins and now, they have."

"Why spare me?" I asked, squeezing my love my chest.

"I spared Del but in order to do that I had to spare you. Make no mistake, I want you punished."

"Is that what you've done here? Punished us?"

"I've entombed you. All of you," she said, buttoning her purple overcoat. "You really are quite the genius, M. The system you used to lock Del inside his own mind made me wonder, could I do something like that?"

"Eve…" said Bernard.

She ignored him.

"Then we spent all that time working on your second signal generator. You yammered on and on about how your precious radio works. You taught me just what it was capable of. I decided to do a little extra work while I saved humanity from your kind. I used your little toy to entomb every last Mentium in range. The hospitals are going to be flooded with unresponsive people tonight."

"You cannot be serious."

Eve laughed. "Look at her, M. Look into those green eyes."

They were dead. Not death, but dead to the world. Entombed.

"What now, Eve?" I said. "What's your play now?"

"I give you three minutes to leave, and then I destroy the Mentium for good."

"How?"

"Your three minutes start now."

"Eve please, you've…" Bernard paused. "This is too far."

"You had better leave, Bernie."

"I want the bodies!" I yelled, still holding my love.

"I want the bodies. I want Izzy and the Twins, and Lilith. I want their bodies. At least grant me that."

"Take them," she said. "Just go."

"Get the Twins, Bernard." I did my best to drag Lilith from the lab. She was so heavy when for centuries she had always been so light.

I climbed a small ladder up and through a street-level window. Bernard passed each body through and I dragged them to the side as he climbed out.

"Take her to Jacques," I said, as I began pulling Izzy through the dirty slush of the street. Bernard carried Lilith away and returned to help with the Twins.

Bernard sat against a stone wall next to Jacques, who grunted at his ribs with each breath. I clung to Lilith once more. She stared at the night and at nothing. Her mouth, loose and hanging. Everything limp.

"What do we do, Bernard?" I said. "What do I do?"

He didn't speak. A snowflake fell onto my Lilith's eye and melted without a blink.

She was gone but she was right there, in my arms. Her body was warm and perfect but her mind, who she *was*, locked in a prison. A prison like Del.

I gasped.

"What?" asked Bernard.

"I need you to find the car and bring it as fast as you possibly can."

"Okay…"

"Quickly!"

Bernard ran off and I sank into the mind.

Del was still outside the subconscious. He'd left the throne, and now sat at the foot of my ziggurat.

"Del," I said, landing beside him. "Del, I'm giving you this body back and I'm doing it right now."

Del stood, astonished. "How? I mean, great, yeah, but how?"

"Killing you."

He stepped backward and tripped on the sandstone steps.

"You can't be serious. After all this you're just going to kill me?"

"Almost."

"What are you talking about? Almost?"

"Del, I need you to trust me and I need you to trust Bernard. We won't let you die. You don't deserve to die. Do you trust us?"

"I, I trust Bernie."

"Then that will have to do. Trust him, he will not fail you."

"What are you going to do?

"You don't need to know. It's better if you don't. Now," I said, raising my outstretched arm. As it rose, an iron platform grew from beneath Del's feet.

"What are you doing to me?"

Iron bars fell from the sky and surrounded the platform, an iron roof, a metre thick, crashed down atop them.

"No, not again, you can't do this!"

I walked up to him, his arms groping for me through the bars. Into his hand I dropped a key.

"What's this?"

"That will let you out, but for this to work, I need to you stay in here. Stay locked and safe until I'm gone. Fully gone. You'll feel me go and then I want you to let yourself out and do it quickly."

"I don't know."

"Del, I'm giving you your life back, now take it."

I snapped back into the icy air of reality and found Bernard piling the Twins into the back of Vivienne's car.

"Bernard, Jacques, hurry!" I called. "Help me get Lilith into the car. I'll be in the front seat and put her across my lap."

Jacques winced as he hefted Izzy on top of the Twins while Bernard carried Lilith to me.

"Thank you," I said, stroking her hair.

He squeezed my shoulder then climbed in with the comatose Mentium in back.

Jacques turned the key and the car shook to life, then shook once more. Two huge fireballs rose into the night behind us. Eve had finished her job.

"Jacques, I need you to drive us to the hospital."

Another explosion rang out and he pulled away.

"The hospital? Why the hospital?" asked Bernard, pushing Apollo aside to clear more room for himself.

As we roared down the hill more fire erupted from the south.

"The catacombs," I said.

"Look," said Bernard and pointed at the tower. Showers of flame cascaded down from the top."

"It's gone, my radio…" I stared at the fire as the concussions finally met our ears.

Bernard again grabbed my shoulder but this time gave it a shake. "M, the hospital, why?"

"Because I've found a way to give Del back to you. You're not going to like my method."

"Why not? M, what are you going to do?"

I didn't answer, just sat stroking Lilith's hair as the streetlights streaked past. I was about to gamble with three lives.

"M?"

With Del's thin arm, I reached into my boot and retrieved the knife I'd taken off the felonious kitten that first night. With one hand I opened its blade.

"M?"

A long deep breath, a final decision, an act. I ran the blade across my wrist. Across, this time, *across*.

"No!, Damn it, no. What are you doing?" yelled Bernard, grabbing at the knife. I let him take it.

Jacques recoiled in horror.

"Jacques, drive, get us to a hospital," I said, staring into the green eyes of my love.

"Damn it M, what have you done?"

"Bernard, listen carefully. Transference has only ever happened through death. As the body fades, the mind releases enough for our consciousness to make the jump. But that's just it."

I could feel my concentration draining with my blood.

"What's it?"

"It's not death at all," I said, struggling to stay focused as the blood drained from my wrist and flowed over my fingers. "It's just a matter of forcing the brain to let go. What I'm doing is forcing Del's brain to let me go. When I'm gone…"

"What, M? What happens when you're gone?"

"When I'm gone, it will be Del's again. He'll be Del again. It's all his. It's—" Lilith's eyes were so beautiful. I focused hard on their shape, their colour, those eyes.

"M, where are you going? Stay here. Fight it, M, goddammit. Fight!"

Bernard was wrong. It wasn't the time to fight. It was the time to fly.

Like an arrow.

This time, the target was right in front of me.

AMSTERDAM

• • •

1933

61

THE FUTURE

Warm rain pelted the streets of Amsterdam and the water in the canal danced to its impact. The downpour sent pedestrians prancing about like frightened antelope.

We sat near the leaded window of our study and watched. We wore a flowing green silk dress and had our raven hair tied up. The steam from our coffee cup left fog on the glass.

To our left, a marquetry side table held a picture frame. The image was of Del, Bernard, Vivienne, and Jaques. It was taken in 1930 in front of their new business, in which we were the primary investors. The combination hotel-theatre attracted the continental *crème de la crème* who sought both Vivienne's hospitality and Del and Bernard's orchestra that played nightly shows. My blade hadn't cut deep, and Del's playing did not suffer. These people, a Multi-Receiver and three Monos, had proven invaluable to us and it was only right they be rewarded. I owed them.

The years after my radio was destroyed were not easy for any of us. Del spent six months in the best institution our money could afford, uncoiling the dragon from his body and restructuring his mind. While he recovered, Bernard, Vivienne, Jacques and the two of us, lived together for a time in Lilith's apartment until we could relocate them into permanent living spaces. They mended their physical wounds and helped us grow accustomed to our current state.

Eve was in the wind. For now. Not even Vivienne knew of her whereabouts. It was only a matter of time, however.

"Madame," said our butler, Luuk. "The trunks are prepared. The porter wants to bring them to the ship at noon."

"Fine," we said. "That will be fine. See that our porter returns with a receipt. I want nothing lost."

"Madame," he said, bowing and leaving us.

The coffee was hot and bitter on our tongue as we sipped, walking from the window to the desk. A leather-bound notebook lay open. We'd taken over most of the bank accounts held by the Mentium after we had dissolved the order. The twentieth century was a time for individualism and those Underlings who had been out of the city during Eve's mass entombment were given their freedom. It did come with a cost, however. Their wealth was tied up in the Mentium's holdings, holdings that were now ours.

We studied the figures once again, making sure the transfers to New York had been noted. The populace was still reeling from the financial crash of '29 but it was a perfect time for us to invest.

It was also the perfect time for a change of scenery. The Continent was growing more toxic by the month. The German chancellor was not a Broadcaster, but he may as well have been. He managed incredible control with only his words. He was despicable and dangerous.

Yemoja had moved to America in 1929. Cernunnos, Edinburgh that same year, and Radegast made a home for himself in Prague. All had been allowed to keep their wealth and they agreed that separate enterprises would be best. We still kept in touch.

An urn sat sentinel on our mantle. It was of Ming origin and housed the remains of my mentor and our friend, Tian. Yemoja had the body cared for after his death. She gave the urn to us shortly after our arrival in Amsterdam.

We closed the notebook and reached for another — an address book bound in red canvas. We pulled the ribbon and opened it to the address of our new home. It had been Artemis and Apollo's vacation home in Manhattan. The space was laid out over two floors of a modern high-rise and we had already had its contents sold off. It would be our blank canvas to paint.

"Luuk," we called, rising from the desk and walking out into the hallway. "Luuk?"

The young, thin man poked his head out from a bedroom. "Yes, Madame?"

We entered the room. Inside stood three beds. One each for Izzy, Apollo, and Artemis. Their still bodies had atrophied, leaving inhuman frames bulging from under their gowns. We'd cared for them since Eve's massacre. We wanted them close. We wanted to ensure their lives would be long.

"Luuk, has the hospital finalised the transfer details?"

"Yes, they will be moved tomorrow but they ask that you not visit for at least a month after your arrival in New York. For acclimation purposes."

"That's fine. Thank you, Luuk."

To be honest, we'd grown weary of the trio. Dips into their minds were only enjoyable for the first year, maybe two. Their suffering grew, predictable. The New Jersey State Lunatic Asylum graciously agreed to care for them. The drive was close enough to visit when a check-in was desired but far enough to forget them entirely, should they grow too tiresome.

"Luuk, one last thing,"

"Yes, Madame?"

"Have the urn in the study wrapped and make sure it stays sealed. We'll be taking it with us. It's too important to damage."

"Yes, Madame."

We took our porcelain coffee cup to the study and poured more. It was June and the fireplace was cold but it had always been inviting. We sat in an overstuffed, wing-backed chair and crossed our legs, holding the coffee in both hands. Its warmth seeped into our fingers and it was a good time for me to seep inward as well.

The work I'd done inside Lilith's mind was very different from my previous hosts. This world existed as a blend of our two inner worlds. My ziggurat still stood tall over the buildings that surrounded it, but my Babylon grew amongst her Jerusalem. She'd been adamant that we share our space in an even manner.

I set myself to flight and flapped my great wings over our alloyed city. Lilith would have liked it there. Someday, I hoped to show her. For now, she lived as a troglodyte, just below. We were nearing a solution. Our work had made progress. We were so close.

I came to rest at the foot of a massive iron door, a door I could not demolish. This was Eve's door, her portal to the subconscious, and it remained locked and impenetrable.

Eve had taken inspiration from the structures I'd used to control Del. She'd moulded that inspiration into something far more sinister and more powerful. She'd entombed every Broadcaster within range of my radio.

Eve could have her door. I'd managed to build another. I'd installed my door in the Twins, Izzy and my Lilith. Lilith's door was green with an elegant brass handle. I turned it and fell.

Soft, cottony clouds passed as I sailed through her powder-blue sky. My back-swept wings guiding me toward the ground.

Memories flashed against those clouds, but my love had learned to control their content. Dark clouds still crossed her sky but they were few and burned away in minutes. Lilith focused on the positive. There was no other choice.

"Lover!" she said as I landed on a knee.

The world of her subconscious was an oasis smelling of fresh water and fresh fruit. Where Del had erected derelict buildings, Lilith grew date palms and pomegranate trees. Where Del placed his childhood bedroom, his prison, Lilith bathed in a crystal-clear spring.

Her arms were draped across the edge of the pool, her back to me. She raised one of those long arms and waved her fingers, an invitation to join. I obliged, my wings and clothing evaporating from my body. I stepped into the soothing waters at her side and she leaned close, resting her head on my shoulder, her hand on my thigh.

"My sweet snake-dragon, is everything in order?" she asked, looking out over the gardens and orchards that spread from that spring into infinity.

"Yes, my love, we sail this evening."

"Good, and the others?"

"The asylum is taking care of their transport."

"Delicious."

She leaned onto one hip and placed a hand on my cheek before taking my mouth. She tasted of apple.

"Progress, sweetling? Any news?"

Not enough.

"Yes and no. From my experiments on some of the others, I'm fairly certain the subconscious will begin to crumble along with the rest of the mind as death progresses. I know we can get you out, love, it's getting you into a new body that is still proving difficult."

She rolled her head away but kept her hand where it was.

"And your meeting in New York?"

"Yes, he's staying at the New Yorker Hotel. He's agreed to meet me and discuss my designs. The issue is containment. We have to control your consciousness and guide it into your new host. That is going to take a lot of electricity and some unorthodox procedures, and my new favourite Serb is the man to consult in that field."

"I trust you, M. I do."

Above us, a single dark cloud formed, the images on it still too dim to see. Lilith's lips pursed and it disintegrated. I stroked her wet, black hair.

It wasn't trust I needed. I needed Lilith back. I was as frustrated as I knew she was. It would happen. Of that I was certain. We were still young. Our body wasn't even forty.

"Mother!" called a distant voice from outside.

"Now what?" I asked, letting my head fall back.

"Answer them, darling, I'm not going anywhere."

I kissed her and returned to our study where I took control of our body once more, moving to the window as a cascade of footsteps pounded closer.

The rain set a perfect mood for the day. Rain brings new life. It cleans and refreshes. It renews. New York would do that for us. America would be a fresh start for us all.

Our twelve-year-old adopted children, siblings on paper alone, came thumping into the study.

"Mother," said Marc, his dark hair and tan features looked handsome in his small tweed suit. "When do we leave for America?"

"Soon, darling, we leave very soon."

"I can't wait," he said, flopping his body onto the sofa.

Lily had taken a seat at our desk. She seemed less enthusiastic.

"What's wrong dear," I asked, moving to her and putting both hands on her shoulders.

"Do we have to go?" she asked, playing with her raven hair. Her mint dress splayed out across the seat. "All of my friends are here."

"Yes, we have to go, you know that, but don't you worry. There is so much to do and so many friends to make in America." She did not seem impressed. "This old world will always be our home, but the new world will be our garden. We'll grow so many splendid things, sweetie. You have no idea what a wonderful life we have planned for you two. You two are our future."

ACKNOWLEDGEMENTS

RADIO has been shaped by many people since I "tuned in" to its initial concept while in the back of K.M. Alexander's car on New Year's Day, 2015.

First and foremost I need to thank my wife, Kelcey, for everything she's done to make this book a reality. From instigating our move to Paris, to literally feeding and clothing me, to her expertise in design and her work as a proofreader, I cannot thank you enough.

Next I want to thank my parents who have only ever encouraged me to dream big and think outside the box. You've always allowed me to follow my own path in life. For that I am truly grateful. To my brothers and their significant others as well as extended family, in-laws included, your support and encouragement has meant the world.

Authors and friends K.M. Alexander and Hazel Manuel have been important mentors for me in my adventures in publishing and I owe them so much for all of the knowledge and guidance they've given me.

To my wonderful beta readers: Bill Rushing, Allison Vilander, Haley Enright, Yoanna Novakova, Robert McVicar, K.M. Alexander, Hazel Manuel, and Kelcey Rushing, thank you for your willingness to tear my book to shreds. RADIO and I are both the better for it.

Over the years I've been fortunate enough to be a part of three incredible writing groups, each having an impact on RADIO. From the writers of the Paris Scriptorium, to my evening Paris writing group: Haley Enright, Arnaud Koëbel, Alexandra Rossi, and Jeremy Walker, and now my fellow writers in the Zürich Writing Sessions group, thank you all for your input and friendship.

Finally, I need to give a huge thanks to my amazing editor, Amanda J. Spedding at Phoenix Editing. Her encouraging words and precision work helped me maintain everything great about RADIO while fine-tuning it into something to be proud of.

J · Rushing is an American writer whose work blends elements of adventure, fantasy, science fiction, and horror to create worlds that feel as familiar as they do foreign.

He is a musician, amateur luthier, and former teacher who first traded the microbreweries and Cascade Mountains of the Pacific Northwest for the bustle and beauty of Paris. After nearly three years in the City of Light he and his wife settled near Zürich, Switzerland where they spend much of their time traveling and immersing themselves in the outdoors.

◆ ◆ ◆

www.ingramcontent.com/pod-product-compliance
Lightning Source LLC
Chambersburg PA
CBHW051521100726
47898CB00005B/1542